NOWHERE TO RUN

Maggie Hudson was born in Bradford and now lives in London with her husband and three dogs. Writing under the name Margaret Pemberton, she is the author of many successful novels including the best-selling *White Christmas in Saigon*, *The Flower Garden* and *A Multitude of Sins*.

MAGGIE HUDSON

NOWHERE TO RUN

HarperCollins*Publishers*

HarperCollins*Publishers*
77–85 Fulham Palace Road,
Hammersmith, London W6 8JB

www.harpercollins.co.uk

Published by HarperCollins*Publishers* 2002
5 7 9 8 6 4

ISBN 0 00 651454 5

Typeset in Sabon by Palimpsest Book Production Limited,
Polmont, Stirlingshire

Printed in Great Britain by
Clays Ltd, St Ives plc

For Mike. From first to last.

Acknowledgements

Again, many thanks to my agent Caroline Sheldon, and to my editor, Anne O'Brien. Also thanks are due to two close friends, Christine Morris and Linda Britter.

Chapter One

'He's coming back!'

Sharyn Bailey stepped into a chaotically untidy room and as her best friend, Angie Flynn, threw herself down on the nearest of two unmade beds, closed the door so that her mother wouldn't be able to earwig in.

'Who's coming back?' Angie rolled on to her stomach, discovered she was lying on a newly purchased Beatles LP and hiked it out of her way.

'Guess.' Though she was fizzing to share her news, Sharyn wanted Angie to be agog to hear it. She leaned against the battered and scarred door, a broad white belt slung decoratively low on a mini-skirt as short as a pelmet.

'Dunno.' Angie had no intention of dancing to Sharyn's tune. She transferred the gum she was chewing from one side of her mouth to the other and pushed a shoulder-length fall of black, water-straight hair away from her face. 'And unless it's John Lennon,' she added, beginning to read the LP's cover with feigned interest, 'I ain't really in a tizzy about it, Sha.'

It was a lie and Sharyn knew it.

'If I told you it's someone sexier than John Lennon and who you haven't seen for ten years, I bet you'd be interested.'

Angie gave a derisive snort. 'Christ, Sha. You do pile it on. Ten years ago I was six. Who could I have last seen then that I'd be interested in seeing now?' Her words tailed off into stunned silence as comprehension dawned. She stopped laughing. Blue mascara'd lashes widened in incredulity and her jaw dropped. 'Johnny's twin? He's coming back home? Back to Bermondsey?'

'That's what Johnny says.'

Eighteen-year-old Johnny Martini was Sharyn's boyfriend – or so she liked to think. The Martini men were not the kind one could ever be sure about. Second-generation Sicilian, they were still regarded as being Mafia-connected by the criminal families they associated with, families such as the Baileys and Flynns. It was a belief reflected in the respect they were always accorded. No one messed with the Martinis, not if they wanted to tell the tale undisfigured – or wanted to live to tell it at all.

'But I thought he was Canadian now?' Angie was no longer sprawled on the bed. She was sitting bolt upright, her thoughts racing. Tony Martini had been eight when, kicking and screaming, he had left England with an aunt who, together with her Scottish husband, had made her home in Canada. That had been after their mother's death. A death no one spoke about – ever.

If Tony was now even a quarter as handsome as Johnny, then she had every intention of moving in on him fast. She'd lost out on Johnny mainly because Sharyn had had the advantage of living next door to him. She wasn't going to lose out a second time. Being Tony Martini's girlfriend would make her a person to be reckoned with. And even at eighteen, he'd have money. All the Martini men had money.

'Even if he is Canadian now, what difference does it make to his coming home?' Sharyn said, answering Angie's question with a grin, knowing exactly what direction Angie's thoughts were taking. 'If you knock him off his feet we'll be able to go out in a foursome. It'll be great. We might even end up having a double wedding!'

Angie gave a shriek of not very convincing protest and sprang from the bed in order to pirouette in front of the dressing-table mirror. 'I don't suppose the girls in Canada are up to much, do you, Sha?' she said, knowing that she was. 'I mean, no one talks about swinging Canada like they do swinging London, do they?'

Hands on hips, she thrust out her chest, admiring the outline of her breasts as they strained against a skimpy white crocheted sweater, the neckline scalloped and scooped. It had been bought the previous Saturday in Carnaby Street and, worn with a purple mini-skirt and low-heeled purple shoes, was the kind of fab gear she was sure was in short supply in Canada.

Especially the part of Canada Tony was coming from.

'He's on a ranch way up north, out in the wilderness,' Sharyn had once said. 'Johnny says it sounds fantastic. Tony has a horse of his own and he goes hunting and fishing with Albie – Albie's his auntie's husband – and once Albie took him camping in the mountains and they panned for gold, just like in the films.'

Angie had tried to look suitably impressed, but inside she'd been shuddering. The furthest north she'd ever been was Yorkshire, and it wasn't an experience she intended repeating.

Sharyn's eyes widened as a sudden thought hit her: 'I wonder if Tony will bring the gun he hunts with? Not legally, of course. He wouldn't be able to do it legally, but he might smuggle it home, mightn't he?'

'Why would he bother?' There was provocative one-upmanship in Angie's voice. 'Guns are easy to get hold of, Sha. Fast-Boy's got one. I've seen it.'

Despite having been determined that, just for once, it was going to be Angie hanging on to her every word and not the other way round, Sharyn's jaw dropped. 'You're joking,' she said in a voice that made it clear she knew Angie wasn't. 'Christ, Angie! Where does he keep it? Does your mum know? Does Johnny know?'

At the mention of Johnny, something flashed in Angie's cat-green eyes and was suppressed at the speed of light. 'No, and don't you go telling him, Sha. Fast-Boy'd kill me!'

The Flynns had known the Martini family for almost as long as they'd known the Baileys, but though Angie's dad and Old Man Martini were on fairly good terms – it not being a good idea to be anything else – her brother and Johnny Martini were not.

Within minutes of their first meeting at Jamaica Road Nursery School, Fast-Boy and Johnny had fought. Throughout primary school and junior school the animosity had continued. On their tenth birthdays they'd joined the same junior boxing club and their fights, gloved and ungloved, had taken on a new intensity. There'd been playground fights and street fights; Saturday-matinee cinema fights and fairground fights. There had been a brief lull when Fast-Boy won a grammar-school scholarship while Johnny sauntered off to wreak havoc at the local secondary-modern, but it hadn't lasted long.

The problem was that, though on many occasions there was one clear victor, it was never the same victor. They were too evenly matched – and both wanted the same thing: to be the king-pin of the Bermondsey streets they'd been born and brought up in.

Because of his dad's reputation, it was a rivalry in

which Johnny had the edge. There was more clout in belonging to a gang led by him than there was in belonging to a gang led by Fast-Boy. The Martini family were the heavy side of crime; the dark side. The Flynns were merely bruisers and not-too-successful burglars. Consequently, Fast-Boy's teenage gang was low-key compared to Johnny's. Not that it worried Fast-Boy. A loner at heart, he liked to keep his head well below the parapet – and he didn't like people knowing his business.

'I won't tell,' Sharyn now said huffily. 'What d'you take me for?'

Angie bit back a tart reply. Fast-Boy didn't know that she knew about the shotgun wrapped in grease-proof paper and stowed in a toolbox in their coal bunker, but he'd soon cotton on if Johnny were to make a snide, taunting remark about it. He'd know that Johnny had got the info from Sharyn and that Sharyn had got it from her, and then the fat would be in the fire.

'You'd better not,' she said, loading the words for all she was worth, wishing she'd kept her mouth shut.

Sharyn grinned, well aware she now had a piece of info Angie had had no intention of sharing. 'So what's Fast-Boy up to?' she said teasingly. 'Going to rob a bank, is he?'

Deciding to put an end to what was becoming a tricky conversation, Angie gave a last appreciative look in the mirror and turned away from it, saying dismissively: 'I doubt it, Sha. He's more likely to be looking after it for someone. How about we go down past the billiard-hall and see if Johnny and his mates are there?'

Not waiting for a response, knowing that Sharyn would follow her because she followed her everywhere, she sashayed out of the cluttered room, wondering how Tony Martini's return home would affect her brother. One thing was for certain. He'd appreciate being fore-warned of it. His being daggers-drawn with Johnny was bad enough, but they were evenly matched and there was balance to it. There'd be no balance at all once Tony returned and he and Johnny became a double act.

As their footsteps receded down the stairs, the mound of blankets on the far bed stirred and twelve-year-old Amber Bailey cautiously poked out her head. She'd kept still for so long she was half-suffocated, but it had been worth it. Sharyn and Angie would never have talked as they had if they'd known she was in the room.

She rubbed a leg to get the blood flowing again and thought about what she'd heard. Which bit had been the most interesting? The bit about Johnny Martini's twin brother coming back home or the bit about Fast-Boy Flynn having a gun?

As the front door opened and then crashed shut she decided she was more interested in Fast-Boy having a gun than she was in someone she didn't know. Not that she knew Fast-Boy well. He always looked totally surprised whenever she said hello to him in the street, as if he couldn't remember who the hell she was – which perhaps he couldn't.

Irked by the memory, she crossed bad-temperedly to the window and watched Sharyn and Angie as they walked, laughing, down the short path into the street. They were laughing so hard they were having to hold on to each other. Her pale-lashed eyes narrowed in resentment. There were occasions – and this was one of them – when she heartily hated them. They were always going out and having a good time, and they never took her with them.

She pushed a fall of tightly curling ginger hair away from her eyes. That was another reason why she hated them. Both Sharyn and Angie had gorgeous hair. Sharyn's was pale blonde and Angie's was blue-black. Neither colour was natural, of course, but what did that matter? And their hair hung sleek and straight to their shoulders. Her hair wouldn't stay straight no matter what she did to it – and she'd done everything, including ironing it.

Moodily she went back to the bed, sitting cross-legged on it, her thoughts returning to Fast-Boy and the gun he had hidden away. Why had he got it? Was it for protection? Was it because someone had told him that Tony Martini was returning home and he thought he'd better get himself tooled-up in case of serious trouble? Not that a shotgun would be much use in a fight – even she knew that. It would be pretty handy for blasting someone down in a pub, though.

She chewed the corner of her lip, remembering how George Cornell, a mate of her dad's, had been shot and killed in the Blind Beggar pub a few months ago. No one had been arrested yet, and she'd overheard her dad saying that he doubted anyone would be.

It was a gangland slaying which might have caught Fast-Boy's imagination and, the more she thought about it, the more certain she was that his having a shotgun was something Johnny should know about.

She swung her legs from the bed. Sharyn may have promised to keep shtum, but she hadn't. It meant she now had something very interesting to do – though she'd need to glam herself up with Sharyn's lipstick and eyeliner before she did it.

*   *   *

Ewan Flynn had been raining blows on to a punchbag in Clyde Scale's boxing gym for fifteen minutes non-stop. Now, as sweat trickled into his eyes and the punchbag continued to swing crazily, he stepped away from it.

'Jeez, but you're fast with your fists,' one of the old-timers who hung about the gym said admiringly as he threw a towel towards him. 'Anyone ever tell you?'

Ewan caught the towel and flashed a glimmer of a grin. 'Yeah. Plenty of people.' It was true. It was the reason for his nickname, and he'd had his nickname ever since junior school – though he'd been fast with his fists long before then.

As he slung the towel round his neck, his grin broadened. He'd certainly been fast with them the first time he'd met Johnny Martini. Even after fifteen years, remembering brought a stab of satisfaction so deep it was almost sexual. He'd been three and a half years old and it had been his first morning at Jamaica Road Nursery School.

'Come and say hello to two other little boys who are starting nursery this morning,' the prissy-looking woman his mum had handed him over to had said. Though he hadn't wanted her to, the woman had taken hold of his hand and dragged him across a vast expanse of green linoleum floor.

He'd never seen twins before; had never known that two people could look as if they were the same person. He'd stood in front of them, a strap of his home-made dungarees sliding down his arm, and had looked from one to the other, seriously disturbed by the strangeness of what he was seeing.

'Say hello to Johnny and Tony nicely, Ewan,' the woman had said, stooping over him so closely he could smell a funny smell; a smell like dead flowers.

Johnny and Tony hadn't said anything. They'd just

8

stood shoulder to shoulder, staring at him wooden-faced. In mutinous silence he'd looked again from one to the other and then his fist had shot out and he'd delivered a belting blow to Johnny's nose. Blood had spurted with such force that his mum had never been able to get the stains out of his dungarees. There'd been uproar, of course. His victim had screamed, Tony had hollered, the woman with the funny smell had shouted and yanked him away from Johnny so hard she'd nearly pulled his arm out of its socket. When his mum had come at the end of the afternoon to take him home, he'd had to endure listening to the woman telling her how violent and uncontrollable he'd been. Not that that had been the worst of it. The worst had been when his mum had got him home.

'You stupid little fuck!' she'd screamed at him when she'd tired of leathering his backside. 'Why did you have to go picking on one of the Martini twins? Don't you know who their dad is, for Christ's sake?'

He hadn't. And even when he was old enough to know and appreciate just who the Martini twins' dad was – and what he stood for – he hadn't cared. He didn't like Johnny Martini and he'd never been sorry that, in their ongoing battles, he'd been the one who had hit out first.

With the towel still round his neck, he mooched off towards the showers. To this day he couldn't work out what it had been about Johnny Martini that had so riled him. He'd always been a smugly good-looking little bastard, of course, but then so had Tony – and he'd never been overwhelmed by the urge to bash Tony into lifeless pulp.

He slung his towel over the shower-room door. If it had been Johnny, not Tony, who'd been whisked out of school and away from home when he was eight, life would have been a lot easier. Fast-Boy would then have been the local gang-leader and Tony would have either had to run with him or run alone. Either way, the two of them would have worked things out and rubbed along OK. Johnny, though . . .

He dropped his sweat-soaked shorts and kicked them aside. Johnny was a different matter entirely. Johnny was a pain, impossible to rub along with. Beneath the handsome exterior – the electric-blue eyes, the thickly curling hair, the toothpaste-ad white smile, Johnny was a sicko. A psycho.

He stepped under the nearest shower and turned the water on. People thought Johnny was hard in the same way his dad, old man Marco Martini, was hard, but Fast-Boy knew differently. He knew stuff about Johnny that no one else knew, not even Tony. Johnny was round-the-bend nuts – had been ever since he was a kid. Why no one else had cottoned to it was beyond him, but they would one day – he'd been looking forward to making sure of it for years.

He raised his face to the steaming jets of water, thinking about his girlfriend, Zoë. If Johnny didn't start minding his manners where Zoë was concerned, the day in question was going to come fast – so fast that Johnny wouldn't know what had hit him.

He lathered his chest and shoulders with soap, the grin back on his mouth. Johnny's reputation would be zapped for good – and he'd never make a comeback. Not in a million years.

Johnny Martini lounged against a paint-scarred radiator and regarded Jimmy Jones with a mixture of bafflement and regret. Jimmy had run with his gang for over a year and, though not the brightest bulb in the pack, was useful at times. Or had been.

'You were seen, Jimmy,' he said again, shifting his stance slightly. 'You were seen hobnobbing with a copper – the same copper – not just once, but three times. And as you weren't with him because you'd been asked to be with him – because you were doing a bit of business with him – there's only one conclusion to be drawn. You were grassing someone up. And that ain't on, Jimmy. Know what I mean?'

The building they were in backed on to the Thames. Once a warehouse, it had been converted into recording studios and they were in one of the small rehearsal rooms on the top floor. Jimmy was there because he and the band he played keyboard with were going to cut a record later in the week and needed all the practice time they could fit in. Johnny was there because he'd known that was where he would find Jimmy. Gaining entry hadn't been a problem. Though it wasn't generally known, the name on the building's deeds was his dad's.

They weren't alone. A handful of other gang members were ranged around the room and two members of the band, the bass player and the lead vocalist, were there – though they clearly didn't want to be.

'Well, I sure as hell wasn't grassing on you, Johnny,' Jimmy said, trying to inject a dismissive laugh into his voice. The result, as his voice cracked and broke, wasn't what he'd had in mind.

'No? Well, mebbe you weren't.' Johnny eased himself away from the radiator and sidestepped a mike. 'Problem is, Jimmy, you were definitely grassing up someone – and to me that's just as bad. Rule number one, learnt at my old man's knee: "Thou shalt not grass." You've broken that rule and so there are consequences. There's got to be.'

He strolled across the room and rammed the bottom half of a grimy sash window as high as it would go, pissed off with the entire scenario. When it came to it, as now, he could be as heavy as need be – but he was too happy-go-lucky by nature for it ever to be the highlight of his day.

'For Christ's sake, Johnny! What yer goin' to do?' There was naked panic in Jimmy's voice.

It was a question everyone was curious about. Certainly no one imagined that Johnny had opened the window to admire the view of the Thames – spectacular though it was.

'Look, I don't think we really want to be here any longer . . .' the bass player said nervously, beginning to edge towards the door.

The gang member who was standing full-square in front of it, a knuckle-duster on his right fist, didn't budge.

Rather than push his luck, the bass player faltered to a halt.

'Johnny! I ain't a grass! I swear I ain't! On my mother's life!'

Jimmy's eyes darted in panic from one face to another. There was stony indifference on the faces of his former mates; appalled incredulity on the faces of the two band members. On no one's face was there the promise of help.

At head height, Johnny's hand tightened on the bottom edge of the fully opened window. Why had the stupid fucker said the word 'mother'? Didn't he know what that would trigger? Didn't he realize?

It was July and even though it was a hot day he was,

as always, smartly suited. He gazed down at the shimmering surface of the Thames, the sun so bright it hurt his eyes. He'd been having a really good day until now. Hell, he'd been on such a high at the thought of Tony coming home, he hadn't even been going to allow Jimmy to spoil it. A bit of a verbal scare, that's all he'd been going to give him.

Six storeys down, an oil slick swirled past the foot of the building. A bit of a verbal scare no longer seemed punishment enough. Jimmy wasn't in the know about the long-firm scam he was in the middle of setting up, but if he had been, the whole complicated project would have had to be jettisoned and then he'd have had nothing on the go with which to welcome Tony home. The colours in the oil slick glinted like fire. He blinked, giving his head a slight shake.

Jimmy, mistakenly thinking that Johnny's silence meant that the worst was over, said with an attempt at brave swagger: 'I mean, Johnny . . . Jesus, what sort of mother-fucker do you think I –'

It was a sentence he didn't finish.

Johnny wheeled around, seizing hold of him with such force that Jimmy half fell. As Johnny began hauling him towards the open window and he began lashing out to free himself, his former mates pitched in to restrain him, seizing hold of his arms and legs. Seconds later Johnny had manhandled him over the sill of the window, so that he was hanging, head down, over the dizzying drop to the river. Now only Johnny had hold of him. And Jimmy was no longer kicking to be free.

'Haul me in!' he was shrieking. 'Get me in! DON'T LET GO!'

On the far side of the river a tug was motoring steadily upstream. 'That's a sight you don't often see now the

13

docks are near-dead,' Johnny said laconically, bracing himself in order to continue holding Jimmy's weight. 'The bloke aboard has seen you, Jimmy. Shall I give him a wave?'

'NO!' There was a sob in Jimmy's voice. 'Don't fuckin' let go of me! Get me in, for Christ's sake!'

Johnny looked down at the point in the river where, if he let go of Jimmy's legs, Jimmy would plummet. The liquid fire of the oil slick was long gone, borne away on a current that was notoriously fast. Jimmy, too, would be carried away fast – so fast that any help the tug-man might give or summon would, in all probability, be too little, too late.

Behind him the lead vocalist was shouting at him to haul Jimmy back into the room, and he could hear Cheyenne, the gang member he'd detailed to bar the door, saying: 'I think mebbe you should, Johnny. You've proved your point and, once the bloke on the tug gets on the blower, the River Police'll be here mob-handed, know what I mean?'

Johnny did. Not only that, but his good mood was back. Whoever Jimmy had been grassing on, it hadn't been him. Christ, even Jimmy wasn't *that* stupid. And how could he stay in a heavy mood when he was so over the moon about Tony coming home? Tony was his twin. His soul mate. His other half. Once Tony was home, the sky would be their limit; together they could achieve whatever they set their hearts on.

Still holding on to Jimmy, he stepped away from the window. Jimmy jerked upwards a couple of inches, his shins scraping the window-bottom as Johnny unceremoniously dragged him back across it. The lead vocalist rushed forward and grabbed hold of a leg. One of the gang members grabbed the other and together they helped Johnny haul his near-hysterical victim back into the room.

'Can we go now?' the bass player asked nervously as Jimmy fell into a weak-kneed huddle on the floor, his shoulders heaving as he sucked in great lungfuls of air.

'Why'd you want to go?' Johnny brushed imaginary debris from his suit sleeves. 'I thought you were here to rehearse?' He eyed Jimmy with amusement, aware that Jimmy had pissed himself. 'You're supposed to be pretty hot on the keyboard, ain't you, Jimmy? Come on, then – give us a tune.'

Maureen Bailey paused in what she was doing, her hands wrist-deep in soapy washing-up water. So Tony Martini was coming home, was he? She remembered the day he and Johnny had been born. She hadn't had any kids of her own then, of course. Sharyn hadn't been born till 1950, when the twins were toddlers, and Amber didn't arrive till 1954. Which meant that Amber wouldn't even remember Tony.

She remembered him, though. He'd been a handsome little devil. While Johnny had taken after his father, there had been something about Tony that was totally his mother. He'd certainly been inseparable from her.

She tried to close her mind to memories of Sheelagh Martini, and failed. Sheelagh had been her friend, just as Angie was Sharyn's friend. They'd grown up during the war years and, even though Sheelagh was asthmatic and not always in good health, they'd gone everywhere together. Marco had been off the scene at the time, held in an internment camp. So instead of dating Italians handsome enough to commit suicide for, she and Sheelagh had gone up West to the Palais Ballroom where there were servicemen in droves. Their favourites were the Americans – the Yanks had the most money – but when it came to sheer dishiness, Polish and Czech airmen came a very close second.

Maureen swished the water around in the sink, lost in thought. It had been a wonderful time. The best time of her life. Then the war had ended. Sheelagh had married Marco and she had married one of his henchmen: Tommy Bailey.

She halted her trip down memory lane with fierce abruptness. What had happened over the next few years wasn't the kind of thing it was healthy to remember. It would lead to thinking about Sheelagh's death, something she never allowed herself to dwell on. Instead she thought about Marco.

Old Man Martini he was known as now. Not that he was old. Fifty-four wasn't old. Not nowadays. Her hands stopped moving as she wondered how he felt about Tony coming home. There'd been a time, of course, when he would have told her.

She lifted her hands from the water, shaking the suds off them, and as she did so the back gate clicked. She looked swiftly through the window, just in time to see Amber scurrying up the path, her face plastered with Sharyn's make-up.

Maureen grabbed hold of a tea-towel. Where the hell had Amber been, tarted up like a little tramp? Though she was going to demand to know, she knew she wouldn't receive a straight answer. Stubbornness was Amber's middle name. She dried her hands, knowing with utter certainty that one day her youngest daughter was going to be real trouble.

And Tony Martini? When Tony returned home, was he going to be real trouble, too?

She chewed the corner of her lip. One thing was for sure. If he was, getting rid of him wouldn't be easy.

Not this time around.

Not even for Marco.

Chapter Two

Tony Martini leaned forward in his seat as the Pan Am jet rolled down the runway of Vancouver's international airport. The hands clasped between his knees were white-knuckled, not because he was afraid of flying, but because the tension of the moment was nearly more than he could bear. After ten years – ten years two months and fourteen days, to be absolutely accurate – he was at last returning home.

The plane began picking up speed. Within hours he would be in Bermondsey again. With Johnny.

The engines changed tone and as there came a great surge of power, he shut his eyes. Johnny. His twin. His other half. The plane left the ground and he was aware of the woman seated next to him giving a small gasp.

Would Johnny have changed much? His stomach muscles tightened. Would they still know what the other was thinking? Would they still be able to anticipate each other's moves? The ten-year separation made it impossible to know. Was Johnny feeling what he was feeling now, for instance? Was he counting the minutes away, too?

'Would you like a drink, sir?'

He opened his eyes, saw that a stewardess was leaning towards him, and flashed her a smile that brought a flush of colour to her cheeks.

'Yep. A whisky and ginger ale, please.'

He'd never flown before and the offer of a drink had

been unexpected, though he didn't let the fact show. He'd never been called 'Sir' before either, and, considering the way he was dressed – yellow T-shirt, black jeans and silver-studded cowboy boots, that, too, had been something of a novelty.

As he was handed his drink he was glad he'd made the decision to fly. Travelling by sea would have been cheaper, but he wasn't into cheap. He was into quick. And there was another reason. When he'd left England with his aunt, it had been by boat, and he hadn't wanted to return that way. It would have brought back too many memories – memories that still gave him nightmares.

He downed the whisky in a couple of needy swallows.

The past was past and this was the present. He had dreams to fulfil and ambitions to achieve. And at the centre of everything would be Johnny. His hand tightened round his empty whisky glass.

Johnny was the reason he was returning.

Johnny was the reason for everything.

'But why can't I come?' Zoë Fairminder was a headmaster's daughter from Blackheath and her middle-class voice was petulant as she leaned against the bonnet of Johnny's yellow Mustang, a luscious expanse of leg showing between the hem of her buttercup-suede mini-skirt and the tops of her knee-high white boots. 'There's no sense in me jilting Fast-Boy if you're not going to take me places with you. Fast-Boy takes me everywhere with him. He always has.'

Johnny grinned, not believing her for one moment. Fast-Boy might be nuts about her, but he wasn't a geezer to be under anyone's thumb, least of all a bird's.

'My picking Tony up at the airport is strictly personal, darlin'. We're going to be meeting again after ten years and neither of us is going to be wanting anyone else around.'

He slipped on a pair of wraparound shades, flicked a speck of dust from his lightweight mohair suit and walked around the car to the driver's door.

'I don't believe this!' Zoë stood upright abruptly. 'You chase after me as if it will kill you if I don't leave Fast-Boy for you – then you're Mr Indifferent!'

'No, I'm not.' He opened the door and grinned at her across the Mustang's roof. 'Be in the Prince of Wales tonight. I'll be there with Tony. It's going to be a belter of an evening.'

'I might be there.' Her sootily made-up eyes flashed fire. 'And if I am, I might just be there with Fast-Boy.'

He slid behind the wheel, happily certain that, even if she was, it would only be a slight hiccup in his long-term scheme of things. He'd seen her reaction the first time he'd taken her out in the car. She'd liked the glamour of it, the looks they had received. Fast-Boy didn't have a tasty motor. He was a bike fiend. Not just any kind of bike, of course. Clad head to foot in tight-fitting black leathers, Fast-Boy rode a top-of-the-range Harley Davidson – and he rode it fast.

It was a very sexy image. What wasn't very sexy was being wind-blasted riding pillion and Zoë, he knew, was fed up with it. Like many girls from respectable families, she liked the thrill of being seen out and about with someone dangerously lawless, but the experience was one she wanted to enjoy in style.

And Johnny had style. It was Sicilian Mafioso style. His father's style, and he loved it. Fast-Boy might slum around in bikers' gear, but he didn't. Emulating the big-time gangsters his father mixed with, he was a very classy dresser. His shoes were handmade by Maclarens in

Albemarle Street. His suits came from Savile Row. And his big American car was a car that turned heads everywhere.

Knowing he looked the dog's bollocks; knowing his arch enemy's girlfriend was his for the taking no matter what negative signs she was at present giving out, he pressed his foot hard on the Mustang's accelerator and surged away from the curb. The journey he was making was one he'd dreamed of for so long, he could hardly believe it was now reality.

He shot down Jamaica Road at speed and into Druid Street, relishing the fact that he was at last on his own. It had been a pretty close call. Sharyn had been on his back for days about driving out to the airport with him, as had a whole clutch of hangers-on. Not his dad, though. Even though it would have been the most natural thing in the world for him to have driven out to the airport, his dad hadn't suggested it.

It was odd that he hadn't, but not so odd as to be sinister. Their dad had always been ice cool when it came to showing emotion. Johnny couldn't even remember him crying at their mum's funeral.

With a screech of tyres, he swung the Mustang into a right-hand turn, surging on to Tower Bridge. It wasn't that their dad didn't care. The reason he didn't show emotion was that he cared too much. He'd worked that out as a small boy. He'd had to, in order to make the unbearable manageable.

Traffic was heavy on the bridge and he was forced to drop speed. It gave him the chance to appreciate the river. It was looking great, as always, slick and sinuous and glistening like tinsel. He tried to imagine what it would be like not have seen it for ten years, and couldn't. He liked to see it every day and the best view was from a bridge. Sometimes from Tower Bridge, as now, often from Southwark Bridge, which gave such a stunning view of St Paul's.

If crossing the river was good, re-crossing it homewards was even better. He always let out a shout of euphoria when he drove over a bridge – any bridge – into South London. Today, the euphoria would be uncontainable. Tony would be with him and they'd never be separated again. Never.

He cruised down Tower Hill into Lower Thames Street, the volume on the Mustang's radio as high as it would go. The Stones were belting out 'Little Red Rooster' and as he held the wheel steady with one hand he beat out the rhythm with the other, the sun glinting on his gold signet ring, his gold cuff-links and the wide bracelet of his gold wristwatch.

Was Tony going to be red-hot enthused about the scam he was setting up for them both? It wasn't an original idea, of course. Long-firm scams were the staple diet of many professional crims – and with good reason. The money was substantial and people rarely got caught. All that was needed for success was a front man with no previous convictions and no history of debt. As no such front man was available to him, he'd fitted himself out with the identity of a bloke long dead. His birth certificate, passport, national insurance number, the lot. And under the hookey name, he'd already rented the necessary premises.

He swooped down into an underpass, emerging seconds later on the Embankment. All he needed to do now was to decide on the type of goods he was going to deal in and suss out the wholesalers. He didn't want to do all the arranging himself, though. He wanted this to be a joint operation. Him and Tony, acting as equals. A partnership. A duo. The Kinks' 'Sunny Afternoon' was blasting out of the radio. He began singing along with it. Tony was coming home and life was good. Life was *great*.

Marco Martini strolled into Bertorelli's in Charlotte Street. A restaurant, Italian café and bar all rolled into one, Bertorelli's also offered the advantage of private dining-rooms and was his favourite Soho watering-hole. Not overly tall, but thick-set and with powerful shoulders, he was a man who always attracted attention. His hair was grazed with silver and was still thick; still tightly curling. His belly was still flat and firm, too, though only just. He passed a strong hand across the front of his immaculately tailored double-breasted jacket as if in reassurance of the fact.

'*Buon giorno, Signore Martini!*' His favourite waitress hurried towards him. She had served in the restaurant as long as he had been patronizing it and they were old friends. She was middle-aged now, but then, so was he. It wasn't a pleasant thought. None of his thoughts, so far that day, had been pleasant.

'Your guests have not arrived yet,' she said, bustling ahead of him to his usual table, a corner one from which he could survey the whole room. 'Would you like a bottle of Barola opened while you wait for them?'

It was his preferred red wine. He never drank white, not even with fish. White wine was for women.

'*Grazie,*' he said, glad that his guests hadn't arrived. He wasn't in the mood for them. He looked down at his ostentatious Audemars Piguet wristwatch. Quarter past one. Johnny would be nearly at the airport by now. He broke a bread-stick in half, wondering why the hell it was that Tony's coming home should be making him feel so old. He was fifty-four, for Christ's sake, not seventy-four. Why, then, was he suddenly feeling that his best years were behind him? And where had those years gone?

The wine waiter approached, a bottle of Barola in his hand. Marco remained sunk in thought. Things had gone wrong for him on a personal level from the day Sheelagh had died. He corrected himself abruptly. Sheelagh hadn't simply died. There'd been circumstances. His face hardened as he thought of those circumstances and of the way they had reduced his family life to ruins.

Having poured a splash of wine into his glass, the waiter was waiting for him to taste it. With a peremptory movement of his hand, he indicated he wasn't going to bother.

What would happen once Tony was home? How were memories, long stifled, going to remain stifled? And what the fuck was Tony going to do? From the little he'd gleaned from his brother-in-law, Tony was only ever happy when riding in the wilderness on a horse – and he certainly wouldn't be able to do that in south-east London.

And what about Johnny's relationship with Tony? Johnny might be over the moon at the thought of Tony being back home, but Johnny never did think about things too deeply. It didn't seem to have occurred to him that once Tony was home he'd no longer be able to have everything his own way – and all his own way was the only way Johnny liked things.

Once the honeymoon of his sons' reunion was over, there would be trouble. He could feel it in his water. For the first time in years he found himself wishing he could share his concerns with Maureen Bailey – not that he ever thought of her as Maureen Bailey. He only thought of her by her maiden name – the same way he thought of Sheelagh.

Maureen Gallagher and Sheelagh O'Shaughnessy. They'd been best friends. Both had come from big Irish families. Both had had the hots for him. He'd married Sheelagh and Maureen had screwed up her life by marrying Tommy.

He took another drink of his wine, barely tasting it. Maureen Gallagher was a woman and a half with a laugh that was the best he'd ever heard. It just spluttered out of her, husky and unchained. It was a laugh her ginger-haired youngest daughter had inherited. The elder girl, Sharyn, didn't have the laugh, but she did have the same fizzing zest for life. For the last year or so Sharyn had been running after Johnny and the thought of what would happen if she caught him was one he found amusing. Maureen would go crackers – and Tommy wouldn't know why.

Marco had never understood why Maureen had wasted her life on a nobody like Tommy. Though she'd just celebrated her fortieth birthday, she was still a good-looking woman. Slender, with incredible cat-green eyes – eyes both her daughters had inherited – and with hair the colour of warm mahogany, how could she not be a throat-tightening sight?

And she wouldn't speak to him.

She hadn't spoken to him for over ten years.

Two shadows fell across his table.

'Hi, Marco. How ya doin'? Are we late? Christ, I didn't realize we were late.'

He raised his eyes from his wine-glass, shrugging himself out of his thoughts as his two guests slid their bulk on to chairs at the opposite side of the table.

'So today's the big day?' said the one who hadn't

spoken previously, reaching for a toothpick. 'Tony's coming home after ten years. Quite a moment, eh?'

'Yeah.' Marco glanced down at his watch. It was one-thirty and, if it was on time, Tony's plane was just landing. His stomach muscles tightened. To say it was quite a moment was the understatement of the year.

For the umpteenth time Johnny's eyes flicked towards the Arrivals Board. The Pan Am flight from Vancouver had landed and its passengers were in baggage retrieval. A couple of people, businessmen carrying only brief-cases, had walked out into the Arrivals Hall, but as yet no one else had followed them.

There was quite a crush of people waiting for friends and family and Johnny wasn't used to being in a crush. Wherever he went, people usually gave him space.

Even though the time was prominently displayed, he checked his watch. The flight had landed fifteen minutes ago. Tony had to walk out into the Arrivals Hall at any second. He had to.

There was such a constriction in his throat, he could hardly breathe. What if Tony hadn't caught the flight? What if he'd changed his mind about coming?

A family emerged, the father pushing a trolley stacked high with luggage. His wife waved to an old lady stand-ing to Johnny's left. The two children with them suddenly shrieked 'Granny!' and broke into a run. Other people were now hurrying down the ramp behind them, some with faces alight at the expectation of being greeted; others quite clearly not expecting to find anyone wait-ing for them.

Johnny's heart began to slam. Where was Tony? For the first time it occurred to him that he might not recog-nize him. He banished the thought almost instantly. They were identical twins, for Chrissakes. How could he not recognize a mirror-image of himself?

There were more families. Another scattering of businessmen. A young woman followed them and a man standing only feet away from Johnny gave a whoop of joy and ducked under the barrier, sprinting to meet her. A bevy of children, all in school uniform, clattered down the ramp. A young hippy with long hair and wearing jeans and silver-studded cowboy boots strolled in their wake, a duffel bag over his shoulder.

Johnny's excitement was beginning to turn to panic. Tony would surely have done everything he could to be first off the plane and first out of baggage retrieval. That being the case, where was he?

The girl standing to his immediate right rushed forward to throw her arms round a middle-aged man. From behind him someone shouted to attract the attention of a woman struggling with a heavily laden trolley

Only a scattering of passengers were still emerging from baggage retrieval. An elderly couple, walking with difficulty. A harassed-looking woman with a baby in her arms. A priest.

And then there was no one else. The ramp was empty and remained empty. The crush around him had dispersed. He was on his own.

The young bloke in the jeans and distinctive cowboy boots was standing fifteen yards or so away and was looking across at him as if trying to come to a decision.

Uncaring of what the hippy's problem might be, Johnny fought to control his panic. So Tony hadn't been on the flight he'd said he'd be on. It didn't mean that he wasn't still coming. He'd missed it, that was all. He'd be on the next one and all Johnny had to do now was find out when the next flight was due in. It probably wouldn't be today, but it could very well be tomorrow . . .

The long-haired youth was strolling towards him, a quizzical smile on his mouth.

Johnny stopped thinking about the next flight in from Vancouver. The ground was beginning to shelve at his feet and the blood was drumming in his ears with such force he thought he was going to pass out.

'Hi, Johnny,' his twin said, coming to a halt in front of him and slinging his duffel bag to the ground. 'I kinda expected a warmer welcome.'

'Tony? Jesus – *Tony!*' Johnny struggled for breath and then, with a choked sob, flung his arms around him.

He was crying. He'd known he would cry. It was the main reason he hadn't wanted anyone to come to the airport with him.

Their emotional bear hug was one in which time rocked still and then ricocheted backwards. He was overcome by the memory of smoke and flames; of cowering in a blazing room, shrieking: 'Me, Mummy! Me! ME!'

A judder ran through him as he fought down the past, dragging himself with super-human effort back to the present.

'Christ,' he said shakily, still gripping Tony by the arms as he stepped away from him enough to look into his eyes. 'Christ, but it's good to see you, Tony. Hell . . .' he began laughing with nervous reaction. 'Hell, I didn't even recognize you!'

The stranger who was his twin shot him a lopsided smile. 'Nor me you, for a couple of seconds.' He picked up the duffel bag and slung it back over his shoulder. 'What's with the flash gear? Who's getting married?'

'No one. It's a statement.' He had himself under control again and as they began walking out of the Arrivals Hall his answering grin was as dazzlingly self-assured as always. 'What about your own gear? Add a couple of flowers and you'd be a hippy. Your hair is nearly on your shoulders.'

'Hippies don't wear cowboy boots,' Tony said easily. 'They wear sandals.'

Once again they looked at each other, their grins deepening.

'You reckon I'm going to look a bit out of place, then?' Tony said as they began walking again.

'Not so you'd notice. London's full of hippies – real hippies. You can't move for 'em in the King's Road. Thing is, though, Bermondsey isn't Chelsea and, even if it was, it wouldn't make any difference to the geezers who hang out with me. They're all pretty sharp dressers. It's part of being who we are. Part of the image, if you know what I mean.'

'No.' Tony sounded bemused. 'No, I haven't a clue.'

They'd been walking across to the Mustang, but as he took on board what Tony had said, Johnny stopped dead.

'You're joking, right?' he said, trying to get his head around the fact that Tony probably wasn't. 'I mean, you haven't forgotten things about Dad when we were kids, have you? I know you were only eight when . . . when . . .' It was a sentence he couldn't continue. 'I mean, you must remember how it always was – how he was such a beautiful dresser and always had big cars and a pocketful of money.'

'I remember the front door being hammered in whenever the police made a raid,' Tony said drily. 'Is that how things still are?'

Johnny hid his alarm at how much catching up the two of them were going to have to do. 'Nah,' he said, beginning to walk once again towards his car. 'The coppers spent years trying to put him away for keeps but they only ever succeeded in making a case stick once, and by the time the hookey witnesses had done their stuff he only got a couple of years.'

He came to a halt beside the Mustang. 'Dad's got enough coppers in his pocket these days to keep him well safe – and he ain't into robberies and front-line stuff like that. He specializes in protection and repossessions.' He took his keys out of his pocket and shot Tony a speculative glance. 'It suits his personality. He likes hurting people. He always has. Remember?'

'Yeah.' Tony didn't meet his glance. Instead he looked at the car in disbelief. 'Is this a joke hire car, Johnny? An American Mustang? In London? I thought everyone drove Minis over here.'

'Not me.' Johnny's grin was back in place again as he unlocked the Mustang's door. 'I'm into over-the-top style.' He thought of Zoë and his grin deepened. 'It never fails, Tony. Trust me.'

Tony slid into the front passenger-seat. 'OK. I've got the picture re you and the old man. What else is new? Are any of the kids we went to school with, still around? What about the Baileys? And Fast-Boy Flynn?'

'Fast-Boy's a fucking lunatic.' Johnny slammed the Mustang into gear and slewed out of the car park. 'You'll never guess what Amber Bailey told me earlier today. He's tooled himself up with a shotgun. She heard Angie Flynn – d'you remember Angie, Fast-Boy's sister? – telling Sharyn about it. There's nothing Fast-Boy would like better than to have me off the scene, so I ain't too happy about it, know what I mean?'

Belying his words, he started chuckling. 'He might really go to town with his shotgun when he finds out I've just taken his girlfriend away from him. She's from

Blackheath – a real class act – and, between you and me, I reckon she's going to be the most important person in my life. I can feel it in my blood and bones.'

'And who is she?' Tony asked, genuinely interested. 'What's her name?'

'Zoë Fairminder. Her old man's a grammar school headmaster. He won't be too happy when he finds out about me, but I'll tell him it could have been worse. I'll tell him it could have been Fast-Boy!'

They careened on to the A4, laughing fit to bust a gut. Tony rested a booted foot on the dashboard, his leg comfortably bent, and dragged a cigarette from a pocket of his jeans.

He was back. This was England. Soft green fields skirting either side of the main road. Hedges. Woods. Everything small-scale. Everything neat and tidy.

Everything safe.

He was glad Johnny had a girl he was mad about. He wanted Johnny to be happy.

'So when do I get to see Zoë?' he asked, flicking ash out of the open window.

'Tonight. I've told her we'll be in the Prince of Wales. D'you remember the Prince? The pub on the corner? I thought we'd call in there now, before going home, so that you can get a couple of brandies in your gut before meeting up with the old man.'

'Good idea.'

At the wealth of meaning in his voice, Johnny flashed him a look, opened his mouth to say something and then thought better of it.

Tony's relief was deep. There'd be time enough to discuss the old man when he more fully had his bearings. For the moment, just being back in England was disorientation enough.

They were heading into a built-up area and, though the countryside had been pretty much as he had remembered it, the streets were far different. Surely they hadn't been so wide when he'd been a kid? Nor so busy. And there were high-rise buildings in the distance. Flats, perhaps. Or offices. Whatever they were, they were no part of the England he remembered.

Not until they were in London proper and approaching Piccadilly did he experience a slamming feeling of recognition. Eros was still there, looking ridiculously small, and Lillywhites, where his mother had bought him a pair of football boots for his seventh birthday. And then they were driving down the Haymarket and into Trafalgar Square and the massive stone lions he and Johnny had clambered on as children were just as he had remembered them, as were the flocks of pigeons and crowds of tourists.

'And now for the river,' Johnny said as they veered into the Strand. 'This is going to be quite something.'

It was. Though he didn't join in with Johnny's American Indian war whoop as, minutes later, they sped over Waterloo Bridge, he certainly understood it. Nothing signified London as much as the Thames and he was well aware that, once it was at his back, he was nearly home.

There were more blocks of flats he had no memory of; some buildings he half-remembered, but which looked so different, he couldn't be sure. There was a cinema at the Elephant and Castle roundabout that definitely hadn't been there when he'd been a kid, likewise a new-looking shopping precinct.

'We're nearly there,' Johnny said to him with charged emotion as they cruised past a building he finally recognized. It was the nursery school where Ewan Flynn had punched Johnny so hard his nose had bled like a river.

Their street was coming up on the left and he braced himself for the sight of the house.

'Pub first,' Johnny said.

Tony nodded, keeping his eyes firmly on the Prince of Wales' signboard, not trusting himself to look beyond it.

'The car park's officially out of action,' Johnny said as he spun the Mustang off the road and into the area beside the pub, taking no notice of the sign that said CAR PARK CLOSED. 'There's a sewage leak,' he added as he avoided a cordoned-off area around a deep pit. 'Workmen have been trying to sort it for days.'

Tony wasn't listening. As the car rocked to a halt he was looking beyond the car park and down the street. Slowly he stepped out of the car.

He could see the house clearly. Strange that he'd forgotten how near it was to the pub.

He stood with the backs of his legs hard against the car, unsure whether, if he attempted to walk, he would be able to.

Though the street looked the same, the house didn't. He'd known it had been re-roofed, of course, but he hadn't expected the roof tiles to still look new – or to be a different colour to those of the houses either side. The new-style window frames looked odd, too, not suiting the house as the original sash windows had suited it. And then something else impinged on his consciousness; something that made his scalp prickle and his breathing become fast and light.

The brickwork around the windows was discoloured and black. Smoke-black.

Johnny was speaking to him, but he wasn't listening. He was remembering fire and choking smoke and the sight of his mother stumbling from the house, Johnny in her arms.

'Ready for that brandy, now?' He finally became aware of what Johnny was saying.

'Yep.' He dragged his eyes away from the house. There'd been times over the last few weeks when he'd wondered if returning to London was the right thing to do. The last few seconds had given him his answer. 'Lead the way, Johnny,' he said, aware that the wheel of fate was turning full circle and that there was no getting off it. Not for him, anyway.

And certainly not for Johnny.

Chapter Three

'I'm revising for my shorthand exam and I don't want disturbing!' Zoë Fairminder shouted down the stairs to her mother.

Satisfied that she would now be left in peace for a couple of hours, she stepped back into her bedroom, closed the door behind her and, ignoring the Pitman notebooks strewn across her bed, threw herself down beside them so that she could think.

Fast-Boy Flynn or Johnny Martini? There was a decision to make and it was a harder one than she'd first thought it would be. Fast-Boy was crackers about her and she didn't have any qualms about losing him – unless, of course, she wanted to. Whereas Johnny . . .

She reached for the battered one-eyed teddy bear perched on the pillow next to her and hugged it to her chest. Johnny was an unknown quantity. He wanted her to leave Fast-Boy for him, but what would happen if and when she did? Would she still be his girlfriend in six months' time, or would he have ditched her as he had so offhandedly ditched all his previous girlfriends?

She chewed the corner of her lip. Johnny said he loved her, but as he wanted her to leave Fast-Boy for him, he would say that. The thing was, was it true?

Still with the teddy bear in her arms she rolled over on to her side. Johnny and Fast-Boy loathed each other and were always trying to score points over each other. Was that the reason Johnny was trying to steal her from

Fast-Boy? So that he'd be ahead in their bizarre game?

If it was, then, much as she yearned to be Johnny's girlfriend, the temptation was one she was going to resist. Being dumped by Johnny, six months down the line, would be too public a humiliation.

But what if there wasn't much chance of that happening? What if he really did love her as much as he said? What if he was as crackers about her as Fast-Boy was?

She rolled on to her back again, staring up at the ceiling. Sexy as Fast-Boy was, there was far more kudos in being Johnny's girlfriend. Johnny's father, Marco Martini, was a face; a full-fledged gangster. In the forties and fifties he'd been Billy Hill's right-hand man – and in books and magazines Billy Hill was still referred to as having been London's King of Crime. People reacted to the name Martini. They showed respect – the kind of respect that was exciting and glamorous.

A frisson of fear touched her spine as she thought of what would happen if her father was ever to find out the kind of company she had begun keeping. He'd kill her. Or he'd try to.

She savoured the fact that, no matter whether she was with Fast-Boy or Johnny, they wouldn't let her father get away with touching a hair of her head. It was a delicious thought. Her last boyfriend before Fast-Boy had been a cadet policeman and he'd been so careful not to offend her father – getting her home on time, etc – that it had been pathetic. He'd been scared of her father. Fast-Boy wasn't. And Johnny wouldn't be, either. Where the Martini family was concerned, it would be her father who would be scared of them.

She began giggling, finding the thought hysterically funny, half wanting it to happen and half dreading it. One thing was for sure: having an up-and-coming villain for a boyfriend was fun. They always had wads of money in their back pocket and were never afraid to spend it. The other girls at her secretarial college thought themselves lucky if their boyfriends spent a tenner on them. Fast-Boy would give her that for a quid cab fare, telling her to keep the change.

As for Johnny . . . Johnny was a seriously big spender. Life with Johnny would be life in the fast lane – and that was what she wanted. She certainly didn't want to be a secretary working for a miserably small pay packet. With a kick of her foot she sent the Pitman notebooks flying off the bed. Her parents could go take a running jump if they thought she was going to settle for the stultifying boredom of that little lot.

And nor was she going to settle for seeing Sharyn Bailey, the little scrubber who lived next door to Johnny and was always running round after him, finally landing him. Which left only one option.

She drew her knees up, sitting the teddy bear on top of them so that they could have a face-to-face talk.

'Have I to do it, Ted?' she asked, determined to come to a firm decision before her evening date with Fast-Boy. 'Have I to jilt Fast-Boy for Johnny?'

Ted's lone glass eye glittered provocatively. *Why not, Zoë?* he seemed to say. *Why not, when you enjoy danger so much?*

With a squeal of euphoria she tossed him high into the air. Ted had given her her answer and she was going to do it. She was going to go to the Prince of Wales tonight with Fast-Boy – and leave with Johnny. Until now she'd simply played at being a moll. With Johnny she really would be one – and she was going to enjoy every wild and wonderful moment of it.

*   *   *

37

'Three more Remy's, *per favore*,' Marco Martini said to the waitress. He liked peppering his speech with a little Italian. It helped fuel the rumours that he was Mafiosi.

'Where's the little bit of business we're taking care of this afternoon?' one of his companions asked, wiping his mouth on a napkin. 'Is it walking distance?'

'No.' Marco's voice was abrupt.

Aware that Marco wasn't in the mood to be chatty, his questioner didn't press the issue or betray his surprise at there being heavy business on the agenda. He hadn't expected it. Not when Marco was about to be reunited with the son he hadn't seen for ten years. What he'd been expecting was a celebration party.

'We're going to Knightsbridge,' Marco said unexpectedly as he nursed his re-filled brandy glass. 'I thought I'd celebrate Tony's return by acquiring a club somewhere other than Soho.'

His companions grinned, well aware that this wouldn't be done by visiting an estate agent or meeting up with a willing vendor.

Marco drained his glass, laid a fan of notes on the table without waiting for the bill and rose to his feet. 'He's Swedish, a legitimate businessman and the only effective shareholder in a holding company by the name of Entertainment Ltd. And what Entertainment Ltd controls is a small but exclusive gambling club a stone's throw from Harrods.'

As the two men walked from the restaurant in his wake they exchanged relaxed glances. When it came to putting the frighteners on, legit businessmen were a piece of cake.

Whether their assumption was right or wrong was of no concern to Marco. He simply wanted to expunge his nervous tension – and the only way he knew of achieving that was through an act of brutal violence.

What he wanted from his victim was the acceptance of the cash offer he was going to make him and a short and simple entry in Entertainment Ltd's company minutes, detailing the sale. There were minor shareholders to take into account, of course, but there was no need for their rights to be affected. They could keep their directorships and their profits. Anyone who didn't like his style of management would be eased out at his convenience.

The nice thing about it was that, not only would it all be legal, but he doubted he'd have to lay a hand on the Swede in order to gain his co-operation. The informant who'd tipped him off about Entertainment Ltd's vulnerable company structure had also mentioned that there was a Thai houseboy in residence at the Swede's Knightsbridge address.

As he stepped out into Charlotte Street, Marco smoothed the front of his double-breasted jacket. He was going to lash the houseboy to a chair and throw him down two flights of stairs. It would be as good a way as any of showing the Swede the kind of treatment he could expect if he didn't co-operate.

And it would be one way of passing the afternoon until he could no longer decently put off returning home.

Two hours later, unable to defer his return any longer, he was driving back across the river and into Bermondsey, wondering why he so stubbornly stayed there when he had the kind of money to enable him to live anywhere he chose.

He cruised at a steady speed down Jamaica Road, musing on the mystery that puzzled so many of his cronies – cronies who had long since moved out to pseudo manor-houses in Essex or Kent. Perhaps the nub of it was that he'd been born and brought up in Bermondsey and that, for him, roots counted for a lot. Even as a small child he'd never been able to understand how his father had torn himself away from Sicily. It was an uprooting he couldn't even begin to imagine.

There were other aspects, of course. As a professional criminal he was far more cautious than his outward flamboyance suggested. Flaunting the proceeds of crime by living in manorial style was a sure-fire way of attracting unwelcome attention – and in his book that was crass stupidity. Not that he didn't enjoy a bit of ostentatious luxury when it suited him. His house in Marbella was the last word in over-the-top opulence. Out in Spain, though, where it wasn't under anyone's nose, it didn't matter.

Decreasing speed, he took a left turn. Another aspect of Bermondsey that suited him was its nearness to Soho and the fact that everyone in the area knew who he was. It made him feel the kind of Sicilian godfather-figure he liked to think his father had been. He enjoyed the hush that fell over a room when he entered it; the tension that existed in a bar until he left.

Not that there were as many bars in Bermondsey as there had once been. The docks were dying, the new-style container-ships were berthing elsewhere, and many of the old streets were being demolished, and the now-unemployed dockers and their families who had once lived there were being re-housed in high-rise flats newly built on the area's outskirts. It had meant a sharp fall in custom for many of the local pubs.

Though some people had been glad to see the back of the Victorian two-up, two-down terrace houses, he hadn't. It was the kind of housing he'd been born and brought up in and he liked the little back yards and the front pavements where people gathered to pass the time of day. They may have been slums, but they'd had character. The house he and Sheelagh had moved into when they had married had been reminiscent of the house he had been born in. Built in 1910 it, too, had been a terrace house, but with its Edwardian stuccoed ceilings and mahogany woodblock floors still intact, it had been very classy terrace housing.

Sheelagh. His hands tightened on the wheel. Since Tony had announced he was coming home, he'd hardly had Sheelagh out of his thoughts. That was when he should have moved away, of course. After the fire. After his wife's death. It was what people had expected and, because of that, he'd stubbornly stayed put.

He turned into Magnolia Street. His street. The street his children had been born in. Well before reaching the front of his house, he drew to a halt, sunk in thought.

''Lo there, Mr Martini.'

He leaned across the passenger seat and lowered the window, regarding Amber Bailey with interest. Not many people would have gone out of their way to attract his attention – and he knew it wasn't Amber's age that accounted for her cheeky forwardness. He recognized fearlessness when he met it – and it was a quality twelve-year-old Amber Bailey possessed in spadefuls.

'Hello, Amber,' he said, a thought occurring to him that hadn't crossed his mind in years. He looked at her hair and decided yet again that it was impossible. 'Is your mother in?'

'I think so.' Amber wasn't too interested as to whether she was, or wasn't. 'Johnny brought Tony back from the airport hours ago. I thought he and Tony were identical twins. He doesn't look a bit like Johnny. He looks more like Bob Dylan.'

It was a startlingly unexpected comparison, but Marco didn't let it throw him from what he'd decided to do. 'Go tell your mother I'd like a word with her,' he said, noticing for the first time that there were flecks of blood on his knuckles.

Amber regarded him for a long moment. He knew what she was thinking. If he wanted to speak to her mother, why didn't he just knock on the front door? He could, he supposed, have told her that ten years earlier her mother had made him vow on Johnny's life that he'd never do so again – but he didn't.

'OK,' she said at last, taking his odd behaviour in her stride. 'Will do.'

She turned away from him and, at a negligent stroll, her thumbs hooked in the front pockets of her jeans, walked across the pavement towards her home. Despite all his inner turmoil he had to suppress a grin, knowing damn well she was aware that people usually did things he asked of them at a run.

Would Maureen come out and speak with him? It was a long shot, but as she'd have heard that Tony had arrived home, it was just possible that she might. She would, after all, be curious as to how he intended handling the situation he now found himself in.

Briefly he thought of how he'd handled it so far, recalling the bruised and battered body of the Thai houseboy and the unharmed Swede's gibbering terror. Then he thought of the sale transaction that had been entered into Entertainment Ltd's company minutes and, with a feeling of satisfaction, dismissed the incident from his mind.

Maureen . . . Surely ten years was long enough for her to be able to draw a line under the past and start all over again? Christ. As a woman who'd hit forty, she should be begging for the opportunity. Gorgeous girls half her age were craving his attention wherever he went. If ever a man could have his pick of women, he could. And did. At the present moment, though, no dolly-bird could give him what he needed, because what he needed was someone with whom he had a shared history. And the only person who adequately filled that category was Maureen Bailey.

Amber told her mother that Mr Martini was parked outside the house and that he wanted a word with her, and then watched her mother's face with interest.

Considering that Mr Martini had been their next-door neighbour since before she'd been born, she found her mother's attitude towards him odd. Her mother was a very friendly and chatty sort of person, but she was never friendly and chatty with Mr Martini. Not, of course, that many people were. He wasn't the kind of man to gossip with and borrow sugar from. Her mother, however, didn't speak to him even if she passed him in the street. And although her dad did a lot of running about for Mr Martini – and got paid well for it – her mother always behaved as if the arrangement didn't exist.

'He wants a word, does he?' her mother said now, her voice clipped and tight. She was wearing a red cotton dress that had shrunk so much in the wash it was stretched taut across her bosom and hips.

'Yes,' Amber said, waiting.

Her mother toyed with the crucifix hanging on a thin gold chain round her neck.

'Perhaps he wants to talk to you about Johnny's twin,' Amber ventured. 'He's home. I saw him going in the house with Johnny about an hour ago.'

'You see too much, young lady.'

Amber shrugged. Whether she did, or didn't, was neither here nor there. 'So?' she said impatiently. 'What are you going to do? Are you going to have a word with him, or aren't you?'

'I'm going and I don't want you with me.' Her mother pushed a mass of shoulder-length hair away from her face. 'No listening in, understand? And no telling your dad or our Sharyn about this, either.'

'I never tell Dad or Sharyn anything, as it goes,' she said, following her mother as she walked towards the door.

Once at the door she came to a reluctant halt, watching as her mother walked down the short path and across the pavement to the car. Though she'd promised not to listen in, she hadn't promised not to watch. By some kind of miracle the street was empty and no one else was watching – leastways, not from the pavement or a garden.

Though her mother had her back to her, Marco Martini, as he leaned across the front passenger-seat to speak to her mother through its open window, didn't. She was just wondering if she would be able to read his lips when he opened the passenger door, obviously with the intention of having her mother join him in the car.

Her mother didn't.

Instead, with a sharp movement of her foot she kicked the car door shut again.

Amber's interest became edged with nervousness. Her mother being stand-offish with Mr Martini was one thing; her nearly taking his hand off in a car door was quite another. What if Mr Martini took the incident out on her dad? Men like Mr Martini expected other men to be able to keep their wives in order – even when they weren't with them.

Her dad, of course, had never been able to keep her mum in order, but she didn't think he'd like Mr Martini knowing about it.

There were a couple of people in the street now, old people, who, in Amber's eyes, didn't really count. Marco Martini opened his car door and, with a face so shuttered she could read no emotion on it whatsoever, stepped out of the car and walked round it to join her mother on the pavement, standing with her in such a way that he, too, now had his back towards the house.

Unable to hear what was being said, Amber let her mind wander. When she'd told Johnny about Fast-Boy having got himself a shotgun, he'd said he much appreciated the info and that if she could get herself into the Prince of Wales that evening – which was where he and Tony were going to be celebrating Tony's return home – he'd buy her a snowball.

Snowballs were her favourite drink, but she didn't think she stood much chance of being able to take him up on his offer. The Prince of Wales' landlord was red-hot when it came to spotting anyone under age drinking alcohol and her hair was so hideously distinctive that she stood out like a sore thumb.

She'd be in the pub, though, snowballs or no snowballs. She wanted to see what Johnny's gang members would make of Tony's shoulder-length hair and ornately studded cowboy boots. She wanted to see how Angie Flynn would go about becoming his girlfriend. And she wanted to know if Fast-Boy would put in an appearance.

'Never!' she heard her mother say explosively. 'Not till hell freezes over!'

In utter finality she turned away from Marco Martini, her high-heeled mules slapping against her bare feet as she marched back to where Amber was still standing, her face so pale she looked ill.

'Mum . . .' Amber began to say, concerned for her.

Her mother didn't even look towards her. Hugging her arms as if against some kind of inner disintegration, she walked straight past her and into the house. Moments later, Amber heard a bedroom door slam shut. Macro Martini must have heard it, too, but if he did he gave no sign of it. Leaving his car where it was, he was walking towards his own house, his hands plunged deep in his trouser pockets, his massive shoulders slumped in weariness.

By nine o'clock when Amber sneaked into the Prince of Wales wearing as much of Sharyn's make-up as she'd been able to get her hands on, it was as crowded as if it were New Year's Eve.

The pub's regulars were all squeezed in around their usual tables; many of them, from the snippets of conversation she overheard, people who remembered Tony Martini's departure ten years ago. Marco Martini was centre-stage at the bar, his arm round Tony's shoulders as he bought drink after drink for the henchmen and hangers-on crowding around them. If his body language had been weary a little earlier, it wasn't any longer. Now there was an intensity about him that made the air positively crackle.

Johnny was a few yards away, the top button of a black silk shirt undone, a silver-grey tie pulled loose. Sharyn was standing as near to him as she could get, Angie Flynn at her side. Both were wearing skirts so short they were nearly non-existent, both had glasses of Babycham in their hands and both were shrieking with laughter in a way that indicated they wanted everyone to believe that they were right in there, at the heart of everything that was going on.

That they weren't was rather obvious as neither Johnny nor his father were sparing them an iota of attention.

Amber squeezed past a friend of her mother's and wondered how near the bar she could get without attracting the attention of Happy Harry, the landlord. Harry's nickname had been coined because he was such a miserable old bugger and, party or no party, if he saw her, he'd throw her out. It was a humiliation she didn't want, not when the pub was so crowded.

Adroitly she eased herself behind the massive bulk of Cheyenne. She now had the advantage of being able to hear an awful lot of what was going on around Johnny, but was shielded from the view of anyone serving at the bar.

'Yeah, man, it's fantastic to be back home,' she heard Tony Martini saying in a drawl that sounded almost American.

Now that she could see him near-to, it was obvious that he and Johnny were identical twins. Their being dressed so differently made it easy to distinguish between them, of course, but Amber knew that, even if they were to dress alike, she would never mistake one for the other. Their personalities were too different.

Whereas Johnny was all happy-go-lucky and full of fun, Tony was reserved, possessing an air of self-containment and self-sufficiency that reminded her strongly of his father. She wondered who the elder twin was and suspected it was Tony.

'Jimmy Jones don't look happy.' The speaker was a suited and booted figure standing close to Cheyenne. 'D'you reckon he's goin' to hold a grudge about what Johnny did to him this morning?'

Cheyenne turned slightly, looking over Amber's head to where a frozen-faced youth was standing near a cigarette-machine, staring mean-eyed at Johnny's back. 'Hold a grudge over what?' he said, not sounding too interested. 'Being held out of the window?' He shrugged his shoulders. 'He might, but where will it get him? If he's got any sense, he'll put up a show of laughing it off.'

'It'd take quite a sense of humour, mate. We were six storeys high! If Johnny had dropped him, he'd be drifting past Southend by now.'

As they both cracked with laughter, Angie, desperate to gain Tony's attention, called out loudly: 'Is London fab after Canada, Tony?'

'Yeah, well, I guess.' Tony looked rather startled, but that was probably because Angie was more exotically made up than Elizabeth Taylor in *Cleopatra*.

The question answered – after a fashion – he returned his attention to his father's friends, leaving Angie still thwarted.

Marco Martini was now rumbling with laughter at something one of his cohorts had said, and Amber's attention turned elsewhere. Her dad wasn't in the pub yet, thank goodness, though no doubt he soon would be. As she looked round, clocking who had put in an appearance and who hadn't, she saw Fast-Boy Flynn enter, dressed in black biking leathers as usual.

He stood for a moment, noting who was there and who wasn't, the same way she had just a moment ago. She saw him register his sister's presence deep in the Martini camp and witnessed a spasm of anger cross his face. It was an unusual face for a tough South Londoner: oddly fine-boned, the nose slightly aquiline, the cheekbones high. A lock of hair, dark and straight, hung across his forehead. It made him look very mean and moody – which, from everything she'd heard about him, he was.

On impulse she began weaving a way through the noisy knots of drinkers, intending to have a word with him.

'Watch it, Ginger Nut,' an ex-boyfriend of Sharyn's said as, in squeezing past him, she jogged his arm spilt some of his light ale.

Amber's eyes flashed fire. Why, just because her hair was the hideous colour it was, did no one refer to her by her proper given name? Why did it always have to be Carrot Head or Ginger Nut or, even worse, Ginge?

Still seething, she came to a halt a foot or so away from Fast-Boy. 'Have you come to say hello to Tony?' she asked bluntly. 'He isn't a bit like Johnny. You'll prob-ably quite like him.'

'Kids your age shouldn't be in pubs.'

It wasn't a very encouraging start, but at least he was speaking to her. 'I do what I like,' she said, wondering whether or not to ask him about the gun hidden in his mother's coal bunker.

Up till now he hadn't even looked at her directly. Now he did so. 'You're Sharyn Bailey's sister, aren't you? Angie says you're a real pain.'

'So's Angie,' she retorted, furious at being spoken of so disparagingly behind her back.

'Yeah.' He shot her an unexpected grin. 'I'd go along with that.'

There was a moment of something very like cam-araderie between them as the noise level in the bar grew even more deafening. 'I'm gonna get a drink,' he said, raising his voice to be heard. 'What are you having?'

'A snowball,' she shouted back unhesitatingly.

He didn't bat an eyelid. 'OK, Red. Wait here.'

As he shouldered a way through to the bar, she remained where she was. Red was a new name to add to the list, but it was a big improvement on Carrot-head or Ginger-nut. For one thing it sounded complimentary, not derogatory, and for another there was something sophisticated and adult about it. Very much to her surprise, she decided she rather liked it.

'So why are you in here tonight?' he asked when he returned and handed her her drink. 'Happy Harry doesn't go for having kids in his bar, you must know that.'

'I'm here because I wanted a closer look at Johnny's twin, and I don't give a stuff about Happy. Cheers.' She raised her glass and clinked it against his pint of Guinness.

He was no longer looking at her. A tall, slim girl with pale-gold shoulder-length hair had just entered the pub and commanded his attention. Grudgingly Amber had to admit that she certainly had style. Her sleeveless linen mini-dress was cyclamen-pink and unadorned, her expensive-looking boots knee-high and white.

'My girlfriend's here,' Fast-Boy said as the blonde began making her way towards him. 'You'd better scarper, Red. I don't want Zoë getting jealous.'

He was making fun of her, but she didn't mind. Though no one else she knew liked him, she rather did. She was even beginning to wish she hadn't told Johnny about his having a gun hidden away.

Drinking her snowball fast, so that she'd neither spill it nor have it taken away from her, she manoeuvred her way back to the corner of the bar where Marco Martini was holding court.

Despite all the loud gales of laughter, there wasn't a great deal of interest going on. Angie looked to be no nearer to gaining Tony's attention. Johnny had moved from where he had been standing so that he was now surrounded by his gang members, making it impossible for Sharyn to drape herself around him. Tony was still standing next to his father, his hands in his pockets, neither drinking nor smoking.

Out of the corner of her eye, Amber saw Fast-Boy's girlfriend say something to him and then begin making her way towards the ladies loo. It was somewhere she, too, now needed to go. The door leading to the toilets was just beyond the cigarette-machine and she hadn't yet reached it when she saw that Johnny, too, was heading in that direction. As they reached the cigarette-machine, Johnny and Fast-Boy's girlfriend converged – and not, as far as Amber could see, by accident.

'So have you finished with him, yet?' she heard Johnny say.

As she hovered within earshot, wanting to hear Fast-Boy's girlfriend's reply, she was aware she wasn't the only person listening in. The youth Johnny's mates had been discussing earlier was still lounging against the cigarette-machine, eyeing Johnny stonily. If Johnny was aware of him, he gave no sign.

'I'm going to ask him to take me outside and then I'm going to do it,' Zoë was saying. 'But only if you're really serious about me, Johnny.'

'I love you, darlin'.' The throb in Johnny's voice indicated that he was speaking the truth. 'Only you, Zoë. Honest. Cross my heart.'

'What if Fast-Boy gets nasty?' There was an edge of real apprehension in Zoë's voice. 'What if he starts slapping me around when I tell him? He's got a wild temper and he really is crazy about me. He once said he'd kill me rather than lose me.'

'Don't worry about Fast-Boy. Finish with him and wait for me in the car park. I'll meet you out there and we'll go off somewhere nice and quiet to celebrate. Know what I mean?'

Even standing a foot or so behind Zoë, Amber could see the fire in Johnny's searingly blue eyes. She wondered if he'd ever looked at Sharyn in such a way, and doubted it.

Knowing exactly what he meant, Zoë gave a little shiver of delicious anticipation.

As Johnny watched her make her way back across the crowded pub to where an unsuspecting Fast-Boy was waiting, he said to Amber, 'I know I promised you a snowball, but what about a glass of champagne? I've got a lot to celebrate.'

'Lovely. I'll have a cherry in it, please.'

'I was talking about proper champagne,' he said, pained. 'Not Babycham muck.'

He moved back in the direction of the bar, people making way for him with alacrity. Amber didn't bother to watch. She was too busy trying to see what was happening between Zoë and Fast-Boy.

The youth who Johnny's gang member thought might have a grudge against Johnny had gone. By standing in the space he had vacated she was able to see Zoë say something to Fast-Boy that drew a frown from him, then the two of them were walking out of the pub, the tension between them palpable.

With the glass of champagne Johnny had bought for her now in her hand, Amber fought down the temptation to follow them. The barney they would be having would be major and Fast-Boy wouldn't appreciate an audience. Another reason for staying put was that there was another barney taking place and, as it was between Johnny and her sister, it was more interesting.

From where she was standing she couldn't hear what

was being said, but the gist was obvious. Johnny was telling Sharyn to quit hanging around him.

It wasn't often Amber felt sorry for her sister, but she felt sorry for her now. Johnny could, after all, have put her straight somewhere he couldn't have been overheard. As it was, though, Tony wasn't a witness to her humiliation, having sauntered off to the loo moments before. But Angie most certainly was and so were dozens of Johnny's friends.

As Johnny finally turned his back on her and began talking to Cheyenne, Amber saw Sharyn push her way free of the group she'd so badly wanted to be a part of, tears streaking her face as she made a beeline for the nearest door. It was a rear door and Amber put her empty champagne glass down on top of the cigarette-machine, about to try and catch up with her.

A heavy hand fell on her shoulder, preventing her from doing so. 'I've told you before!' Happy Harry thundered. 'No under-age drinking in my pub! Got it?'

As Happy twisted one of her arms high up her back, Tony Martini walked past them on his way back to the bar. His only reaction as Happy began frogmarching her towards the pub's main door, as if he were a copper and she a violent criminal, was one of amusement.

He wasn't the only person amused by her predicament. Scores of people were either sniggering or calling out the kind of jokey helpful advice she could well have done without. She caught a glimpse of her father and knew she'd have hell to pay later, at home. Then, in utter mortification, she saw that Fast-Boy was back in the bar.

'OUT!' Happy hollered, playing up to his customers for all he was worth as he opened the door leading to the street and hurled her out on to it.

'FAT PIG!' she hollered back, vowing never to forgive him.

From inside the pub came shouts of laughter and then the door slammed shut and she was out in the darkness, alone.

She stood for a few moments, so angry that she was panting. How *dare* Happy make such a laughing stock of her? Why couldn't he just have politely asked her to leave? She rubbed her bruised wrist and cautiously wiggled her shoulder to make sure it hadn't been wrenched from its socket.

It was gone ten o'clock and dark, but she didn't want to go home. Her mum would want to know where the hell she'd been and, even if she managed to avoid a ruck with Mum, Sharyn would be crying about Johnny all over the place.

Moodily she wandered round the corner of the pub and into the pitch-black car park. She needed a wee-wee and there'd be a certain satisfaction in pissing against Happy Harry's property.

She kicked some rubble out of the way, undid her jeans, wriggled them down past her knees and squatted with her back against the wall of the pub. Then, as her eyes adjusted to the darkness, she saw the booted foot.

The boot was elegantly heeled and white and in a curious position, sole upwards. It didn't seem to be connected to a body.

Forgetting all about relieving herself, Amber stood up, adjusting her jeans. Then she took a step forward and, stumbling on another piece of rubble, fell to her knees. Her hands shot out to break her fall and smacked against an edge of jagged concrete rimming a yawning black void.

Down below her she could see the outline of a body –

a body that had fallen into the void headlong, leaving only one foot protruding over the pit's lip.

A body whose head was at an improbable angle.

A body wearing a mini-dress that, even though it was too dark to see for certain, Amber knew was cyclamen-pink.

A body that was very, very dead.

Chapter Four

Six months later, as Angie made her way to the Take Six recording studios for a clandestine rendezvous with Johnny, it was typical December weather, dank and freezing cold. It was also dark and the cobbled streets surrounding the now dead and dying docks made walking in flimsy-heeled fashion boots difficult.

'Bugger,' she said vehemently as, yet again, she went over on her ankle.

Why Johnny liked meeting her in such a creepy place was beyond her. He said it was because no one would see them together there – and by no one, of course, he meant Tony. If her regular boyfriend had been anyone else, she knew that Johnny wouldn't have given a flying fuck whether they were seen or not.

She pulled the imitation fox-fur collar of her coat as high as it would go in order to keep her ears warm. Once, she'd been to the recording studios with Sharyn during the day and the atmosphere, then, had been very different. There'd been all sorts of interesting-looking people buzzing in and out. Sharyn had been on a high, of course, full of the fact that they were only there because Johnny now took her everywhere with him.

'Nearly, Sharyn,' she'd wanted to say. 'Nearly, but not quite.' A smirk tugged at the corner of her mouth as she turned into a narrow road lined with warehouses. Johnny certainly didn't bring Sharyn with him when he and she met up in the studios and shagged each other senseless on the carpeted floor of his father's private sanctum.

Only once had anything happened to spoil the furtive excitement of it all. That had been the time when, his eyes closed and his face contorted by passion, he'd called out Zoë's name.

She came to an abrupt halt, searching her handbag for cigarettes and lighter. It had probably been understandable, but she hadn't liked it. She'd never known if he'd been aware of his slip because, if he had, he never mentioned it. She wondered if he ever called out Zoë's name when he was with Sharyn.

Zoë.

She slid a Marlboro from its packet, reflecting on the strange and nasty Zoë business.

Because of the circumstances there'd had to be an autopsy and the coroner's verdict had been one of accidental death. What had been nasty was that it had been such a preventable accident. The deep drop left by the council workmen, exposing the sewer they were repairing, was one that had been clearly and appropriately barricaded off by them, but the barricade had been kicked away.

Because the pub's car park had been closed to cars the night Zoë had died, very few people had crossed it in order to enter the pub and it had been impossible to determine just when this act of vandalism had taken place.

A local bookmaker had stated that the barricade was still in place when he had taken a short-cut to the pub at about nine o'clock. After that, no one was sure. All that was absolutely certain was that it hadn't been there when, following her row with Fast-Boy and after he had re-entered the pub without her, Zoë had walked into the unlit car park and fallen in the pit, breaking her neck and dying within seconds.

Angie lit her cigarette and inhaled deeply. From where she was standing she could see the converted warehouse where the Take Six recording studios had its home and she could also see that Johnny's Mustang was not yet parked outside. With nothing else to occupy her mind, she continued thinking about the hideous days that had followed Zoë Fairminder's death.

The worst time had been the immediate aftermath when the words 'foul play' were being bandied about and when her brother had been questioned for hours at a time at London Bridge Police Station. Then had come the inquest and relief at the result had been vast. It hadn't prevented people from suspecting that Fast-Boy was responsible for the accident, though.

He'd been seen having a barney with Zoë in the pub. He'd been seen leaving the pub with her and had been overheard continuing his barney with her on the pub's doorstep. If it hadn't been for Tommy Bailey, Sharyn and Amber's dad, making a statement saying he'd been behind Fast-Boy when he had walked back into the pub and that, as they had done so, Zoë had been flouncing away, things could have been worse than nasty. They could have been dire.

'Fast-Boy was only out of the pub for a few minutes,' Tommy Bailey had said, wading in on Fast-Boy's behalf. 'He couldn't have kicked the barricade away without the Zoë girl being there when he did it. And if she was there when he did it, she wouldn't have gone anywhere near the drop, would she? Not even if he'd asked very, very nicely.'

It was a point of view the police also came round to eventually, but they weren't happy about it – and they'd let Fast-Boy know that they weren't.

Then there had been the lingering effects of the fight

that had taken place between Fast-Boy and Johnny in the hours after Zoë's death. A private encounter, the result was public knowledge. Fast-Boy had stumbled into St Thomas' Casualty Department, his face a mask of blood, and Johnny had staggered into Casualty at nearby Guy's. Fast-Boy had copped for a reef of stitches in a wound that had nearly cost him an eye, and Johnny had had two broken ribs tightly bound and a dislocated jaw re-set.

Whether Johnny had taken on Fast-Boy one-to-one because he believed Fast-Boy to be responsible for Zoë's death, and whether Fast-Boy had tried to annihilate Johnny because Zoë had told him that Johnny was the reason she was finishing with him, Angie didn't know. Certainly the fact that Zoë had been about to become Johnny's girlfriend wasn't generally known. Sharyn, for instance, still didn't know – at least not for sure.

She knew because Johnny had told her.

She wasn't certain, but she thought perhaps she was the only person he had really talked to in the weeks following Zoë's death.

'Tony's been great about it,' he'd said to her, looking oddly dishevelled, his tie pulled loose, his face showing lines of strain. 'Without Tony, I don't know how I'd have got through this last couple of weeks. The thing is, though, he's never had a girl he's been really batty about, the way I was batty about Zoë. Me and Zoë, we'd have been together forever, Angie. It was written in the stars, know what I mean?'

Though Johnny had talked to her at length about his grief over Zoë, her brother hadn't said a word to her, nor, as far as she knew, had he spoken to anyone else. Always reticent, in the months after Zoë's death he had become even more withdrawn; not mixing with anyone, not finding himself another girlfriend, not letting on to anyone where he was spending his time or where the money he was never short of came from.

When another gun, a .38 Colt, had joined the sawn-off shotgun in the coal bunker, she hadn't told anyone about it, not even Sharyn.

Johnny's grief had been very different. More than once he'd cried into his lager when talking about Zoë. It had been an unnerving sight, but no one had taken the piss. If Johnny wanted to warble on about how Zoë was now an angel in heaven, then that was his prerogative. Only Jimmy Jones had been heard to sneer – and he'd sneered from a very safe distance.

Sharyn, well aware of how interested in Zoë Johnny had been, was over the moon at the way her rival had disappeared from the scene so suddenly and so permanently. Not that she let anyone know, apart from Angie.

'And it's a lie that Johnny was crazy about her,' she had said stubbornly. 'He wasn't, Angie. He's sorry she died like that, but he'd be sorry whoever it had been.'

It wasn't true, but she had no intention of putting her choice position in jeopardy by telling Sharyn so.

She took another deep draw on her cigarette. Choice. It was a lovely word and it summed up her present situation perfectly. She'd become Tony Martini's girlfriend, just as she'd intended she would be even before she had met him. And she was sleeping with his brother as well. When it came to choice, she had it – and very nice it was, too.

She saw Johnny's Mustang nudge into the street from the far end, but remained where she was in order to finish her cigarette. It didn't do to seem too eager where Johnny was concerned. It was a lesson Sharyn would have done well to learn.

Being Tony's girlfriend wasn't the mind-blowing experience she'd led Sharyn to believe. He was far too carelessly indifferent and, when it came to the bed department, he didn't have a quarter of Johnny's to-die-for expertise. It had been a disappointment, but she hadn't allowed it to faze her. What mattered was that she was the girlfriend of one of the Martini twins and, as such, had the kind of status she'd always craved.

Sharyn, of course, believed herself to be Johnny's steady girlfriend and it was true that, as the weeks after Zoë's death had merged into months, Johnny had begun paying attention to her again. He had also, when Sharyn wasn't around to see him, begun paying attention to Angie.

She'd slept with him because she'd always wanted to sleep with him; because it was such fun to be doing so when Sharyn didn't have a clue about it, and because, unlike his twin, he fucked absolutely brilliantly.

Which was why, at this moment in time, she was about to meet him at a rendezvous where there was no chance of them being seen by Tony.

She dropped her cigarette butt to the pavement and crushed it into extinction. There were times when she wondered if Johnny only made love to her because Tony did, too. The fact that she was Tony's girlfriend – and Tony's only girlfriend – certainly seemed to give him a buzz. He was always asking questions about Tony's performance in bed – and she was always winding him up by telling him that Tony was absolutely ace.

There was a smirk on her face as she crossed the road to the recording studios entrance. She was playing the notorious Martini twins as if they were a pair of pianos. And the only thing she had to worry about was what her brother would do if he found out about her and Johnny.

She remembered the handgun that had joined the shot-gun in Fast-Boy's secret stow and a lick of fear ran down her spine. Fast-Boy was such an unknown quantity – even to her – that there was no telling what he might do. Or who he might do it to.

Savouring the excitement of skating on such thin ice, she walked into the building.

He was waiting for her in an area beyond the door that had been tarted up with pot plants and a reception desk.

'Hi, Babe,' he said with the down-slanting smile that sent her heart somersaulting. 'Where does Tony think you are? With Sharyn?'

'He might,' she said, wanting to keep him on his toes. 'And then again, he might be looking for me. Who knows?'

'Quit teasing,' he said, an edge to his voice as he pulled her into his arms.

She leaned against him willingly, raising her face to his. The next moment his hands were hard upon her body, her mouth dry as his tongue slipped past her lips. He didn't lower her to the floor to make love to her and nor did he take her into the carpeted office. He simply eased her back against the wall and took her where she stood.

It was an immediacy that she loved. As her fingers tightened in the coarseness of his hair and her breath came in short, urgent gasps, she knew that Sharyn's days as his girlfriend were numbered and that she would soon be ditching Tony; that before long it was going to be her and Johnny. What Johnny had been so sure was writ-ten in the stars wasn't Zoë's name entwined with his. It was hers.

He just hadn't realized it yet, that was all.

*　　*　　*

Tony Martini strolled into the Prince of Wales, his only concession to the chilly December evening, a zip-up bomber jacket. After living for ten years in a country where winters were truly ferocious, he couldn't get his head around the fact that, in Britain, 5°C was regarded as being seriously cold.

'Hi, mate. What can I get you?' Happy Harry managed something that passed for a welcoming grin. If Tony was in the pub, Johnny might be joining him – and if Johnny was joining him, it meant the Prince would soon be heaving with dozens of Johnny's hangers-on.

'A Coke.'

Though he'd sometimes ask for a whisky and ginger ale, Coke was his usual request and one Happy still flinched at. 'Right you are,' he said, wondering how Johnny coped with having a twin who was so near tee-total. It was almost as bad as the way he dressed. Johnny and the blokes who ran with him were all snazzy dressers: Italian suits, crocodile shoes, silk socks, heavy gold watches and signet rings were pretty much a uniform with them. It set them apart and made them look distinctive, and Johnny liked to look distinctive. He certainly looked distinctive these days, going around with his twin, but Happy doubted that it was in a way that he liked.

Six months after arriving back in England, Tony was still wearing the black jeans and silver-studded boots he'd been wearing when Johnny had met him at Heathrow. Happy slid a bottle of Coke and a glass across the bar top, thankful that Tony wasn't also sporting a cowboy hat.

Tony poured the Coke into the glass and, not wanting to get into a tedious conversation with Happy, walked across to a corner table near the cigarette-machine. Apart from himself and a handful of elderly locals, the pub was empty. Which was the way he liked it.

He parked his behind, sitting with one leg akimbo across the other, a hand resting comfortably on his booted ankle. By rights, he should have been out with Angie, but she'd rung him a couple of hours ago saying she had bad period pains and was going to bed, and that she would see him tomorrow.

He took a swig of his Coke, amazed at how dozy some girls could be. The last thing he wanted to know about was her periods, for Christ's sake. Not unless, of course, she stopped having them. If that happened, the situation would just have to be sorted.

He wondered if, in continuing to go out with her, he was being fair to her. Knowing that he wasn't, he tried to stop thinking about it.

He couldn't.

One of the first things that had become obvious to him on his return home had been that, unless he armed himself with a regular girlfriend, he would be pestered to death by girls everywhere he went. The solution had been Angie and, to do her justice, their relationship hadn't been devoid of interest.

For one thing, she remembered his mother. 'Me and Sharyn must've been five or six and we were always in and out of your house – not that I'd expect you'd remember. You and Johnny were usually running the streets with a gang of Johnny's mates. Sharyn's mum was best friends with your mum and whenever she called in for a chat, we'd go with her. Your mum made yummy scones – and Irish soda bread. My mum never bothered making anything. All me and Fast-Boy got was bread and jam – and that was only if we were lucky.'

She'd laughed, but he hadn't.

His mum's soda bread. She'd brought back memories of it so vivid he'd thought he was going to cry. His hand tightened around his glass. That had been the hard part about being back home. The memories he'd been forced to face up to.

There'd been the attic bedroom, for instance. The room he and Johnny had been trapped in when the fire had started. How he'd forced himself to step through its door again, he still didn't know. For a few seconds he'd had to hold on to the door jamb till a wave of sickness had passed. The room was totally different, of course, to how it had been when he and Johnny had slept in it. Back then it had been a small room, identical to the one adjoining it, but during the rebuilding work the two rooms had been made into a single room big enough to take a full-size snooker table.

He'd walked around it, trailing his fingertips across the green baize, wondering if it had been where one of the legs of the snooker table now rested that he'd stood transfixed with terror as Johnny had shrieked, 'Me, Mummy! Me! ME!' It had been impossible to know for sure. But there was no uncertainty as to the exact point where, from the window, he had watched his mother stumble from the flames with Johnny in her arms.

Johnny.

His being reunited with Johnny had, for ten years, been nearly all he'd thought about. And now that they were reunited, it was just as wonderful as he had dreamed it would be. It was also strange in ways he hadn't expected.

He drained his glass, wondering why he'd never realized just how much of a crim Johnny had become. Their letters to each other had always been pretty stilted and inadequate, which wasn't surprising when both of them were so crap at putting words on paper. Why Johnny couldn't do it, he didn't know. Johnny had, after all, gone to school until he'd left the day he turned sixteen.

He hadn't been so lucky.

A nerve began to throb at the corner of his jaw.

He hadn't been lucky at all.

He squeezed his eyes tight shut against the memory of Albie hauling him from bed at the crack of dawn for another eternally long, grindingly hard day of manual labour on the ranch. School was a paradise he'd only enjoyed for a handful of scattered weeks each year. When Albie had needed an extra pair of hands, he'd had to supply them, no question.

If anyone came round from the school authorities, asking why he was absent, Albie always made him squat in a rat-infested hidey-hole in the barn roof. He could hear Albie telling them he was away, visiting relatives. It was the same hidey-hole he was locked in whenever it was punishment time – and punishment time with Albie came round with heart-stopping regularity.

'Wotcha, Tone. How ya' doin'?'

Cheyenne grinned down at him, jerking him abruptly and mercifully back into the present.

'Fine,' he lied, not betraying the truth by even a flicker of an eyelid.

'Coke, is it?' Cheyenne nodded towards his empty glass.

'Yeah. Fine.' Tony struggled to look affable. He hadn't wanted his privacy invaded, but Cheyenne was more bearable than some of the other members of Johnny's team.

As Cheyenne sauntered across to the bar, he thought about Johnny and the extreme way that, for several weeks after Zoë's death, Johnny had grieved for her. A few people had, he knew, thought Johnny was putting on something of a show.

It wasn't a mistake he had made. They were twins and, even if they didn't dress alike any more or want the same things out of life, there was still an uncannily deep bond between them. He'd known when Johnny had first told him about Zoë that he was serious about her and that, if Zoë hadn't died, she and Johnny would have been together long-term – perhaps long-term enough for Johnny to have settled down.

He chewed the corner of his lip, wondering if Johnny might even have embarked on a more legit lifestyle. It was possible. He suspected that a straight middle-class girl like Zoë would have become disillusioned with being a moll just as soon as the reality of what it entailed hit in. A couple of dawn raids by the police, having her front door axed off its hinges and her home turned over, and she'd soon have been wanting Johnny to become a straight go-er.

That, though, wouldn't happen now.

As Cheyenne returned, a glass of brandy in one hand, a Coke in the other, he wondered what Johnny's reaction was going to be when he told him about the law course he intended taking. His completing it and going on to law school would be a long uphill struggle when his formal education had been so sporadic, but he knew he was fiercely bright and he knew he could do it.

His mouth twitched in a smile as Cheyenne handed him his drink. The old man would have ten fits. Hell, if he were to achieve his ambition and become a criminal lawyer his dad would be so mortified he'd probably leave the frigging country!

'Cheers,' he said to Cheyenne, in better spirits than

he'd been for weeks. 'So what's new? Is Johnny still running you ragged over his long-firm scam?'

Amber dug her hands deep into her pockets against the December cold. She'd spent the evening at a friend's and it was now nine-thirty and she was unwillingly on her way home. Why her mum was so fussed about her being home by ten was beyond her. What did it matter what time she got home, as long as she got up for school each morning? Which she always did – eventually. Plus, she was now thirteen and a teenager. A sensible mother would surely have let her use her own judgement about what time she got in, but her mother wasn't sensible. Having watched her closely for weeks, she'd come to the decision that her mother was, in fact, decidedly odd.

Why, for instance, did she go to such lengths to avoid Mr Martini? If her mother got to the front gate and saw that Mr Martini was anywhere in the street, she immediately hurried back in and, whatever her errand might have been, she didn't set out on it again until she was sure the coast was clear. Obviously her mother and Mr Martini had once had a huge barney over something – but what had that something been?

Still with her hands deep in her pockets, she slouched around a corner, leaving Jamaica Road and its ceaseless roar of cars and brightly lit buses behind her. That her mother and Mr Martini had once been on friendly terms she knew because of the photograph album stuffed with pictures of Sharyn as a baby, then as a toddler, and then at primary school. That her mother had never bothered to keep photographs of her in a similar album had always riled her. It was as if Mum had run out of enthusiasm for album-keeping after she'd been born – and photograph-taking, too, for there were far more photographs of Sharyn than there were of her.

She had recently spent a moody half-hour flicking through Sharyn's album and, with her new awareness of just how carefully her mother avoided running into Mr Martini, she'd been surprised to see how many days out their two families had enjoyed together before she had been born, when it was just Sharyn and the twins.

Mr Martini's wife had been alive then, of course, and Mrs Martini and her mum had been best friends. As well as the photographs of her mum with Sharyn and the twins, and of Mrs Martini with the twins and Sharyn, there were lots of pictures of her dad and Mr Martini. Most of them looked as if they'd been taken at the seaside, at Margate perhaps, or Ramsgate. Amongst the photographs tucked loosely in the back of the album there was even a photograph of Mr Martini holding her as a baby.

She didn't know why she was so sure the baby was her, but she was. She was swaddled in a shawl and could have only been a few weeks old. There was no one else in the photograph and, unlike so many of the others, it hadn't been taken at the seaside but in a field, with woods in the distance and a horse grazing. Who had taken it? Her dad? Her mum? It was an odd photograph and looking at it made her feel strangely uncomfortable. Did Mr Martini remember that someone had once taken a photograph of him cradling her in his arms? She hoped he didn't, because she found it too embarrassing for words.

She was approaching the Prince of Wales now and she slouched to a halt. It was still way off ten o'clock and on principle she had no intention of walking into her home a minute before her deadline. The problem was, though, it was too cold for hanging around to be a pleasure. She looked speculatively at the door of the pub and then dismissed the idea. Unlike the night of Tony's welcome home party, six months ago, there was hardly any noise coming from inside the Prince and she judged it was probably half empty – which meant she stood no chance of sliding in unobserved.

On a whim she turned into the alley that divided the back gardens of the houses on her side of the road from the back gardens of the next street. It was narrow and dark, the only light coming from a lone, old-fashioned streetlamp, but it suited her mood perfectly. Why was being thirteen no different to being twelve? She'd expected that, once she became a teenager, life would have become instantly more interesting, but it hadn't. Sharyn still never took her anywhere with her. Her mother still went haywire if she wore make-up and flatly refused to let her wear anything approaching a mini-skirt. Even worse, no one would mull over the whys and wherefores of Zoë Fairminder's death with her.

'It was an accident, got it?' was all Sharyn said whenever she attempted to talk to her about it. 'Some kids kicked the barricade away from the hole and the silly cow fell in. I'm sick of people trying to make out that Johnny had anything to do with it, and Angie's sick of people saying Fast-Boy gave her a helping hand.'

'Or you,' she had retorted maliciously the last time Sharyn had been high-handed about it with her. 'Are you sure it wasn't you, Sha? I was there, remember? You making out Zoë wasn't about to become Johnny's girl-friend won't wash with me, 'cos I know different. She went outside with Fast-Boy to finish with him; if she'd walked back in, she'd have come back in as Johnny's girlfriend. And don't make out you didn't know that was on the cards, 'cos you did. It's why you rushed out, crying. And if you were still outside when Zoë went outside you'd have had a real ruck with her, wouldn't you? I bet you –'

Before she could finish the sentence, Sharyn had laid into her with a shriek of outrage, slapping, kicking and punching, and it had taken their mother – who could slap and punch with the best of them – to break it up.

Still mulling over Zoë Fairminder's fateful accident, she walked past her back gate, continuing to the point where the alley exited into the street parallel to her own. She didn't seriously think Sharyn had done for Zoë Fairminder – at least not intentionally. She wouldn't have put it past her sister to have removed the barricades around the pit, though, if she'd known Zoë was going to be out there in the dark, waiting for Johnny. What Sharyn would have been hoping, of course, was that in falling Zoë would have ruined her Mary Quant dress, messed up her hair and emerged looking a fright.

As she pondered the fact that her sister might have a lot on her conscience, she heard the sound of a motor-bike fast approaching the bottom end of the alley. It wasn't an unusual event as the Flynns lived in the next street and the gates of their back yard were just below the alley's lone streetlamp.

She stopped, waiting to see if the bike was Fast-Boy's Harley.

It was.

He slewed into the alley, bringing the bike to a halt below the lamp. He was wearing his leathers, of course, but there was also something that looked like a length of curtaining bunched up round his waist.

She was just about to call out to ask him what it was, and to let him know that she was there, when, as he dismounted from the bike and stepped into the lamp's yellowish pool of light, she saw his face.

Her eyes widened and her jaw dropped.

He was wearing make-up. Sooty black eyeliner and glossy sizzling-pink lipstick. And the gaudy material bunched around his waist, over the top of his leathers, wasn't curtaining.

It was a skirt.

Chapter Five

Johnny crushed a couple of pound notes into the hat being proffered by a carol-singer as he made his way down Deptford High Street towards his favourite billiard-hall. Life should have been good, yet it wasn't. He dug his hands deeper into the pockets of his Crombie overcoat. He still thought about Zoë, of course, and that didn't make for a happy frame of mind. He and Zoë would have made a great couple. She'd had class. Real class.

He crossed the busy road, distancing himself from the off-key strains of 'Silent Night', certain that if Zoë hadn't fallen and broken her neck he wouldn't now be feeling so pissed-off about everything. Tony, for instance. What the fuck was wrong with the guy? Why couldn't it be the way it was when they were kids? Hell, not only had they wanted to do the same things then, they'd thought the same things. Now there were times when it was hard to believe they were even brothers, let alone twins.

He mooched into a doorway beside a men's outfitters and mounted a flight of uncarpeted stairs heavy-footed. Not only was Tony refusing to have any involvement with the scam he'd set up for the two of them, he'd enrolled at a college as a mature student and was studying for a clutch of exams.

At first when Tony had told him what he was doing, he'd thought he was having him on. Then, when he realized Tony wasn't joking, he'd thought perhaps his twin had lost the plot because of his having been in the wilds of Canada for so long. The trouble was, as Tony never talked about Canada, there was no way of knowing for sure.

'I just want you to keep the firm's books for a little while,' he'd said, unable to get his head around the fact that Tony wasn't interested in a scam that was an absolute dead cert. 'This isn't Dad's kind of villainy. You're not going to have to hurt anyone. All we have to do is get the stock in, trade as if we're legit for a few months, and then cash in and do a runner. I've got the false ID all set up, a warehouse rented. All I need is someone who's sharp with figures to do the bookwork.'

'Why don't you do it yourself?' had been Tony's answer – which just went to show that if Tony had been able to read his mind when they'd been kids, he certainly couldn't now.

'Because I ain't got the patience for it,' he'd replied exasperatedly. 'You have, though. You'd be ace at being a company manager for a few months. Trust me.'

'Oh, I trust you, all right,' his twin had said. 'But this isn't for me, Johnny. Sorry.'

And that had been that. All the fun of setting the dummy firm up had gone flying out of the window. He hadn't called it off, though. For the last five months, under the name of a geezer who had been dead and buried for thirty years, Pomeroy Electrical had been up and running, legally registered at Companies House and with Cheyenne doing a reasonably good job acting as its manager. He hadn't let Cheyenne do the book-keeping, though. That he'd done himself.

'Hiya, Johnny,' someone called out as he strolled into the billiard hall. 'How ya doin?'

He grunted to indicate he was doing OK but wasn't going to be chatty about it.

Cheyenne was playing a game at a far table with another of his sidekicks, Little Donnie. They made a bizarre couple, Cheyenne being an easy six foot five whilst Donnie scarcely cleared five foot. It was Donnie who, when delivery lorries arrived at Pomeroy Electrical, shifted the loads into the warehouse. Strong wiry little blokes never ceased to puzzle him. Where did their strength come from? Though he wasn't a short-arse, Fast-Boy Flynn was, like Donnie, whippet-thin and by rights shouldn't have been able to pack a punch at all. Yet Fast-Boy's punches were lethal.

He remembered their last run in, mere hours after Zoë's death, and a pulse began to throb at the corner of his jaw. A lot of people thought they'd been fighting because each held the other responsible for Zoë's death, which was bollocks. He hadn't left the pub after Zoë had left it – and Fast-Boy knew that. And he'd seen the expression on Fast-Boy's face as he re-entered the pub without Zoë. Unless the guy was a hell of a lot more peculiar than even he gave him credit for, Fast-Boy hadn't just killed. He hadn't had that look in his eye – a look Johnny was familiar with and would have recognized. Christ, if he'd thought for one minute that Fast-Boy was responsible for Zoë's death, he wouldn't have settled for trying to batter him into next week, he'd have killed him. Slowly. No question.

'Has Tony shown yet?' he asked Cheyenne, knowing that one day he would do for Fast-Boy permanently – and knowing that the pleasure of that day would have to wait until his affair with Angie had burnt itself out.

'Nah. I didn't know you was expecting him. I thought the three of us were just going to have a meet about

Pomeroy.' Cheyenne, having potted a red and then missed the black by a yard, walked around the table towards him, holding his billiard cue as if it were a javelin.

'Yeah, well. Tony might have some thoughts on things,' he said, knowing that any thoughts he had, Tony would keep to himself.

As he shrugged himself out of his coat, he wondered where he and Angie Flynn were going. In the beginning he'd merely enjoyed the fact that he was regularly shagging his twin's girlfriend senseless. It had been a way of getting back at Tony for scuppering the plans he'd had for them both.

Lately, however, he'd become aware that he'd want to be shagging Angie even if she wasn't Tony's girlfriend. She was far more entertaining company than Sharyn – and far more gutsy. He had a feeling he'd be able to take Angie out on a job with him and she wouldn't let him down. He'd even speculated about training her up to be a get-away driver. She wasn't old enough, yet, to have a driving licence, but she'd shown him how well she could drive and the thought of her acting as his stoppo amused him – as did the bluebird tattooed on her right buttock.

'So have you called it a day, paying the invoices and running Pomeroy legit?' Cheyenne asked as they watched Donnie heave himself up over the edge of the table, nearly rupturing himself in order to play a shot.

'Yeah. You should be beginning to get reminders for payment.'

'I am. That's why I asked.'

Johnny dragged his thoughts away from bluebirds. The time had come for Pomeroy Electrics to hit the dust – the question was: how? Originally, he'd intended the usual: having lulled the company's many suppliers into a false sense of security by paying their invoices on the dot month after month, he would place massive orders on the strength of his good credit and then stage a gigantic, wham-bam, cut-price-for-cash sale, leaving Pomeroy's creditors squealing for payment from a bloke who'd been dead for thirty years.

And then he'd begun thinking about fires. An insurance claim after a fire would mean he'd make not just one killing but two. It would be a nice earner, if it could be wangled.

'A fire,' he said to Cheyenne musingly. 'Do you think if we fired the warehouse we could clean up on the insurance?'

Cheyenne's eyebrows shot high. 'Christ, Johnny! Don't you think that's a bit risky? At the moment all we have to do is walk away once we've had the sale. With a fire there'd be a real in-depth investigation, there always is. And it's me whose been signing all the delivery notes and whose face is known to the drivers. I'd be in a real dodgy position, know what I mean?'

'Yeah. I suppose.' Johnny watched Donnie carefully eye up a shot. He'd always known when to let a subject rest and, not wanting Cheyenne to get twitchy about things, he judged he should let this one rest now.

He wasn't going to forget about it, though. It was too cheeky a wheeze. Besides, he knew more about fires than Cheyenne would ever know.

Tony skirted his way around a stack of Christmas trees propped outside a greengrocers in Jamaica Road. He was supposedly on his way to meet up with Johnny at the billiard hall in Deptford High Street, but wasn't sure he could be bothered making the trek. Not that it was far to go. Fifteen minutes and he'd be there. He tucked his fists into the pockets of his windcheater jacket. The trouble with Johnny was that he only ever wanted to talk business. His kind of business. And Tony didn't want to be drawn into it. When he'd returned to England, he'd returned with a clear-cut agenda of what being back in London would mean to him – and it didn't include involvement in his old man's protection and repossession rackets, or with Johnny's desire to be a big-time villain.

He slowed to a halt, suddenly aware that in another half-dozen steps he would be outside Clyde Scale's boxing gym. It wasn't a gym he'd ever been a member of. The minimum age for the gym's junior boxing club was ten and he'd been eight when, traumatized with shock, he'd left England with his aunt. Johnny had been a member, though. Like Fast-Boy Flynn, he'd joined the first day he'd been eligible.

He stood for a moment, wondering whether to continue walking on into Deptford, or to check out the gym. A flash of lighting and a rumble of thunder decided the matter. He turned in at the gym's doorway and mounted the stairs.

Even before he reached the top he was almost overcome by the smell of stale sweat and wintergreen. He took a deep breath. Whatever the smell, it couldn't be worse than the smells he'd grown up with on the ranch. Memory brought a rise of panic into his throat – panic he immediately battened down on. Canada and Albie were thousands of miles away. He'd escaped. He was home. And he had an agenda – an agenda he was going to follow undeviatingly.

He kicked open the door at the top of the stairs and, with his hands still tucked in the pockets of his bum-freezer jacket, sauntered into the room beyond. It was humming with activity. In one corner was a full-size boxing ring. Ranged elsewhere were punchbags and speedballs. All were in use. A few people, when they looked across at him, did a double take. He knew why. Even with long hair and dressed as he was, he was still Johnny's mirror image. If he ever cut his hair in a French crew-cut and got himself kitted out in a single-breasted mohair suit, he'd have been able to pass for Johnny any time he wanted.

'Wotcha, cock. Can I 'elp yer?' said an elderly geezer with a towel slung around his neck.

Assuming him to be either a coach or a cleaner, Tony shook his head. 'Nope. Just checking the place out, that's all.'

His eyes were on the two fit-looking blokes sparring in the ring. One of them he knew. Had once known very well. Since he'd been back in London, though, opportunities for a get-together with Fast-Boy – even though he was dating Fast-Boy's sister – had been few and far between.

'What does he think about you and me?' he had once asked Angie, genuinely curious.

'Not much,' she had said with a giggle.

He'd known it was an understatement. Though, according to Angie, Fast-Boy still didn't know that Zoë had ditched him in order to become Johnny's girlfriend, he must suspect that Johnny was the reason – especially with all the gossip that had been on the go since the moment she had died. Certainly the long-term animosity between Fast-Boy and Johnny had deepened even further since Zoë's death.

On Johnny's part, Tony knew it was jealousy at Zoë having been Fast-Boy's girlfriend for so long when, the moment she had decided to become his girlfriend, fate had sent her tumbling to a broken neck. But on Fast-Boy's part? Gossip was that Fast-Boy *had* known the reason he was being ditched – and if he had, it was no wonder he had laid into Johnny with such venom that he'd broken two of Johnny's ribs and dislocated his jaw.

'If you want a coffee, there's a machine out the back,' a young kid said helpfully.

'Ta.' He didn't make a move to check out the coffee-machine. Instead, he continued to watch Fast-Boy sparring. Fast-Boy was good, but then he'd always been good. If he'd been built differently, with shoulders a yard wide like himself and Johnny, and had carried more bulked-up muscle, he'd have been heavyweight championship material, no doubt.

'He's the best we have,' said a perspiring bloke who'd just come away from a still-swinging punchbag. 'Back before Johnny stopped coming to the club, he bested Fast-Boy a couple of times – but that was all. The thing about Fast-Boy is he can land dead perfect punches. No matter how defensively his opponent is fighting, he can always get one in on the cheekbone – just under the eye – or on the chin. And those are the nerve centres. Hit those and it's goodnight, baby.'

Tony, well used to people he'd never met before coming up and talking to him as if they'd known him for years – which, in a way, via Johnny, they had – made a noise in his throat which could have meant anything.

His companion took it for friendly agreement, flashed him a grin and mooched away.

'OK, that's enough, you two!' It was the elderly man with a towel round his neck. This time his shouted instruction was directed at Fast-Boy and his sparring partner.

Fast-Boy's sparring partner clapped him on the back

and then ducked between the ropes, passing their trainer as he clambered up to Fast-Boy and began unlacing his gloves. Tony saw him speaking but was too far away to hear. Whatever it was, Fast-Boy suddenly looked directly over to where he was standing.

Tony kept his hands tucked in his pockets and let a smile tug at the corner of his mouth. Something approaching amusement sparked in Fast-Boy's eyes. Seconds later he was ducking out of the ring and walking towards him. Not for the first time, Tony was struck by the similarities in their appearance. Like the Martini twins, Fast-Boy had black hair and blue eyes. There was no Sicilian in him, though. His skin was too pale and he simply didn't have the manner.

The manner he had, however, was one Tony found intriguing. Fast-Boy's self-containment and self-sufficiency were qualities he recognized in himself. Whether, like himself, Fast-Boy also had a slower psychological pulse than most people, he didn't yet know. What he did know was that Fast-Boy was a loner – and he strongly suspected he was a loner with ice in his veins.

'What brings you here?'

There was nothing belligerent in Fast-Boy's tone.

Tony shrugged. 'I was passing, that's all.'

'And it's pissing down with rain?'

'Yeah.' The grin tugged at the corner of his mouth again. 'I guess that had something to do with it.'

Fast-Boy chewed the corner of his lip for a moment and then said: 'I'm going to shower. Why don't you hang about for a while? There's a greasy-spoon next door that does great fry-ups.'

'Yeah. Sure.'

As Fast-Boy began walking in the direction of the locker-room, he strolled alongside him. There were plenty of curious looks from people – gossip about Fast-Boy and Johnny's fisticuffs after Zoë's death had reached a wide audience – but no remarks were thrown. Tony doubted if snide remarks ever were thrown in Fast-Boy's hearing.

Fast-Boy yanked a metal locker-door open and took out a towel. 'Five minutes,' he said. 'Don't get too pally with the guy you were talking to earlier. He's a fairy.'

'Ta.' Tony was appreciative. When it came to things sexual, he always liked to know exactly where he stood. For the second time in thirty minutes memories of Albie and the hideous hidey-hole in the barn threatened to overwhelm him.

He clenched his jaw – and the cheeks of his arse. Never again. He closed his eyes tight. Never. Never. Never. It was over. It was history. He was home and he was safe. When he opened his eyes again, perspiration was beading his lashes. He blinked it away, focusing on the photograph Fast-Boy had Sellotaped to the inside of his locker-door. It was Zoë.

She was seated on a low wall, leggy and doe-eyed and wearing the pink mini-dress she'd been wearing the night she'd died. He wondered if Fast-Boy realized and, if he did, wondered if that was the reason he had chosen this particular photograph of her for his locker-door.

'Still unmolested?' Fast-Boy said when he returned, naked except for the towel round his waist.

'Yeah.' It was a remark that could have sounded taunting. Coming from Fast-Boy, it didn't.

Fast-Boy dropped the towel, climbed into a pair of Y-fronts, hauled on a pair of black jeans and tugged a black turtleneck sweater over his head.

'OK then,' he said, sliding on a pair of black suede loafers. 'Let's get some chow.'

As they walked out of the gym together he suddenly said: 'About your mum, Tony . . . When we were kids, you were sent off to Canada so quick I never got the chance to tell you how sorry I was about what happened, but I was sorry. I liked your mum. What happened was a real tragedy.'

For several seconds Tony was completely beyond speech and then he said, with difficulty, 'Tragedy isn't a big enough word. Nothing is.'

Fast-Boy flashed him an uncomfortable glance and then, as they walked into the café, which was literally next door to the gym, he said awkwardly: 'But your mum would have died young anyway, wouldn't she? I remember my mum saying that, what with your mum being so severely asthmatic, she'd never make old bones.'

Tony sucked his breath between his teeth and then said tautly. 'I know you mean well, Ewan, but I can't have this conversation with you. I can't have it with anyone.'

The skin was stretched so tightly across his cheekbones that he looked ill.

'Sure. Right. Look, let's sit over in the corner. I'll get us in a couple of mugs of tea. The grub in here wouldn't make a food hygienist happy, but it's good and it's cheap. What say we have a couple of all-day breakfast fry-ups?'

'That's fine by me.' As they sat down at the Formica-topped table he said, 'Is it important to you that the food is cheap?'

A workman at the next table had pushed a folded-up *Evening Standard* to one side of his plate and the headline, **ARMED ROBBER'S THIRD PO RAID IN THREE WEEKS**, was clearly visible. Below the headline, the words *young . . . lone . . . shotgun . . . daring* and *effrontery* could also be read, as could *Clapham . . . Wandsworth* and *Eltham*.

'No. I'm not short of cash.' Aware of what it was that had caught Tony's attention, Fast-Boy looked across at the headline and then, having read it, said blandly: 'Sounds like he's a busy boy.'

'Yeah. Doesn't it just?' Tony's eyes held his across the table. 'How do you think he makes his get-away? On a Harley?'

'Dunno. Does it say? The print's too small for me to read more than the headline.'

A beefy-armed waitress came up to take their order. 'Two sausages, eggs, bacon, tomatoes and mushrooms,' Fast-Boy said succinctly.

'It's too small for me to read, too,' Tony said as the waitress moved off with their order. 'Beats me why crims do it,' he added, aware that Fast-Boy was letting him know his guess as to the robber's identity had been correct. 'I wouldn't risk being locked up . . .' there was the merest tremor in his voice '. . . being locked away – not for anyone.'

Fast-Boy looked at him with deep curiosity. 'I'd heard you'd come home purer than driven snow, but I thought it was some sort of joke – or a smoke-screen. It's for real, then, is it?'

'Yeah.' Tony speared a sausage with his fork. 'There's only two kinds of villainy. My old man's kind – protection, bullying, poncing off other thieves – and Johnny's and the fella we've just been talking about, the one holding up post offices with a shotgun. I don't go for either. Dad's lifestyle has always sickened me because I remember how it sickened my mother.'

He speared another sausage and took a long time eating it.

'Is that right?' Fast-Boy wasn't eating. He was too fascinated by the unexpected insight he'd been given into Marco Martini's marriage. 'And what about the bloke holding up post offices? What about that kind of villainy?'

'What's the point of it? A load of dosh until he's caught, and then years locked up. Why would anyone want to risk it?' He put his knife and fork down. 'Why do you risk it, Ewan?'

It was the second time Tony had called him by his proper name and the experience was so alien to Fast-Boy that he almost looked over his shoulder to see if someone was standing behind him.

'Because the hours are good and there's plenty of time off,' he said flippantly. 'What d'you expect me to do? Become a brain surgeon?'

'You could become something – learn a trade and become a plumber or a carpenter, get yourself an office job, even go to adult education classes. Like me.'

Fast-Boy was now looking at him as if he'd come from another planet. 'Education classes? Christ, if that's what you're doing it's no wonder you and Johnny ain't inseparable any more! What kind of classes, for fuck's sake?'

Tony reached for a steaming mug of tea. 'English. Maths. I'm doing whatever it takes so that one day I'll be able to study for a Law degree.'

There was a beat of stupefied silence and then Fast-Boy cracked into a roar of laughter. 'Christ All-bleedin'-mighty!' he gasped, when he could finally speak. 'I wish I could hear what your old man thinks about that!'

'Laugh all you like,' Tony said, ignoring the last remark, 'but long term, I'll have far more dosh than you or Johnny – and I won't be constantly running the risk of getting nicked and locked away.'

'You'll never have more dosh than me, Tony.' Fast-Boy chuckled. 'And from the sound of it, you're never going to have enough for my sister, either. This "I want to be a lawyer and a straight dude" crap won't be impressing Angie. She's like Sharyn. She likes life in the fast lane.'

Tony shrugged. He'd never taken what Angie liked into account, and he wasn't about to start now.

Fast-Boy slid his plate to one side and regarded him with interest. 'You're not that bothered about Angie, are you? I mean, if she's hoping for an engagement ring, she's going to be disappointed, right?'

'Right,' Tony said equably, amused at the thought of Fast-Boy ever becoming his brother-in-law. 'And I suppose you're now going to get all indignant on your sister's behalf?'

'Nope. But you've made it easier for me to tell you something.'

'Such as?'

'Such as Johnny feeling exactly the same about Sharyn Bailey as you do about Angie. She's wallpaper, know what I mean? He can take her or leave her. She might think she's on her way to becoming Mrs Johnny Martini, but she ain't.'

'Yeah, well. That isn't exactly earth-shattering news. Everyone who knows Johnny knows that.'

'Except Sharyn.'

'Except Sharyn,' Tony agreed, wondering why on earth Fast-Boy was even remotely interested in Johnny's relationship with Sharyn Bailey.

'There's something else Sharyn doesn't know . . .' Fast-Boy's body language was still as relaxed as ever, but at the expression in his eyes Tony's amusement began to evaporate. 'She doesn't know that Johnny's cheating on her with a bird he *really* interested in.'

86

Tony shrugged, finding the conversation bizarre. He was Johnny's twin and if he weren't overly interested in Johnny's love-life he couldn't for the life of him see why Fast-Boy should be.

'So?' he said indifferently. 'Who cares?'

'I care.' Fast-Boy's slate-blue eyes were suddenly so hard they looked to be black. 'I care, because the bird in question is my sister. You're being two-timed, Tony. Johnny and Angie are red-hot. They meet a couple of times a week, nine or ten o'clockish, at the Take Six recording studios. If you'd been serious about her, I wouldn't have told you. As you aren't, I don't suppose you're too trashed about it, are you?'

Amber twanged a wooden gold angel hanging from the Christmas tree her mother had put up in the sitting-room and moodily watched as its swinging movement sent another half-dozen baubles shimmering and shaking. She was bored. She had a noxious concoction on her hair that, according to the Trinidadian girl in her class at school who had sold it to her, would leave her hair curl and kink free. As she pulled the towel a little closer to her neck, she was hoping fiercely that it would work. It had to be left on her hair for another half-hour yet and the smell was appalling.

She twanged the angel again, wondering where Sharyn was, knowing she would either be with Angie or Johnny. She certainly wouldn't be on her own. Spending time alone simply wasn't Sharyn's scene. She had to have someone with her, even if it was someone she didn't like very much.

Where Angie and Johnny were concerned, of course, that wasn't the case. Angie was her best friend and Johnny she would die for. Amber wondered what would happen if and when Sharyn found out what Angie and

Johnny were up to behind her back. Not that she would find out, unless she was told. Sharyn's powers of intuition were nil. Hers weren't. Hers were exceptional and yet even she had only realized what was going on when she'd seen them down by the Thames one evening and had followed them back to a warehouse that had been tarted up as recording studios.

It was possible, of course, that Johnny was trying to turn Angie into a pop star, but Amber doubted it. Angie Flynn had many talents, but singing wasn't one of them.

With another bored sigh she checked the time. There was still twenty minutes to go before she could rinse the yuk off her hair. With nothing better to do, she went back to thinking about Sharyn's probable reaction if she discovered that Johnny was two-timing her with Angie. Which of them would she forgive first? Assuming that she could forgive either of them. Sharyn had inherited their mother's Irish temper in full measure and, when she lost it, she lost it spectacularly.

As did their mother.

Lately, both her mother and Sharyn had been losing their tempers with increasing regularity, with each other. It didn't make for a happy Christmassy atmosphere and Amber was fed up with it. The cause of all the rows was their mum's insistence that Sharyn ditch Johnny, and Sharyn's insistence that she would never give him up.

'I'm going to marry him!' she had shrieked defiantly at the end of last night's row.

'Over my dead body!' their mum had shouted back, slapping her across the face.

'Merry Christmas, you two!' Amber had yelled sarcastically at them.

It hadn't made a scrap of difference. The barney had gone on for hours.

Once again she checked the time. There were still another ten minutes to go, which seemed an age as the stuff on her hair was now stinging her scalp like red-hot needles. She visualized the eventual result, her hair straight and shiny and sleek, and gritted her teeth, determined to stick out the full thirty minutes.

According to Sharyn, things were tense next door as well. The problem in the Martini home, however, wasn't Johnny's relationship with Sharyn – it was his dad's relationship with a dolly-bird.

'Old Man Martini's always had girlfriends young enough to be his daughter,' Sharyn had said on one of the rare occasions when she had bothered to confide in her. 'This time the girl is only seventeen. Can you imagine? *I* can't imagine going out with a bloke in his fifties. What makes it worse is that she's always in his car when he nips home for anything. She's becoming quite a fixture outside our house. You must have noticed her. I know Mum has. And Mum thinks like Johnny. She thinks it's disgusting. I can tell from the expression on her face when she has to walk past the car.'

Amber had found it all very interesting and had wanted to know how Tony felt about his dad's dolly-bird girlfriend. Sharyn hadn't known.

'Tony's a closed book,' she had said, as if telling Amber something she didn't know already. 'He keeps things to himself.'

As she checked the time yet again, seeing with deep relief that the thirty minutes were up at last, the front door opened.

It was Sharyn.

'Great,' Amber said, intending to put her to good use. 'Do me a favour and wash this gunge off my hair for me.'

'Why should I?' Sharyn looked at the concoction on

89

Amber's hair with distaste. 'Wash it off yourself, why don't you?'

The reason she didn't want to wash it off herself was that it was stinging so much she was certain that if she got it on her hands she would come out in a rash. As this reasoning would hardly encourage Sharyn to go within a foot of her, she resorted to bribery: 'Because I'll share some gossip with you, if you do.'

'What kind of gossip?'

'Gossip about the night Zoë Fairminder died. I know who it was that kicked the barricade away from the workmen's pit.'

In actual fact, she didn't. All she'd done, after thinking about things for a long, long time, was hazard a guess that, for her at least, made sense.

Sharyn's eyes narrowed. 'OK,' she said, well aware how talented a people-watcher and eavesdropper Amber was. 'So long as you're not going to come out with any crap about it being Johnny.'

'No.' Amber remembered the look in Johnny's eyes and the throb in his voice when he had been talking to Zoë on the night of her death. Johnny had been nuts about Zoë. He wouldn't have kicked the barricade away with malicious intent – and that it had been kicked away with malicious intent was the only scenario that interested her. 'No,' she said again, remembering who else had been within hearing distance of that conversation. 'It wasn't Johnny. I think it was Jimmy. Jimmy Jones.'

'Jimmy Jones?' Sharyn looked at her as if she'd taken leave of her senses. 'The Jimmy Jones who used to be in Johnny's gang? Talk sense. Why on earth would he have kicked the safety barricade away? He's a grown man, not a ten-year-old vandal.'

'I'm not suggesting he kicked it away for the sheer fun of it.' Sometimes Amber despaired of her sister's thought processes. 'I think he did it on purpose. He did it because he knew Zoë was going to go out to the car park to meet Johnny, and he thought that if he hurt Zoë he'd be somehow getting his own back on Johnny.'

Something in Amber's voice prevented Sharyn from shrieking that Johnny had never had any intention of meeting Zoë in the car park. 'Why would Jimmy Jones want to get back at Johnny?' she asked, her curiosity caught. 'What do you know that I don't?'

'A lot,' Amber was tempted to say, but didn't.

Instead she said, 'Johnny held him from a window. I heard Cheyenne and one of the other guys talking about it the night of the party. They were wondering if Jimmy was holding a grudge about it. I mean, it wouldn't have been surprising, would it? I wouldn't like to have been held out of a sixth-floor window, would you?'

'And?'

'And I was standing near to Jimmy a bit later on in the evening when Zoë walked past me on her way to the loo – or supposedly to the loo. She never actually went into the Ladies. She met up with Johnny.'

'I know. I saw them.' The skin across Sharyn's cheek-bones had become oddly tight.

It was as near to admitting that Johnny had fancied Zoë as she had ever come.

'And if I heard what was said – and I did – then Jimmy Jones will have heard it as well. And that's what they were doing: arranging to meet outside in the car park.'

'You really think Jimmy Jones went out there and kicked the barricade away in the hope she'd fall in?'

Amber tilted her head to one side, eyeing her sister

speculatively. 'To be honest, Sha, I know I didn't mean it when I lost my rag with you and said you might have done it, but I've been thinking about it and you could have, couldn't you? But if you didn't, then, yes, I think it was Jimmy Jones. Now will you wash this gunge off my hair for me?'

'No, I bloody won't!' Outrage blazed in Sharyn's eyes and angry colour stained her cheeks. 'So you seriously think *I* could've kicked the bloody barricade away? Do you realize what would happen to me if that got back to the coppers? Your trouble, Amber Bailey, is that you've got ears as big as a bloody elephant's and a mouth big enough to garage a plane!'

'And you can't see what's in front of your bloody eyes!' Amber shrieked in retaliation, aware she was going to have to wash her hair herself. 'Johnny's seeing Angie! They meet at Take Six studios, down by the river. So what are you going to do about *that*, Sharyn? Or shouldn't I ask in case it gets back to the coppers?'

Sharyn stormed into the bedroom she shared with Amber, slamming the door behind her so hard the whole house shook. Her little sister was a cow – and worse. How *dare* she say that Angie and Johnny were cheating on her behind her back? It wasn't true. It couldn't be true.

She flung herself on her bed. What worried her was that it wasn't often Amber came out with blatant untruths. She was always so clued up about who was doing what, where and with whom, that she never needed to. And Angie had always fancied Johnny. Plus, Johnny could be a prize bastard when he wanted to be.

The night Zoë bloody Fairminder had broken her neck, for instance. He'd told her he was fed up with her draping herself around him and that her presence was no longer wanted. She'd known why, of course. She'd seen him meet up with Zoë near the cigarette-machine and she'd guessed the kind of conversation they were having.

Her nerves began to throb. What if it was starting all over again, only this time with Angie? What would she do then? Angie was her best friend. How could she let herself be betrayed by her best friend? Or by Johnny? Her nails dug deep into her palms. What would she do if Johnny ditched her? Especially if he ditched her for Angie. How would she ever be able to bear seeing the two of them together? She wouldn't be able to. She wouldn't be able to bear such pain. She wouldn't be able to survive it.

Which meant she would have to do something – anything – to make sure it never happened.

Chapter Six

Fast-Boy eased the stolen Wolseley 690 to a halt bang outside the post office and glanced down at his watch. It was late afternoon and though the pavements were busy with Christmas shoppers, the post office was empty.

Which was the way he hoped it would stay.

Too many people present and there was always the risk that one of them would be a have-a-go merchant yearning to make a name for himself as the bloke who stopped a robbery. The 'I wanna be a hero' brigade were dangerous – to themselves, to him, and to any bystanders.

He smoothed his false moustache with a thumb and forefinger, tugged his pigskin gloves a little tighter and glanced down at his watch. As a rule, this time of day would have been a no-no for a profitable raid. Cash was usually delivered first thing in the morning – but not at this sub-post office. Some weeks ago his eagle eye had registered that Friday's money arrived late on Thursday afternoon and, unlike most other sub-post offices, this branch stayed open for trading on Thursday afternoons.

He re-positioned the sports bag that was lying in the passenger-seat footwell and took a pile of envelopes and sheet of stamps from the glove compartment. Dressed as he was in a camel-hair coat typical of the overcoats worn by city businessmen, his long hair concealed by a wig, the slimline moustache adding years to his age, he looked the image of respectability; a gent on his way home from the office, dropping off the day's mail.

It was a fiction that could only be sustained for a short period of time. Once he'd stamped the envelopes he could spend a further few minutes apparently checking the accuracy of the addresses, but after that his continued presence in the car, parked where it was, would begin to attract the postmaster's attention.

He moved again in order to begin sticking down stamps and this time the movement was uncomfortable – which wasn't surprising, considering the sawn-off shotgun stowed in the mega-deep pocket he'd sewn into the overcoat's lining.

Thankful that the weather was cold enough for him to be wearing such a bulky coat without it looking odd, he looked through the driving mirror again.

The cash-delivery van was approaching. It was nearly lift-off time.

As his nerves stretched and tightened he flicked through the envelopes as if checking them. Behind him, the van slid to a halt.

One of the two men in it stepped on to the pavement, a large box chained to his wrist. In perfect synchronization Fast-Boy stepped from the Wolseley, envelopes in hand.

The security guard gave him a keen glance and then, looking away from him, checked the street from right to left.

Fast-Boy strolled towards the pillar box, knowing the box in the guard's hand was one he could ignore. It was merely the 'screamer' – an alarm. The cash-box was still with matey in the van.

As the security guard walked into the post office to give it a quick once-over, Fast-Boy began posting his letters, aware, without having made eye contact with him, that matey had barely registered his presence.

From the open door the guard gave the nod to his colleague that the pavement was safe to cross. With the cash-laden postman behind him, Fast Boy turned from the pillar box and strolled into the post office, his excitement coiled to explosion point.

This was it. Another two or three seconds. Maybe even less.

The moment he'd passed the security guard, leaving both men ranged together behind him, he dived for the shotgun, wheeling round on them as he did so, uncaring of the postmaster's shouts of panic and the security guard's frantic activation of his alarm-box.

'One wrong move and I'll blow your fucking brains out!' he yelled as, almost deafened by the screaming of the alarm siren, he brought the muzzle of the sawn-off up against the side of the cash-delivery man's jaw, sending him reeling.

With his companion sprawled half-senseless on the floor and the shotgun's muzzle mere inches from his chest, there was no way the unarmed security guard was going to make a move, wrong or otherwise. In activating the alarm-box he'd done what he was paid to do and, as far as he was concerned, it was now up to the police to arrive and do what they were paid to do.

Grateful for his common sense, Fast-Boy scooped the cash-box from where it had fallen and, with the speed that stood him in such good stead in the ring, was through the open door and across the pavement in seconds.

Yanking open the Wolseley's door, he threw the cash-box into the sports bag, tossed the shotgun on top of it and gunned the Wolseley's engine into life.

There was never any telling how soon police cars

would converge on the scene of a robbery. If a patrol car was in the vicinity of the post office in question it could be far too quick for comfort. Which was why he planned his escape routes so very meticulously.

This time the post office he had raided was only streets away from Hither Green train station – and running underneath the station was a tunnel providing pedestrian-only access to the road on the south side of the tracks.

Fast-Boy screeched round a corner, off the main road. As he swooped down the side road he could hear, in the distance, the wail of a siren. Aware that his luck was out and the patrol car was nearly on top of him, he threw the Wolseley round another corner and sliced down the road towards the station. It was a road traversed by two residential streets and, if the police car veered in on him from one of them, blocking his route to the station, there was no way out. It would be good-bye freedom, hello jail.

He careened over the first junction as the police car slewed into the far end of the road behind him. Never before had the cozzers been on his heels so quickly. He roared across the second intersection at full pelt. Now there was only the dead-end of the station.

With tyres screaming, he brought the Wolseley to a shuddering halt, grabbed the handles of the sports bag and was out of the car, sprinting for the tunnel as the police car sped across the first intersection.

The car he'd parked in readiness at the far side of the tunnel was a stolen Cortina. As he yanked the driver's door open, throwing the bag on to the front passenger-seat, Fast-Boy could hear the sound of feet sprinting through the tunnel. They were after him on foot. But they weren't going to be able to catch him. Not now.

Throwing the engine into gear, he screeched away from the kerb, taking the whole width of the road to straighten out before he reached the corner, knowing he had only a heartbeat before other police cars would be either hard on his heels or ahead of him, cutting him off. A short hill with a left turn into a main road and then a distance of a hundred yards or so led to Hither Green Hospital.

He covered the ground in a minute and a half, taking the sharp right-hand turn into the hospital car park at a speed that had him disappearing from view before the first of the chasing police cars even had him in their sights.

By the time the police had finished roaring past the hospital entrance in the direction of Lewisham, sirens wailing, he had rid himself of his first disguise and was pulling out a second – another wig, a pair of high-heeled shoes and lipstick – from a giant carrier bag on the Cortina's rear seat.

No one using the car park so much as looked towards him as he carried out his transformation. Once it was complete, he stuffed the overcoat, shoes and wig number one into the carrier bag, zipped up the sports bag containing the cash-box and shotgun, and stepped from the car, an elegant brunette in a trouser-suit and sexy high-heeled shoes. The carrier bag and sports bag he was carrying didn't look odd; there were a number of people entering or leaving the hospital carrying suitcases or large bags.

He was nearing the hospital gates when, realizing their quarry had given them the slip, the police began retracing the route of the chase. A patrol car swerved into the hospital grounds and, seeing the Cortina, squealed to a halt. While the driver radioed in the Cortina's location, three policemen piled out – passing within inches of Fast-Boy. Five minutes later, he was on a bus heading for Lewisham.

He never took loot back home with him. It was far too risky and his mother and Angie were far too nosey. Instead he took it straight to Jed's. Jed, his elderly trainer at the gym, lived in a block of high-rise flats in Lewisham. Even 'guised-up, Fast-Boy could walk in there at any time of the day or night without his presence causing comment. There were other plusses to Jed's gaffe. He could leave his bike and biking leathers there, ready to change back into them and return home in his normal manner. Which was what he was now about to do.

His certainty that he'd pulled off a successful raid never wavered all the time he was at Jed's and all the time he was riding the Harley home. Even two hours later, the adrenaline buzz from the car chase was still surging in his veins. It had been a close call. If he'd not had the Wolseley for his get-away he doubted he would have reached the foot tunnel – and if he hadn't, he would now be sitting in a cell, which was why he would use a Wolseley 690 again. They were powerfully fast cars. More than that, they were traditional police cars. That was why he had stolen the 690 in the first place. The connection had amused him.

Through the dark of early evening he cruised at a modest speed from Lewisham into Deptford, and then on into Bermondsey. The haul from the raid had been good, and what was even better was that he didn't have to split it with anyone. Working alone was no picnic – grabbing a cash-box or money-bags while holding a shot-gun steady wasn't easy – but it was profitable.

As he had every intention of hitting the town that evening, he didn't turn in at the alley. There was no sense in garaging the Harley in the back yard if he was going out again in half an hour or so.

Confident that everything had gone his way, he brought the bike to a halt outside the front gate of his home, dismounted and began strolling up a path lit only by the fairy lights on the Christmas tree standing in the window.

Then all hell broke loose.

From either end of the street came two speeding police cars, siren wailing, lights flashing.

Fast-Boy didn't have long to wonder who or what their target was. As the cars swerved to a halt nose to nose, with only his Harley between them, he affected a laconic stance, his mind racing.

How the *fuck* had they guessed his identity? The descriptions given by the post office staff couldn't have led them to him, and all the coppers in pursuit had seen was a moustached and hatted figure driving a car and sprinting through the foot tunnel. As he had nothing incriminating on him, all he had to do was to keep shtum.

The sirens and lights had brought half the street to their doors and windows. Fast-Boy only hoped they were enjoying the show. As the cozzers piled out of the cars and across the pavement, and as his mother wrenched the front door open so that they wouldn't need to hammer it off its hinges, he was beginning to feel a flicker of amusement himself.

They wouldn't find anything. The cash-box and shot-gun were at Jed's, as was his handgun. The cozzers were on a hiding to nothing.

'In the house, Flynn!' one of them shouted, seizing him by the arm and whipping it up behind his back as he frogmarched him across the doorstep.

Which meant they weren't arresting and charging him. If they had been, they'd have had him cuffed and marching in the opposite direction, into a police car and away.

'Wipe your feet, you fuckers!' his mother was screaming as six officers barged over the doorstep behind Fast-Boy and his captor. 'I've just shampooed this fucking carpet ready for fucking Christmas!'

'This is a funny time for a raid, ain't it?' Fast-Boy said to the lot of them in general as Angie came pounding downstairs in a hastily dragged on dressing-gown, her hair dripping wet, bath foam clinging to her legs and feet.

'Not if it's a success,' the officer manhandling him through the house and into the kitchen said grimly. 'And trust me, sonny, this one is going to be.'

'What's going on?' Angie shrieked, rounding the foot of the stairs and pummelling her way through the crush. 'Leave my brother alone! Get the fuck out of here, you bastards! Mum? *Mum?* They haven't hurt you, Mum, have they?'

Her mother, who had experienced more police raids than she'd had hot dinners, snorted derisively at the very thought.

'Christ, but they've both got mouths on them like dockers,' one of the coppers said as Angie succeeded in reaching her mother's side. 'Now just keep out of the way, ladies, and let us get on with what we're here to do.'

What they were here to do was quite obviously not the usual blitzing of the house. Not one copper raced up the stairs. All of them piled through the kitchen and into the back garden.

And all of them made a beeline for the cement-built coal bunker.

As half a dozen powerful torches illuminated it, Fast-Boy worked hard at keeping his expression indifferent.

They'd been tipped off that he kept a sawn-off in there. He'd been grassed up. The question was: who by?

Across the melee, as the coal bunker's contents were ransacked, his eyes met Angie's. Her horror was so blatant it was obvious she knew the bunker was his stow – and that she knew what was usually stowed in it.

So . . . who had she told? The most likely person was Sharyn. And if she'd told Sharyn, then, as night followed day, Sharyn would have told Johnny. And there was the answer to his question. Johnny 'never grass on anyone, not even enemies' Martini had grassed him up. He'd told the police where to look for his shotgun – a weapon that, had it still been there, would have tied him into a dozen robberies and seen him put away for more years than he cared to count.

'Not a thing,' one of the coppers was saying in disgust as the bunker yielded nothing but a few lumps of coal.

'Search the house,' the officer in charge said crisply, flicking off his torch.

There was a general retreat indoors with some of the cozzers sprinting up the stairs to search the bedrooms, while others began blitzing the downstairs rooms.

'Mind that Christmas tree!' his mother yelled, pursuing them into her front room. 'And those are Christmas presents, you bastards!'

Uncaring, the police were ripping tinsel bows and festive wrapping paper off everything that lay beneath the tree.

'This is all down to you,' Fast-Boy said through gritted teeth to Angie as the policeman who'd had hold of him released him in order to help with the search and their mother's shrieks of protest and abuse collapsed into sobs of genuine distress. 'You blabbed to Sharyn, or you blabbed to lover-boy yourself.'

'Tony?' she tried to look bewildered and failed. 'Why would I . . . ?'

'Not bloody Tony.' From upstairs there came the sound of beds being overturned. 'I know who you've been meeting at Take Six. And this is his doing.'

In the hallway a policeman started prizing floorboards up.

Fast-Boy sucked his breath between his teeth. 'Christ,' he said, his voice shaking with passion, 'but I'm going to kill you for this, Angie. I swear to God, I'm going to fucking kill you!'

'I could kill you, Johnny. Honest I could.' The tears were hot and aching behind Sharyn's eyes. For two days she hadn't been able to find him and, now that she had tracked him to the Drum, a pub down near the river, he was being as offhand towards her as he'd been in the bad old days when he'd always had Zoë bloody Fairminder on his mind.

'You're taking liberties, Sha.' Johnny's voice was easy, but his eyes were granite-hard. 'I've been busy and I'm still busy. When I want you, I'll call you.'

She knew that the wisest thing to do was to force a smile, say OK, and breeze out of the pub with her dignity more or less intact. But she couldn't. Not after the things Amber had said. What if Johnny really was seeing Angie behind her back? What if the reason he was being so offhand was because he was thinking of finishing with her?

'You don't look busy,' she said mulishly, eyeing the pint of light and bitter he was drinking.

'Christ, but you can be a stupid bitch.' It was true. Probably the truest thing he'd ever said to her and the knowledge amused him. 'Look, Sha,' he said, with more patience than anyone who knew him would have believed, 'I've got a meet with a geezer tonight. OK.'

It was a statement, not a question. It was also a lie. He'd called in at the Drum because it was only round the corner from the recording studios and he was meeting Angie there at nine.

'I'm not stupid.' There was rare defiance in Sharyn's voice. 'I'm not so stupid that I don't know more than you about who caused Zoë bloody Fairminder's accident.'

She hadn't intended to say it. She'd just wanted to say something that would hold his attention and impress him.

It certainly did the job.

'Run that past me again, will you?' He'd breathed in so deeply that his nostrils were white.

Frantically Sharyn tried to remember exactly what it was Amber had said to her. 'It was Jimmy,' she said with a toss of her head, as if she'd thought the whole thing out for herself. 'Jimmy Jones. He was standing near you and Zoë while the two of you were having your sneaky little confab in the Prince. I know you keep telling me you never arranged to meet her in the car park, but I don't believe you. You did, and Jimmy Jones heard you.'

'And?' His eyes had grown so dark they were almost black.

'And because you'd upset him . . .' She faltered, wondering whether or not to throw in what Amber had told her about Johnny having held Jimmy out of a window, and decided against it. 'Because you'd upset him, he kicked the barricades round the pit away in the

104

hope that when Zoë went out to meet you, she'd fall in and hurt herself. It was his way of getting back at you without having to front up to you.'

'Who told you?'

'I . . . no one.' Sharyn wasn't going to admit that it had been her kid sister. She flicked a fall of daffodil-blonde hair back over her shoulder. 'I worked it out for myself.'

It was highly unlikely, but as he stared through her unseeingly he was too busy remembering to want to pursue it.

Jimmy *had* been within earshot while he and Zoë were making their arrangements to meet up in the car park. And Jimmy did have a score to settle with him – a score he wouldn't dare settle face to face.

'I don't suppose he meant for her to break her neck,' Sharyn added, realizing too late the repercussions that would follow. 'So in a way it *was* an accident . . .'

'One word, *one word* in defence of whoever caused Zoë's death and you'll never breathe the same air as me again. Got it, Sha?'

Sharyn sucked in her breath, hardly able to believe he could be so unfair. Hadn't she just done her best to put him in the picture? Why couldn't he be nice to her? She was always nice to him.

'Now beat it,' he said, aware it was already after nine and that Angie would be waiting for him.

This time she knew better than to argue. She also knew that she didn't believe a word he'd said. He wasn't having a meet – at least not a business meet with a geezer. Any meet he was having was with a woman. And as the recording studios were only round the corner from the pub, it didn't take a genius to work out where the meeting was going to take place.

And who it was going to be with.

She swung away from him, not wanting him to see the tears stinging her eyes. She wasn't going to let him get away with this. And she certainly wasn't going to let Angie get away with it.

Once out on the cold dark pavement she didn't head towards Jamaica Road and home. Instead, her heart hurting so much she thought she'd never survive the pain, she plunged into the warren of warehouse-lined back streets that led to the recording studios and the river.

Angie looked at her watch impatiently. She'd arrived at the studios early – so early there were still musicians in one of the rehearsal rooms – and with Johnny being late she felt she'd been waiting for ever.

Apart from the reception foyer, the building was usually in darkness when she arrived. Consequently, she'd never had the opportunity to explore the place on previous occasions when she'd arrived before Johnny and been let in by the night-watchman. Now, though, with other people still in the building, several corridor lights were on and in order to kill some time she'd been wandering around the different floors, having a look-see in a few rooms.

She was fairly familiar with the second floor, because that was the floor with the luxuriously kitted-out room that they used for their secret trysts. Lushly carpeted, it had deep sofas, a fab music system and a well-stocked cocktail cabinet. Though she'd never been in a room at the Ritz, she thought it was probably just as good.

The rooms on the third and fourth floors were nearly all recording studios, and on the fifth and sixth floors were the rehearsal rooms. Not all the corridors were lit, of course, but she turned their lights on before walking down them and then turned them off when she had finished her exploration. Even though she was aware that there were other people in the building, it was an experience that, had she not been so sick at heart, she would have found too eerie to be pleasant. As it was, with her footsteps echoing on the bare wooden floors, she wandered in and out of the maze of rooms, wondering if Fast-Boy was right and if it had been Johnny who had tipped the police off about his shotgun.

If, when they'd entered the house, the cozzers had just carried out a normal raid, then it would have been possible to assume that they were acting on a hunch. But they hadn't. They'd made straight for the coal bunker. And the only person who had known that Fast-Boy used the bunker as a stow, apart from herself, was Sharyn. But since Sharyn wouldn't have had the nerve to grass even if she'd had a reason to – which she hadn't – the only possible conclusion was the one Fast-Boy had come to.

Sharyn had told Johnny and Johnny had told the police.

She stood by a window on the sixth-floor landing, looking out at the spectacular sight of London by night, knowing she was going to have to confront Johnny with what had happened, and dreading the result of that confrontation.

What if he admitted to having grassed up Fast-Boy? What would she do then? How on earth would she be able to carry on having an affair with him? Blood – as Tony was always telling her when discussing his relationship with Johnny – counted. She and Fast-Boy might row like crazy, but he was her brother. And in her own way, she loved him.

The trouble was, she loved Johnny, too.

Below her, on the fifth floor, a door opened and half a dozen musicians noisily clattered down the stairs towards the foyer and the street, laughing and joking after what had obviously been a successful rehearsal.

Slowly she began walking down the stairs in their wake, wryly aware that, if nothing else, the present problem put her other concerns in the shade. Until now, she and Johnny had managed to keep their affair secret, but it wasn't a secret that could be kept indefinitely. For some time she'd been fretting over what would happen when the shit hit the fan and Tony and Sharyn found out they were being two-timed. From having both the Martini twins as lovers, would she find herself facing a future without either of them?

As the entrance door banged shut after the musicians, she paused on the fifth-floor landing, pondering the mystery of Johnny's relationship with Sharyn. Careless of Sharyn's feelings though he was, there was some sort of a tie there that Angie couldn't fathom. He had never, for instance, suggested that he might finish with Sharyn. Which was why she'd never taken the risk of finishing with Tony. Unsatisfactory as her relationship with Tony was, she hadn't wanted to burn her boats.

She began walking down the dimly lit stairs again, brooding on the way she and Johnny seemed to have been made for each other in a way neither of them were made for their present partners. Johnny needed someone as wild and reckless as himself. And though Sharyn liked to think she was a wild child, in reality she was nothing but a doormat. As for Tony . . . Even after months of on/off intimacy with him she was still no nearer to figuring out just what kind of a girl Tony needed – or if he needed one at all.

She glanced down at her watch, saw that it was twenty past nine and began walking a bit faster. Johnny surely couldn't be much later and, when he arrived, he wouldn't want to have to come shouting through the building in order to find her.

As she turned the corner of the stairs on the fourth landing she heard someone moving about. Not Johnny. Johnny wouldn't be tiptoeing about the building. If he was there, he'd be shouting her name. Not one of the musicians either, because the movement was coming from below her and, if one of the musicians had stayed behind, he would still be up on the fifth floor.

She shrugged, not too concerned. Take Six was a rabbit-warren of rooms and corridors, and the person she'd heard was most likely a cleaner or the rarely seen night-watchman.

Five seconds later, as she reached the third-floor landing, the lights went out. Not just the stair lights, but the foyer lights below.

She sucked in her breath, fumbling blindly for the wall, hoping that the power-cut was only going to be fleeting.

For a long moment she waited, standing absolutely still in the pitch-blackness.

Nothing happened. No lights went on, and from where she was standing there was no window from which she could see if the streetlights were out as well.

'Bugger,' she said, knowing she was going to have to make her way down the remaining two flights of stairs as best she could.

Cautiously, running one hand against the wall, she turned the corner of the landing, the darkness so complete it felt like a physical force pressing in on her. For the first time she wondered if there were rats in the building. Bubbles of panic began rising in her throat. Take Six was a riverside warehouse. All riverside warehouses had rats. And rats *liked* the dark. They would be leaving wherever it was they hid when the building was lit by daylight or electric light. They would be scurrying along the night-black corridors and down the stairs. What if one brushed against her legs? What if one *bit* her?

There came the sound she had heard earlier. The sound of someone, *something*, moving in the darkness not too far from her. With panic now completely unleashed, she abandoned caution, feeling frantically with her foot for the first of the stairs leading down to the second floor. As she found it, she stepped forward fast, certain of the number of steps to the next landing.

Something whip-like smacked across her ankles, tripping her with such momentum that nothing could have saved her.

With a terrified scream, her hands shooting uselessly in front of her, she plunged head first, her momentum so violent it was like being jettisoned over a cliff. There was no slithering and rolling, no breaking her fall by grasping at banisters or rails. Only when she smashed into the concrete facing wall on the second-floor landing did her body finally come to a crumpled halt.

Which was where, ten minutes later, under blazing lighting, Johnny found her.

Chapter Seven

Marco Martini stared through his kitchen window, a mug of coffee in one hand, his hard-boned face grim. It was seven-thirty in the morning and he'd spent a restless night. That Johnny had told him about Angie Flynn's near-fatal tumble down the stairs at the studios hadn't been a surprise. Unlike Tony, Johnny always told him everything.

'She's got a whole host of broken bones,' he'd said tersely. 'I had no choice but to call the ambulance out. Christ, until the ambulancemen said differently, I thought she'd broken her back.'

Marco had just grunted. If the girl had broken her back it wouldn't have surprised him. More than most, he knew the kind of injuries that could result from a forceful fall down a long flight of stairs.

It had been an accident – and a serious one. And serious accidents, on premises that he owned, Marco did not like. He had enough problems avoiding being questioned about accidents he had engineered without having to take on board genuine ones.

The other problem – the real problem – was what was going to happen if and when Tony discovered that his girlfriend's accident had happened in a Martini-owned building she had no valid reason for being in, other than her secret assignation with Johnny.

'She has to be told not to tell Tony where it happened, or that you called for the ambulance,' he'd said. As it was obvious Johnny couldn't go back to the hospital and wait for her to come round after surgery in order to prime her how to handle things, that presented a problem.

It was this problem he was now mulling over. The ideal person to have spoken to Angie would have been her father. Danny Flynn wouldn't blink at the fact that his daughter had been two-timing Tony with Johnny, and certainly wouldn't bat an eyelid at asking her to lie as to where and under what circumstances her near-catastrophic accident had happened.

Unfortunately, Danny was presently a guest of Her Majesty in Brixton, on remand.

He took another sip of his coffee and saw Maureen walk out into her back garden. Even though they lived next door to each other, catching sight of her was a rare event. She was wearing high-heeled mules, a white towelling dressing-gown tie-belted at her waist. As she scattered bread for the birds he continued to watch her, wondering why the fuck he was so emotionally tied to a woman of forty when he had a gorgeous girlfriend not yet twenty.

As he wondered what Maureen's reaction would be if she got to know that his son had been two-timing her daughter with her daughter's best friend, his eyebrows pulled together in a frown. Somehow, before Tony and Sharyn were told of Angie's accident, a framework of lies had to be put in place.

'I don't want Fast-Boy knowing where it happened and that I found her,' Johnny had said. 'It'd just be too much unnecessary hassle. Know what I mean?'

Remembering the heightened tension there'd been between Johnny and Fast-Boy after Zoë Fairminder's fatal fall, Marco had known exactly what he meant. If

Angie's brother had been anyone but Fast-Boy, Johnny wouldn't have given a stuff. Fast-Boy Flynn, though, was a force to be reckoned with. Anyone prepared to go beyond the limit always was. Marco, of all people, knew that.

So . . . who could get hot-foot to Guy's Hospital to be at Angie Flynn's bedside in order to make sure she told an acceptable story to her family and friends? As he watched Maureen walk back into the house, hair the colour of molasses spilling loosely around her shoulders, the answer came with blinding obviousness.

Amber.

And in preparing the ground for speaking to Amber, he was being given a perfect excuse to speak to Maureen again.

He waylaid her half an hour later as she left the house for work. 'A minute of your time, Maureen,' he said, stepping from the car in which he'd been waiting.

Even to him it sounded a ridiculously false way to open the conversation. He didn't want a minute of her time. He wanted all of her time.

'Sod off, Marco.' She swung away from him, beginning to walk swiftly up the street towards the bus stop, her mane of hair corralled into a shiny French pleat, a sculptured wool coat skimming knee-high black boots.

'It's about Angie Flynn,' he said, his face tightening as he reflected that if anyone else had spoken to him like that, they'd have been dead meat. He raised his voice slightly so she could still hear. 'She's in hospital with serious injuries after a fall.'

It stopped her in her tracks, as he had known it would.

'Angie's in hospital?' She swivelled to face him. 'Which hospital? How do you know?' Beneath her make-up her creamy skin was pale. Angie had been her daughter's best friend for years. She was almost family.

He shrugged massive shoulders.

'One of the hospital cleaners is married to a contact of mine. She knows Angie is Tony's girlfriend, so she rang me with the news first thing this morning. Apparently Angie was taken in last night after falling down a flight of stairs at London Bridge Station. I haven't been able to get in contact with Tony – he was up and out early – but I thought you'd want to let Sharyn know.'

'Sharyn left for secretarial school ten minutes ago,' As she tried to take in just how badly Angie had been hurt, Maureen's voice was dazed.

'Oh? I hadn't realized.'

It was a lie. He knew exactly what routine the Bailey house followed. Sharyn left first. Then Maureen. When it was term-time, Amber left fifteen minutes after her mother. When, as now, it was a school holiday, she would still be in the house, the volume of her record-player turned up as loud as it would go the instant her mother was out of earshot.

'Thanks for telling me, Marco.'

It was the most civil she'd been to him in a decade.

Taking advantage, he said, 'Let me give you a lift. You'll have missed your bus now and the traffic on the main roads is nearly at a standstill. I can get you to New Cross, through the back doubles, in ten minutes, maybe less.'

She worked in an old people's home just behind Goldsmith's College and he'd often reflected that her presence there must be making a lot of old men very happy.

She stared at him as if he'd taken leave of his senses, civility vanishing fast as light. 'You must be joking! The day I warm a passenger-seat for your dolly-bird is the day I shoot myself!'

It was a taunt too far and, as she spun on her heel, about to stalk away from him, he seized hold of her, swinging her to face him so that they were again eyeball to eyeball. 'What the fuck is it with you?' he roared, goaded beyond endurance. 'Why shouldn't I have dolly-birds when you won't have anything to do with me!'

'Can you blame me after what happened last time?' There was an edge of near-hysteria in her voice as she wrenched herself free of his hold. 'There's not a day goes by I don't suffer torments of guilt! If it hadn't been for us . . . If it hadn't been for me . . .'

There was a beat of stunned silence.

And then another one.

At last he said with incredulity, 'Christ Almighty . . . you're talking about Sheelagh's death? You think *I* was responsible for it?'

She swayed slightly, her skin no longer pale, but ashen. 'The fire wasn't an accident, Marco. Everyone knows that. What was an accident was the twins being in the house when they should have been at a birthday party. A party you thought they had gone to.'

Never in his life had he been so utterly pole-axed. He stared at her like a vertigo sufferer for whom the world was tilting crazily and who was waiting for the dizziness to pass. When at last he trusted himself to speak, he said hoarsely, 'And that's what's been the matter all this time? You've been having nothing to do with me because you think I started the fire? That I did it because of us? That I did it hoping Sheelagh would die?'

She held his eyes and, as she read the expression in them, for her, too, the ground felt as if it was shelving away. 'It wasn't you?' Even as she asked the question, she could read her answer in his face. 'But if it wasn't you . . .' She began to tremble, the enormity of the realization almost more than she could comprehend. 'If it wasn't you, Marco, then who was it? Who, in God's name, was it?'

From her bedroom window, Amber watched the exchange with interest. For an incredulous moment, as the conversation came to an end, she actually thought her mother was going to get into Mr Martini's car. She didn't, though. Instead, looking as if she were sleep-walking, she set off up the street, towards the main road and her bus stop.

And then Mr Martini did something that almost robbed Amber of breath.

He walked up the front path of her house and knocked on the door.

'And you're Angela Flynn's sister?' a staff nurse asked when, an hour and a half later, Amber asked which bed Angie was in.

'Yes,' Amber lied, hoping to God that Fast-Boy wouldn't storm on to the ward before she'd done what she had promised she would do.

'I want you to make sure Angie doesn't spill the beans to Tony – or to Fast-Boy and Sharyn – about where the accident really took place and who called the ambulance,' Mr Martini had said to her, after explaining that Angie's headlong plunge down a flight of stairs had happened when she was in a place she shouldn't have been, waiting to meet Johnny. 'Tell her she's to say that her accident took place at London Bridge Station and that it was a member of the station staff who rang for the ambulance. That way a lot of difficulties will be avoided.'

'Sure,' she'd replied, knowing exactly the kind of difficulties he had in mind, flattered that he was treating her as a confidante. 'Cool.' She hadn't, though, wanted him to think he was telling her anything about Johnny and Angie that she didn't already know.

Tilting her head to one side slightly, she'd regarded him through pale eyelashes. 'This accident that Angie is to say took place at London Bridge Station . . .' she'd said speculatively. 'Did it actually happen at the Take Six recording studios?'

It had been a guess, of course, but as Mr Martini's heavy eyebrows shot nearly into his shock of silver-streaked hair, she'd known she'd been spot on.

'How the devil?' he'd exploded, an expression flashing through his eyes that most people would have been afraid of.

She hadn't been afraid, though. How could she be when, as a baby, he'd so comfortably held her in his arms?

'I have eyes in my head and I'm not stupid,' she'd said, answering the question he hadn't finished asking.

'And is this guess of yours one you've kept to yourself, or have you told other people?' he'd asked.

She'd known that lying to him would be a dangerous thing to do, but the lie had come glibly all the same. 'It's one I've kept to myself,' she'd said, seeing no reason to tell him that she'd told Sharyn.

Incredibly, he'd seemed to believe her. Leastways, he'd given her money for a cab to Guy's Hospital and now here she was, being led across to the bed where a comatose Angie had been brought up from theatre.

It wasn't an ordinary bed. It was one equipped with a daunting array of ropes and pulleys. Angie's left leg was encased in plaster from the hip to the ankle and hoisted at an improbable angle. Her left arm, also encased in plaster, was similarly held high, and her right shoulder and her chest were bandaged and strapped.

'It will probably be a while before your sister comes round from the anaesthetic,' the staff nurse was saying. 'If your mother or father arrive before she comes to, you'll have to leave. It's one visitor to a bed when patients are in recovery. Understood?'

She nodded, knowing that Angie's dad was kicking his heels in a cell in Brixton and that Mr Martini was ensuring Angie's mother wouldn't be down to the hospital for hours yet, so there was no need for her to worry. What she didn't want to happen, though, was for Fast-Boy to find out about Angie's accident and come haring to the hospital.

As she pondered how likely this was, a large black woman pushing a trolley paused by the foot of Angie's bed and asked if she wanted a coffee.

She accepted gratefully, still thinking about Fast-Boy. She hadn't had the chance of a matey conversation with him since the night she'd seen him arrive home in the dark, a skirt half tucked into his biking trousers, but she knew that the bad blood between him and Johnny had become even worse since Zoë Fairminder's death.

And though he hadn't said so, she knew it was because of that bad blood that Mr Martini didn't want Fast-Boy knowing who his sister had been waiting to meet when she'd pitched headlong down a flight of stairs.

There were just a tad too many similarities.

Apart from one, of course.

Unlike Zoë, Angie was still alive.

As if to prove it, there was a slight sound from the direction of the bed.

'The young lady is comin' round,' the orderly said as

Angie made a struggling noise in her throat. 'I'll tell the nurse. See that kidney-basin on her locker top? Hold it near her mouth, honey. She's sure goin' to need to use it.'

'Dad tells me Angie's had an accident and is in Guy's,' Tony said laconically to Johnny. 'Fancy coming with me to visit her?'

It was eleven o'clock and the Prince had just opened for business. Johnny had been propping the bar up well before the doors had opened to the general public. Tony had strolled in only a moment ago.

'Christ! Has she? What kind of an accident?' With all the skill at his command, Johnny tried to simultaneously affect shock, concern and curiosity.

Clad in a beige polo-neck sweater, black leather jacket, jeans and the eternal silver-studded cowboy boots, Tony slid on to a bar-stool.

It wasn't exactly the behaviour of a bloke worried out of his mind about the girl he loved and Johnny felt a twinge of uneasiness. What if Amber Bailey hadn't done her stuff? What if she hadn't been allowed on the ward? What if . . .

'Dad says she fell downstairs late last night at London Bridge Station.' He took a packet of Marlboros out of his jacket pocket. 'I can't imagine what she was doing there. I mean, where do you reckon she was going to, or coming from?'

His interest, as he tapped out a cigarette, seemed almost academic.

'Christ knows.' Johnny ran a hand over his close-cropped hair. 'Who told Dad? Do you know how badly Angie's hurt herself? Shouldn't you be getting the hell down to Guy's to see her?'

'Yeah, well . . . Thing is, Johnny, I reckon she was meeting another guy. D'you get my drift?'

As he lit his cigarette, he looked directly at Johnny – and Johnny knew the game was up. Tony knew. The question was: how much did he know?

He shot his twin a lopsided smile. 'You always were sharp enough to cut yourself, Tony,' he said, as if ruefully amused. 'You're spot on that she was meeting another bloke. She was due to meet me, but when she didn't show I figured she'd got other fish to fry. Thing is, Angie wants to break into the music business and I've been giving her a bit of help. Giving her access to the rehearsal rooms down at Take Six, that sort of thing.'

There was a flicker of something indefinable in Tony's eyes and then he began giving a slow, sarcastic handclap. 'Nice try, Johnny. A very nice try. But as Angie's never once mentioned any ambition to go into the music business, I don't believe a word of it – especially as she can't sing a note. I'll be happy to listen to her, though. It should be a real treat.'

A nerve began pulsing at the corner of Johnny's jaw. He wasn't used to being mocked and he didn't like it. Particularly coming from Tony.

'Watch it,' he said warningly. 'I don't take lip from anyone, Tony. Not even you.'

'Is that right?' There was no amusement between them now, feigned or otherwise. 'But I'm supposed to stand for you shafting my girlfriend? Just as, when we were kids, I had to stand for you roping me into all the shit you got yourself into? Well, I've got news for you, Johnny: I'm not going to. I'm going to treat you the same way you'd treat me if I'd been having it off with one of your women. I'm going to give you the fucking thrashing of your life.'

Overhearing Tony's last sentence, Happy Harry removed himself from the danger zone. Most fisticuffs he would have handled with the expertise that came with his job description. He had, after all, been a landlord for a long time. Fisticuffs between Johnny Martini and his twin, however, was another matter. He'd never crossed any of the Martinis yet and didn't intend starting now. Plus he was pretty sure that a fight between Johnny and Tony wouldn't stay at a fist fight. Despite his boxing expertise, fist fights weren't Johnny's style. Knives were more Johnny's style.

As Harry beat his retreat there was a brief second in which Johnny stared at Tony, hardly able to believe what he was hearing.

It was a second Tony put to good advantage.

With all the force he could summon, he whacked Johnny straight in the mouth.

He didn't have the fight experience Johnny had, but his days on the ranch had been spent in hard physical labour and the blow was a pile-driver. Totally unprepared for it, Johnny went flying, chairs and tables crashing around him as he made spectacular contact with the floor.

The second he landed, Tony hurled himself on top of him, aware that if Johnny regained his feet the fight would be over before it had started, leaving him pulverized. Straddling Johnny as he'd done in their childhood fights, he struggled to hold him by the throat with one hand in order to deliver a terrific blow across his mouth with the other.

With a roar of rage Johnny bucked free, fisting him on the jaw with such force he felt as if his head was leaving his shoulders. Blindly he hit out in retaliation and then, as another punch caught him just below the cheekbone, began lashing out with his feet as well as his fists, fighting like the very devil for survival.

'Fucker!' Johnny was yelling at him as they wrestled and rolled across the pub. 'Fucker! *Fucker! FUCKER!*'

It was never a fight he was going to win, but he regained the advantage with a kick to Johnny's gut, leaving him gasping for air and doubled up in agony. For a second, despite the blood pumping from a split eyebrow and a busted lip, he thought he was going to be able to finish the fight. All he needed was to smash just one more pile-driving punch into Johnny's jaw . . .

Still gasping for breath, white with pain and fury, Johnny was on him before he'd even drawn his fist back to deliver the blow. More tables and chairs toppled and skittered as Johnny's next blow sent him skidding across the floor.

Somehow, his breath rasping in his throat, he managed to regain his feet, trying the oldest trick in the book as he did so. 'Cheyenne!' he shouted hoarsely, his eyes flying to the door in the hope that Johnny would turn his head so he'd be able to get in a blow below Johnny's ear where, with luck, his jaw would break like eggshell.

'Bastard!' Johnny sucked in air, not fooled for an instant. 'Cunt!'

The next blow to his forehead sent him staggering backwards until he slammed into the bar, and then Johnny was on him again, only this time with a knife.

'You've been asking for this, Tony!'

The knife was at his throat.

'Ever since you arrived back from fucking Canada not wanting to fit in – not wanting to be like a proper fucking twin – you've been asking for this!'

He could feel the tip of the blade pierce his flesh, knew that blood was beginning to ooze. With difficulty he dragged air into his lungs. 'Christ, but you don't change, do you?' He held Johnny's eyes, struggling not to betray fear or capitulation, his voice raw. 'You always did fight dirty. There was no keeping to boxing-club standards for you, Johnny-boy, was there? It was always blades or razors or knuckle-dusters. And the old man supplied them, didn't he? What will he do if you cut my throat? Give you a fucking medal and dance at the funeral?'

He saw Johnny's pupils dilate and knew he was only a beat away from having his jugular punctured.

The moment seemed endless and then suddenly, his chest heaving, all passion spent, Johnny dropped the knife.

'What the fuck,' he asked wearily, 'do you mean?'

Tony allowed his legs to give way. Nearly senseless with relief he slid down against the bar until he was sitting on the floor, legs splayed.

'I mean that the old man didn't want me to come back,' he said, as blood continued to trickle from his eyebrow and mouth. 'Didn't you know? Hadn't you worked it out for yourself?'

'Bollocks.' With the fight as forgotten as if it had been one of their many childhood scraps, Johnny collapsed exhaustedly beside him.

It was the first moment of true camaraderie they'd known since Tony's return.

'Dad always favoured you, not me.' Johnny pushed his fingers through his hair. 'Look how he saw to it that you always had the best of everything. When it came to one of us going to Canada and living on a ranch with horses and cowboys, it was you he sent, not me. I never had the chance to learn to ride and shoot and pan for gold. I had to stick here, being bored to death. You were the lucky one. You were always the lucky one.'

'Yeah.' Tony leaned his head back and closed his eyes. 'Yeah, I was the lucky one, all right.' To Johnny's bewilderment, he began to laugh. He began to laugh so much that tears began mixing with the blood trickling down his face.

Johnny didn't know what the joke was – and didn't care. What mattered was that he and Tony were comfortable with each other again, just as they'd been when they were children, in the days before the fire; before they'd been separated; before the world, as they'd known it, had come to an end.

He fished a handkerchief from his pocket and handed it to Tony, saying as he did so: 'You know the night Zoë died? Did you notice if anyone was listening in when me and her were having our little chinwag near the cigarette-machine?' It was a question he'd been wanting to ask for a while and he saw nothing incongruous in asking it now.

Tony pressed the handkerchief to his eye. 'That geezer Cheyenne said used to run with you – Jimmy Jones – was earwigging. He didn't look too happy.' He lifted his shoulders in a shrug. 'He left the pub straight afterwards. Why do you want to know?'

'Nothing.' Johnny had got the answer he wanted and he'd made up his mind what he was going to do about it. As it wasn't anything Tony was likely to be happy about, he saw no sense in burdening him with it. There was something else that needed saying, though. Something that was going to really cost him.

'You were right about Angie and me,' he said, knowing there was no longer any point in denying it. 'But it's over. It's history. OK?'

'Yeah.' Tony avoided his eyes, aware of just how high

a price Johnny was paying in order to make things right between them.

He took the handkerchief away from his eye and pressed it to the corner of his split lip. If concessions so mammoth were being made, perhaps it was time he began making some, too.

'About your Pomeroy scam . . .' he said, crossing the Rubicon he'd fought shy of for so long. 'How's it going? Can I be of help?'

Chapter Eight

Sharyn stared at her mother, a half-dozen conflicting emotions within her. 'Angie fell *where?*' she said at last, disbelievingly. 'She has *how many* injuries?'

'Multiple,' her mother said succinctly, taking off her coat and hooking it over the newel-post at the foot of the stairs. She had just returned home from work, entering the house only minutes after Sharyn. While her daughter stood gaping at her, she walked through to the kitchen, picked up the kettle and filled it at the sink.

'But Angie can't have fallen down the stairs at London Bridge Station.' Sharyn's confusion was obvious as, still wearing her coat, she followed her mother into the kitchen. 'Angie wasn't *at* London Bridge. She was . . .' She stopped short. She couldn't say where Angie had been without opening a whole can of worms for herself. 'Who told you about her having fallen?' she asked, wondering if Johnny knew; if his reaction to the news – the depth of his concern – was going to destroy her.

'Marco,' her mother said, lighting a gas hob and putting the kettle on it.

Sharyn blinked. There was only one Marco: Johnny's father. Very few people ever took the liberty of referring to him as Marco, though. It was always Mr Martini. Not that her mother was so respectful. Her mother's usual way of referring to Marco Martini was to use words that turned the air blue.

'Marco who?' she asked, wondering if she was losing

touch with reality entirely. Why, for instance, was it being said that Angie's fall had taken place at London Bridge Station? It hadn't. Angie had been at the recording studios. She knew that for a fact.

'Marco Martini,' her mother said, turning away from the stove and looking at her as if she needed certifying. 'What other Marco is there?'

It wasn't a question that needed an answer and though her bewilderment was deepening by the minute, Sharyn had the sense to make no response. Instead she said, 'And he told you this morning? Does that mean Johnny and Tony know? Has anyone been to visit her? Which hospital is she in? What ward?'

Her mother rinsed a teapot out with hot water and put three caddyspoons of Typhoo into it. 'I don't know whether Johnny and Tony know, though I imagine they must, by now. And there's no point in you rushing off to Guy's – which is where she is. Amber's with her. She phoned me at work and said that Angie is days away from being able to chat to visitors – she's fractured the neck of her pelvis, crushed her pubic bones, broken a leg, dislocated her shoulder and goodness knows what else.' Her voice was unsteady and, as she lifted two cups off a shelf, her hand shook. 'God only knows how she could have fallen with such force – or how long it's going to be until she's on her feet again.'

A spasm crossed Sharyn's face as, for the first time, she took on board just how badly hurt Angie was. The terrible thing was that she didn't know whether to be glad or not. Yesterday, when she'd realized that Amber had been telling the truth about Johnny cheating on her with Angie, she'd wanted to kill Angie. What if Amber had got it all wrong, though? What if Angie had just been meeting Johnny to talk to him about Tony? What if she'd been having problems with Tony that she didn't want anyone else, apart from his twin, to know about?

As the kettle began to boil and her mother took it off the hob and brewed the tea, Sharyn reflected on just how far back she and Angie went. It was a long, long way. *She* was the one who should be sitting with Angie, not Amber – especially as Angie didn't even like Amber!

'It's me Angie will want to have with her,' she said, knowing how bad it would look if she weren't at Angie's bedside. 'Why is Amber at the hospital, anyway? You shouldn't have told her about the accident, Mum. Not till you'd told me first.'

'I didn't.' There was an odd note in her mother's voice. Something Sharyn could neither place nor understand. 'Marco told her.'

Once again Sharyn felt as if she were being unutterably stupid. 'You mean Amber was with you when he told you? I still don't see why she took it on herself to hare down to the hospital. I mean, it isn't as if Angie is *her* best friend . . .'

'Marco spoke to her after he'd spoken to me – after I'd gone to work.'

'Amber waylaid Mr Martini in the street?' In spite of trying not to be, Sharyn was shocked. People with sense avoided Marco Martini. They didn't trundle up to him as if he were their favourite uncle.

'No.' As her mother poured herself a much-needed cup of tea, Sharyn saw that the lines of strain around her mouth had deepened. 'He came to the house to speak to her. And please don't ask me why, Sharyn, because I don't know.'

And with that, cup of tea in hand, her mother walked past her, out of the kitchen. A moment or so later there was the click of a bedroom door closing. And then silence.

Sharyn drew in a deep, steadying breath. Was the world going mad or was she losing her grip? Had Angie been at Take Six last night, or had the person she'd assumed was Angie been someone else? It had, after all, been dark. And why on earth had Marco Martini trolled up their front path to speak to her kid sister? It was odd enough that he would speak to her mother about Angie's accident, but that he would go out of his way to tell Amber was bizarre. *She* was the one who was Angie's best friend. If he'd been going to tell anyone, why hadn't he told her? And how had he known about it, anyway?

Just trying to puzzle it all out made her head ache. She needed to speak to people. Most of all Johnny. She needed to know what he knew about Angie's accident. And she needed to speak to her brat of a sister to find out just what Marco Martini had said to her. Plus she needed to be with Angie, so that Angie could tell her what she remembered of how and why and where she had fallen.

Ignoring her steaming cup of tea, she walked out into the hallway, picked up her handbag from where she'd dropped it, and swung out of the house. She'd go to the Prince of Wales first, on the off-chance that Johnny was there. If he wasn't, she'd take a bus to the hospital. And she wouldn't panic about anything yet.

There was probably no need.

Not if she kept her mouth shut.

Jimmy Jones was running scared. How the fuck could Johnny Martini think he was responsible for Zoë Fairminder's death? He hadn't even known her; had never even spoken to her.

'But you knew she was about to dump Fast-Boy for Johnny,' Cheyenne had said to him when he'd run him to ground at the White Swan in Deptford. 'And you knew Johnny was crazy about her.'

'No, I didn't!' His protest had been so vehement he'd spilled half his pint of light and bitter. 'Christ, why should I have? I ain't exactly in Johnny's pocket any more, am I?'

'You earwigged in on the conversation Johnny had with her in the Prince the night she fell and broke her neck,' Cheyenne retorted. 'You knew what was in the offing, Jimmy. And Johnny knows you knew.'

'So . . . ?' he said belligerently, still seeing no sense to what Cheyenne was saying. 'So what? They weren't exactly exchanging state secrets. The pub was packed that night. Half a dozen people were probably standing near enough to overhear what they were saying.'

'Yeah . . . maybe they were.' Cheyenne took a deep drink of his beer. 'Thing is, though, they wouldn't all be wanting to do a number on Johnny, would they? You were.'

'Oh, sure!' he jeered. 'So why didn't I, then? A minute ago you were saying it was his bleedin' girlfriend-to-be that I'd snuffed.'

'I'm still saying that,' Cheyenne replied, 'or at least, that's what Johnny's saying. He reckons you wouldn't have had the bottle to try and iron him out. And let's face it, Jimmy – you wouldn't. But Johnny's old lady would be a different matter.'

'So what am I supposed to have done?' he'd said, the panic he'd been battening down beginning to break free and bubble up into his throat. 'Break her neck with a karate chop and stuff her down the workmen's pit?'

Instead of laughing at the ridiculousness of it, Cheyenne merely shrugged. 'It could have been done like that,' he said. 'Johnny thinks you did it a bit sneakier, though. That knowing she was going out into the car park to meet him, you kicked the barrier away in the hope she'd fall headlong into it. And because he thinks that, he's on the hunt for you. And when he finds you, it'll be curtains, Jimmy. Know what I mean?'

He'd known exactly what Cheyenne meant and he'd done what everyone south of the river always did in such a situation. He'd moved north of the river sharpish – very sharpish.

It wasn't a foolproof solution, though, and he knew it. The big boys north of the river, the Krays, wouldn't be interested in taking him aboard and offering him protection. He was a small-timer. Christ, even in Johnny Martini's outfit he'd been a small-timer.

So what the fuck was he going to do? Arrange a meet with Johnny in a safe place and try to reason with him? He jettisoned the thought fast. Where Johnny was concerned, there wasn't such a thing as a safe place. Johnny would arrive mob-handed and tooled-up, and how the fuck could anyone reason with a psycho?

And he couldn't get him off his back by killing him. He simply didn't have the back-up and there'd never be an opportunity. Johnny wasn't a loner. He never went anywhere without an entourage – and with his entourage around him there'd be as much chance of popping him off as flying to the moon.

Which left only one option. Hiding. But for how long? Johnny would know he was now north of the river. What if he got his old man to have a word with the Krays? If that happened there wouldn't be a pub or a club in the East End or Soho where he would be safe.

Birmingham. Perhaps he should go to Birmingham.

He wiped a bead of sweat away from his upper lip.

Or perhaps he should take the rattler to Glasgow.

Even Glasgow, though, might not be far enough.

America, then? Or Canada or Australia?

Fear churned in his belly. He didn't have a passport and he'd have to get one. He'd have to get one fast.

Amber picked up the magazine the woman in the next bed had said she could borrow, and flicked through it for the umpteenth time. Angie was asleep again. Or unconscious. Or comatose. Amber didn't know the difference. She only knew that poor old Angie was in a very bad way indeed.

When she'd first come round from the anaesthetic, she'd been sick. Not normal sick, though. 'It's bile,' the nurse had said conversationally as she'd removed the kidney bowl from beneath Angie's chin. 'There's a clean bowl on her locker top if she needs one again.'

Angie had.

Even worse than witnessing Angie's sickness had been witnessing her pain. Every time she'd surfaced from the remnants of the anaesthesia she'd moaned and whimpered. The surgeon who had operated on her had made his rounds and checked on her, and shortly afterwards a staff nurse had given her an injection.

Amber, ever curious, had asked what it was. 'Morphine,' replied the staff nurse. 'Don't be too worried about her. She's actually doing very well. Just don't stress her by trying to talk to her.'

Mindful of the reason she was there, it was advice she'd ignored. In one of the brief periods when Angie had been conscious enough to register her presence, she'd held her hand, saying urgently, 'Angie, it's me: Amber. Mr Martini wants you to say that your accident happened at London Bridge Station. He thinks it best, under the circumstances.'

Angie had merely groaned.

'You actually fell down the stairs at the recording studios,' she'd added, doubtful whether Angie even remembered what had happened to her, let alone where. 'You were waiting for Johnny – but Mr Martini doesn't want Tony knowing that, or Fast-Boy,' she said, wondering when Fast-Boy was going to show at the hospital. Now that she'd told Angie what she was supposed to say, it didn't matter when Fast-Boy showed. Or it wouldn't if Angie remembered what she'd been told.

'Do you understand what I'm saying, Angie?' she asked, concerned. 'It's just that it might be important. Know what I mean?'

Angie hadn't been up to making a verbal response, but her fingers had tightened reassuringly on hers.

An hour or so later, still without opening her eyes, Angie said quite clearly, 'Amber? Are you there? The lights went out, Amber. The lights went out and a snake smacked against my legs.'

For a second she'd been too startled to react and, when she had, asking Angie if she was talking about her fall, it had been too late. Angie had been unresponsive, sunk again into deep unconsciousness.

'Another coffee, sweetheart?' the orderly with the tea-trolley asked Amber as she trundled it to a halt at the foot of Angie's bed. It was the sixth time that day that she'd made the offer and had it accepted, and the two of them were getting to be quite good friends. 'It's general visiting hour now, honey. When that's over, I think you'll be asked to leave. Still, at least you'll have someone to leave with. Your brother came five minutes ago and he's speaking to the doctor. Guess the doctor's tellin' him just how bad hurt your sister is.'

Amber flashed a quick look towards Angie, about to hiss the words 'London Bridge Station' again, but Angie's eyes were still closed, her skin so pale it was almost translucent.

Hoping that Angie would stay in morphine-induced unconsciousness for a little longer she looked down the length of the ward, watching as Fast-Boy came out of the Sister's office and began walking towards her.

He was wearing a sheepskin-lined flying-jacket, tight black leather trousers and black motorcycle boots. It was nearly eight o'clock at night, peak visiting time, and several people turned their heads to follow his progress. Amber didn't blame them for staring. Fast-Boy was the nearest thing to a James Dean lookalike she'd ever seen.

He came to a halt at the foot of the bed, visibly shocked by the amount of plaster-casting Angie was encased in, and by the number of pulleys and slings and tubes and drips she was attached to.

'Don't worry too much,' Amber said, repeating what the staff nurse had said to her earlier. 'She's actually doing very well.'

'Then I'd hate to see anyone who wasn't,' he said tightly, a pulse throbbing at the corner of his jaw. 'How, in Christ's name, could she have done all this to herself just by falling down some stairs?'

'I 'spect the stairs were stone – station stairs usually are, aren't they?'

'And is that where it happened? At a station?'

'Yes,' she said, her eyes holding his, wondering why some people found it hard to lie convincingly when she could do it as easy as falling off a log. 'She was at London Bridge. Did the doctor tell you what it is she's broken and fractured?'

'He gave me a fair idea.' He moved round to the side

of the bed furthest from her and sat down on one of the uncomfortable chairs provided for visitors. 'From what the doctor said, you and me are now related. As kid sisters go, I suppose you could be worse. Why'd you lie? Wouldn't they let you in otherwise?'

'No . . . and I thought she'd want someone with her when she came round from the anaesthetic.'

He slouched as comfortably as he could on the upright chair, resting one leg akimbo across the other, holding it in place by the ankle. 'And you were told what had happened by . . . who?'

The question was casual, but his eyes weren't. They were narrow and speculative and very, very suspicious.

'By Mr Martini,' she said, lapsing into truth and knowing it didn't matter as she was still only giving out a version of events that Mr Martini had okayed. 'A friend of his works in Accident and Emergency. Knowing Angie was Tony's girlfriend, he rang Mr Martini so that he could break the news to Tony.'

'Did he now?' Fast-Boy's eyes were, if possible, even more suspicious. 'And as Angie wasn't in any condition to give anyone her home address and phone number, that's how my mother got to know as well – via Mr Martini? Surprising how much of a Samaritan he can be when he wants to, ain't it?'

'Angie is Tony's girlfriend,' she said blandly, ignoring his sarcasm. 'I suppose that's why he went out of his way to tell your mum. Anyway, Mr Martini can be quite nice when he wants to be.'

Fast-Boy cracked with laughter. 'Yeah,' he said, genuinely amused. 'And they tell me Hitler was quite a decent bloke too, on his good days.'

Remembering the photograph of herself as a baby in Mr Martini's arms, Amber decided to change the subject.

'Where's your mum?' she asked. 'I thought she'd have been here by now?'

His good humour vanished. 'Yeah. Thing is, Red, she was given to understand Angie wasn't allowed visitors until tomorrow. I said that was bollocks – which is why I'm here. You, though, you've been here how long?'

'Since late this morning,' she said, knowing there was no point in lying when it was something he could so easily check on.

'If you don't mind me saying so, I find that a little strange, Red. If it had been Sharyn who'd been with her, I could understand . . .'

As if on cue, and with only twenty minutes of general visiting time left, Sharyn walked into the ward, Tony at her side.

For the first time that she could remember, Amber was sincerely glad to see her.

'Sharyn's here,' she said, cutting across him. 'And Tony . . .' Anything else she might have been going to say was lost as her jaw dropped in shock.

Tony looked as if he'd been in a battle. His right eye was swollen and beginning to turn a rich black, the cut above it so deep it was only held together by half a dozen stitches. There were grazes and bruises on his right cheekbone and his lip had been split and was as swollen as a pumpkin.

As he and Sharyn reached the foot of Angie's bed, a nurse hurried up. 'I'm sorry,' she said briskly, 'but it's only two visitors to a bed, and Miss Flynn isn't really in a condition for *any* visitors . . .'

Sharyn drew breath, about to throw a wobbly, and Amber chose that moment to rise speedily to her feet. 'I'm off,' she said, to no one in particular.

'Me too.' Fast-Boy stood up, his thumbs hooked

nonchalantly in the pockets of his leather trousers. 'You look as if life's been interesting lately, Tony. What did you do, walk into a door?'

'Something like that.' There was a glimmer of amusement in Tony's voice and Amber looked from him to Fast-Boy, her eyes widening. Because Johnny and Fast-Boy were arch enemies, she'd always assumed that there was no love lost between Tony and Fast-Boy, either. Now, for the first time, she realized she'd been wrong.

Sharyn sat down unsteadily on the chair Amber had vacated. 'Oh, *look* at poor Angie!' she said, her eyes beginning to fill with tears. 'Doesn't she look strange without her make-up? And what are all those pulleys and things for? Has she been speaking to you, Amber? Where did she fall? How did she do it? What has she said?'

'She fell down the stairs at London Bridge Station.' Amber's eyes, as she looked at her sister, were as speculative as Fast-Boy's had been when they'd held hers a little earlier. 'The doctor said she mustn't talk, so if she comes round again, don't go pestering her with questions, Sha.'

'Course I shan't.' Sharyn gave her shoulders a wiggle, all affronted indignation at the very thought.

Tony said, 'If you and Fast-Boy are going, Amber, you'd better leave now before we all get turfed out.'

It was a sensible remark and, though she was dying to find out who he had been in a fight with, she knew that now wasn't the time to ask.

'OK.' She picked up her coat, gave a last concerned look towards Angie and, without another word, began walking away.

Within half a dozen yards Fast-Boy was at her side. 'Want a lift, Red?' he asked, pushing open the doors at the end of the ward.

As the doors swung shut behind them, she halted,

looking at him with renewed interest. 'On the Harley?'

'Natch. You can wear my crash helmet.'

'OK.' She tilted her head to one side, looking measuringly at him. 'But only on one condition . . .'

'Which is?' There was amusement in his eyes again and not for the first time it occurred to her that when he looked amused he also looked very, very nice.

She hesitated, not wanting to scupper the chance of a ride on the Harley and then, reckoning that it was a risk she was just going to have to take, said, 'Why do you wear women's clothes and make-up? Are you some kind of a perve, or do you do drag acts in clubs, like Danny la Rue?'

Angie drifted back to consciousness but didn't open her eyes. The voices she could hear were no longer Amber's and Fast-Boy's. They were Sharyn's and Tony's, and the pain she was in was far too deep for her to want to speak to either of them.

What on God's earth had she done to herself? Every part of her body seemed to be trussed and bound. The only things she'd been able to move – the only things she'd had the nerve to *try* and move, were her fingers when she had acknowledged what Amber had said about Mr Martini wanting her to say that her fall had taken place at London Bridge. Well, that was fine by her. She could quite well see why he wouldn't want Tony knowing that she'd been meeting Johnny at the recording studios. She didn't particularly want him knowing about it, either.

The pain was so intense that, despite trying not to, she moaned. She could hear Sharyn's near hysterical reaction, and Tony calling for assistance. Seconds later she sensed the presence of a nurse. Something cold and hard and wet was pressed against her lips – an ice-cube? Whatever it was, she was grateful for it. Then she felt her arm being swabbed and knew that she was about to receive the blissful relief of a painkilling injection.

Before she sank again into oblivion there was something else she knew she had to think about: Johnny. Was it Johnny who had found her and got her to the hospital? And where was he now? When was he going to visit her? Amber hadn't mentioned him, and Sharyn and Tony weren't mentioning him, either. There'd been something very important that she'd wanted to say to Johnny when she'd gone to the recording studios. What had it been?

She could feel herself sinking into what felt to be a bottomless pit of cotton-wool – and she wanted to sink into it. She wanted to sink into it and never come out of it. Johnny, though . . . why was it so important that she spoke to Johnny?

And then, as she felt herself succumbing to the morphine, she remembered. There'd been a raid. Fast-Boy was convinced Johnny had grassed him up and he was out to get him. She'd been intending to warn him – still had to warn him. And she had to ask him if Fast-Boy's assumption was correct, because, if it was . . . if it was, then when he visited she was going to have to finish with him.

Just as she floated free from consciousness there came another thought.

If.

If he visited her.

That he might not was a prospect so bleak even morphine couldn't make it bearable.

Sharyn stared unhappily at her friend's closed eyelids. She'd visited people in hospital before, but they'd always been sitting up in bed, reasonably perky. There was nothing perky about Angie. She looked like a corpse. Unbidden came the thought that she could very easily have been one. She had, after all, fallen a much greater distance than Zoë Fairminder, and Zoë had died instantly.

She looked across at Tony wondering if he, too, was recalling what had happened to Zoë. Then she remembered that, as he hadn't known her – he'd only arrived home a few hours before she had died – it wasn't very likely.

'It doesn't look as if Angie's going to be talking to us this evening, does it?' she said to him, wondering how long he was going to stay; wishing he hadn't suggested accompanying her.

There were times – and this was one of them – when Tony made her feel uncomfortable. Why, she didn't know. He was always perfectly civil to her. Unlike a lot of the guys in Johnny's gang, he never treated her as if, where Johnny was concerned, she was more of a groupie than a girlfriend.

Sometimes she thought that perhaps the trouble was his being so intelligent. All the stuff about him going to college so that he could pass exams and go to university made her feel weird. Why would he want to do such a peculiar thing? It made no sense to her. Not when he could rake in money by the bucketful by being useful to Johnny or his father.

'Nope, I don't reckon she is,' he said now, in answer to her question. 'But we might as well stay until visiting time's over. There's only another ten minutes or so to go.'

He took a paperback out of his bomber jacket pocket and flicked it open. The title on the front cover was *Giovanni's Room* and it was by someone called James

Baldwin. Sharyn couldn't even begin to think what kind of a book it was or what it might be about.

She looked away from him and towards Sharyn. Tony wasn't showing too much concern for Sharyn's injuries, but then he wasn't someone who showed his feelings – which was another reason why she was often uncomfortable in his presence. At least with Johnny it was obvious whether he was in a good or a bad mood; whether he wanted her around or not. Tony was never so easy to fathom. He was always a mystery.

The scene she'd walked in on a couple of hours ago at the Prince, for instance. Tony had been bleeding like a stuck pig from the cut above his eye and his busted lip – yet he'd been grinning, one arm slung round Johnny's shoulders, more relaxed and at ease than she could ever remember seeing him.

At first she'd thought the two of them had just fought off a gang of liberty-takers – but then Johnny had said that they'd been settling a little private dispute.

'You've been fighting each other?' she'd asked, wide-eyed.

They'd both cracked with laughter.

'And now we're going down to Guy's to get some stitches in Tone's eyebrow,' Johnny said. 'Shouldn't you be down there as well, Sha? Visiting Angie?'

'Yes,' she'd said when she'd got her breath back. 'Yes, I should.'

That he knew about Angie's accident and wasn't distraught about it – as he would have been if there'd been any truth in Amber's allegation – was such a relief she'd almost burst into tears.

Johnny had thought the tears were welling out of her concern for Angie. 'Don't worry, babe,' he'd said, moving away from Tony in order to slip his arm round her waist.

'She'll be all right. Angie's as tough as they come, ain't she, Tone?'

It had been the first time she'd ever heard Johnny call his brother 'Tone', and it had certainly been the first time she'd sensed such an overpowering closeness between them. Something cataclysmic must have happened between them, but what?

As she sat looking at him across Angie's bed, she tried to put it out of her mind. It wasn't as if she'd be able to work it out for herself and, whatever it was, it couldn't possibly be as cataclysmic as what had happened to Angie.

Her eyes grew dark as she looked towards her friend. From the look of her, Angie was injured for life.

Her throat tightened.

No one had said so yet, but she rather thought Angie would never walk again.

Chapter Nine

May 1971

Amber leaned against the embankment railings outside the Trafalgar pub at Greenwich, her face raised to the warmth of the sun. It was her lunch-break and she was meeting a friend who worked in an estate agent's near to her own office in William IV Street for a drink and a sandwich.

Her friend, Tilly, was late, but she didn't mind. It was the first decent summer since Zoë Fairminder had died and just being by the Thames was so blissful she wasn't sure she wanted to spoil the magic of it by listening to Tilly's chatter about her anxieties over her latest boyfriend.

She turned, resting her arms on top of the railings, so that she could stare out over the glittering surface of the fast-flowing water. How many years had it been since that last lovely summer? Four? Five? She'd been twelve when Zoë had died and she was now seventeen, so it must have been five years ago. It occurred to her that, though in some respects an awful lot of changes had taken place in those five years, in other respects not much had changed at all.

Sharyn, for instance, had barely moved on in any way, apart from trading typing classes at college for a position as a typist with a local printing company. She was still in love with Johnny; still always at his beck and call; still adamantly insisting he wasn't serially unfaithful to her.

He was, of course – though it was unfaithfulness constantly dogged by bad luck. Deirdre Crosby, Little Donnie's sister, had been killed in a road accident when their steamy relationship was only weeks old. Another girl, Abbra Hornby, had fallen off the platform of a moving bus and, but for a taxi-driver's extremely quick-off-the-mark emergency stop, might very well have met the same fate as Deirdre.

'Christ, but a girl would have to have a death wish to go out with you, Johnny,' Cheyenne had once joked. Everyone in the Prince of Wales had laughed, but Amber, who had been there, had thought that behind his rueful chuckle of agreement, Johnny hadn't found the remark even remotely amusing.

Other things in Sharyn's life hadn't changed, either. Angie was still her best friend, though since her fall at the recording studios had left Angie with a limp she was self-conscious about, they no longer went out to discos together and their nights out in a foursome, with Tony and Johnny, were also a thing of the past.

Amber knew why, of course. It was because Johnny and Angie's affair was well and truly at an end – had been at an end since the night of her fall – and Angie's hurt over it was far too deep for her to want to be in Johnny's company, pretending otherwise.

Like Sharyn, Johnny hadn't changed much either, except that he'd carved an even bigger reputation as someone to be wary of. He and Fast-Boy still never spoke a civil word to each other, but despite Fast-Boy's conviction that Johnny had grassed on him over his gun cache, there'd been no major confrontation. 'They're too evenly matched,' Tony had said to her when she broached the subject of their permanent stand-off. 'And even if Johnny unbalanced that, by going for Fast-Boy mob-handed, Fast-Boy's retaliation – when he could walk again – would be to kill Johnny. And Johnny knows it.'

If Fast-Boy and Johnny were still daggers-drawn, Tony and Johnny were inseparable. Though Tony was now studying for a degree, he was also Johnny's chief confidante and, if gossip was to be believed, the brains behind most of Johnny's crooked business operations. The most disconcerting aspect of their new-found closeness was the way Tony occasionally emphasized his and Johnny's identical looks by jettisoning his jeans and cowboy boots in favour of a single-breasted mohair suit and hand-made shoes. It wasn't something that happened often, but when it did, the effect was unnerving.

A flock of seagulls skimmed the river as she pondered on other things that had changed. Her dad, for instance, was no longer out and about acting as one of Marco Martini's more minor sidekicks. He'd landed a six-year sentence for affray. Fast-Boy and Angie's dad, on the other hand, was out of nick, propping up the bar at the Prince lunchtimes and evenings, seven days a week.

Her eyebrows pulled into a frown as she watched the seagulls settle on the river and reflected on the one relationship that had changed out of all recognition: her mother's relationship with Marco Martini. Not that it was a relationship many people were aware of – and with good reason. It would be damaging to Marco Martini's reputation if it became known he was on over-friendly terms with the wife of a man who was 'away' – especially when the man in question had, for years, made himself useful to him.

Not that she knew for a certainty that her mother was on over-friendly terms with Marco Martini, but it was the only explanation she could think of for their lunching together in pub-restaurants so far-flung from their home ground that they might confidently have expected not to have been seen.

She had seen them, though. She often went out with Fast-Boy on his new Harley and once, when they'd roared down the A20 to Shoreham, she'd seen her mother and Marco Martini sitting outside the Wheatsheaf pub, enjoying a summer-evening drink together. Another time, when they had been heading for a favourite meeting-place for bikers, the Burford Bridge Hotel at Box Hill, they had stopped off at Reigate, intending to have a quiet drink en route, and there, seated at a window-table in an Italian restaurant, they had seen her mother and Marco Martini deep in what looked to be a very intimate conversation.

One of the things she liked about Fast-Boy was that he'd made no comment. Absolutely none. All he'd done, when they'd finally reached Burford, was to buy her a double snowball.

Her frown deepened as she pondered what had become a very troubling mystery. Her mother had never, for as long as she could remember, had any truck whatsoever with Marco Martini. So what were they doing together now? It was, after all, a very odd time to choose. With the Krays off the streets – Ronnie serving a minimum of thirty years for gunning down George Cornell in the Blind Beggar, and Reggie serving a similar term for killing Jack-the-Hat McVitie – Marco's reputation had become more high profile than ever.

As, of course, had Johnny's.

'Johnny's nothing like the same calibre as his old man,' Fast-Boy had once said in the tight voice he always used when talking about Johnny. 'He's like Ronnie Kray – careless. And just as Ronnie's luck ran out when members of his firm turned Queen's Evidence and started making statements about what happened at the Blind Beggar, so Johnny's will run out where Jimmy Jones is concerned. Too many people knew that Ronnie had killed Cornell and too many people know that Johnny's done away with Jimmy Jones. One day, when Jimmy's body turns up – and there's a situation where it'll save their own skins – they'll talk. Just you wait and see.'

'Even Cheyenne?' she'd asked, sick to her stomach at the guilt she carried where Jimmy Jones' disappearance was concerned.

'Even Cheyenne,' he'd said, and that had been the end of the conversation. She hadn't told him how responsible she felt for whatever it was that had happened to Jimmy Jones – and she'd certainly never told him why she carried such responsibility.

Now, looking out over the railings at the sun glistening on the river, she regretted for the hundredth time ever letting Sharyn in on her half-baked idea that it was Jimmy Jones who had moved the barrier away from the pit Zoë had fallen into. It had been nothing but a wild surmise and, if only she had kept it to herself, Sharyn wouldn't have passed it on to Johnny as being near fact, and Johnny would never have abducted Jimmy as he scurried out of the Passport Office in Petty France.

What had happened to Jimmy after Johnny abducted him, no one knew – or if they did, they weren't telling. But as Jimmy had never been seen again, the guess was that he was very, very dead.

'A penny for them,' a familiar voice said.

As his shadow fell over her, she forced her dark thoughts back to where they had come from and turned to face him, truly pleased to see him.

'They're not worth it. What are you doing in Greenwich? Up to mischief?'

'Nope,' Fast-Boy said easily, seeing no reason to tell her he'd been checking on a get-away route from the Barclays Bank in William IV Street. 'I'm just bored, Red, that's all. I thought I'd go down to Box Hill for an hour or two. Fancy coming?'

Even at the speeds Fast-Boy favoured, Box Hill was a good forty minutes away. If she went, she wouldn't be able to return to work until mid-afternoon. And if she was that late back from lunch, she'd be fired.

'Course I'm coming,' she said, not finding the decision hard to make. Tilly was so late it was pretty obvious she wasn't going to show, and what did it matter if she was fired? She could always get herself another job – maybe even a job with Mr Lampeter, the estate agent Tilly worked for.

She eased herself away from the railings. 'You did a ton on the A24 last time we went to Box Hill,' she said, sliding her arm through his, 'but that was in the evening. D'you reckon you'll be able to do the same again, or will there be too much traffic this time of day?'

Inside the Trafalgar, Tony stood at one of the windows overlooking the Thames, watching as Amber mounted the Harley behind Fast-Boy in his leather trousers and motorcycle boots, a fringed leather waistcoat over the top of a black T-shirt.

He was still watching as, seconds later, Fast-Boy revved the Harley's engine hard and the two of them sped away.

Tight-lipped, he wondered where they were roaring away to. Wherever it was, he envied them. Ever since the old man had given him the news that Albie was paying a visit to London and would be staying with them, he'd have given everything he had to have been able to roar as far away as possible.

The prospect of being in even the same city as Albie was bad enough. That he would again be sleeping beneath the same roof was nothing short of nightmare.

Johnny's total ignorance of what the news meant to him had only increased the ghastliness. 'Christ, that's blinding,' he'd said as he grilled bacon for a late breakfast. 'I can't wait to meet him – I was always jealous as hell about the good times you used to have with him, out in Canada. Just don't start thinking about wanting to go back there, Tone.'

It had been said as a joke, but he hadn't been able to raise even the ghost of a smile.

Weeks and weeks of Albie. He'd never be able to survive it. Not that it would be the same as when he'd been a kid, of course. He turned away from the window, his hand tightening on his almost empty pint-glass, sweat breaking out on his brow. If Albie laid one hand on him again, either to beat him or to fuck him, he'd be a dead man. But Albie wouldn't. He'd be able to crucify him in another ways, though. He'd be able to make snide references that no one but Tony would understand. References to the cubbyhole in the barn roof and what had gone on in there.

He was holding his glass so tightly that his knuckles were white. As he squeezed it even harder it shattered explosively, shards flying, lager spraying.

'Careful, mate!' the geezer standing nearest him shouted as he stepped speedily backwards out of range of the glass, 'what d'you think you're fuckin' doin?'

Tony didn't answer him. He merely set the jagged base of the glass down on the nearest table and, as a barmaid hurried towards him to clear up the debris, shouldered his way past her, out of the pub.

Once on the pavement he wiped the sweat from his face, knowing that people were staring at him; knowing that he had to get himself under control; that he had to stop remembering.

He couldn't.

With the river on his left-hand side he began walking fast – so fast he was almost running. Despite the breeze blowing from off the water and the bright sunlight, he was again, in memory, choking in an airless, dark, coffin-like space.

Somehow, some way, he had to extricate himself from the hell he'd plunged into; he had to control his breathing; fight down the panic that was drowning him.

The effort was beyond him. He felt like a little kid again; totally helpless, totally vulnerable. He'd been eight years old, for Christ's sake. *Eight.* One minute he'd been the apple of his mother's eye, a young hooligan happily running wild in the streets as he and Johnny played war games on bomb-sites, Johnny always in the role of a ruthless German officer. The next, an aunt he barely knew had hauled him off to the other side of the world to the horror of life with Albie.

And all because of the fire.

All because his mother had died.

All because, when the chips were down, his mother had loved Johnny the best.

He kept walking fast, dimly aware he was heading down-river, away from Greenwich and away from Bermondsey.

Canada had been cold enough when he arrived. A few months later, with the onset of winter, it grew cold beyond all imagining. He hadn't had the clothes for such weather, and no one had spent money buying him any. With snow drifts ten-feet high and more to battle with, all he'd had for protection were clothes for a London winter. Even though he'd piled on every article of clothing he possessed, he'd still nearly died.

Later, when Albie had introduced him to the cubby-hole in the barn, he'd wished he had died.

He floundered to a halt, his heart palpitating, his breathing harsh.

He'd told his auntie, of course, but only the once; only after the first time. He'd been bewildered and hurt, bleeding from his nose where Albie had hit him; bleeding from his backside where Albie had fucked him.

She'd screamed the place down.

Screamed that he was a liar.

Screamed that she wasn't surprised his dad had made her take him with her when, after his mother's funeral, she'd returned to Canada.

Screamed that the old man hadn't wanted him in the house. That he hadn't wanted him influencing Johnny; turning Johnny into the same kind of psycho he was.

He hadn't understood a word of it; not then.

What he had understood, though, was that there was no one in the world who was going to help him. That he was going to have to retreat into himself if he were to survive. And that one day he would have his revenge.

It was why he had become so focused.

It was why he was still so focused.

As he looked down-river, towards Woolwich and the ferry, his breathing began to steady. He'd set his course years and years ago. Now, where Albie was concerned, all he had to do was to stick to it.

And he was going to.

There were going to be no deviations.

Not from now until the end of time.

Angie sat on the edge of her bed, a lit cigarette in her hand. She had a lot to think about and none of it was pleasant.

A baby.

How could Sharyn have been so insensitive and brain-dead as to have come rushing round to the house late last night to tell her that she was pregnant? Under the circumstances, it was unbelievable.

When, after her accident, she'd been told by the doctors that her pubic bones had been so badly damaged she would never be able to have a successful pregnancy, Sharyn had been the first person she had told.

Sharyn had wept buckets with her over it, but that had been then. This was now, and Sharyn's memory was short.

Hers wasn't.

Before the accident, her only thoughts about babies had been praying that she wouldn't fall for one.

Not now, though. Now that she knew she could never have one, wanting one and longing for one was practically all she ever thought about.

And Sharyn was pregnant. Not with just anyone's baby, but Johnny's.

The bleakness she felt was almost unbearable.

With all her heart she wanted to turn back time. She wanted to go back to that winter night in 1966 when she'd so heedlessly set off from home to meet Johnny at the recording studios and she wanted to halt when she reached the end of the street. She wanted to change her mind about going to the studios. She wanted to go into the Prince of Wales instead.

She wanted it to be *then*, not now. *Then*, when having any kind of physical disability was inconceivable; when if she'd wanted to have a baby she could have had one; when Johnny had been crazy about her and anything and everything had been possible.

She took a deep draw on her cigarette, bitterly aware that the past could never be reclaimed. She *had* gone to the studios. She *had* wandered to the top of the bloody building. And she *had* fallen down the nightmare-long flight of stairs, smashing her body spectacularly and irreparably.

But had she fallen accidentally, or had someone ensured that she'd fallen? Had someone laid something across the top step and fused the lights so that, in the darkness, she would hurtle to grave injury or perhaps even to her death?

In the days immediately after her fall she'd had no such dark thoughts. All she'd been able to think about was the pain she was in and that, though Amber, Fast-Boy, Tony and Sharyn were visiting her, Johnny wasn't.

It was Amber who had prompted memories she'd been unaware of having. 'You said there was a snake around your legs, Angie,' she'd said to her when she was no longer fuzzy from the after-effects of anaesthetic and morphine. 'It was the afternoon you came back from theatre. You were in and out of consciousness, and you said quite clearly to me, "The lights went out and a snake smacked against my legs."'

'Did I?' she'd said, totally perplexed. 'I must've been having a nightmare.'

Both of them had let it go at that, but though she could bring back no memory of what had happened to her in the seconds before she had fallen – other than that the lights had gone out – she hadn't forgotten about it.

It had troubled her and it continued to trouble her.

Months later, when she had recuperated sufficiently to be able to walk without the help of crutches, she'd revisited the recording studios, posing as a member of a group using one of the rehearsal rooms. Johnny hadn't known about the visit and neither had anyone else.

She'd wanted to see, by daylight, just how far she had fallen. And though she hadn't admitted it to herself, she'd wanted to trigger memories of those last few seconds before she'd fallen.

Her first thought, standing on the third-floor landing again, had been that, though the flight of stairs in front of her was long, she would probably not have fallen to the very bottom of them if she'd merely lost her balance. Somehow or other she would have managed to break her fall and ended up slithering down them and coming to a halt. It was the momentum with which she had plunged – the force with which she had smashed into the facing wall of the second-floor landing – that had been responsible for the multiplicity and severity of her injuries.

So why had she fallen with such force?

There'd been no obvious reasons visible. No loose telephone wires or electric cabling so badly positioned it could have come loose; nothing to explain why she had apparently said to Amber that something snake-like had smacked against her legs.

Exhausted from the climb, she sat down on the top step at the point from which she had fallen. The stairs looked as if they hadn't been cleaned for a decade: the corners were thick with grime, the plasterwork at the foot of the walls either side was peeling and pitted. On the right-hand side, at ankle-level, were the remains of an old gas pipe, the filthy coating of grime and dust it had accumulated disturbed halfway along its length, as if something in the not-too-distant past had been tied around it and wrenched free. On the other side of the step, at a corresponding height, was an air vent.

She had looked from the air vent to the piping and then from the piping to the air vent several times. If a piece of abandoned electrical wiring had been looped from the piping to the air vent, it would certainly account for the sensation of something snake-like whipping against her legs. Though the possibility was feasible, it was also bizarre. So bizarre that she hadn't even told Amber about it.

As the days after her visit to the studios had lengthened into weeks and the weeks into months, she had begun to doubt the conclusion she had come to. It was too unfeasible. Too fanciful. And it raised too many issues she didn't want to face. Issues such as who, apart from Johnny, had known that she would be in the building that night and who, knowing she was there, would have wanted to harm her? And why?

That, above all. *Why?*

Even after months of puzzling, she had never come up with a remotely satisfactory answer. Finally, in order to stay sane, she had forced all thoughts about it to the back of her mind, only brooding over it when something happened to bring it all back – like Sharyn's news that she was having Johnny's baby.

The cigarette was beginning to burn her fingers and she rose from the bed, crossed to the open window and tossed it outside. Her bedroom looked out over the back yard and there was, as usual, no sign of Fast-Boy's bike. It wasn't surprising. Though Fast-Boy still lived at home, he was seldom in evidence. Where he spent his time – and what he did with it – she had no idea. Fast-Boy had always followed his own agenda and their only point of real contact was their mutual friendship with Amber.

Where she was concerned, it was a friendship that infuriated Sharyn. 'Just because Amber was the first person to visit you in hospital doesn't mean she has to suddenly become your best friend!' she'd raged jealously. '*I'm* your best friend, Angie! Amber's only a kid!'

At the time, of course, it was true, but what was important to her was that Amber had known the truth of where she had been when she had fallen – and who it was she had gone there to meet. She'd been able to talk to Amber about Johnny in a way she couldn't talk to anyone else, and the bond it had forged between them was deep.

Amber's friendship with Fast-Boy was another matter. It puzzled everyone, even her.

'I don't care whether he's your brother or not!' Sharyn had stormed in a rage of rare sisterly protectiveness. 'If he's sleeping with my kid sister, I'll bloody kill him!'

That Sharyn, when her temper was in full flood, was capable of killing someone, Angie hadn't doubted for a moment. She was sure, though, that where Fast-Boy and Amber were concerned, Sharyn's fury was misplaced.

'They're just friends,' she'd said.

It was what, on different occasions, both Fast-Boy and Amber had told her and, though she wouldn't have staked her life on anything Fast-Boy said, she was certain Amber wouldn't lie to her about it.

'Ewan doesn't want a girlfriend,' Amber had said, her use of Fast-Boy's Christian name startling the socks off her. 'He's never really got over what happened to Zoë. I thought you'd know that, Angie.'

She hadn't. Fast-Boy never spoke to her about his private life and it hadn't been something she'd ever thought about. She'd simply assumed that his having no regular girlfriend was simply part and parcel of his being a loner.

Now, remembering that conversation with Amber, she had no option but to remember Zoë as well. And what she most remembered about Zoë was the way she had died. It had been in the dark. It had been a headlong fall. And it had been classified as a tragic accident.

The similarities to her own accident were glaring.

She tried not to think of them and instead found herself thinking of the other accidents suffered by Johnny's girlfriends: Deirdre Crosby had died in a car crash; Abbra Hornby had nearly died falling from the platform of a moving bus . . .

It was a sinister tally and the temptation to brood over it was strong. She didn't give into it. What good would it do? No amount of thinking would make sense of it. The bottom line was that, unlike Zoë Fairminder and Deirdre Crosby, she was alive.

She dug her nails deep into her palms.

Alive was the way she was going to stay.

Chapter Ten

Marco Martini reached for the cigarettes and lighter on the bedside-table. It was mid-afternoon and, though the cream-coloured window blinds were pulled down, the hotel bedroom was full of subdued light.

Beside him, amid the tumble of pillows and rumpled sheets, lay Maureen.

'What time is it?' she asked huskily as he tapped two cigarettes from a packet.

'Three o'clock.' He lit the cigarettes, handed one to her, and then rested on his elbow, looking down at her.

She smiled. The languorous smile of a woman satiated by lovemaking. 'I have to be on my way.' There was regret in her voice. 'I'm supposed to be at the dentist's, and my manager isn't going to expect it to take more than a couple of hours out of my working day.'

'Screw him,' Marco said succinctly, his eyebrows pulling together in a frown of irritation.

She knew what the frown signified. If she wasn't careful, they would again be having words over her refusal to give up her job. 'No thanks,' she said, throaty laughter in her voice as she tried to gloss the moment over. 'I'd rather screw you.'

His hard mouth tugged into a glimmer of a grin. 'For Christ's sake, Maureen – I'm fifty-eight. I need a ten minute rest-break!'

'Rubbish,' she said lovingly, her fingers moving slowly

across his chest and down towards his stomach. 'You're just playing hard to get.'

As sexual excitement began pulsing through him yet again, his grin deepened. How was it that Maureen could make him feel like a nineteen-year-old, with all a nineteen-year-old's sexual energy, when girls who were nineteen barely stirred him at all?

It was a mystery, but one he had no intention of wasting time trying to unravel. All that mattered was that he at last had a real woman in his bed – a woman who had known him ever since he was a young villain on the up and up; a woman who knew things about him no one else, not even his children, knew; a woman he had loved for a quarter of a century and whom he loved still.

His head moved down, kissing the hollow of her throat. Gentleness of any kind was foreign to him – but not when he was with Maureen. With Maureen he came dangerously near to being a man no one who knew him would recognize, and whom he barely recognized himself.

As he eased his weight once again on top of her she gave a moan of pleasure that sounded as if it had been torn from her heart. Desire flooded through him in a white-hot tide. She was his without reservation and she was going to stay his. He wasn't going to lose her, no matter what the cost, and neither was he going to spend time apart from her.

Living together in London was out – what had happened to Sheelagh, and why it had happened, had seen to that – and so he was planning to do what scores of others in his profession had done before him. He was going to live permanently in southern Spain. He was going to sell off his London interests and, with his vast bundle of liquidized assets, move into the kind of ventures that close proximity to Tangiers made easy.

'I love you, Maureen,' he said hoarsely, as her breasts pressed softly against his chest and her long legs coiled around his. 'Christ knows why we've wasted so much time. I don't.'

Her eyes had been dark with the heat of desire, but now something changed in them. 'Yes, you do, Marco,' she said quietly, her arms still round him. 'We both do.'

He'd been about to enter her, but now he halted, his eyes holding hers, knowing exactly what she meant, exactly what she was thinking. 'You expect me to sort it, don't you?' he said, hating the fact that he, Marco Martini, a man whose name alone was enough to cripple people with fear, was, in this instance, almost powerless.

She bit her bottom lip, thinking of Sharyn's heedless commitment to Johnny. Thinking of what had happened to Sheelagh – and to Zoë Fairminder and Angie.

'Who are you most frightened for?' she asked, her voice unsteady. 'Johnny or Tony?'

For a long moment he said nothing, but she could feel the difference in his breathing, sense the tension running through him.

'Johnny,' he said at last, a nerve pulsing at the corner of his jaw, his eyes as hard as granite. 'Definitely Johnny.'

Sharyn was seated on a bar-stool, fidgeting restlessly as she waited for the moment when she would have Johnny to herself so she could tell him that she was pregnant.

It was late afternoon and, though lunchtime drinking was officially over and the pub was closed, Johnny and his entourage were still playing pool, discussing business and slashing pints of beer and brandy-chasers down their throats.

From a few yards' distance she watched them, certain that, now she was pregnant, Johnny would marry her. He was, after all, half-Sicilian. He'd have to marry her. Family meant a lot to Sicilians. She'd heard Johnny say so tons of times.

She didn't want him to wait months and months before he put a ring on her finger, though. She didn't want to look as big as a hippopotamus when she walked down the aisle. She wanted to look slim and svelte and stunningly beautiful. She would wear white and she would have Angie and Amber as her bridesmaids. Johnny would undoubtedly ask Tony to be his best man, which left only the question of who would give her away. Her dad wouldn't be able to do the honours. He was still only halfway though a six-year prison sentence.

As she watched Johnny line up a ball and pot it, she wondered if she'd be able to persuade him to ask his dad to give her away. If Marco Martini agreed, it would make the wedding a huge gangland event.

She thought of her mum's reaction to such a scenario and flinched. Although her mum no longer ranted on about Marco Martini the way she used to, Sharyn reckoned it was only because she'd reached the point where she couldn't bring herself to say his name. She certainly avoided bumping into him in the street as much as ever, and what would happen when she was told she was to be Johnny's mother-in-law was anybody's guess.

'So there's an outstanding business debt of thirty grand owing to me,' a middle-aged, soberly suited man she had never seen before was saying to Johnny. 'I've gone through all the usual channels to try and call it in, but the result's been zilch. I need some assistance and I've been told you're the man to give it.'

As Sharyn began thinking about wedding dresses, she saw Johnny shrug in acknowledgement.

Would she wear a long dress or a short one? A short dress – really short – would be more fashionable. She could wear it with white boots and a veil.

'I just want the person involved frightened,' the soberly suited bloke was saying, an edge of nervousness in his voice. 'He should play along then. If he doesn't . . .'

Sharyn chewed the corner of her lip. Perhaps, even with a dress as short as the shortest mini-dress, she could wear a really long veil? A veil that would float into a train behind her?

'If he doesn't,' Johnny was saying, 'do you want someone to do the business? Do you want him really hammered?'

'Y-e-ss.' There was doubt now as well as nervousness in the man's voice.

It was the sort of doubt Sharyn had heard in straight-goers' voices many times when they sought out Johnny's services. They just never knew how far Johnny was prepared to go – and whether, if things went pear-shaped, they'd be roped in to any nasties that might ensue.

Of course, there were times when people came to Johnny wanting someone croaked, no messing. What Johnny did then, she wasn't sure. In most cases she thought he probably told them to do the dirty them-selves. In others, as when a man had come to him because his little girl had been raped by a so-called family 'friend', she knew he handed things over to Marco.

And what Marco did in those kind of circumstances was not something she'd ever wanted to ask about.

As money changed hands between Johnny and the businessman, she wondered what colour bridesmaids' dresses to have. With Angie's blue-black hair, a vibrant colour such as sapphire or searing pink would suit her. Neither sapphire nor searing-pink would, however, do much for Amber's turbulent mass of carrot-red curls. The only colour that suited Amber was green – and she wasn't going to be followed down the aisle by bridesmaids wearing a colour as unlucky as green.

For a wild moment she wondered if she could get away with not having her kid-sister as a bridesmaid. Then she remembered Angie's limp. If Angie was walking side by side with Amber, her limp wouldn't be as noticeable as it would be if she were to walk down the aisle behind her unaccompanied. Amber, then, was a necessity. She frowned, wondering if turquoise might be a suitable compromise. Or yellow.

'I'll be hearing from you then, Mr Martini,' the businessman was saying to Johnny, according him careful respect even though he was at least twenty years his senior.

It didn't strike Sharyn as being in the least odd. Most people gave Johnny the same kind of respect they always gave to his father.

Minutes later the man had gone and, as the game of pool drew to a close, she drew in a deep breath, readying herself for her big moment.

'So you want a couple of us to have a word with the Tiger Tyres man?' Cheyenne was asking Johnny as he slotted his pool cue in the rack. 'Been a bit naughty, has he?'

'Yeah. Donnie will fill you in on things on your way over there.'

Johnny's voice was disinterested. The kind of business under discussion wasn't really the kind he got a buzz out of, but if someone needed a debt collecting, if a business had to be wrecked or a club destroyed, he arranged the details like any other professional providing a service. And he prided himself on giving value for money. Any time. Any place. Anywhere. That was his business slogan. It didn't bring in major money – major money came from his long-firm scams – but it kept him high profile where his father's friends were concerned, and that was important to him.

Knowing that at any minute Johnny might make arrangements to go off somewhere without her, Sharyn slid to her feet and walked across to him, slipping her arm through his.

'Can we have some time together, Johnny?' she asked, her voice taut with excitement. 'There's something really, really special I want to tell you.'

'Sure, babe.' He was in a good mood. Tony was in the City, registering yet another new company under a fictitious name. It was the first step in their latest long-firm scam, and he had no doubt at all that it would be going smoothly. In the four years that Tony had been managing the setting up and running of the operations, they'd never encountered serious difficulties. Things simply kept on rolling, the effort on his part minimal.

'What do you want to tell me?' he asked as he walked her towards the door. 'Been shopping again and over-spent?'

'No.' There was a giggle in her voice. Overspending on the kind of money Johnny gave her would have been difficult, even for her. 'But I soon will be shopping, Johnny.'

She paused for dramatic effect and he looked towards her, an eyebrow quirked.

She stood still as the pub door swung shut behind them, wrapping her arms round his waist. 'I'll be shopping for baby things, darling.' Her face was radiant. 'Isn't it wonderful news? Isn't it terrific?'

There was a beat of silence as he grappled with incredulity that any girl – even one as dim as Sharyn – could be so stupid as not to be fearful of how such news might be received.

There was a second beat of silence as amusement kicked in. One thing about Sharyn, she always ran absolutely true to form. She'd be expecting an engagement ring now. A white wedding. The whole works. The decision he had to make was whether he was, or wasn't, going to indulge her.

Unknown to her, he was also dating someone else, someone who, in many ways, reminded him of Zoë. Tilly Conway was a friend of Amber's and, like Zoë, was a straight girl from a straight family. The one major difference was that, whereas Zoë had always sought the thrill of having a rascal for a boyfriend, Tilly's boyfriends had, until now, always been respectability personified.

His thoughts swivelled back to Sharyn. What was he going to do? Make her happy, or endure the tedium of her crying all over him whenever he ran into her – occasions which would, to say the least, be frequent.

A kiddie might be fun. Hell. It *would* be fun. If it was a boy, he'd call him Marlon. Marlon Martini. It was a name with a great ring to it.

He shot her his down-slanting smile. 'You're right, sweetheart. It is terrific news. What say we meet up with Tony and crack open some bottles of Louis Cristal to celebrate? Being an uncle is going to suit him. He'll be thrilled to bits.'

It wasn't true, and, as she squealed in delight and threw her arms around his neck, he knew it. Tony, when he told him he was going to marry Sharyn, was going to think he'd taken leave of his senses.

*   *   *

165

Breaking the news wasn't the easy matter he'd thought it would be. For reasons he couldn't fathom, Tony didn't show after his appointment at Companies House. So, to give himself something to do, Johnny took an ecstatic Sharyn to a jeweller's at Hatton Garden and bought her an engagement ring. The jeweller owed him a favour and the solitaire diamond didn't cost him – a nicety Sharyn was unaware of. Later, they went up to Chinatown for a celebratory dinner and then on into a different part of Soho for an evening of nightclubbing and gambling.

Not till next morning did he speak to Tony – and when he did, his twin's reaction was just as he'd expected it would be.

'You're *what?*' Despite the anxiety he was battling with where Albie's impending visit was concerned, Johnny had Tony's full attention. 'You're *marrying* her?' His disbelief was total. 'But why, for fuck's sake? What's the bloody point?'

Johnny shrugged. Barefoot and wearing only a singlet and trousers he was cooking a fry-up of egg, bacon and tomatoes. ''Cos she's having a kid – *my* kid.' He flashed a sudden grin. 'And because I'm such a decent bloke and always do the right thing.'

'Yeah, enough of the funnies, Johnny. You've been taking Sharyn for granted for years –why the sudden difference? Don't tell me she's suddenly become the love of your life, because I don't believe you.'

'Me and Sha are OK, Tone. And she's got one thing going for her, no one else has.'

'Surprise me.'

Johnny did so.

He tossed the spoon he'd been stirring the tomatoes

with into the sink and, no longer grinning, said: 'She's the only girlfriend in over four years who's managed to avoid having a major accident or getting killed. That being the case, I reckon I should stick with her, don't you?'

The question had so floored Tony, he hadn't even tried to answer it. What he had done was to wonder if the time was now ripe for asking Angie to marry him. Not a double wedding, of course. Since the day of their fight, when the price for things being OK between them again had been Johnny ending his affair with Angie, Johnny had never once admitted just how hard the sacrifice had been for him. He'd known, though. He'd always known what Johnny was experiencing. It was one of the benefits of being a twin.

So, a double wedding was out of the question. It simply wouldn't be fair to Johnny. Whether it would also be unfair to Angie was a question he didn't allow to surface. As far as he was concerned, he'd made his choice of a girlfriend a long time ago. If he'd been going to end the relationship, he would have ended it the day he and Johnny had had their fight – and he hadn't. Nor had he discussed it with Angie. She knew that he knew – and he was aware she knew that. It had been enough.

When she had finally come out of hospital she'd been reluctant to resume their relationship, but he'd persisted and his persistence had paid off. With a little effort on both sides, it had been almost as if her affair with Johnny had never happened. She wasn't the same girl, though. The livewire recklessness that had been such an integral part of her personality was curbed almost to the point of being extinguished. She was quieter. More introspective. It was a difference he'd coped with.

What he hadn't done was ask her to marry him. There'd been too many difficulties – difficulties that were all to do with the way Johnny still felt about Angie. With Johnny now so committed to Sharyn that he was going to marry her, those difficulties were a thing of the past.

He would, then, suggest to Angie that they got married. The only thing was – would it be best to do it before Albie arrived, or after?

At the thought of Albie, his pulse began to race and sweat broke out on his brow. How was he going to endure Albie's visit? How was he going to survive it? He fought to control his breathing, his chest feeling as if it were being crushed by bands of steel.

Becoming engaged to Angie before Albie arrived would be the best option. By doing so he'd be making the most blatant statement possible about his sexuality. It would be protection – of a kind.

As he thought of who and what he was – a six foot, muscular, twenty-three-year-old with a surname that was synonymous with violence – the insanity of his fear where Albie was concerned slammed into him with all the force of a pile-driver.

What the fuck was he afraid of? The days when Albie could do with him whatever he wanted were long gone.

The memories hadn't gone, though. The memories were still raw; still bleedingly alive.

And on top of the old fear – the fear born of habit – there was fresh fear. The fear of anyone discovering just how terrified he had been – and of how, in Canada, he'd come to terms with that fear.

That, though, wouldn't happen. He had his life in order. He had his girlfriend. He had his studies. Despite his present little sideline arranging Johnny's long-firm scams, he had a brilliant career in the law ahead of him. Above all, where his years of terror with Albie were concerned, he had revenge to brood over. All he needed to do, in the long term, was to remain focused.

And in the short term, to persuade Angie to become Mrs Tony Martini.

'I know you and Johnny Martini are wrapped together arse-tight,' Detective-Sergeant Rob Gowan was saying to Donnie Crosby in a corner of a pub that was way off Donnie's usual manor, 'but if you don't prise yourself loose, you're heading for big, big trouble.'

'Oh yeah?'

Little Donnie regarded Gowan with contempt. Years ago they'd been in the same class at school and, though they'd never been close mates, it was a contact Gowan was always trying to make the most of now he was in CID.

'Jimmy Jones' body is going to surface eventually,' Rob Gowan said, as if stating the obvious. 'And when it does, the person in the frame will be Johnny. And as Johnny never does anything without his sidekicks – and with you and Cheyenne Goody being his chief sidekicks – the two of you have a lot to be running scared from, don't you think?'

Donnie gave a snort of derision. 'Christ, but you're a tosser, Rob. You always bleedin' were, and you 'aven't changed. I'll be running scared from what, for Christ's sake? A murder rap? When ain't there bin a bleedin' murder? Do me a favour. Jones is the one who's running scared. That's why he took off four years ago and ain't been seen since. He upset Johnny and didn't want to stay around to take the consequences, so 'e did a runner. Plain and simple.'

It was a lie and they both knew it.

'Bollocks,' said Rob. His pint-glass was empty, but he wasn't going to make a trip to the bar and risk coming back to find that Donnie had done a disappearing act. He'd been trying for months to corner Donnie somewhere they weren't likely to be seen, which of necessity meant somewhere far from Donnie's usual haunts in Bermondsey and Soho. Now that he'd finally done so, he didn't want Donnie scarpering before anything useful had come of it. 'Jimmy was going to do a runner, I'll give you that. He was last seen picking up a passport from Petty France. A passport he was so desperate for he didn't want to wait the couple of days it would have taken for it to be posted to him.'

'Because he was running scared,' Donnie reiterated. 'I know. It ain't a secret. Everyone knows. And when 'e 'ad the passport in 'is 'and, 'e was away on 'is toes. Canada, America – who knows? Who bleedin' cares?'

'I care,' Rob said bullishly, 'because I don't believe he left the country – and neither does his family. Since the day Jimmy went to Petty France they haven't heard a peep from him.'

Donnie gave a hacking laugh. 'Christ, I wouldn't read too much in that! Jimmy was probably as glad to see the back of 'is bleedin' family as 'e was to see the back of Johnny.'

'And his name didn't appear on the passenger list of any flight leaving that day, or the next few days,' Rob continued remorselessly. 'There's no evidence that he left the country by boat, either. Initially, we had a couple of witnesses who saw a young man matching Jimmy's description being bundled into the back of a car only yards from the Passport Office. The person manhandling him was described as being approximately six foot tall and broad-shouldered with dark hair worn in a French crew-cut. He was wearing an Italian-looking suit and expensive sunglasses.'

With the air of someone resting his case, Rob slid his hands into his trouser pockets. 'The description of the hair-cut alone is enough to point the finger at Johnny. Who else wears their hair so short these days? Even I don't, and I'm a copper.'

'You're a wanker,' Donnie said, casting yet another look round the pub to make sure there was no one there who knew both him and Gowan. 'If the coppers 'ave witnesses that Johnny 'iked Jimmy from off the pavement, why are yer talking to me about it, four years down the line? Why didn't you build up a case and press charges?'

'You know bleeding well why.' Rob's easy-going chatty manner was fast disintegrating. 'The next time the witnesses were questioned, they rescinded their statements. They hadn't seen what they'd said they'd seen. There'd been a bit of confusion on the pavement, that was all. The bloke wasn't being forced into the back of a car, he'd had a lunchtime drink and was being helped. They were sorry for wasting police time. And there's been nothing else to go on. But there will be.'

'Yeah, yeah,' Donnie said mockingly. 'Don't tell me, I know – when the bleedin' body surfaces.'

Rob shrugged. 'Be as cocky as you like about it, Donnie. The truth will come out eventually. There's just too much gossip for it not to. It may be impossible for us to get statements as to what happened outside the Passport Office, but everyone who's on nodding terms with Johnny knows what happened. The only thing not generally known is exactly how and where Jimmy's little car ride ended. But you know, Donnie, don't you? So why don't you tell? It's guaranteed to get you off the hook no matter what – and that's a message you can pass on to Cheyenne, because the same goes for him. You'll both get immunity. You have my word.'

Donnie rolled his eyes skywards. 'You're a detective-sergeant, Rob. Not the Chief Commissioner. Your word ain't worth shit.' He shifted his stance, reckoning he'd given quite enough of his time and having no intention of giving much more.

Rob wasn't overly put out. He'd done what his guv'nor, Detective Inspector Colin Ramsden, had asked him to do. He'd sown a seed re the possibility of immunity and that was enough. He didn't want to antagonize Donnie. His job was to stay on as near chummy terms with him as possible.

'So . . . how's your sister?' he asked, trying to make as much out of the fact that they'd all been kids together as possible. 'Are she and Johnny still an item behind Sharyn Bailey's back?'

The expression in Donnie's eyes, which had been so scoffingly derisory all the time they had been talking, changed. Something raw flashed through them and Rob felt a quickening of interest. He'd unwittingly touched a nerve, though he was buggered if he knew why.

'Nah.' A shutter came down over Donnie's thin, high-cheekboned face. 'She's dead. She's bin dead nearly three years. If you weren't so fuck-useless as a copper, you'd've known.'

'I didn't. I'm sorry.' There was sincerity in his voice. He'd never known Deirdre well – she'd been younger than Donnie and they'd never been in the same school together, but he remembered her as being a more attractive personality than her brother. 'How did it happen?' he asked with interest. 'Was she ill? Was it an accident?'

'An accident.' The flare of emotion in Donnie's eyes

had gone. 'Silly cow drove off the road coming 'ome from a club in New Cross. And that's all you're goin' to get, 'cos I don't like talking about it.'

'That's OK.' Rob raised a hand in surrender, well aware he could get all the necessary details from the accident report. 'I don't blame you. If it had been my sister, I wouldn't want to talk about it, either.' He paused for a moment and then said, as casually as possible, 'So who's Johnny seeing now – besides Sharyn, of course.'

'What the fuck's it got to do with you? I've 'ad it up to 'ere –' Donnie drew a line graphically across his throat – 'with you coming the old pal's act. Piss off, why don't you? Go spoil someone else's day.'

Not wanting to jeopardize their relationship further, Gowan had done as Donnie suggested. Still off-duty, he had driven off in search of a more pleasant watering-hole and more congenial company.

Thirty minutes later, he was in the Mitre in Greenwich, having a late lunchtime drink with his brother-in-law, an estate agent whose office was in nearby Church Street.

'So Johnny Martini seems to have spectacular bad luck where his girlfriends are concerned,' he said dryly, wiping crumbs away from his mouth. 'He only started going out with Deirdre Crosby when the other girl he was crackers about died after a fall in a pub car park.'

'And then he started going around with Abbra Hornby,' his brother-in-law said knowledgeably. 'I know all about that because at the time her parents were looking to sell their flat in Deptford and buy a house in Greenwich, and they went out of their way to let me know they had connections – presumably in case I tried to swindle them in any way. She nearly ended up in a wooden box as well.'

'Who?' Rob was suddenly very still. 'Mrs Hornby? Or Abbra?'

'Abbra. She took a tumble from the platform of a bus as it turned a corner in Trafalgar Square. Her mother was hysterical about it. Said Abbra had come within a hair's breadth of being killed – which was probably no exaggeration, knowing what traffic's like round there. Are you ready for another drink? This draught Guinness is first class.'

'No. I'm fine.' Rob's attention was one hundred per cent elsewhere. Two girls dead and another very nearly dead. And all girls Johnny Martini had had the hots for.

It could, of course, be bad luck. Or coincidence. But what if it wasn't? What if Johnny Martini was just as much a psychopath as his old man? What if he hadn't only murdered Jimmy Jones but a couple of girlfriends as well? What if he had murdered a whole string of them?

His heart slammed at the enormity of what he might have stumbled on.

One thing was for sure. He was going to find out.

He was going to find out, starting today.

Chapter Eleven

'And I'm having a baby and we're getting married!' Sharyn flung the words defiantly at her mother and sister, triumph in her eyes. 'Do you like my engagement ring? Isn't it *gi-normous*? I bet even Elizabeth Taylor would be jealous of a ring like this!'

There'd been too many rows for too many years about Johnny and her relationship with him for Sharyn to imagine that her mother was going to be pleased at the news and, as she flashed the diamond solitaire, she did it from what she judged to be a safe distance.

There was a beat of stunned silence; a moment of time in which she saw Amber's eyes widen and knew, with intense satisfaction, that though her sister usually knew everything before being told about it, she hadn't this time. It wasn't Amber's reaction she was waiting for, though. It was her mother's.

She didn't have to wait long.

'You stupid, *stupid* bitch!' Maureen's voice was so dangerously unsteady that even Amber took a step backwards to be nearer the door and a speedy exit. 'I've been warning you off him for years and you've never listened! Why did you think I was doing it, Sharyn? Did you think it was just because I didn't like him very much? Because I wanted you to find someone who was legit? Someone respectable?' She snorted scoffingly. 'Why would I have been so bothered when your dad's never been legit in his life?'

'Because you don't like Mr Martini!' Sharyn's voice rose into a shriek. 'You've *never* liked Mr Martini! You're like everyone else – you think Johnny's dad is some kind of a psycho and you're *frightened* of him!'

The distance Sharyn had hoped would be safe proved not to be safe at all. Her mother closed it in what seemed to be a millionth of a second, saying explosively as she smacked her across her face, 'Christ Almighty! Anyone *not* frightened of Marco would have to be brain-dead!'

As Sharyn let out a howl of pain, Maureen knew she was almost out of control. She corrected herself. She *was* out of control. If she hadn't been, she would have stopped there, but she couldn't stop.

'It isn't Marco who's the psycho!' With eyes blazing, the words poured out of her in a bitter torrent. 'It's your precious Johnny! Didn't you ever wonder why Tony was sent to Canada? Didn't it ever *occur* to you there was something sinister about it? Well, as you're too dense to ever work anything out for yourself, Sharyn, I'll spell it out for you: Marco sent Tony to live with his sister and her husband because he was scared stiff what might happen if he didn't. Because he was certain Tony wasn't *safe* living with Johnny. And Christ knows he had plenty of cause to think that, because no one else was safe! Not even cats survived more than a week in that house!'

The words were hurled from a place so deep she'd almost forgotten it existed. She panted for breath, her chest heaving, aware of the appalled silence. Amber was staring at her in stunned incredulity. Sharyn was stumbling backwards, panic-stricken uncertainty on her face.

It was uncertainty that didn't last long.

'Liar!' she shouted as she collided with the door. '*Liar!* You're saying anything you can to spoil things between me and Johnny! You just don't want me to be happy! You've *never* wanted me to be happy!'

'That's not true – and I'm not lying!' Maureen ran an unsteady hand through her hair, pushing it back away from her face. 'Hamsters, rabbits, cats – they all came to hideous ends. Sheelagh couldn't understand it. And by the time she did, it was too late.'

If she'd hoped that this would carry weight with Sharyn, she was disappointed.

Sharyn merely laughed. 'And I'm Dusty Springfield,' she said derisively, 'and Mr Martini is the Pope! I'm not hanging around to listen to any more of this pathetic old rubbish. My Johnny is as likely to torture a cat as Amber is to win Miss World!'

Before Amber could think of a suitably blistering retort, Sharyn stormed out of the room, slamming the door so hard it rocked on its hinges. Seconds later there came the sound of the front door being slammed, and then the gate.

For a long moment neither Amber nor Maureen spoke. Then Maureen said wearily, 'I went too far, didn't I? She didn't believe me.'

'Of course she didn't believe you.' Amber's relief that her mother had simply been spinning Sharyn a line was so intense her legs felt weak. 'Not even Sharyn's thick enough to believe that Mr Martini sent Tony away because he was frightened Johnny would kill him, or torture him, or do whatever it is you were trying to make out he'd done to the cats. Johnny really suffered when he and Tony were separated. You don't seem to realize how close identical twins are, Mum. They're not really like other people at all.'

'Those two aren't, that's for sure.'

Maureen's voice was clipped and curt, her eyes dark.

She wasn't certain, but she thought that twins ran in families. And Sharyn was pregnant. The thought of being grandmother to carbon copies of Johnny and Tony brought her out in gooseflesh. She rubbed her arms, wondering if Marco knew yet that Johnny and Sharyn were engaged and that Sharyn was pregnant. If he didn't, she'd have the unhappy task of putting him in the picture.

And what Marco's reaction would be was anybody's guess.

'You knew about the baby, then?'

Tony and Angie were in Greenwich Park. Angie was sitting on the grass, her arms hugging her legs. Tony was lying beside her, hands behind his head. Below them, at the foot of the grassy hill, lay the magnificent panorama of the Queen's House and, beyond it, the glittering, snaking curve of the Thames.

It was Tony who had asked the question and Angie nodded, carefully keeping her eyes firmly on the view as she said, with as much disinterest as she could summon, 'Yes. Sharyn told me days ago.'

'He's going to marry her.' He paused, watching her averted face as she made no response to his news. 'I never thought the day would come, did you?'

It was a loaded question. That she and Johnny had once been unable to keep their hands off each other was something that always lay unspoken between them.

Knowing that she had to say something, she gave a slight, dismissive shrug of her shoulders. 'It isn't something I've given much thought to,' she lied. 'Sharyn's been Johnny's girlfriend for so long that his marrying her isn't really such a surprise.'

'No. I suppose not.'

He was still watching her and she knew that he was the one now telling a porky-pie, because of course Johnny marrying Sharyn was a surprise. Hell, it was the very last thing anyone who knew Johnny would have imagined him doing. Sharyn was just a convenience to him. Everyone knew that. The girls Johnny had really had the hots for all possessed far more style and liveliness than Sharyn. Girls like Zoë Fairminder. Girls like Donnie's sister Deirdre, who had been a model. Girls like herself.

She clamped down on the thought swiftly, not wanting it to show on her face. Johnny could have had her for keeps, but the minute he'd thought there was a chance Tony would find out about their affair he'd washed his hands of her. He hadn't wanted her enough to risk a permanent rift with Tony. And there was another reason, too, why her fall at Take Six had doomed their relationship.

Ever since the accident, she'd limped. And a girlfriend with a limp was definitely not Johnny Martini's style.

'Their getting married has given me an idea.' As he spoke, Tony pulled her down beside him.

The last thing she wanted was to be in a close embrace, but neither did she want him aware of just how much her mood had changed – in case he guessed why.

'Yes?' she said, looking upwards to where the leaves of a tree were dancing and fluttering high above their heads.

He rolled over on to his side, resting his weight on his elbow so that he could look down at her.

'I reckon we should steal their thunder. Marry before they do. What d'you think?'

'Marry?' Her eyes flew to his. 'You and me?' There was stunned incredulity in her voice.

'Sure.' His mouth twisted in ironic amusement as he registered her reaction. 'Why not?'

She forgot all about Johnny and Sharyn, able to think of a hundred reasons, not least the fact that, though their relationship had endured, it had never been one that had seemed to be going anywhere. There had always been something lukewarm about it, something make-do.

From her point of view, of course, it was because she'd always regarded him as being somehow second-best. But from his point of view? Why had she always had the feeling that he, too, was simply marking time? It was a puzzle and, like other puzzles that troubled her, one she had no answer for.

'Well?' he prompted.

'Because there's no way on God's earth Johnny will stand for being Fast-Boy's brother-in-law!' Hysteria bubbled up in her throat at the very thought. 'Or that Fast-Boy will stand for being Johnny's brother-in-law! Or that your dad will wear becoming Fast-Boy's father-in-law!'

He shrugged, his eyes unreadable. 'They'll have to swallow it, just as I'm going to have to swallow having Sharyn as a sister-in-law.'

She tried to think of something to say, but couldn't. He was serious. Unbelievably, incredibly, he was *serious*. Angie Martini. Sharyn would be so furious at having her thunder stolen she'd probably never speak to her again. And what about Fast-Boy? He'd have a coronary. Or perhaps he wouldn't. It was, after all, Johnny that her brother loathed, not Tony. If anyone would have a coronary, it would be Johnny.

She thought of Johnny's reaction to having her for a sister-in-law and to finding himself related by marriage to Fast-Boy, and knew she was going to say yes. How could she not? Tony had cash. She didn't know exactly what it was he did for Johnny, but he always had a wad of notes in his back pocket thick enough to choke a pig. And one day he wouldn't just have hookey money. When he got his Law degree, he'd be a solicitor or a barrister. He'd be both hookey *and* respectable. And he had kudos. Everyone knew who he was; who his father was; who his twin was. And when her name was Angie Martini everyone would know who she was, too.

Other thoughts came fast and furious. Even though he wasn't the most demonstrative of boyfriends, he'd never treated her badly; never knocked her about the way some of Johnny's gang members did their girlfriends. And an even bigger plus in his favour was that he'd never allowed her limp to embarrass him. As she thought about that – and what it said about him – she realized how she'd always undervalued him. He didn't have Johnny's charisma, but he did have something far more important. He had a decency that, even in the days when she'd been blindly in love with Johnny, she'd always known that Johnny had lacked.

Never once had Tony given her cause to feel seriously uneasy about him, as, where her accident was concerned, Johnny had – and still did.

The things about Tony that she'd always thought of as being more of a minus than a plus – the way he never attempted to be anything other than second-lieutenant to Johnny; the tediousness of his studying for a degree; the way he was always so reserved emotionally – were, she saw now, all points in his favour.

Johnny would, no doubt, be wildly exciting as a husband, but he would also be profoundly disturbing and perhaps even dangerous.

There would no such drawback with Tony.

What about her, though? Where marriage was concerned, she came with a drawback. A bloody great drawback. For a fleeting moment she wondered if she could get away with not telling him about it, knowing that, if Sharyn were in her position, Sharyn would most certainly stay shtum.

Only she wasn't Sharyn.

She took a steadying breath and said, 'I can't have children.' Avoiding his eyes, she looked up at the leaves. 'It's because of something that happened when I fell. I never mentioned it before, because there wasn't any need and I don't like thinking about it, let alone talking about it.'

There was silence.

The leaves continued to quiver and sway. Two sparrows alighted on a low branch, wrangling noisily.

At last, when she thought she wasn't going to be able to bear the tension a second longer, he leapt to his feet.

'Jesus!' he erupted explosively. 'Jesus *Christ!*'

He walked a yard or so away from her, his thumbs hooked in the pockets of his jeans as he looked unseeingly down towards Greenwich and the glistening white colonnades of the house built by King James I for his queen.

Angie remained motionless, looking bleakly up into the tree. She'd wrecked everything – and knowing that she'd had no choice didn't make the pain any easier to bear.

She closed her eyes tight shut, wishing for the thousandth time that she'd never heard of the Take Six recording studios; wishing she'd never stepped foot inside them.

High above her head, the squabbling birds flew off to continue their disagreement elsewhere. Somewhere in the distance dogs barked. Then she heard Tony turn round and walk back towards her.

'I'm sorry,' he said as his shadow fell over her.

He sounded as though he meant it.

She opened her eyes. 'Yes,' she said. 'So am I.'

The sun was behind him and, despite his ponytail and jeans and T-shirt – clothes Johnny never, ever wore – he looked so like Johnny that she felt a rush of panic. Johnny might still hold all the aces where raw, over-powering sex appeal was concerned, but ever since she'd seen the sinister marks at either side of the step from which she'd fallen, he was also someone she avoided being alone with.

Swiftly, before her thoughts could go down a road she'd no desire to travel, she scrambled to her feet.

'So that's it, I suppose,' she said, avoiding his eyes as she vigorously brushed grass seeds from her skirt. 'We're finished. Through. Kaput.'

'Nope. Those words aren't in my script.'

Her hand fell to her side. 'Oh?' Uncertain as to his meaning, she took a step backwards, leaning for support against the rough bark of the tree. 'Then what is?'

'That we walk down to Greenwich Registry Office and fix the first date possible to get married. We don't want a lot of fuss, do we? Just you, me and the Registrar. What d'you say?'

He'd moved close to her, one hand resting on the trunk of the tree above her head.

She thought of the expression on Sharyn's face when she heard that Angie had married into the Martini family before her. She thought of Johnny's reaction. She thought of just how much she had underestimated Tony's feel-ings for her, and how deep those feelings must be if he was prepared to marry her, knowing she could never have children. How could she have been so blind for so long about his true worth?

'Yes,' she said, sliding her arms up and around his neck as he lowered his head to hers. 'I say yes, Tony. Yes. Yes. *Yes.*'

'So me marrying Sharyn ain't nothing for you to worry about, darlin',' Johnny said, his arm round Tilly Conway's shoulders as the Thames launch *King Henry* pulled away from Greenwich Pier and headed up-river, towards Westminster. 'Things will be just the same between us, I promise.'

'But how can they be?' They were sitting on the open deck, at the very rear of the boat and, as the breeze blew her silver-blonde hair across her face, Tilly's eyes were overly bright. 'You'll be *married,*' she said, fighting back tears. 'Things are *bound* to be different!'

Johnny grinned and, taking advantage of the fact that they were alone on the deck, slid his hand up her fake snakeskin skirt. 'They won't be, Tilly. Trust me.'

Tilly wanted to, but she was a streetwise seventeen-year-old and didn't. 'I just don't see why you have to *marry* her,' she said stubbornly. 'What if the baby isn't yours? It might not be. Amber's always telling me how Sharyn fibs and exaggerates.'

Johnny's winged eyebrows pulled together in a slight frown. That Tilly and Amber worked together was something he kept forgetting about. 'Yeah, well, when Amber yacks to you about Sharyn, don't go giving secrets away about you and me. It'll only cause problems. Understand?'

She nodded, pressing closer to him. His fingers were inside her panties now and she didn't want to think about his marrying Sharyn any more. She didn't want to think about anything other than that she wanted him to make love to her – right here, right now, on a boat in the middle of the Thames.

Forty minutes later, as he parked his Chevrolet behind his dad's equally distinctive Mark 10 Jaguar, Johnny still had a smile on his face. Little Tilly Conway was a cracker. Her hair was the same silver-blonde colour Zoë's had been and just as long and silkily straight. Like Zoë, she came from a respectable family. Her dad was a magistrate who, if he ever got to know the kind of company his daughter was keeping, would go absolutely ape-shit.

Still smiling, he slammed the car door behind him, wondering why he was so turned on by respectable girls with middle-class accents. Was it because, when they were outrageous, it always seemed doubly unexpected and arousing? Tilly, for instance: wanting, and willing, to be shagged in broad daylight in the middle of the Thames. Tilly thought Sharyn cheap and common, yet Sharyn would never have been up for a stunt like that, not in a million years.

He strolled up the short path and stepped into the house, instantly aware, from the voices he could hear, that both his dad and Tony were home. And then he heard another voice: Angie's.

He came to an abrupt halt outside the sitting-room door. Tony very rarely brought Angie home – and never when there was any likelihood of anyone else being in the house. The old man regarded the family home as a citadel. He never held meets there and never allowed anyone else to do so. Business operations were discussed and planned in the office of one of the many massage parlours, drinking clubs, or recording studios that he owned.

When he heard his old man give something that could very nearly be described as a chuckle, his uneasiness deepened. What the fuck was going on? For a hideous second he wondered if Tony and the old man had a project on the go that they weren't letting him in on. The idea was so ludicrous, he rubbished it almost instantly. Not only had the old man never confided in Tony in that way, Tony wouldn't be party to anything that didn't include both of them. He was too loyal. Too much his other half.

A shiver ran down his spine as he remembered a time when it had been very different; a time when their mother had been alive. Christ, that had been terrible – being sent to bed while she let Tony sit on her knee and listen to *Journey into Space* on the radio; coming into the house unexpectedly and hearing her laughing with Tony in the kitchen; trailing behind her in the street as she held Tony's hand, not his.

With a start he realized he was perspiring as if he'd been running. He wiped his forehead with the back of his hand, let his shoulders relax and, with every appearance of careless self-assurance, entered the room.

'Hi,' he said, flashing a laconic smile. 'What gives?'

'Angie and Tony are getting married next Thursday.' If Marco was unimpressed by the news, he didn't allow it to show on his face or in his voice.

'And we don't want anyone else knowing about it,' Tony said, one hand hooked into the pocket of his jeans, the other holding a cigarette. 'Not even Sharyn. Not till it's a done deal.'

It took enormous self-control, but Johnny kept his smile firmly in place. 'No problem, Tone,' he said, walking across to his twin and punching him on the arm. 'I think it's great news. Terrific news. Absolutely belting.'

As Angie avoided his eyes, he kissed her on the cheek. 'Welcome to the family, Angie darlin'. I can't think of anyone I'd rather have as a sister.'

Angie flushed.

A nerve began pulsing at the corner of Tony's mouth. Marco cleared his throat.

Johnny beamed round at them all. 'Christ, but Sha's goin' to be pissed off when Angie starts flashing a wedding ring around before she does. What say we open a bottle of champagne for a little advance celebration? Come on, Tone, let's see if there's one in the fridge, nicely chilled.'

As he walked out of the room, heading in the direction of the kitchen, he still didn't know what line he was going to take with Tony once they were on their own. One half of him wanted to let Tony know how pissed off he was at having his and Sha's wedding upstaged; the other half wanted to give the impression that he didn't give a toss about it.

As for how he really felt about having Angie as a sister-in-law . . . He clenched his jaw so tightly a muscle began to twitch. He wasn't going to let anyone in on that one.

'So?' he said as the kitchen door clicked shut behind them. 'Why all the urgency? Why next Thursday?' He opened the fridge, studied the array of bottles lying on the middle shelf, and pulled out a bottle of Louis Roederer Cristal. 'Why couldn't we have gone for a double wedding?' he asked, having decided to play things very offhand. 'Sha would have loved that.'

'D'you reckon?' Tony shrugged, as if regretful that he hadn't thought of the idea himself. 'It's too late, now. Everything's fixed.'

'It's a bit of a surprise.' Johnny closed the fridge door

and leaned against it, one foot crossing the other at the ankle. 'I mean, I'd have thought you'd have said something to me earlier. Before you'd made any arrangements. Know what I mean?'

Tony opened a cupboard door, lifting champagne flutes off a shelf, two in either hand. 'You mean like you did before you proposed to Sharyn?' he asked blandly.

'Yeah, I guess.' Johnny laughed and the tension ebbed. 'OK, so I did act the same way – it's just that me and Sha getting married isn't quite the same as you and Angie getting married. I mean, you must be really *serious* about it, or you wouldn't be doing it.'

Tony's shoulders stiffened. 'And you're not?' he said, turning away from the cupboard so that they were again facing each other.

Johnny shot him a blinding grin. 'Christ, Tone, course I'm not. What d'you take me for? I've been out with someone else this afternoon. Her name's Tilly Conway and she's class. Real class. Wait till you see her – she's the spitting image of Zoë.'

Something flashed through Tony's eyes too fast for Johnny to decipher. It could have been shocked disapproval, incredulity, or even relief. Whatever Tony's reaction to his offhand attitude to marriage, it didn't matter. He'd got his equilibrium back. So what if Tony was going to marry Angie? What did he care? He had one girlfriend he was going to marry because he knew for a fact that she'd stand by him through thick and thin and never cause him any hassle, and another girlfriend who was game for anything and had the kind of looks that turned heads everywhere he took her.

All Tony had was a girlfriend who limped.

'Come on, mate,' he said, throwing an arm round his twin's shoulder. 'Let's slash some bubbly down our throats. Has the old man told you he's thinking of jetting off to the villa once Albie arrives?'

He nudged the kitchen door open with his foot, adding, as they walked down the hallway towards the sitting-room, 'Whether he's planning on taking Albie with him or not, I ain't sure. Perhaps we could all go. A bit of the highlife on the old Costa del Sol would go down a treat. Do you think Angie could be talked into passing Tilly off as a friend? That way I could have both her and Sha out there.'

They were still laughing as they re-entered the sitting-room. Angie, who hadn't enjoyed being on her own with her future father-in-law, tried to catch Tony's eye and failed. She tried not to mind. The champagne being opened was expensive and that was how life was going to be for her from now on; everything the best that money could buy. It was a prospect she wasn't going to let anything mar; not even Johnny and Tony standing in such close proximity that the sight made her eyes hurt.

Even after the champagne had been poured and handed around, Johnny still had an arm slung affectionately round Tony's shoulders. Awkwardly, wishing she could move away but feeling that to do so would look odd, she continued standing next to Marco.

'I take it your brother doesn't know about the wedding yet?' he was saying to her as, from the street, there came the distinctive sound of a black cab drawing to a halt.

'No. Not yet.' She tried to keep her voice as casual as possible, as if Fast-Boy's reaction, when he was told, was unlikely to matter very much.

There came the sound of the cab's door being opened and then slammed shut. 'Ta, mate,' the driver called out cheerily. 'Enjoy your stay in England.'

Then came the sound of footsteps approaching the Martinis' front door. Only then did Angie realize how unlikely such a sound was. People didn't casually call on Marco Martini – or the twins.

'It sounds like Albie's arrived,' Johnny said, lifting his arm from Tony's shoulders. 'I'll go let him in.'

As he strolled out of the room, Angie was aware of a feeling of relief. The visitor didn't signify trouble – always a possibility where her father-in-law-to-be was concerned – and his arrival had cut short a conversation that could have become difficult.

'This is nice,' she said brightly, flashing Tony a smile as, from the hall, there came the sound of laughter and greetings and heavy back-slaps.

It was then that she saw he looked ill.

'Come into the sitting-room, Albie,' Johnny was saying. 'And stop blinking at me as if you can't believe I'm not Tony. He's kept his hair long so that people can tell us apart. What the fuck have you got in this suit-case? The *Encyclopædia Britannica*?'

When they walked into the room, and Albie said: 'Well, well, well, so here I am at last,' in an accent that was heavily Glaswegian despite the years he'd spent on the other side of the Atlantic, her surprise at it was so great it surmounted even her concern for Tony.

Albie grinned across at his brother-in-law. 'How many years has it been, Marco? Fourteen? Fifteen?'

Marco covered the few yards between them in a couple of swift strides. 'Fourteen, you bastard,' he said, hugging him in a way that was totally Italian. 'Tony's been home four years and was with you ten.'

Angie watched the little scene, intrigued, aware for the first time that Albie and Marco weren't just brothers-in-law but old cronies, too. Taking stock of Albie's cracked front tooth and grizzled, prison-style hair-cut, she wondered if that was how Marco's sister had met him – via Marco, when Albie had been one of his cohorts.

As Albie stepped free of Marco's bear-hug he looked directly at her. 'And who's this?' he asked, his eyes full of prurient interest.

'Angie Flynn.' There was no expression whatever in Marco's deep growl of a voice. 'She and Tony are getting married next Thursday. Johnny is engaged to Sharyn, one of Tommy Bailey's girls.'

At the mention of Tommy Bailey, Albie shot Marco a swift, startled glance. Then he was in front of her – standing too close – shaking her hand and saying: 'Pleased tae meet you, Angie. Tony always had the devil's luck in Canada and, if you're going tae marry him, it seems he's still got it.'

Only then did he finally turn to Tony. 'And how are you, laddie?' he asked, cocking his head to one side. 'Missed me, have you?'

Tony made a noise in his throat that could have meant anything.

Johnny had brought out another bottle of Louis Cristal and an extra champagne flute. As Albie stepped closer to Tony, Johnny popped the cork, pouring the fizzing champagne into the glass.

'Here you are, Albie,' he said, holding the glass out towards him. 'Welcome back to London. It's great having you here.'

He could have been speaking to thin air. 'And you, Tony?' Albie was saying, ignoring the proffered glass. 'Do think it's great having me here?'

Tony didn't answer. Instead, putting his champagne flute down on the nearest available surface, he turned and left the room, stumbling slightly at the doorway and then making a headlong charge up the stairs to the bathroom.

Seconds later there came the unmistakable sound of vomiting.

'He's ill,' Albie said, stating the obvious. 'He was always throwing up as a kid. Leave him tae me. I'll soon have him right.' And as if his doing so was the most natural thing in the world, he left the room, crossed the hall and seconds later was taking the stairs two at a time.

Angie was the first person to move. Wanting to be with Tony, she hurried after Albie, coming to a halt at the foot of the stairs as, from the bathroom, she heard him say: 'Don't worry, laddie. Albie's here. Just like in the old days.'

Then the bathroom door was closed.

A key was turned.

And there was silence.

Chapter Twelve

'You're too imaginative to be a copper, Gowan. You should be a ruddy journalist. Most of 'em don't know how to spell facts, let alone stick to 'em.'

Detective Inspector Colin Ramsden pushed Rob Gowan's carefully composed file back across his desk-top.

It was an action Rob had expected. He'd been more than aware of how thin his argument looked when set down in black and white, accompanied only by three accident reports and two coroner's reports.

'I don't think the idea should be dismissed, sir,' he said stubbornly. 'We suspect Johnny Martini of having murdered Jimmy Jones. We have statements from two members of the band Jimmy played in describing an incident in 1966 when Johnny held him out of a sixth-floor window by his ankles – seemingly without even losing his temper over it. We *know* he's violent – Christ, half the heavy door-men and repo-men in London are hired out by him. And in the last four years, two of his girl-friends have died in accidents and another has almost died. That's astronomical bad luck for any bloke, but when the bloke in question is Johnny Martini . . .'

He gave an expressive shrug.

Ramsden, bearing in mind that Gowan wasn't in the habit of making a mountain out of a molehill, exercised patience.

'Let me spell it out,' he said heavily. 'One –' he held

up a nicotine-stained forefinger – 'not one of the victims – Zoë Fairminder, Deirdre Crosby and Abbra Hornby – was Martini's steady girlfriend. That dubious honour belongs to Tommy Bailey's eldest girl.

'Two –' he held up another stubby finger – 'though he was in the vicinity when the Fairminder girl fell to her death, he wasn't in the car park with her. A pub full of people were agreed on that. And he most certainly wasn't in the car Deirdre Crosby died in, and, as no other vehicle was involved in the accident – something else for which there are reliable witness statements – neither was he the cause of it. Deirdre Crosby was a newly qualified driver who, driving a car whose brakes were faulty, and with well above the legal limit of alcohol in her blood, swerved off the road and hit a lamp-post head on. As for the Hornby girl . . .'

He raised yet another finger. 'She was wearing three-inch high stiletto-heeled shoes when she lost her balance on the crowded platform of a bus as it turned a corner in Trafalgar Square. It happens every week. Her bad luck was to fall in front of a speeding taxi. Her good luck was that she escaped serious injury. No witnesses, either on the bus or in the street, mentioned anything about anyone pushing her or behaving suspiciously.' He tapped his finger decisively. 'Conclusion? They were all accidents. Pure and simple.'

'I agree that none of the girls supplanted his steady girlfriend, sir,' Rob persisted doggedly, 'but they were all in a sexual relationship with him when they died.'

'*Two* of them were. Zoë Fairminder was Fast-Boy Flynn's girlfriend – and had been for quite some time.'

'And at the time of her death she'd ditched Flynn for Johnny. Donnie Crosby told me that, and I've no reason to think he was spinning me a yarn.'

'You're the one who's spinning a yarn, Gowan. Christ, where's the bloody motive? Where Zoë Fairminder is concerned, Flynn had more of a motive than Johnny. Violent as Johnny undoubtedly is, there's no record of his ever having been violent towards a woman – at least not in a way they've ever complained about. If we were talking about his father, it'd be a different matter.'

Aware of the kind of man Marco Martini was – and not interested in him in the way he was interested in Johnny – Rob tucked the rejected file beneath his arm. 'Are you thinking of any particular incident, sir?' he asked, aware that some show of interest was called for.

Ramsden pulled at his ear lobe. 'Yes, Gowan. I am. I'm thinking of the house fire that nearly did for the Martini twins when they were nippers. Their mother died of smoke inhalation after rescuing one of 'em. It was a clear case of arson, but no one was ever charged.'

Rob felt a tingling at the base of his skull. This was interesting. He didn't know quite in what way – not yet – but he definitely wanted to know more.

'Are you saying the fire was Marco's way of getting rid of his wife and that he wasn't bothered if the children went up in smoke, too?' he asked, struggling to keep the incredulity out of his voice.

'Not quite.' Ramsden squinted as he tried to recall the circumstances surrounding the Martini house fire. It had happened fifteen years ago, when he'd still been an ambitious detective-sergeant. 'As I remember it, the twins should have been at a birthday party, only the birthday kid fell ill and the party was cancelled. It was assumed the arsonist didn't know and thought the only person at home was Mrs Martini.'

He chewed the corner of his lip. 'Only she wasn't. She'd left the twins on their own and gone shopping.

When she returned, the house was ablaze. She rescued one of the twins – and then collapsed and died. A fireman rescued the other.'

'And Marco was responsible?'

'Not being in the house himself at the time – and knowing the sort of character he is – he was the likeliest suspect. It was a Roman Catholic marriage, remember, and the divorce laws in the mid-fifties weren't quite as easy-osy as they are today. It was generally thought he wanted a quick out and that this was his way of getting it. The scenario had only one flaw . . .' The scepticism in Ramsden's voice spoke volumes. 'According to the statements of half a dozen witnesses, he was at a race meeting in Northumberland at the time.'

'And so he got away with it?'

'He did – if it was him that started the fire. The alternative was that it was a gangland retribution attack. Marco was always hurting people. The firing of his home could easily have been someone's way of getting back at him. Certainly that was the line the officer in charge of the case finally took. Not that any name ever surfaced, but then you wouldn't expect it to, would you? If Marco knew who was responsible, he kept the knowledge to himself – and no doubt dealt with it himself.'

That his method of dealing with it would have been extremely nasty – and final – didn't need to be said.

'And the third possibility where the starting of the fire was concerned, sir? The most obvious one? What about that?'

'Two young kids left alone in a house and playing with matches? No, Gowan. That scenario had no mileage in it. The fire was started with petrol-soaked rags. It wasn't kid's stuff, It was intentional. Whoever did it wanted to kill the person believed to be in the house at the time. And that person was Sheelagh Martini.'

Aware from the finality in Ramsden's voice that the discussion was at an end, Rob made his exit. Two things were blindingly clear: One was that Ramsden believed Marco Martini had been the arsonist, the other was that he'd utterly failed to convince him that Zoë Fairminder, Deirdre Crosby and Abbra Hornby's 'accidents' warranted investigation.

Back at his own desk he realized something else. He hadn't asked the question now uppermost in his mind.

Which twin had Sheelagh Martini saved from the fire at the cost of her own life?

Had it been Tony?

Or Johnny?

Amber and Angie were seated at a corner table in the Prince of Wales. It was lunchtime and reasonably quiet. There was no sign of the twins or any of Johnny's cohorts, and no sign of Sharyn, either.

'So you're not going to have anyone with you at the Registry Office tomorrow? Not even Johnny?' There was blatant fascination in Amber's voice.

'That's right.' Angie took a sip of her vodka and lime. 'It's just going to be me and Tony.'

'Wow!' Such an extremely private exchange of wedding vows seemed, to Amber, romantically dramatic; almost as if Tony and Angie were eloping to get married in Gretna Green. 'But what about witnesses, Angie?' she said, remembering having been to a wedding where her mother had acted as one of the witnesses. 'Surely you have to have witnesses?'

'Tony's going to ask a couple of the Registry Office workers if they'll act as witnesses and, if they're not allowed to, he's going to pull in a couple of people from off the street.'

'Blimey.' Fascinating though such a scenario was, Amber also thought it unnecessary. She could have acted as one of the witnesses – she would have liked to see Angie marry Tony – and she found it incomprehensible that Johnny and his father wouldn't be there. 'Have you always wanted this kind of a wedding, Angie?' she asked curiously. 'You know – no frills, no fuss, no friends, and no family?'

Angie put her glass of vodka and lime back on the small round table in front of them. Since her accident she'd given mini-skirts a wide berth and had embraced maxi-length fashion whole-heartedly. It suited her. She was wearing a Miss Belville print patchwork dress, the colours all plum and raspberry, deep and rich. Her hair, too, was worn in a way drastically different to her old Cleopatra cut. Below shoulder-length, she wore it in a wild, crinkled frizz that came from sleeping with it in braids. She wasn't an out-and-out hippy, but she'd certainly acquired a look that was distinctively Pre-Raphaelite.

'No,' she said slowly in answer to Amber's question. 'No, of course I didn't.'

'Well, then?' Wearing inky blue, skin-tight denims, a T-shirt emblazoned with the American flag and a sequinned jersey beret crammed over her crackly red hair, Amber waited for an explanation.

Though she didn't live in Angie's pocket the way Sharyn still did, their friendship was by far the deeper one, with secrets shared that neither of them would have dreamed of sharing with anyone else.

'It wasn't actually my idea to have such a quiet wedding. It was Tony's.' She saw Amber's cat-green eyes widen and added hurriedly: 'But you can see the sense of it, can't you? If Tony had his family there, I'd have to have my family there. And Johnny and Fast-Boy in the same congregation . . . ? That would be asking for trouble. This way, at least we know there won't be a fight.'

'So Fast-Boy doesn't know yet, and neither does Sharyn?'

'That's right.' Angie shot her an impudent, face-splitting smile and Amber was reminded of the Angie of the old days; Angie before her accident. 'If Sharyn knew, the whole of South London would know. Besides, I can't wait to see her face when I flash my wedding ring. She's going to be *livid* at me marrying before she does. Trust me.'

'Oh, she'll be livid, all right.' As she thought of just how livid, Amber winced. Angie didn't have to live with Sharyn. She did.

'Another round, girls?' Happy Harry called across to them from behind the bar.

Angie nodded. Amber, who had never forgiven him for the way he had ejected her from the pub the night Zoë Fairminder had died, didn't even look towards him. She was still only seventeen and, though he had apparently decided to pretend that she was eighteen and old enough to be served alcohol, she'd no intention of coming the old pals act with him. He was a miserable old bugger and she only came in the Prince because everyone else did.

'It's a bit of a shame for Tony's auntie's husband, isn't it?' she said as Happy unceremoniously plonked two more drinks down in front of them. 'I know he didn't come all the way from Canada because you and Tony were getting married – he couldn't have, because he didn't know about it – but now he *is* here, it seems a bit of a shame not to take advantage of it and have him at the wedding. After all, he was like a father to Tony, wasn't he? He did more or less bring Tony up.'

'Y-e-s.'

There was such doubt in Angie's voice that Amber's interest was caught. 'What's the matter?' she asked. 'Don't you like him very much?'

'I don't like him at all – he's too smarmy by half.'

Amber shrugged. Men being smarmy – especially when they were as old as Albie – was nothing new. 'Sharyn quite likes him.' Her tone of voice indicated how little this opinion was worth. 'She and Johnny are even thinking of going to Canada for their honeymoon.'

'Are they?' Angie was unimpressed. 'I wonder if Tony knows. I don't think he'll be envious. I get the feeling he was overjoyed when he left and never wants to return. I also get the feeling that, far from Tony thinking Albie's the greatest thing since sliced bread, he actually doesn't like him very much. In fact I'd go further. I think he hates his guts.'

Amber spluttered disbelievingly on a mouthful of Bacardi and Coke. 'But Albie was wonderful to Tony!' she said when she'd recovered the power of speech. 'I remember Johnny telling Sharyn about the camping trips Albie took Tony on; of how they went hunting and shooting and fishing together – and how, once, they even went panning for gold.'

'Well,' Angie said dryly, 'if they did, I don't think Tony enjoyed it as much as he made out.' She shrugged. 'Or maybe it's just my imagination playing tricks. Tony's had food poisoning since the day Albie arrived, so we haven't had the opportunity to go anywhere with him.'

Amber's eyes widened. 'My God, Angie! You can't get

married tomorrow if Tony's still got food poisoning! What if he has to run to the loo when you're only halfway through exchanging your vows?'

The image was so ridiculous they convulsed into giggles.

'And another thing,' Amber said, still giggling even though the possibility that had just occurred to her wasn't particularly funny: 'when Sharyn finds out that you married without telling her about it beforehand, she's going to be childish and cry off having you as her bridesmaid. Which means I'll have to walk down the aisle behind her on my own.'

This time Angie's shrug was philosophical. Not being a bridesmaid when Sharyn married Johnny would be a relief of massive proportions – though she hadn't hinted as much to anyone; not even Amber.

Amber picked up her glass again. 'You know I've always fancied Johnny something rotten, don't you?' she confided. 'And I never thought he'd marry Sharyn. I always thought that, when I was a bit older, I'd be in with a chance.'

It was frivolous girl-talk and she'd expected a saucily flippant retort. What she got was silence.

'Angie?'

As Angie remained silent – and very, very still – she remembered that Angie, too, had once fancied Johnny something rotten, and that there'd been a time when she'd done something about it and had nearly taken him away from Sharyn. What had never occurred to Amber, until now, was that Angie still had unresolved feelings for him.

'Sorry,' she said sincerely, wondering just how much of a chance Angie and Tony's marriage was going to have. 'I didn't realize Johnny was still a sensitive subject.'

Angie didn't shrug the remark away, as Amber had half expected her to. Instead, she said slowly, her entire mood suddenly different: 'I'm not sensitive about Johnny, Amber. At least, not in the way that you mean. I'm . . .' She made a slight movement with her hand, searching for the right word. 'I'm . . . uneasy.'

'Uneasy? About his marrying Sharyn?' Amber gave a gurgle of laughter. 'I expect most people are. Johnny doesn't have a track record for faithfulness.'

'I'm uneasy about something more serious than that.' Beneath her cloud of blue-black hair, Angie's face had drained of colour.

Amber stared at her, appalled. 'What on earth's the matter, Angie?' Fear made her throat dry. 'Have you heard that Johnny's about to be arrested for something? Or that someone's got a contract out on him? Is it Fast-Boy?' The fear became crippling. 'Because if it's Fast-Boy . . .'

'No.' Angie shook her head. 'It's something that happened the night I fell. Or at least, something I *think* happened the night that I fell.'

'You mean the snake-thing you thought had smacked against your ankles?'

Angie nodded. It was something that hadn't been mentioned between them since she'd left hospital, when they'd agreed her words had been spoken in delirium, an after-effect of her anaesthesia. Even when – later – she'd begun to think differently, she'd never said so.

Now she said, 'When I came out of hospital, I went back to the studios. I wanted to see just where I had fallen from – to see if I could work out how it had happened.'

'Well, that makes sense. It's what I would have done, especially if I'd thought my fall had been caused by some kind of negligence. What did you find? Were there cables strewn all over the stairs and landings?'

'No. And I don't think there would have been any the night I fell, either. There's no reason for there to be cables on stairs and landings.'

'Well, no, but . . .'

'On one side of the step from which I fell was a piece of old piping, and on the other, at exactly the same height – ankle-height – was an air vent.'

Amber blinked, not seeing what Angie was driving at. 'So?' she said, the sudden anxiety she'd been feeling ebbing fast. 'It's an old building, Angie. It used to be a warehouse, remember? It'll be littered with old piping. And unless it was piping you fell over – and it couldn't be if it was still fixed to the wall – I don't see why you're so het up over it.'

Angie met her gaze with tortured eyes. 'I'm het up, Amber, because the pipe was an inch thick with dust and dirt and grime – except for an indentation sliced right through it as if something had been tied or looped around it. And if something had been tied or looped around it, it could only have been in order that it could be stretched across the step and tied to the air vent. I've thought and thought about it, and I just can't come to any other conclusion. I said something snake-like had smacked across my ankles, didn't I? Well, if wire or flex had been tied across the step, from the pipe to the vent, that's exactly what it would have felt like. And if that's what I tripped over, then no wonder I plummeted down those stairs with such force.'

Amber opened her mouth to speak, but no words came.

'And if it was done on purpose,' Angie continued remorselessly, 'it was either done by someone absolutely mental who didn't care *who* tripped and was killed or crippled, or it was done by someone wanting to kill or cripple me.' Her voice shook. 'I know it's a crazy conclusion, but what other conclusion can there be? I keep thinking about what happened to Zoë, about how, like me, she was waiting for Johnny when she fell. And how, like me, she was thought to have fallen by accident.'

Amber's face was now almost as white as Angie's. 'The conclusion being that Johnny arranged both accidents?' she said, disbelief in her voice. 'No, Angie. Never. Absolutely not.' The pain behind her eyes was now intense. 'For one thing, why would he have wanted to? He was crazy about Zoë and, though it's just possible he may have already decided to end his relationship with you, you were never likely to cause any major difficulties about it, were you?'

'No.' Angie's fine-boned face was like a mask. 'But if my fall *wasn't* accidental, the person who fixed the wire across the step had to have been in the building with me, because it had to have been put in place after I went up the stairs, after the musicians came down, and before I came back down. They had to know *when* I was on my way back down in order to know exactly when to fuse the lights. And they had to be there to be able to remove the wire before the ambulancemen arrived.'

Her eyes held Amber's. 'And the only person who was definitely in the building within minutes of my fall was Johnny. It was Johnny who found me. Johnny who rang for the ambulance. Johnny who never visited me all the months I was in hospital.' Her voice cracked and broke. 'And Johnny was the only person who knew I was in the building that night.'

The pain behind Amber's eyes was now almost unbearable.

Angie was wrong in her last assumption. Amber, too, had known that Angie was meeting Johnny at the studios – or at least she'd guessed.

And she'd told Sharyn.

Sharyn, who had been consumed with jealous rage. Sharyn, who had then had every reason to have wanted to hurt Angie. Just as, on the night Zoë died, she'd had every reason to want to hurt Zoë.

She knew she should tell Angie, but she couldn't. Sharyn was her sister and, no matter how demented her actions, the relationship was one that demanded absolute loyalty. And it wasn't as if the situation would ever arise again. Not now that Johnny had asked her to marry him and Sharyn was no longer in terror of losing him.

'I think,' she heard herself say, her voice sounding as if it was coming from a vast distance, 'that you're suffering from pre-wedding nerves, that's all. Your imagination is all over the place. Shall we have a couple more drinks? It is your last night of freedom. We could call in at a club for a couple of hours, go dancing . . . Come on, Angie, shake off the heebie-jeebies. They're nonsense and you know it. Let's hit the town and have some fun.'

The club Fast-Boy strolled into wasn't one of his regular haunts. It was more of a nightclub than a general drinking club, with a dance-floor no bigger than a postage-stamp, garish-coloured lighting and R&B music so loud that conversation was impossible. It didn't bother Fast-Boy.

He hadn't come to talk to anyone.

He'd come looking for a fight.

Wearing a black turtleneck sweater, black jeans and a black leather jacket instead of his usual biking leathers, he squeezed his way across to the bar and ordered a whisky mac. It was the sixth club he'd been in on and around Wardour Street and, as he did a quick recce, he still couldn't see the face he was seeking.

Johnny Martini.

Johnny might not give a flying fuck about Tony marrying Angie, but Fast-Boy did. And what he cared about was that Johnny knew about tomorrow's wedding – had known for days – while he'd been kept in the dark and had only found out because of something he'd overheard. For Johnny not to have gone ape-shit over it meant that, sick in the head as usual, he'd decided the situation was funny. Funny at his expense.

Deep in the pockets of his jacket, his knuckles clenched until they shone white. If he'd had any sense he'd have done for Johnny years ago. God knows he'd had enough reason. There'd been the situation that had erupted with Zoë on the night of her death. She'd finished with him – or tried to – and Johnny, with his flash name, flash reputation and flash American car, had been the reason.

Then there'd been the incident when, if the shotgun he'd used in the post office robberies had been in its usual stow, he'd have gone down for so long, he'd probably still be in nick. It had been Johnny who had grassed on him – thanks to Angie blabbing to Sharyn about things that were none of her business. A pulse began throbbing at the corner of his jaw. Well, Angie had felt the force of his anger over that – and she'd feel it again for making him a relation-by-marriage to Johnny.

The disc-jockey was playing a slow number now and he leaned back against the bar, wondering where his next port of call should be. Johnny liked Soho. It was where he did business and where most of his business was. Every club had protection on the door – and the firm Johnny ran provided nearly all of it. It meant, of course, that when he did find Johnny, he wouldn't be able to do for him terminally – there were too many of Johnny's tame gorillas around for him to be able to achieve that particular life-long ambition.

What he would be able to do, though, was to give vent to the fury that had been consuming him ever since he'd overheard his mother vowing a neighbour to silence over the secret she was sharing with her.

If he'd heard about the wedding in a normal way – if Tony or Angie had told him that they were getting married but didn't want anyone with them at the cere-mony– he knew that, however extreme his reaction might have been, it wouldn't have been as bad as when he real-ized, thanks to his mother, that the Martini family were in on the secret.

It was the fact that Johnny knew about it that had made his rage so incandescent.

His first thought had been to find Angie and lay violent hands on her, but his terrified mother had said that Angie was out on a hen night with a girlfriend. Tony, he'd felt no anger towards at all. Which had left Johnny.

Johnny, who was no doubt laughing himself senseless at his expense.

Johnny, whom he hated and whom he had always hated.

Johnny, who, when at primary school, had taken Fast-Boy's puppy, and 'accidentally' killed it whilst pretend-ing to be a German concentration camp doctor.

Rage raced through his veins as fresh now as it had been then. He had got his own back, of course, or at least he had made a damned good attempt to get his own back. The final reckoning had never, as yet, come. It would, though, eventually. It was something he'd looked forward to for so long, he could practically taste it.

The music had changed again – this time dramatically. The record being played was 'Voodoo Chile' by the Jimi Hendrix Experience, and beneath flashing lighting the dance-floor was packed with bodies gyrating to the music.

It was then, as the club plunged from a haze of red to blue and back again, that he saw his quarry. Not the one he'd had most recently in mind.

Not Johnny.

Angie.

He didn't stop to think. He didn't even want to think. He simply wanted – *had* – to give vent to emotion that had reach explosion point.

He catapulted away from the bar so fast that the people standing on either side of him spilt their drinks. Angie was standing on the far side of the dance floor and he didn't bother trying to circumnavigate his way round it. Instead, he plunged straight into the crush, shouldering a way through, heedless of the number of dancers being knocked and slammed out of his way.

Not until the very last minute did she see him, and by then it was too late for her to escape. He saw realization flare through her eyes – and fear – and then, as she looked wildly around for help, he seized hold of her so violently that her cry of pain was audible even above the wail of Hendrix's guitar.

'What the fuck do you fucking mean, not telling me about tomorrow?' he roared, propelling her forcefully in the direction of the nearest wall and swinging her around and hurling her against it. 'Did you think it funny, making me some kind of an in-law to Johnny without giving me any warning? Not even by so much as a fucking day?

'No!' Angie's denial was a sobbed shout. 'I just wanted

a wedding where there wouldn't be any trouble! Where you and Johnny wouldn't be at each other's throats! And the only way was by not letting you know about it!'

'But you fucking well let Johnny know!'

Even though the club was jam-packed and space was at a premium, people began edging away from their immediate vicinity.

'*Tony* let Johnny know!' Over his shoulder, Angie could see Amber emerging from the Ladies; could see her registering the ruckus and trying to push a way through to them. 'And he did it because he and Tony are twins!' she sobbed, hating the way her hen-night was ending; hating the fact that she and her brother were rowing like this on the eve of her wedding. 'They're not like us, Ewan! They're close! They're –'

He slapped her open-handed across the face so hard that her head nearly left her shoulders. Then he slapped her again with such viciousness that she fell.

There were screams of consternation from some of the girls who were near enough to see what was happening; shouts of outrage from others.

Half a dozen pairs of hands were grabbing at him in order to haul him away from her and, as he twisted away from them, Fast-Boy's rage was total. He kicked out, sending Angie, who'd been on her hands and knees trying to regain her feet, sprawling.

As she screamed, tears flooding her face, snot dripping from her nose, the club's doormen finally forced their way through the crush, laying the kind of hands on Fast-Boy that even he couldn't twist away from.

The doormen weren't alone in getting to the forefront of the scene.

Amber had pummelled a way through the crowd and was now kneeling at Angie's side. Her eyes, though, weren't on Angie as, using her for support, she pushed herself up into a sitting position. They were on Fast-Boy.

For nearly five years she'd thought of him as her friend – and for the last couple of years as being far more than just a friend.

Now it was as if she'd never seen him before. Never known him.

There was no need for her to hurl her contempt at him. As the doormen began hauling him away, everything she was feeling blazed in her eyes.

Beneath the garish lighting his face was chalk-white and she knew that, until the second their eyes had met, he hadn't known she was there; hadn't known she had seen what had taken place – and that he would have done anything in the world for her not to have seen it.

And she knew that everything between them was at an end – and he knew it too.

'Come along, sweetheart,' she said thickly to Angie as she helped her to her feet. 'You're getting married tomorrow. Let's get some arnica to take the bruising away and get the swelling down around your eyes. I know you were going to keep it simple and not wear a veil, but I think you might want to reconsider.'

Chapter Thirteen

Rob Gowan strolled past St Alphege's Church in Greenwich, a reasonably happy young man. It was his day off, the summer sun was shining, and he'd just received notification that he'd soon be going in front of a promotion board. It would be a tough interview, but he was already mentally psyched up for it.

With his hands deep in the pockets of his rather unfashionable slacks, he crossed the road, heading in the direction of his brother-in-law's office. As he stepped on to the pavement, he caught sight of his reflection in the window of a shop and grimaced, aware that he was probably the only twenty-six-year-old in London not sporting a Zapata moustache and bell-bottomed trousers. Hell, even his sedate brother-in-law had begun wearing a frilled shirt and a velvet jacket to the office.

He gave a philosophical shrug. Being fashionable and being a policeman weren't compatible. He had to wear his curly hair short and be clean-shaven, for a start, and, without a heavy moustache, fashionable gear just didn't seem to look right – or at least it didn't look right on him. He could have worn jeans, of course, and, with a broad-buckled belt emphasizing his snake-slim hips, often did. Not today, though. Today, as he swung into David Lampeter's office, he looked as square as a Boy Scout leader, and as he saw the vision seated at the reception desk, he groaned, knowing he stood no chance.

She looked more like a model than a Greenwich office

girl. Long-legged and doe-eyed with honey-blonde hair flowing waterfall-straight down to her waist.

'Yes?' she said, aware of his presence but not bothering to raise her eyes from the photographs she was looking at; photographs that were not of houses his brother-in-law was attempting to sell, but of a wedding.

'Is David around?' he asked, thinking that he should perhaps make it clear that he wasn't a prospective client. 'I'm his brother-in-law.'

'Really?' The doe eyes still didn't look up from the photographs. 'He's in the back office. He'll be out in a minute.'

Not only was her voice totally disinterested, it was also flat and unattractive. Rob sighed, reconciling himself to the fact that nothing in life was perfect.

'Who's the bride?' he asked, wondering if she was always so offhand with David's clients and, if so, how the hell David ever managed to sell any houses.

'She's the sister of the other girl who works here.' Tilly at last raised her head and looked at him. 'D'you want to have a look?'

Rob nodded, not overly interested but happy to be able to move a little nearer to her incredible figure.

'This is me –' The uppermost photograph was a large group shot and, even if she hadn't been pointing to herself, she would have been unmissable. The last figure on the right, she was wearing a cerise-pink mini-dress and a matching hat topped by a huge white rose.

She'd been so offhand about everything that he didn't notice the tightness that had suddenly entered her voice.

Even now, two weeks after the wedding, Tilly still couldn't quite believe that Johnny had had the nerve to invite her – or that she'd had the nerve to go. Officially, of course, she'd gone as Amber's friend. Unofficially, she was there as the bridegroom's girlfriend. Not, of course, that anyone knew that. There'd been times when she'd wondered if Amber had guessed that there was something going on between herself and Johnny, but if so, she hadn't said.

'And the bride is . . . ?'

'Pregnant.'

'I meant her name,' Rob said, startled.

'Her name's Sharyn. Sharyn Bailey.'

It was a question he hadn't needed to ask. He'd recognized the groom immediately – and half of the wedding guests. At six foot four, Cheyenne Goody would have been impossible to miss and, at the opposite end of the spectrum, so would Little Donnie. What was stupefying him was that one of Tommy Bailey's girls worked for David. Why on earth hadn't the silly sod said? Surely he must have known it would have been of interest to him?

He flicked through the rest of the photographs, intrigued by a couple of the men standing close to Marco Martini whose faces he didn't recognize. What he needed was to get his hands on a copy of the photographs – which was surely something David, being the younger Bailey girl's employer, could manage for him.

'Who are the rest of the guests?' he said, hoping to God that David hadn't told his staff his brother-in-law was a copper. 'Some of them look pretty distinguished.'

What some of them actually looked was Mafiosi.

Tilly shrugged. 'I don't know,' she said, uninterested. 'I'm not really a friend of the family. I just know . . .' She hesitated, longing to be able to say that she knew Johnny and to say it in a meaningful way. Instead she said, 'I just know the bride because of being friends with her sister.'

'Hi, Rob.' David Lampeter strode into the shopfront-cum-office, a girl with sizzling red hair a foot or so behind him. 'I didn't realize you were here. D'you mind hanging on for another ten minutes? I've a couple of phone calls to make before we disappear for lunch.'

'Take all the time you want,' Rob said sincerely, wanting more time to commit some of the faces in the photographs to memory.

It was an opportunity he wasn't given.

'I gave those photos to Tilly to look at, not the general public,' the redhead said, swiping them unceremoniously from out of his hand.

'Hey, steady on!' If the blonde was apparently unaware of just how interesting the photographs were, the petite tornado now stuffing them into a white patent-leather shoulder bag clearly wasn't. Not that he reckoned she knew he was a policeman. One look at the set of her jaw and he was pretty sure that, if she had, she wouldn't have used the words 'general public'. She'd have used something much more derogatory.

Having stared once at her, he kept on staring. Even without their little altercation, it would have been impossible not to. She was wearing narrow-cut black vinyl trousers with a short-sleeved, short-waisted black vinyl jacket and high-heeled black boots. The jacket was piped in white and was zipped – or rather, half-zipped – up the front. If she was wearing anything underneath it, it wasn't in evidence. What was in evidence was a delectable cleavage and flawless skin the colour of cream.

A pair of white-framed sunglasses were pushed up into a turbulent riot of titian-red curls. Her eyes were the most startling shade of green he'd ever seen on anything other than a cat; her nose was too short for classical beauty; her mouth too full and wide. She seemed to literally fizz with an inner effervescence and was absolutely gorgeous.

And she was old lag Tommy Bailey's youngest daughter.

Not to mention Johnny Martini's sister-in-law.

He took a deep, steadying breath, counted to ten, told himself the words he was about to utter were only in the line of duty, an attempt to find out more about some of her sister's wedding guests, and said, 'I'm going across to the Mitre to wait for David. Do you fancy joining me for a lunchtime gin and tonic?'

Amber looked at his unfashionably short hair, his nondescript jacket and appallingly unhip slacks, and wondered what the odds were of her reputation being ruined by association. Then she looked at his gold-flecked eyes, tousled curls and attractive jawline and decided that it was worth the risk. Not, though, for a gin and tonic.

'I drink Bacardi and Coke,' she said, slipping the white bag over a shoulder. 'And at this time of day, I like a decent ham sandwich to go with it.'

'You're on.' He grinned, feeling suddenly on top of the world. As they stepped out of the office and on to the pavement together, he said casually, 'So tell me about your sister's wedding. Recent, was it?'

'Fairly.'

Reminiscing about Sharyn's wedding was not Amber's idea of a fun topic of conversation. It had been more a day to forget than to remember. Sufficient time had elapsed between Tony and Angie's non-event of a wedding and Johnny and Sharyn's full-blown extravaganza for Sharyn to have got over her outrage at not being asked to be Angie's bridesmaid and, with bad grace, to have persisted with the arrangement that Angie be one of hers. Though, as she was now a married woman, Angie hadn't been a bridesmaid, she'd been the Maid of Honour.

Fast-Boy hadn't disrupted the event, as she and Angie had feared he would. Ever since the hideous scene in the nightclub, he'd kept such a low profile that no one was even sure whether he was still living at home or had moved out and off.

'He's probably moved in with Jed, his boxing trainer,' Angie had said in the days immediately after her wedding, her face still swollen from the force with which he had hit her. 'Mum won't mind. He was hardly ever at home anyway.'

Amber had said nothing. She couldn't speak about Fast-Boy yet. Not even to Angie.

As she strolled across the road towards the Mitre with her boss' brother-in-law – a dude who, where looks and dress-sense were concerned, was the very antithesis of Fast-Boy – she wondered if she would ever get over the shock of the moment when Fast-Boy had slapped Angie so viciously and then, even more incredibly, when he had kicked her as she lay in a crumpled heap at his feet.

Until then, it had never occurred to her that he was capable of violence towards a woman. Ever since she could remember, of course, she'd known about his reputation for being fast with his fists. And she knew he was a criminal – a criminal who, according to Angie, had committed robberies armed with a shotgun when he'd been little older than she was now.

But being a criminal and being violent towards women didn't necessarily go hand in hand. Hell, her dad was a criminal. The judge who had sentenced him to the present stretch he was serving – six years for affray – had said so in his summing-up in no uncertain terms. But he'd never been violent towards her mother. Or to any other woman, as far as she knew.

And neither had the twins. Tony, of course, didn't really come into the equation because, as far as she could see, he wasn't really a criminal at all. Johnny's name, however, was synonymous with violence and intimidation, yet she couldn't imagine Johnny doing to his sister – if he'd had one –what she had seen Fast-Boy do to Angie.

Not that she'd ever convince Angie of that. As she remembered the accidents Angie suspected Johnny of engineering, Amber's tummy muscles contracted in a churning, sickening sensation. Her not being able to set Angie's mind at rest where Johnny was concerned was another reason why she had found her sister's wedding such a strain.

Standing alongside Angie, behind Johnny and Sharyn as they'd exchanged vows at their nuptial mass, had not been a pleasant experience – not when she was so aware of what Angie believed the groom capable of.

There had, though, been nothing she could do about it. She couldn't tell Angie that if anyone was off their rocker, it was Sharyn, not Johnny. There was no knowing where such a revelation might lead – to Sharyn on a manslaughter charge, probably.

As they stepped from the bright sunlight into the near-claustrophobic dimness of the Mitre's saloon bar, the churning in her stomach increased until it was a physical pain. Not for one minute did she believe that Sharyn had intended to kill Zoë Fairminder. All Sharyn had wanted was for Zoë to fall amongst rubble and ruin her stylish clothes. It had been jealous rage carried to a mindless extreme with appalling consequences.

Why, though, had Sharyn learned no lessons from it? Why, when jealousy had again consumed her, had she reacted with a near carbon-copy bout of rage? Only someone mentally sick could have done what Sharyn did to Angie that night at the recording studios. Which left her with a problem: what was to be done about it? She couldn't tell Johnny. If he knew Sharyn was responsible for Zoë's death, not only would his and Sharyn's marriage be over in seconds, but Sharyn would be dead meat.

She thought about the way Jimmy Jones had disappeared from the scene and felt sicker than ever. If Johnny had killed him because he thought Jimmy had caused Zoë's death, then he'd killed an innocent man.

'Are you OK?' Rob asked as she stumbled against him slightly.

'Fine. It's just a bit dark in here, after being out in the sunshine.'

The only person she could possibly tell was her mother – and her mother was now on such sinisterly friendly terms with Marco Martini that confiding in her was not a safe thing to do. If her mother told Marco, he would very likely have a word with Johnny and the result would be the same – absolute disaster.

'Bacardi and Coke and a ham roll?' Mr Clean-Cut was asking her as she sat down on shabby velour bench in the pub's far corner.

'Yes, please. The drink with ice and the roll with mustard.'

Nothing in her voice – which was as perky as ever – revealed her inner turmoil. As he strolled off in the direction of the bar, she gave herself a good mental talking to. Now wasn't the time to drive herself batty thinking about her sister's terrible secrets – nor to go into a mood thinking about Fast-Boy. She was out having a drink with the first bloke who'd even halfway appealed to her – Fast-Boy apart – since . . . she couldn't remember when.

The fact that he was quite obviously not the slightest bit crooked was a nuisance, because it meant she'd have to be ultra careful what she said. It did, however, have a certain novelty value about it.

'So . . .' she said, flashing him a gamine smile that had his heart turning somersaults as he set their drinks down on the table in front of her. 'What's your name?'

'Rob. Rob Gowan.'

Remembering that it would look a bit odd if he was already familiar with her surname, he said, 'And I know your name is Amber, but what's your surname?'

Amber wasn't in the habit of bandying her surname about. It always made her feel as if she was being questioned by a policeman, but there was no trying to hide it on this occasion as he could easily find out from his brother-in-law. 'Bailey,' she said. 'And what do you do, Rob Gowan? Are you a teacher? You look like one.'

'No.' He took a swig of his gin and tonic. This was decision time. Either he was going to be truthful with her, or he wasn't. And if he told the truth, not only would he never pick up any interesting information from her, she would most definitely never date him. And he wanted to date her. He wanted to date her very much.

'I'm a civil servant,' he said, comforting himself with the thought that it wasn't a million miles from the truth.

Amber raised her eyes to heaven. How could a man who had such attractively gold-flecked eyes and such an enticingly sensual mouth be anything so utterly boring?

She gave a mock groan. 'Don't tell me any more. The excitement might kill me. Is having a lunchtime drink in the Mitre the highlight of your week?'

'Nope.' He grinned, enjoying himself more than he'd

done for yonks. 'Sometimes I ring the changes and drink in the Trafalgar.'

She spluttered with laughter, suddenly not wanting anyone else to join them; especially her boss.

Reading her thoughts and sharing her feelings, he said, 'Let's give David the slip. What say we wander down to the pier and have our lunch on one of the boats that go between here and Westminster?'

'You're on.' She was fizzing with *joie de vivre* again, all her dark thoughts firmly under lock and key. 'I was born within sight of the Thames. I love it so much I'd live on it if I could.'

Rob's grin deepened. This was where he scored, *really* scored.

'I do,' he said truthfully. 'I have a houseboat.'

With one accord, they stood up and moved away from the table, leaving their drinks barely touched. She took hold of his arm and said teasingly, 'I knew one day my prince would come! You are, of course, going to show it to me?'

'Oh yes,' he said, forgetting all about his initial reason for asking her out for a drink; not a thought of the Martinis and their friends in his head; deaf to every alarm bell ringing there. 'I most certainly am. And there's no time like the present.'

'I think we're going to have to nail this little game on the head for a while, Tone,' Johnny said reflectively as they strolled across a warehouse floor stacked high with enormous bolts of cloth. 'Donnie says this copper he used to go school with is determined to pin something on me. He says he offered him everything going if he'd be chatty about Jimmy.' He gave an uncaring shrug. 'Well, Donnie ain't goin' to be chatty about Jimmy, and neither is anyone else.' He flashed Tony a blinding smile. 'And as no one's going to be digging Jimmy up from where I dropped him, this Gowan bloke is on a hiding to nothing. No body, no case. Know what I mean?'

Tony knew exactly and didn't bother making any comment about it. Instead, he said with a frown, 'I don't see how this DS trying to nail you for Jimmy is a problem where the long firms are concerned. Our name's never come up in connection with any of them. If it had, we'd have had word.'

'True.' Johnny ran a finger along a head-high roll of Donegal tweed. 'And that's the way I want to keep it. Let the cozzers think my only business interests are security and protection, and let them sweat their balls off trying to finger me for something naughty that way. The long firms are too lucrative to put at risk. Let's take a break from them till we've got this geezer Gowan sorted.'

They'd reached the end of the canyon made by the hundreds and hundreds of stacked rolls of cloth. In a corner, next to a door that led out on to a flight of dusty stairs, was a glass cubicle that served as an office.

Johnny pushed open the door with his shoulder, kicked a couple of empty cartons out of the way, and seated himself behind a shabby desk piled high with invoices.

'Taking a breather won't do any harm,' he said, putting his feet up on the desk and taking a silver cigarette-case from the inside pocket of his single-breasted Italian suit. 'Especially as Donnie says his old school mate seems to be making me his own personal crusade. I s'pose he reckons if he can collar me for something – anything – it'll give him a leg up the promotion ladder. According to Donnie, he's about to be made up to detective inspector.'

'But he isn't one yet.' Tony perched on the corner of

the paper-strewn desk, one leg swinging free. 'Which is why I still don't get a handle as to why you're being so cautious, Johnny. The bloke's a detective-sergeant, he can't instigate his own investigation. All he's doing is trying to kick-start an old and tired investigation, knowing that, if he gets a result, it will help speed up his promotion. It just isn't worth losing sleep over, especially as Donnie said the bloke was a tosser.'

'He didn't, actually.' Johnny lit a cigarette and blew a stream of blue smoke towards the nicotine-stained ceiling. 'Rather the opposite. What he said was that Gowan was razor-sharp.'

This time it was Tony who lifted a shoulder in an indifferent shrug. 'So what? If the police high-ups haven't cottoned on to the fact that you're into long firms, a detective-sergeant ferreting about in his spare time certainly isn't going to. Look at all this –' He indicated the mound of paid invoices on the desk with a wave of his hand. 'We've just reached the point where it's time to recoup on this little lot. You're surely not suggesting we walk away from it, are you?'

Johnny shot him his distinctive down-slanting smile. Today was one of the rare occasions when Tony, too, was suited and booted. It was something Johnny liked to see. It made them, apart from the hair, indistinguishable.

'Course not,' he said, noticing for the first time that, unlike himself, Tony wasn't wearing a wedding ring. Wondering why, he added: 'Far from walking away from the present set-up, I intend cashing in on it in a way that will double our profits. Everything is up to snuff, isn't it?'

Tony nodded and tugged a sheaf of letter-headed invoices from beneath the heel of one of Johnny's hand-made shoes. 'Yup. These are all the invoices from the suppliers and they've all been paid on the dot. The pile of invoices over there, near your left hand, are for goods I've sold cut-rate to shops and a few other customers. Small ads have been running in the trade papers for six months. Our credit is good and Joseph Bee, whose name everything is in, is well and truly dead.'

Johnny's grin deepened. 'Just as a matter of interest,' he said, 'how long did Joseph live?'

Without moving from the corner of the desk, Tony leaned backwards a little in order to tug the top-hand right drawer open. 'Not sure,' he said, pulling out copies of a birth certificate and death certificate. 'Here – take a butcher's for yourself.'

Johnny did so, reminded, for no reason he was aware of, of Tilly. He was meeting her in little over an hour and, at the thought, his prick stirred in anticipation, excitement pulsing through him. Tilly was his secret. A secret even Tony was no longer privy to.

'It's over,' he had lied to him, bored out of his mind by Tony's disapproval. 'So no more Sunday School lectures. They're not needed.'

Now he scanned the certificates Tony had given him, saying: 'Poor little bleeder, he only lived three years. Born 6 May 1947, Lewisham Hospital. Died 2 November 1950, Catford.'

Tony slid the certificates back into the drawer, wondering why the powers-that-be didn't realize the scams that could be pulled when the nation's birth and death certificates were kept in different files. It meant that, armed with the birth certificate of someone who had died and who, if they had lived, would be the right age for the purpose, a whole array of false documentation could be obtained. Hell, it was the way most moody passports were obtained.

Not that he was into the selling of moody passports, profitable though they were. Any time he obtained the passport of a dead person, it was only to facilitate the opening of bank accounts: current and business. He'd have other documentation in the dead man's name, of course. A driving licence. Various club memberships. Then, when he'd put enough cash into the bank accounts for them to look stable and healthy, he'd think up a suitable name for the dead man's company, register it at Companies House, get some letter-headed stationery printed and tell Johnny he could begin trading.

Not that Johnny ever did any of the trading. He would do as much as possible himself, over the telephone, contacting suppliers of whatever goods the company was trading in. Nine times out of ten, this was electrical stock: TVs, fridges, top-of-the-range cookers. If it became essential for personal contact to be made, one of Johnny's many minions was sent round to act out the part of the dead man in whose name they were trading.

For a few months Tony would run the operation as a legitimate company. It was the part of the scam he most enjoyed. Then, six or nine months down the line, with the bank and creditors lulled into a false sense of security, came lift-off time. Maximum orders would be placed with all the suppliers – none of whom would ever be paid for the goods they so trustingly delivered. He and Johnny would organize a gi-normous grand-slam 'liquidation' sale – strictly for cash and nearly always to criminal clientele – and then that would be the end of that particular company.

All cash in the company's bank accounts would be withdrawn. The warehouse, rented in the dead man's name, would be abandoned. Suppliers' bills would be sent in vain. Eventually, the police would be called in.

But, without one genuine name to go on, they would be hamstrung.

Over the last few years it was an activity he'd perfected to a fine art. And now Johnny was saying he wanted to call an indefinite halt to it.

'How's Sharyn?' he asked, stalling for time as he wondered if the Gowan bloke really was such a danger to them.

Usually, Johnny was only too happy to be sidetracked into talking about Sharyn's pregnancy. Faithless though he was to Sharyn, he was over the moon at the thought of becoming a father. 'It's going to be a boy,' he'd say, his eyes as alight as a kid's at Christmas. 'And we're going to call him Marlon. Marlon Martini. It's got a great ring to it, ain't it? Sounds English, but not too English, if you know what I mean.'

This time the ruse didn't work.

'Seein' as how this present company is all cloth,' Johnny said, his attention undiverted, 'It means we can put into practice an idea I've had for ages.'

'Which is?'

'A fire,' Johnny said tersely. 'The stock is insured – had to be to keep the bank happy – so let's capitalize on that insurance. For once, we ain't dealing in electrical stock. Cloth is so combustible it's a gift from heaven for a wheeze like this. We place maximum orders with all the suppliers, as per usual. Have our cash-in sale, keeping back enough remnants of stuff to be found charred in the fire. Torch the building, and bag the insurance. That way, we'll get double the money. Say, twenty grand from the sale of the stock and another twenty from the insurance company for "lost" goods.'

He grinned wickedly. 'As Guy Fawkes rackets go, it'll be a winner.'

Tony was still sitting on the corner of the desk, but the foot that had been swinging was now still. There was tension in every line of his body. His jaw. His shoulders. His hands.

'A fire?' he said, his voice oddly brittle. 'You reckon you can start a major one successfully, do you?'

Johnny's grin deepened. 'Come off it,' he said, swinging his legs from the desk and standing up. 'Course I can. I'll have this place shooting flames hundreds of feet high before you can blink.'

He strolled over to the office door. 'Let's get going,' he said, pausing for a moment and looking back towards Tony. 'There are plans to make.' Taking a coin out of his trouser pocket he flipped it into the air and caught it. Then, whistling, he turned on his heel and ran lightly down the flight of stairs that led to the street.

Tony remained seated on the edge of the desk, as still as a statue.

Even when the outside warehouse door banged open and then, seconds later, slammed shut, he remained where he was.

He remained where he was for a long, long time.

Chapter Fourteen

Amber and Sharyn were sprawled on the twin beds in Amber's bedroom. Even though Sharyn had moved out months ago, when she'd become Mrs Johnny Martini, some of her old make-up still littered the dressing-table and several pairs of her shoes lay in an untidy pile in a bottom corner of the wardrobe.

'I don't know how you survive, living with this old-fashioned wallpaper and furniture,' she said now, a cigarette in her hand as she looked round the room that had been hers for twenty years. 'Can't you tell Mum the fifties are long gone, it's the seventies now?'

From her cat-green eyes Amber shot her sister a look that would have slain a lesser person. 'I like this room just the way it is,' she said as Sharyn eased a body made bulky by pregnancy into a more comfortable position, making the bedsprings creak. 'Mum papered it for us herself when I was at primary school, remember?'

She surveyed the faded, chintz-patterned wallpaper. A Persian-looking design of birds and flowers and trellis-work, it had been an oddly sophisticated choice for young children, but she'd loved it the instant her mother had shown it to her in the wallpaper shop, and she loved it still. The curtains were a dusky pink that matched the pink of the birds' breasts, and the furniture – dressing-table, wardrobe and twin chest of drawers – were made of plain wood that their mother had painted the colour of buttermilk.

'It still suits me,' she said, eyeing Sharyn's stomach with a twinge of alarm, wondering if she'd got her dates right. 'And I much prefer it to the public-lavatory white you and Johnny have gone for in the flat. Have you got anything in there with any colour in it? It's more like a hospital ward than a home.'

'It's fashionable.' Sharyn's voice was tight. She didn't like the decor that had been imposed on her any more than Amber did, but she wasn't about to admit it. 'We didn't do it ourselves, you know. We had bloke in to do it. An interior designer who's done rooms for Mary Quant.'

Despite her exasperation at the airs and graces Sharyn had begun affecting, Amber giggled. 'Mary Quant? Really? I bet the nearest your interior designer came to doing anything for Mary Quant was washing her windows.'

Sharyn's eyes flashed fire. 'You're just jealous. You can't bear the fact that me and Angie both have garden flats in the smartest, newest block this side of the Thames, and that our flat is so big, it even has a wine cellar!'

'I don't notice either of you or Johnny spending much time at Conway Court or Castle Court, or whatever the flats are called,' Amber snapped back. 'Johnny's always next door – And I bet when Marco trolls off to Spain at the end of the week, Tony will be back next door, too.'

Sharyn frowned, not following Amber's reasoning. 'Why should his dad going off to Spain for a month or two affect how often Tony's next door? There's not been a row between the two of them that no one's told me about, has there?'

'No, but there's something very dodgy going on

between Tony and Albie. Haven't you noticed the lengths Tony goes to in order to avoid him? And when they are in the same room, or pub or club together, you could cut the tension – where Tony's concerned – with a knife. Albie's going out to the villa as well, isn't he? Well, once he's sunning himself on the shores of the Mediterranean, you can bet Tony will be next door just as often as Johnny is.'

Sharyn stared at her, well aware of Amber's track record for accurately summing up people and situations. 'Rubbish,' she said, but with doubt in her voice. 'Albie was like a second father to Tony. He used to take him . . .'

'Don't tell me, I already know.' Amber's voice was exaggeratedly patient. 'Camping, hiking, hunting, shooting, panning for gold. You and Johnnie should cut a record together.'

'But it's true. Johnny's always been jealous to death of all the fab things Tony did when he lived in Canada.'

Amber couldn't be bothered persisting with the subject. She was sure of what she was sure of, and it really didn't matter whether anyone agreed with her or not. Tony's relationship with his uncle was between him and Albie and wasn't important.

Something else, however, was.

Two days ago in Greenwich, during her lunch hour, she'd seen Tilly with Johnny. They'd been walking up the gangplank of a Westminster-bound ferry and he'd had his arm round her waist. As shocks go, it hadn't been a particularly seismic one. She'd had her suspicions where Johnny and Tilly were concerned for a long time.

What *did* concern her was how Sharyn would react when she eventually found out about it.

She should, of course, have had the sense ages ago to realize that marriage would make not a jot of difference to Johnny where girlfriends were concerned. All through the years, as Sharyn had clung so perilously to her position as his steady girlfriend, he'd had a string of other girls. Some, like Tilly, had been stunningly beautiful but scarcely out of the schoolroom. Others had been glamorous sophisticates; models and starlets who enjoyed being seen out and about on the arm of a well-known villain and, thanks to his surname and personal security business – supposedly legitimate, but in fact far from it – Johnny was certainly that.

So, knowing what she did about Johnny, why hadn't she confronted Sharyn over the wicked way she had caused Angie's fall? How could she possibly have thought that she didn't need to? How could she have imagined that Sharyn would never again be so insanely jealous? What Sharyn had done once – she remembered Zoë and winced – what Sharyn had done *twice,* she was quite capable of doing again. Especially now Johnny was not merely her boyfriend but her husband.

And this time the girl heading for a fatal, or near-fatal, fall would be Tilly.

She drew in a deep, steadying breath and turned to look at her sister. 'There's something I have to talk to you about, Sharyn,' she said, her throat dry and tight. 'Something deadly serious.'

'About Tony and Albie?' Sharyn had taken to wearing her blonde hair swept up in a glamorous chignon of looped curls, à la Dusty Springfield, and as she gave Amber her avid attention a hairpin fell loose. She jabbed it back into position. 'Has Angie told you something? Because if she has, I'd like to know why she hasn't told me! *I'm* her best friend, not you.'

'Then you've a damn strange way of treating her.'

At the sudden venom in Amber's voice, Sharyn's mood

changed instantly. 'And just what the hell d'you mean by that?' she demanded, sitting up sharply, or as sharply as her condition allowed.

Amber swung her legs from the bed, sitting on its edge. 'I'm talking about four years ago,' she said, her voice hard. 'I'm talking about Angie's accident at the recording studios.'

Sharyn blinked, taken totally by surprise. 'I thought you were going to tell me something about Tony and Albie? What's Angie's accident got to do with them?'

'Nothing.' There were times when Amber wondered where she got her patience from. 'I'm not talking about Tony and Albie, Sharyn. I'm talking about you and Angie.'

'Me and Angie?' Sharyn's heavily made-up eyes were totally without understanding. 'What about me and Angie?'

Amber paused for a moment, praying for strength. Then she said, 'We had a row the night of Angie's fall, remember? I told you Johnny had been seeing Angie. That they used to meet up at the recording studios.'

'Why are you bringing all that up?' There was blank incomprehension in Sharyn's voice. 'It was *ages* ago, and Angie never really meant anything to my Johnny. It was just a couple of silly dates. He's never had anything to do with her since – not in that way.'

'No. You made as damn sure as you could of that.'

Sharyn, too, swung her legs over the side of the bed. 'What the *fuck* do you mean?'

Amber eyeballed her. 'I mean that you went to the recording studios that night, knowing Angie was there waiting for Johnny. And you thought you'd teach her a lesson – that you'd try the same trick you tried with Zoë.'

'Christ! Are you feeling all the bleedin' ticket?' Sharyn's eyes were wide with incredulity. 'You're not *still* trying to make out I moved the workmen's soddin' barricades, are you? I thought when you last threw that accusation at me it was because you were in a paddy over something and just being fucking stupid!'

'I probably was – at the time. But I've given it a lot of thought since and, after what you did to Angie, I know it must have been you who caused Zoë's fall.'

'You're fucking mental!' Sharyn heaved herself to her feet, hysteria edging into her voice. 'The lights fused and went out when Angie was coming down the stairs and she fell. It was nothing to do with me. It was nothing you do with *anyone*. It was an accident. It could have happened to anybody.'

'Only if they'd tripped over wire or cord that had been fixed across one of the steps.'

There was silence.

Sharyn opened her mouth to say something, but no words came.

'You didn't know Angie realized what caused her fall, did you?' The words fell into the silence like a whiplash. 'Well, she did, Sharyn. Almost the first thing she said when she came round from the anaesthetic was that a snake had smacked against her legs and that that was why she'd fallen. Later, when she was well enough to think clearly, she realized what the "snake" had been.'

'And Angie thinks . . . Angie thinks *I* did it?' The blood had drained from Sharyn's face, leaving it as white as death.

Too late, Amber remembered her sister's condition. If the shock she'd just dealt her brought on a miscarriage, she'd be to blame. Hastily, she said, 'No. Angie doesn't even know you knew she was in the habit of meeting

Johnny there. The only person Angie can think of who could possibly have done it is Johnny.'

'Johnny? *My Johnny?*' Sharyn began to hyperventilate. 'She should look closer to home,' she gasped, 'that's what she should do! I wasn't the only person who followed her to Take Six that night! So did her precious Tony! It wasn't only me that knew she was meeting Johnny there!'

The hysteria in her voice escalated. 'If anyone was out to teach her a lesson that night, it was Tony, not me! Why else would he never have admitted to being there? And he *was* there! I *saw* him.'

Blindly she made for the door. 'No one ever thinks anything bad of Tony, do they?' Her voice cracked in a sob as she wrenched the door open. 'It's always my Johnny who's blamed for everything, but it wasn't my Johnny who started the fire that killed his mother – so just take that on board, Amber! It was Tony who started the fire – Johnny told me. It's why Tony was sent away to Canada. And if you don't believe it, ask their father!'

Sobbing so much she could no longer speak, she stumbled down the stairs, more distressed than Amber had ever seen her.

Her own legs, as she finally rose from the bed, were unsteady. Sharyn had always been a monumental liar, but this time she had surpassed herself. Not for one minute did she believe a word of what Sharyn had said about Tony and the fire – or about Tony being at Take Six the night Angie had nearly fallen to her death – but her distress at knowing that her nasty little tricks had been rumbled had been genuine enough.

As she thought about the effect Sharyn's hysterical reaction might have on the baby, she felt decidedly queasy.

People didn't miscarry because they became hysterical – did they? If they did – and if Sharyn miscarried . . .

Disorientatedly she looked around the room, trying to locate her cigarettes and matches. They were on the crowded dressing-table. She fumbled with the box, trying to look on the positive side of things. One thing was now crystal-clear: Sharyn *had* been at Take Six the night Angie had fallen. She'd admitted it when she'd tried to incriminate Tony.

She struck a match and lit a cigarette, seeing, with shock, that her hands were trembling. What if Tony *had* been there? What if, just for once, Sharyn hadn't been lying?

It was, after all, perfectly possible that he'd become aware of what was going on between Angie and Johnny.

And if he had?

Her hand began to shake more violently still. No matter how quiet and reserved Tony was, he was still a Martini; he was still half-Sicilian; still very much an unknown quantity.

She inhaled deeply, well aware of her dilemma. Did she tell Angie what Sharyn had said about Tony, or did she keep it to herself? There was always the chance that Sharyn would confront Angie herself, but somehow she didn't think it likely.

She closed her eyes, exhaling through her nose, struggling to bring logic to her whirling thoughts. The one thing that had always made sense to her was that Zoë's accident, and Angie's, had been occasioned by the same person. And that person could not have been Tony because he had only been in England a few hours when Zoë had fallen to her death. Tony hadn't known Zoë. Hadn't even met her.

The realization that flooded through her was one she

didn't particularly want to explore. Sharyn was still the only person with a motive and, as she'd been at both the Prince of Wales and the recording studios, she'd presumably also had ample opportunity.

She cupped an elbow with a hand, the cigarette still burning as she stared unseeingly out of her bedroom window, wishing there was someone she could confide in. Once, of course, she would have confided in Fast-Boy, but he no longer had any place in her life.

The knowledge brought a stab of pain so sudden and so violent that it made her gasp.

With difficulty she steadied her breathing and fought back the tears rising in her throat.

She wouldn't think about Fast-Boy. She couldn't. It hurt too much.

For a fleeting moment she wondered if she could confide in Rob, and almost immediately dismissed the idea. In the short space of time that she'd known him, it had become obvious how conventional and law-abiding he was. Telling him that her sister was a mental case responsible for the death of one girl and for the near death of another would have him running for the hills.

Never someone who took long to make up her mind about things, she'd already decided about Rob Gowan. Though she'd one day have to break the news to him gently – very gently – that her dad was an old lag serving time in one of Her Majesty's prisons, she wanted him in her life.

He was no replacement for Fast-Boy, but he was attractive and intriguing and fun to be with.

And that, for the moment, was enough.

It was the middle of the afternoon and Marco and Maureen were in bed in a small hotel a stone's throw from Buckingham Palace. Of all the hotels that they'd used since resuming their affair, this one, quaintly named the Tiltyard, was their favourite.

'So, are you coming with me to Spain on Friday or not?' The edge in Marco's voice was one most people would have been instantly wary of.

Maureen, her naked body sheened with perspiration after their passionate lovemaking, rolled over, lying on one elbow.

'I don't know,' she said, looking down at him, her mahogany-red hair tousled but still beautiful. 'It's not just a big decision, Marco. It's a huge decision.'

'Why? Because your adult daughters and my adult sons might not like it?'

'It's not that simple.' Her eyes, as they met his, were dark with concern. 'Once our relationship becomes public knowledge, people are bound to wonder when it actually started. How long ago. And they might start to be aware of the resemblance.'

'Between me and Amber?'

He reached for the bedside table and his cigarettes and lighter. 'Perhaps it would be no bad thing if they did.' He shrugged powerful shoulders. 'I'd quite like the truth out in the open where Amber's concerned.'

'*You* might.' It was her voice, now, that had a dangerous edge to it. '*I* wouldn't.'

She pushed herself up against the pillows. 'One of our agreements was that Tommy wasn't to know about us until he came out of prison – and that isn't going to be for a while. As for Amber and thinking she could ever be told the truth . . .'

As she thought of the enormity of such a disaster, words failed her. Beneath the sheets she pulled her knees towards her chest, hugging them tight. 'That's never been part of any agreement, Marco. Tommy may not be the greatest father-figure in the world, but, as far as Amber is concerned, he's her dad. Telling her that he isn't – and that you are – is not on. Not now. Not ever.'

Marco, who had never seriously imagined it would be, lit a cigarette and handed it to her. 'Calm down – it was only a passing thought. Spain, though, isn't.' He lit the second cigarette and blew a smoke ring towards the ceiling. 'I intend being out there for quite a while this time. Three months. Maybe more. And I want you with me.'

His last sentence was under-shot with steel.

She didn't meet his eyes. Instead she looked down at her knees, her hair falling forward and curtaining her face. This was it. Decision time. Decision time in a big, big way.

She'd been in love with Marco for at least twenty-five years – ever since she'd been seventeen, the age their daughter was now. He hadn't been in love with her, though. Not then. Not way back in the forties, when the war was coming to an end and she'd been wild and reckless. In those days Marco had been so wild and reckless himself that it hadn't been a quality he'd wanted in a woman. It had been her sweet-natured, quiet friend he'd fallen for and married. And – because there had seemed so little alternative – she'd settled for his side-kick and married Tommy.

She breathed in deeply, forcing herself to remember a period of time that she'd spent years trying to forget. The years when she, surprisingly enough, had been the bride who had been reasonably happy, and the years when Sheelagh hadn't been happy at all. The years, after the twins had been born, when she and Marco had begun their affair.

She turned her head slightly, looking down at him as he waited, cigarette in hand, for her response to his last, quite categorical, statement.

Even though he was now in his fifties, it was a handsome, hard-boned, sensual face; the cheekbones high and wide; the nose Roman; the mouth thin-lipped, betraying the brutality in his nature.

It was a brutality that, for reasons she didn't know and didn't care to know, had always sexually excited her.

It hadn't excited Sheelagh.

The reality of marriage to him had been far more than Sheelagh's gentle nature had been able to bear. Though he'd never brought his work – nor business methods – home with him, she'd known about them. She'd known about the people he terrorized in order to obtain protection money; about the people he hurt in the course of his 'repo' business – forcibly repossessing money or goods from anyone and for anyone, as long as the pay was substantial enough. And she'd known, too, about the people who, if they crossed him, conveniently disappeared.

Always asthmatic, her attacks had grown worse and more frequent. The twins had been born and she'd become obsessed with the fear that they would grow up mirror images of their father. It was then that she'd begun favouring Tony. Tony, who, unlike Johnny, seemed to have so little of his father in him.

And it was then, of course, that Marco had at last turned his eyes towards her. She hadn't resisted. Even though Sheelagh was her best friend, she hadn't resisted for an instant.

She unclasped her hands, reaching out to where her cigarette was burning itself away in an ashtray on the bedside-table. Why had it never mattered to her what kind of a man Marco was? It wasn't as if she was a criminal. She'd never stolen anything. Not even as a school kid. And she'd never sold her body for sex, either.

She tapped the ash off her cigarette. So . . . not a thief. And not a whore. But a woman who was, most definitely, amoral. A woman who liked the fact that the man who bedded her was a man other men were afraid of. A woman who liked the hush that fell across any room he entered and who revelled in the tension he created around him. A woman who, after Sheelagh's death, had for ten years denied herself the pleasure of his love-making – and who knew she hadn't the will-power to deny herself again.

'Yes,' she said huskily as he blew a second smoke-ring through the first. 'Yes, I'll come to Spain with you and Albie. Yes, I'll stop pretending I can hardly bare looking at you, let alone speaking to you. Yes, to anything and everything, except to ever giving Amber a clue about the truth where you and she are concerned.'

'Agreed.' He crushed his cigarette to extinction in the ashtray and then, his eyes dark with heat, reached out for her, easing her down beside and beneath him with the strong, brutal hands that she loved.

Fast-Boy was on his way to a job, adrenaline coursing through his veins, nerves taut. Normally he would also be totally focused, not allowing his concentration to deviate for an instant. Now, though, despite the balaclava tucked in one of the outside zipped pockets of his motor-cycling leathers, and the snub-nose revolver tucked in an inside one, his concentration was anything but focused.

It was two o'clock in the morning on Bank Holiday

Monday and, as he roared over a nearly deserted Westminster Bridge, the only sound to be heard was the thumping engine-note of Ruby, the bike he now used on jobs. His up-to-the-minute Harley was too distinctive – and, as far as the police were concerned, he was too closely associated with it for it to be of use on occasions such as this.

He garaged Ruby in a lock-up near to Jed's. She was old but fast, cornering like a single-seater fighter plane, despite a wheelbase of almost two strides.

At the end of the bridge he turned left into Parliament Square, checking the time on Big Ben as he did. Timing, on a job such as the one he was heading towards, was crucial.

The disgruntled employee of a super-chic department store had tipped him off that on nights prior to public holidays – Christmas Day, Easter Monday, Bank Holidays, etc – security staffing was at a minimum, with only two men on duty.

'And while me and the other night cleaners are in the building, the alarm system's turned off so as not to cause us any inconvenience,' his informant had said with relish. 'From ten-thirty at night until half past twelve in the morning, we're on the ground floor and first floor. From half past twelve to half past two, we're on the first and second floor. From half past two to half past four, we're way up out of the way on the fourth and fifth floors. And as icing on the cake, some nights the staff entrance ain't even locked. Stupid bleeders, ain't they?'

If it were true – and he had, of course, no way of telling – then the management certainly were stupid bleeders. As always, he'd checked on everything that could be checked. On two previous public holidays he'd kept watch on the rear staff door and had noted who entered for night duty – and at what times. He'd also checked to see at what time the staff door was finally locked. His informant had been right about the lax security. On the second occasion, the door hadn't been locked at all.

'But it's still protected,' his informant had warned. 'One or other of the security blokes is in position there all the time we're doing the cleaning. Sometimes both of 'em are there, having a ciggie and a chat.'

The information hadn't deterred him, not when the prize – the ground-floor jewellery department with its display cabinets housing hundreds of designer gems – was so mouthwatering.

And his first sight of the security men as they reported for duty hadn't been daunting, either. Unlike the guards Johnny Martini hired out – thugs willing to meet violence with violence without a second's hesitation – the department store's security men were middle-aged and respectable, employed because the references they had supplied, with regard to their honesty, were so excellent.

Not for one minute did he doubt his ability to handle them.

He sped past Buckingham Palace, well aware that, ideally, he should be going into the building with at least two other people for back-up – and he wasn't. Always a loner, he was going in single-handed.

As he veered off in the direction of Hyde Park Corner, he mentally went over the equipment he'd brought with him: crowbar, hammer, strong adhesive Gaffer-tape – the kind used by builders – blindfolds, rope. Everything was in a sports bag in the pannier he had strapped to the back of the bike. The hard bulk of the handgun was snug against his chest. All he had to do now was focus on the job in hand.

And all he could think about was Amber.

Amber being made love to by Detective-Sergeant Rob Gowan.

In jealous rage he slewed the bike around Hyde Park Corner. Did Amber know her boyfriend was a copper? A copper who had a decided interest in Johnny?

From somewhere in the distance came the faint sound of a police car siren. It was too far away to be chasing him, but exerting great self-control he slowed down to an inoffensive speed, knowing that if he were stopped by the police, tooled-up as he was, he'd never see the inside of any department store. Not for years.

Amber. Why the *hell* hadn't he realized that if Angie was in a nightclub, Amber was bound to be with her? Why the *fuck* hadn't he controlled his temper? He hadn't even been out looking for Angie. He'd been out looking for Johnny.

But Angie had been there – the perfect substitute to unleash his rage on. And Amber had witnessed that rage. She had seen him punch and kick Angie and, from that moment on, had been lost to him.

Now she was with Rob Gowan – a copper, for Christ's sake.

But did she know he was a copper? And if she didn't – and if he told her – what would happen then?

He eased the bike into a long, brilliantly lit stretch of Kensington Gore, wondering what would happen if he told her a few other things. That Johnny was screwing her friend, Tilly, for instance.

He slowed Ruby down until the engine was merely a dull throb and turned off into a darkened side street that led to a square a stone's throw from the department store's rear entrance.

There was no one about; not even a tramp or a drunk.

He parked up and hoisted the sports bag from the pannier.

As he began walking towards the store's rear staff entrance, he pulled the balaclava from his pocket and yanked it over his head.

And as the rough wool scratched his skin, he finally stopped thinking about Amber.

From Kensington Gore and nearby Cromwell Road there came the dull sound of intermittent traffic. Somewhere not too far away a street fox barked. High above him, on the second and third floors, lights flicked off. On the fourth and fifth floors, as the cleaners moved upwards, they flicked on.

He looked down at the luminous hands on his watch. It was two-thirty and he was going to give himself thirty minutes. Not a second more.

He reached out and tried the door.

It was locked.

It made absolutely no difference to him.

With icy calm, he raised a gloved hand and knocked with all the belligerence of a householder locked out of his own home. A minute or so later, as he heard steps approaching from the other side of the door, he reached into his leather bomber jacket for his gun.

The footsteps at the other side came to a halt.

He knocked again. 'Come on, mate!' he shouted, calculated impatience in his voice. 'Open up, for Christ's sake! I'm late enough without you making me any bleedin' later!'

'And you are?'

The voice was so punctiliously correct that for a brief moment Fast-Boy wondered if he was being over optimistic about his chosen method of entry.

'I'm a late cleaner, you eejit,' he shouted in response. 'Now open the friggin' door, will yer?'

There came the sound of grumbling and then he heard the rattle of keys as, from among many, one was selected and, with painful slowness, inserted in the lock.

Once it turned he didn't wait for the door to be opened.

He barged it open with such suddenness and ferocity that the man on the other side of it was sent stumbling to his knees.

One of them. That was what he registered as he kicked the door shut behind him, jammed the gun below the man's ear and dropped the sports bag to the floor. Only one security guard had come to answer the door.

'Stay on your knees and do exactly as I say!' With his free hand he yanked the strong adhesive-tape from the bag. 'Hands behind your back and clasp them tight.'

'Don't shoot me! Please God, don't shoot me!'

The man was easily in his fifties and his knees kept collapsing beneath him as, with one-handed expertise, Fast-Boy whipped the Gaffer-tape round his wrists.

'Where's the other guy?'

'What . . . what other . . . guy?' It was a brave try from a man terrified out of his wits, but Fast-Boy wasn't in the mood for brave tries.

'Your mate! Where the fuck is he?'

The man's attempt at defiance abandoned him. 'The k-k-k-kitchen,' he stuttered. 'He's in the k-k-k-kitchen, m-m-m-making tea.'

Fast-Boy knew where the staff kitchen was, just as he knew where the store-room nearest to the staff entrance was. It was all part of the almost military precision with which he planned any job.

'The kitchen is at the end of the first corridor you come to,' his informant had told him helpfully. 'Bang next to the service lifts. There's a small store room, used for Royal Mail parcels, immediately to the right of the staff entrance door.'

Satisfied that he wasn't being lied to, Fast-Boy slapped Gaffer-tape across the man's mouth and then hissed: 'On your feet.'

It was a command the petrified man needed help with. Well aware of how the minutes were ticking away, Fast-Boy hauled him upwards and manhandled him towards the small store room, pushing him inside so roughly that he fell. 'Stay on the floor.'

How long had he taken so far? Five minutes? Six? As he began rapidly taping the man's knees together and then his ankles, he glanced at his watch. It was two thirty-six.

He threw the roll of tape back into his sports bag, took a precious second to ascertain that no footsteps were heading down the passage towards him – which meant security guard number two was still unaware of anything amiss – and, bag in one hand, gun again in the other, began running on rubber-soled feet in the direction of the staff kitchen.

'Who was it at the door, Marty?' asked the man standing with his back towards him, pouring boiling water from a kettle into a mug.

Fast-Boy didn't answer him. With the speed which had given him his nickname, he closed the distance between them and, just as the man finally began to turn his head, jammed the pistol against his temple. 'On your knees! Don't make a sound!'

The kettle clattered to the floor, water shooting from its spout in a scalding stream.

'Okay! Okay!' Despite the gun at his head, the man lifted lightly shod feet from the floor in a skipping movement to avoid the boiling liquid. 'Whatever you say – just tell me you haven't hurt Marty!'

Fast-Boy had no intention of wasting his breath saying any such thing. How many minutes had ticked away now? Nine? Ten? 'On your knees!' he roared savagely as the kettle rolled away into a corner.

'Fuck!' the man said with passion as he did as he was told. 'Fuck. Fuck. *Fuck*.' He was younger than his colleague and Fast-Boy knew that, if it hadn't been for the gun, he would have put up a fight.

'Hands behind your back. Clasp them tight!'

The Gaffer-tape did its magic. Hands bound. Knees bound. Ankles bound. Mouth sealed. Then, just for good measure, a blindfold tied tight. As he ran for the door, he took a swift glance at his watch. It was two forty-three. The time he had allotted himself was running out fast.

He began to run in the direction of the store proper. He knew exactly where the jewellery department was – had recce'd it many times. He knew which top-flight designers had display cabinets there and he knew roughly the kind of jewellery he would find in them. Jed was his fence and Jed had told him exactly what he wanted: 'Gold chains, gold bracelets, diamond rings, amethysts, pearls, wristwatches. Nothing too individualistic. Nothing with stylized engravings. Nothing instantly traceable.' Well, once again, on his visits to the store as a would-be customer, he had done his homework. The only snag was, he had so little time to smash his way into the cabinets.

He ran out of the staff corridor and this time, instead of a gun in one hand, he had a powerful torch. He sprinted though the haberdashery section; through the handbags and gloves section; through perfumery. It was a run he could have done in complete darkness if need be. No alarms went off. No lights burst on. He was in the jewellery section. Display cases glinted in the torch-light. Jewels shimmered.

He drew to a panting halt, threw the sports bag to the carpeted floor and yanked the crowbar and the hammer from its depths. This was the moment – the moment when the sound of splintering glass shattered the silence – that brought even his nerves to a crescendo pitch.

He honed in on the display cabinet he had earlier decided was to be his first priority, lifted the hammer and brought it down with a God Almighty crash. And again. And again. The noise and the reverberations seemed to go on for ever.

Even though they were on the fourth and fifth floors and probably had a score of hoovers going, surely the cleaners would hear the mayhem he was wreaking? Whether they could or not, he'd no intention of stopping. He scooped watches by the score out of the cabinet and into the sports bag. Gold chains. A pearl-and-sapphire choker.

What was the time? Two-fifty-five. Two fifty-six. The next cabinet needed an attack with the crowbar after it had been smashed with the hammer. He was running over time – something he *never* did.

Rings spilled free.

Engagement rings; eternity rings; dress rings; signet rings. Solitaire diamonds; baguette diamonds; cabochon diamonds. Sapphire hoops; emerald clusters; amethyst crossovers; opal twists. Blood-red garnets; sizzling-blue aquamarines; honey-gold topaz.

With a wide sweep of his arm he showered the cabinet's entire contents into his bag. There were other cabinets. Lots of cabinets. And no alarms going. No sirens approaching. It was one minute past three. Two minutes past three. It would take him four minutes, perhaps five, to get clear of the building. That would take him ten minutes over the time he had allotted himself. He couldn't stay a minute longer. No matter how rich the pickings still remaining, he had to leave. He had to leave *now*.

Again he was running. Running back through perfumery. Running back through the handbags and gloves section. Running back through haberdashery. Into the staff area. Down the steps. Into the corridor that led to the staff entry and exit door.

He sped past the kitchen, from which no sounds of any sort came. Christ, but he hoped he'd taped the geezer's mouth properly and that he hadn't accidentally suffocated him. There was movement from the small storage room next to the door. He didn't pause to check, but his instincts told him that Marty was well on the way to freeing himself from his bonds.

He dragged the door open and half fell into the blessedly empty, blessedly dark street. There were still no alarms; still no sirens. He sprinted towards the bike, his heart hammering like a piston, his hands sweating inside his gloves as he crammed the sports bag into the pannier. He'd done it! Christ Almighty, but he'd done it! He'd single-handedly carried out a mammoth jewel raid, *and he was going to get away with it*.

He kicked Ruby into life and roared out of the square, heading for Cromwell Road. He mustn't speed. He mustn't ruin everything now. Nice and decorous, that was how he had to ride. Jed would be waiting up for him in his council flat at Rotherhithe and in fifteen minutes, maybe less, his haul would be glimmering and gleaming on Jed's kitchen table.

Very faintly he thought he could hear the sound of police sirens. Had Marty managed to reach one of the department stores' phones? Were police cars already screaming down into Knightsbridge?

He dragged his balaclava off and stuffed it inside his motorcycle jacket. It didn't matter if they were. He was halfway through Chelsea now, heading for the spangled lights of the Albert Bridge.

As he zoomed over the dark, liquid beauty of the Thames only one thing marred his almost orgasmic euphoria.

Amber wouldn't be at Jed's waiting for him.

Amber had vowed never to wait for him ever again.

He cruised past Battersea Park, his eyes narrowed, his lips tight, determined that, in the morning, *he* would be waiting for *her*.

Chapter Fifteen

'I'm off and I won't be back till early afternoon,' David Lampeter said to Amber and Tilly as he lifted his jacket from the hat-stand that served as the office cloakroom. 'I've a number of properties to value and I might as well do them all in one fell swoop. Amber, if Mrs Ainsworth comes in, asking for the keys to 17 Rushden Place, she can be given them. Contracts were exchanged Saturday. I really appreciate you girls coming in when it's a Bank Holiday, but this business isn't like most businesses.' He shrugged himself into his jacket. 'Bank Holidays are when couples take advantage of an extra day off together and like to browse for properties at their leisure. With a bit of luck, the two of you will be kept busy.'

'Silly sod,' Tilly said as the glass door closed behind him and he strode off up the street in the general direction of Blackheath. 'Anyone looking for houses on Bank Holiday Monday needs their head seeing to.'

Amber, who never minded working Bank Holidays as long as she was suitably rewarded financially for doing so – which she was – slammed a filing cabinet drawer shut and turned to face Tilly, saying as she did so: 'When it comes to people needing their heads seeing to, Tilly, you're first in line.'

Tilly's delicately pencilled eyebrows shot upwards.

'*Excuse* me?' she said, as if unable to believe that she'd heard correctly. 'What bee's got into your bonnet this morning? Is that boring boyfriend of yours giving you

250

a hard time because you're working today when you could both have been down at Southend or Brighton?'

'Rob isn't boring and he's meeting me later on and taking me to the fair,' Amber said tartly, well aware that as Johnny was, for once, spending the day as a family man with Sharyn, Tilly was the one with her nose out of joint.

She leaned against the filing cabinet, her gold-brocade-trousered legs crossed at the ankle, her arms folded across a yellow T-shirt emblazoned with a gigantic diamanté butterfly. 'And this little chat isn't about me, Tilly. It's about you. You and my brother-in-law.'

Tilly gave a gasp of shock and then, rapidly trying to turn it into a gasp of outrage, said indignantly: 'I don't know what you're talking about. I don't mess with married men. If I did, my mum would have my guts for garters.'

'I don't suppose your mum knows. But I do.' Amber unfolded her arms and crossed the room. 'I've seen you with him,' she said, seating herself on the corner of Tilly's reception desk and eyeballing her grimly. 'And even though my sister's having a baby – and I think you're a slut and a slag – I'm not about to pull your hair out in clumps over it. I've known Johnny ever since I was born and, believe me, if he wasn't being unfaithful with you, he'd be being unfaithful with someone else.

'That's not true! Johnny . . .'

'Shut up and *listen*, Tilly!'

At the ferocity in Amber's eyes and voice, Tilly abandoned all thoughts of either continuing to deny her affair with Johnny or attempting to defend it. Instead, shoulders rigid, she remained silent, her lips in a mutinous pout.

Amber breathed in hard. Putting into words her fears

where Sharyn was concerned wasn't going to be easy, but it had to be done – for Sharyn's sake, as well as Tilly's.

'When girls go out with Johnny, Tilly, they get *hurt*. They –'

Tilly snorted in derision. 'By Johnny? That isn't true – and it just shows that you don't know him half as well as you think you do! Johnny is very tough and he frightens a lot of people, but he'd never hurt me, not in a million years. He *loves* me, and . . .'

'Wise up, Tilly! I'm not talking about *Johnny* hurting the girls he two-times Sharyn with – I'm talking about *Sharyn* hurting them!'

Tilly opened her mouth to continue saying how much Johnny loved her, registered what Amber had just said, and gaped at her, goggle-eyed.

Then she began to laugh.

'You think I should be frightened of your sister? Do me a favour, Amber. Sharyn wouldn't *dare* hurt me. For one thing, she'd be frightened of what Johnny would do to her if she did and, for another, I'm quite capable of looking after myself, thank you very much.'

'Johnny doesn't know what Sharyn's done,' Amber said bluntly, hoping the day would never come when he would have to be told. 'But *I* know. And the girls in question were very, very seriously hurt, Tilly.'

She paused, knowing that if she told Tilly one of the girls had been killed and the other had been lamed for life she would most certainly have Tilly's attention, but realizing that she couldn't, for, if she did, Tilly would tell Johnny. And what Johnny would do if he knew Sharyn had been responsible for Zoë Fairminder's death was something she didn't want to even imagine.

'Well, *I'm* not going to be hurt.' Tilly folded her arms

and brazenly locked eyes with her. 'And I don't care that you know about me and Johnny. In fact, I'm glad. He's going to leave your sister – he's only staying with her till the baby's born because he feels sorry for her. Once it's born, he's going to take me to Spain.'

Amber knew that out of loyalty to Sharyn she should be giving Tilly the slapping of her life. And, if it hadn't been for Tilly suddenly looking past her, towards the door, and saying, 'There's a customer about to come in,' she probably would have.

'Just watch your feet when you're on an edge with a long drop below you or when you're standing at the top of a flight of stairs,' she said grimly as the door to the street opened behind her. 'Because if you're not careful, Tilly, you might have a very nasty fall.'

Tilly wasn't listening to her. She was looking at the customer who had just entered and, seeing the expression in Tilly's eyes and the unpleasant little smile that was on her face, Amber swung round.

'I'd like a word,' Fast-Boy said, all insouciant cool in a black leather bomber jacket, black T-shirt, black metal-studded jeans and motorcycle boots.

Amber held her tongue, determined not to argue the toss in front of Tilly.

'I'm taking a coffee-break,' she said, without looking at Tilly. 'I'll be back in fifteen minutes.' Then, without bothering to look at Fast-Boy either, she strode out of the office.

Seconds later, the door reverberating behind him, he was beside her on the sun-scorched street.

'I don't need this, Ewan,' she said fiercely, knowing that a vicious slanging match was inevitable and not wanting to have it in the middle of a pavement thronged with holiday-makers.

She began heading in the direction of the quieter area around the Naval College, adding for good measure: 'I particularly don't need this today, OK?'

'Why? Because you're having to work when you'd rather be with the new boyfriend?' His voice dripped venom.

Tears stung the backs of her eyes. It had been so good between them, once. He had been her friend – her *real* friend. Angie apart, she'd never had a close girlfriend. Somehow, because of having Fast-Boy in her life, she'd never felt the need of one. Then he'd become her boyfriend – though no one had known, at least not for sure. And now he was – nothing. Not a friend; not a boyfriend. Nothing.

'I've no intention of discussing my private life with you,' she hit back waspishly, avoiding a child with an ice-cream as she rounded the corner into Nelson Road.

'Fine by me, because I reckon you don't know enough about it to discuss it with anyone.'

She came to a halt outside a crowded wine bar. 'Just what the *hell*,' she demanded, swinging round to face him, 'do you mean by a crack like that?'

He shrugged, his thumbs hooked nonchalantly in the front pockets of his jeans, his night-black hair falling in a cow-lick over his forehead. 'What do you know about your boyfriend?' he asked, looking so damn sexy her ache of longing was a physical pain. 'Do you know where he works? Where he goes and what he does when he's not with you?' He paused, a malicious glint in his eyes. 'Do you know *why* he's dating you?'

Amber stood very still, aware of her breath coming fast and light and aware of very little else. Though she no longer liked him – *couldn't* like him after what he had done to Angie – she knew Fast-Boy. She knew the way he went about things and she knew that he would know the answer to every question he was asking – and that the answers were going to be very unpleasant or he wouldn't be going out of his way to make her wise to them.

'I know enough,' she said tightly, as a crocodile of tourists threaded past them, following their guide to the river frontage and the *Cutty Sark*. 'So he's a civil servant and not a flashy criminal? So what? *You* might equate earning an honest living with being boring, but *I* don't. I've had enough of thieves and thieves' ponces, thank you very much. What good has being a villain ever done my dad? And what Rob does and where he goes when I'm not with him is none of my affair. Or yours.'

People kept bumping into them as they entered or left the wine bar. It was an affront Fast-Boy would normally have reacted to. But he was as oblivious as she was to what was going on around them. 'And when did this little transformation take place, Red?' he asked nastily. 'Before you started dating a copper, or after?'

For all its grandiose name, Nelson Road was only a short linking road between King William Walk, which led to one of the bottom entrances to Greenwich Park, and Greenwich Church Street, which led to the Thames and the *Cutty Sark*. As a consequence, on any day of the week it was busy with tourists. Today, a Bank Holiday, it was packed with them.

As far as Amber was concerned, it could have been as barren as the moon.

'Rob isn't a copper,' she said through dry lips. 'He's a civil servant.'

'Coppers are civil servants.' Fast-Boy cocked his head to one side. 'Seems to me that lover-boy has been fudging the truth a little.'

There was something else in his eyes now besides the gleam of maliciousness. There was speculation. 'He's a Detective-Sergeant working out of Tower Bridge nick, and if you want to know why he's lit on you for a girl-friend, he's a cozzer with a very special interest in Johnny Martini. 'Nuff said? Get the picture?'

As her eyes held his, a wave of nausea almost engulfed her. Telling him he was a liar would be pointless. Fast-Boy had never lied to her and she knew that he wasn't lying to her now. The label of cozzer was one that fitted Rob all too well, with his unfashionably short hair, old-fogey dress-style and straight-down- the-line attitude to life.

She remembered her nervousness when she'd told him that her dad was an old lag and her relief when he'd merely shrugged, as if her old man being in prison didn't matter to him one jot.

How secretly amused he must have been by her confession, for he would have known, from their very first date, that her dad had a criminal record as long as a gorilla's arm.

From the nearby river there came the sound of a tug's horn and from somewhere else, probably the park entrance, there came the insistent jingle of an ice-cream van's bell.

'How do you know Rob has a special interest in Johnny?' she asked, her voice seeming to come from as far away as the ice-cream bell. 'Do you really know, or are you just guessing?'

'I really know. If you doubt my word for it, have a word with Donnie Crosby. You've never let him – or Johnny, or any of Johnny's friends – know who your boyfriend is, have you? Why don't you give it a whirl and see what reaction you meet with?'

'Maybe I will,' she said tautly, her face as white as a cameo as she remembered the situation in which Rob had first asked her out for a drink. Tilly had been showing him a photograph taken at Johnny and Sharyn's wedding and she had smartly plucked it from his hand. He had known then, of course, who she was. How could he not, when she had been standing beside Sharyn, dressed as her bridesmaid?

He had known and, typical cozzer, had seized his opportunity. What had he done when he had returned home after every one of their dates? Had he filled in a report form? Were details of their relationship common knowledge amongst his colleagues at Tower Bridge nick? The realization of how she must have been laughed at slammed into her with crucifying force. Then another thought came so hard on its heels that whirling black spots distorted her vision. *What had she told him that would be useful to him? So useful that he had wanted to make his relationship with her a long-standing one?*

'About me losing my temper with Angie . . .' Fast-Boy was saying, his hand on her arm, his eyes dark with intensity. 'It was out of order, Red. It shouldn't have happened and I just want you to know that I'm . . .'

She wasn't listening to him. She had to see Rob Gowan to tell him exactly what she thought of his information-gathering technique. And she had to see him *now*.

Without even giving a thought to what David Lampeter's reaction was going to be when he returned to the office to find her long gone – and long gone without any explanation – she twisted away from Fast-Boy and began to run.

Weaving in and out of holiday-makers, she sprinted back into Greenwich Church Street where there were several bus stops – one of them for a bus that would take her straight to Tower Bridge.

There was no way she could know if Rob would be on duty – their arrangement for the day had been that they would meet at the Prince of Wales pub on the Heath at six o'clock and then go on to the fair – but that he would be there was as good a guess as any other.

There was a bus just drawing away from the stop and, careless of life and limb, she hurled herself on to its platform.

'Careful, young lady!' the conductor shouted as the bus sped round a corner and she struggled to regain her balance. 'What are you trying to do? End everything?'

Heaving for breath, her heart slamming, Amber didn't bother answering him. The question was spot on, though. She *was* going to end everything. Not her life, which was what he had sarcastically meant, but everything in her life relating to Rob Gowan.

Rob was typing up a report, but his mind wasn't on it. It was on a rape case that had been adjourned because a key prosecution witness had failed to turn up. The case in question wasn't one he'd had any part in bringing to court. He had only become involved when his guv'nor had asked him to escort the victim to a similar trial at the Old Bailey – the idea being that time spent in the public gallery would help make courtroom procedure seem a little less strange and intimidating to her when she had to give evidence on her own behalf.

'And make no mistake, Gowan,' DI Ramsden had said grimly, 'rape victims are given a very rough ride in our courts. The defence lawyers will present her to the court as a liar, or as a woman of loose morals. The girl in question is eighteen, but a young and inexperienced eighteen. When she was first interviewed she didn't even know the correct terms to describe some of the things that were done to her. A WPC had to explain them. So I want her forewarned about the ordeal she'll face in the witness box, and the best way of doing that is for her to see someone else undergoing questioning of a similar kind. It'll come as a shock to her, believe you me.'

It had come as a shock to him, as well.

He yanked the finished report out of his typewriter. Seeing a woman go through the hell of having to describe, in distressed detail, every appalling act that had been perpetrated against her – while the perpetrator lounged in the dock only yards away – and then to be a witness to her anguish as she was sneeringly branded a pathological liar and attention-seeker by the defence counsel, had not been a pleasant experience. Not for the first time, it had occurred to him that some witnesses were put under more stress than anyone should be expected to handle.

He flipped the report into his out-tray, well aware of other types of witnesses too stressed to function as they should, too scared to give statements. The type of witnesses who made it impossible for charges to be successfully brought against men such as Marco and Johnny Martini.

'It's the Sicilian in them,' a fellow DS had said darkly when the investigation into Johnny Martini had ground to a halt. 'Scaring the living shit out of witnesses and promising victims death if they blab is second nature to them. Take that Thai houseboy a few years back: we know for a fact it was Marco Martini who beat him to pulp and then tied him to a chair and threw him down two flights of stairs. But would the Thai press charges? Would he, fuck. Everything he said when we interviewed him in the hospital, he retracted the minute it came to his giving a signed statement. The same thing always happens with Johnny. Ask a witness to give a statement and they haven't seen anything. They weren't beaten up. They weren't robbed. As far as they're concerned, Martini is a drink with an olive in it. So, unless we get someone to grass on him in a big, big way, we're never going to get him behind bars.'

Rob pushed his chair away from his desk bad-temperedly. For months he'd hoped Little Donnie would be the chink in Johnny's armour; that something would eventually happen between Johnny and Donnie that would make the latter so resentful he'd come running to him and spill the beans – especially the beans about Jimmy Jones' disappearance. Donnie, however, hadn't come running – and didn't seem likely to do so.

Even though he tried not to let them, thinking about Johnny sent his thoughts swivelling to Amber.

Oblivious of the comings and goings at the other desks in the big room, he mooched across to the nearest window and stared broodingly out of it, his hands thrust deep in his pockets. A relationship that had started, on his part, purely as an exercise in information-gathering, had almost instantly changed into something far different.

In old-fashioned parlance, Amber Bailey was the girl for him. He knew it in his blood and bones. And he also knew that he couldn't have both Amber and a high-flying career in the Force. The two were simply not compatible.

You're marrying Johnny Martini's sister-in-law? He could just imagine his Chief Inspector saying. *Congratulations, Gowan. I hope the two of you will be very happy.* It was a scenario as likely as hell freezing over.

Even if it weren't, once she knew he was a copper, Amber would never, not in a million years, accept any proposal of marriage that he might make. Time and again he'd tried to get her to open up to him about Johnny Martini – in the beginning because he'd wanted information, later because he'd wanted to hear her condemn Johnny's way of life – and never once had she said a dickie-bird.

It hadn't been the silence of fear. He was familiar with that kind of silence and would have recognized it immediately. It had been the silence of condoning complicity. Though not a criminal herself, she had pledged her loyalty to criminals. Where her father was concerned it was at least understandable. Where Johnny and Marco Martini were concerned, there could be no excuse. And, unbeknown to her, Rob was deep in the enemy camp. Once she knew the truth about him, not only would she refuse to marry him, she'd probably refuse ever to see him again.

And once his superiors knew the nature of his relationship with her, it would be goodbye not only to his promotion hopes but to plainclothes as well. He'd be back in uniform, back on a beat, as fast as Ramsden could blink.

His jaw tightened. It was an impossible situation and it left him . . . where? Up shit creek without a paddle was the crude answer. If he wasn't careful, he was going to end up with no career and no girl, either.

'Coming down the canteen, Rob?' one of his colleagues shouted across to him.

The thought of canteen coffee wasn't particularly inspiring, but it was better than nothing and he certainly wasn't in the mood for more paperwork. 'Yup. I'll be right with you,' he said, turning away from the window.

As he did, a movement at the far side of the street caught his eye. A bus had just drawn up and the girl jumping from its platform looked amazingly like Amber; she had the same riotous mane of sizzling red hair, the same petite, curvaceous figure . . .

Christ! He swung back to the window again. It *was* Amber. And she was sprinting hell-for-leather across the busy road, uncaring of the traffic veering to avoid her as she headed, in an unerring beeline, for the front entrance of the police station.

He moved so fast he almost fell. Whatever the reason for her visit, it certainly wasn't to report a cat stuck up a tree. Somehow she'd learned that he was a copper and that he could be found here, at Tower Bridge nick.

'What the fuck, Rob!' someone said indignantly as he barged past them, sprinting for the door and the stairs that led to the street.

Unheedingly he began running down the stairs, taking the bottom three in a flying leap. He had to get to her before she came into the reception area; before she spoke to the desk-sergeant; before the kind of scene he knew was about to take place unfolded in front of his colleagues.

'What's up, Gowan? Do you need help?' the desk-sergeant asked as he flew past.

'No!' he roared as the palm of his hand hit the swing door. Christ. Help was the last thing he needed. What he needed was privacy. What he needed was for what was happening not to be happening at all.

As he burst out on to the pavement she was only yards away, hurtling toward him at what seemed to be the speed of light, her breasts heaving beneath a skimpy citrus-yellow T-shirt and the blaze of a diamanté butter-fly.

'Amber! Just listen to me for a moment . . . please!'

As they came to an abrupt collision he grabbed hold of her.

Eyes blazing, panting for breath, she spat full in his face.

'Amber! For Christ's sake . . . !' He let go of her with one hand in order to fumble for a handkerchief. 'Amber . . . let me at least explain . . .'

'You don't need to explain!' she shouted as fellow pedestrians hastily began giving them a wide berth. 'I *know!* You're filth, Rob Gowan. *Filth!* What did you put in your reports? Did you detail every time we made love? And where? No wonder you were always so interested in my family! In Johnny! You're scum, do you know that? You're lower than any of the criminals I know! You're . . .'

What else he was, she didn't get chance to tell him.

As he desperately tried to get a word in edgeways in an effort to calm her down so that they could at least begin talking rationally, a motorbike roared towards them; screeched to the kerb; came to a halt, engine running.

'I love you,' he said fiercely as she finally paused for breath. 'I love you and I want to marry you! I don't care about the job. I don't care about . . .'

She wasn't listening to him. He was offering her the rest of his life; forfeiting all he'd ever worked for and dreamed about *and she wasn't even listening*.

'Come on, Red!' the James Dean look-alike on the bike was shouting. 'Let's go!'

She went. Without another word. Without a backward look. One minute she was a human tornado, spitting abuse at him; the next she was sprinting towards the bike.

'Amber!' he shouted disbelievingly. '*Amber!*'

Though he raced after her, he was too late. She was astride the bike; her arms were around the waist of the leather-clad rider and they were speeding off down the road, way over the speed limit for a built-up area.

Out of habit, he noted the registration number of the bike and then, forcing his heartbeats down to something approaching normal, he turned and began to trudge back towards the station.

'That was a bit of a tidy scene,' the desk-sergeant said as he shouldered the doors open. 'I could hear it even in here.'

With all the timing of a stand-up comedian he said nothing else until Rob had crossed the reception area, then added: 'Reckon the Guv'nor could, as well. His office looks out over the street and, on a day like this, his windows will be open. He wants a word with you, anyway. And smartish.'

Rob gritted his teeth. One thing was for sure, even if he had to tell Ramsden about his relationship with Johnny Martini's sister-in-law, he could at least tell him, with utter truthfulness, that the relationship was now as dead as a dodo.

'Take me straight home,' Amber said fiercely to Fast-Boy above the roar of the Harley's engine. 'I don't want to talk. Not to you. Not to anyone. I just want to be on my own, okay?'

'That's fine by me, Red.' Fast-Boy carefully kept the elation he was feeling out of his voice. Things were going to be just like they used to be. He had his girl back and Rob Gowan was history.

He dropped her off outside her front gate, thought about saying something and then, seeing the expression on her face, decided against it.

Grateful for his silence, Amber let herself into the house, wanting only a strong cup of tea and bed. She might as well have wished for the moon.

'Amber? Is that you, Amber?' With hysteria in her voice, Sharyn came storming out of the kitchen. 'You will never believe this! You will never believe what Mum has just said she's going to do!'

Through the open kitchen door Amber could see her mother leaning against the sink, a mug of tea in her hand. If Sharyn seemed nearly out of her mind with distress, their mother looked remarkably calm and cool.

'What?' she asked wearily, wondering if the kettle was still hot. 'What is it Mum has just said she's going to do?'

'She's going to go and live in Spain with Mr Martini!' Tears of disbelief were spilling down Sharyn's face. 'With Johnny's *dad!*' she said, as if there could be the remotest doubt as to which Mr Martini this could be. 'With my *father-in-law*!' she finished for good measure on a howl of anguish.

Amber stood very still. Her own private life was in such hell, she wouldn't have thought any news could grab her attention – but this did.

Her mother and Marco.

It was something she'd been suspicious of for years. She remembered the first time she'd seen them together, when she'd been with Fast-Boy, riding through Shoreham.

Over Sharyn's shoulder, her eyes met her mother's. 'Is it true?' she asked stonily. 'Are you and Marco having an affair?'

Maureen nodded.

'And are you going to go to Spain with him? Are you going to live there?'

Maureen put her mug of tea down on the draining-board and walked out into the hallway, towards them. 'Yes, I'm going to Spain with him, but we're going for three months or so. I'm not going to live there permanently.'

'And what about Dad?' Her throat was so tight she could hardly get the words out. 'Where does he figure in this cosy little arrangement?'

'My relationship with your dad, is mine and your dad's business, Amber. Not yours.'

Maureen's voice was flat and bleak, and Amber knew her mother wasn't enjoying the scene now taking place any more than she and Sharyn were.

'Why are you being so *calm* about it, Amber?' Sharyn shrieked, her distress even deeper than when Amber had accused her of being responsible for Zoë Fairminder's death and Angie's fall. 'What if she divorces Dad and marries Marco? Have you thought of that? How can my mother be my husband's stepmother? What's my Johnny going to say when *he's* told about it? It's disgusting, that's what it is!' She barrelled past Amber towards the front door. 'Mum's *forty-two!* She shouldn't be having sex with anyone – and even if she is, she shouldn't be having it with a man like . . . like *Marco!*'

She yanked the door open and then slammed it behind her.

It was suddenly very quiet in the hallway.

Amber drew in a deep, steadying breath and then said words she never thought she'd hear herself speak. 'I'm with Sharyn on this, Mum. Absolutely. Dad might not be the most brilliant husband in the world, but he loves you. You're out of order. Way out of order.'

Her mother flinched and said nothing, presumably because she had nothing else to say. Sick at heart, Amber went up to her room and closed the door.

For a long time she did nothing but sit on the edge of the bed. It had been a pearler of a day. First there'd been the scene with Tilly, then the scene with Fast-Boy. Then the scene with Rob had put everything else into the shade – or it had until she'd come home.

What would happen when her mother and Marco returned from Spain? Would they then live together openly? Would her mother perhaps move in next door? And what would Johnny and Tony's reactions be, if she did? They'd adored their dead mother – and their mother had been her mother's best friend. It would raise all kinds of questions and resentments.

Pain beat above her eyes and she lay down on the bed, longing for sleep.

Forty-five minutes later, the ringing of the telephone in the hall jarred her awake. As she heard her mother walk out of the sitting-room to answer it, she wondered if the caller was Marco.

She was just closing her eyes again when her mother screamed.

Terrified, she jack-knifed from the bed and raced out of the room. As she reached the head of the stairs, her mother looked upwards, horrified eyes locking on hers.

'It's Johnny,' she gasped, the telephone receiver still in her hand. 'He's found Sharyn at the bottom of the steps that lead into their wine cellar. The ambulance is on its way, but he thinks she's going to lose the baby. Oh God, Amber! What if she does? What if it's all my fault? What if she fell because she was upset and crying and couldn't see properly?'

As Amber hurtled down the stairs, her mother dropped the receiver. 'Johnny says the ambulance will be taking her to St Thomas',' she said, shaking uncontrollably. 'Will you drive me there? I'm in no state to drive. Oh, please God, don't let Sharyn lose the baby! I couldn't bear it! I'd blame myself till the day I died.'

'Give me the car keys, Mum. Let's get going.'

Outwardly calm and efficient, inwardly Amber felt as if her head was about to explode. Stairs. *Stairs.* The word hammered in her brain as the two of them ran out of the house. It was stairs again. Yet another fall. Yet another accident.

She yanked the car door open and threw herself behind the wheel, aware that this time it wasn't a fall stage-managed by Sharyn. It couldn't be. No matter how much of an attention-seeker Sharyn was, she would never do anything that might harm her baby. This time the fall was an accident. It had to be. There was no alternative.

Or was there?

Her fingers slippery with sweat, she turned the key in the ignition, the monstrous question ricocheting around her brain like a time-bomb: what if there was? Dear God in heaven, *what if there was?*

Chapter Sixteen

'So how did it happen, Johnny?' Tony asked as they surveyed the almost empty first floor of the warehouse. 'What was she doing, going down into the cellar in the first place? Wine isn't Sharyn's tipple, is it?'

Johnny slid his hands into the pockets of his expensively tailored trousers. 'Maureen had just told her about her plans for going to Spain – so she was upset, natch. And I don't only keep wine down in the cellar, Tone. I keep spirits down there, as well.'

As they continued walking across bare, dusty floorboards, he chewed the corner of his lip. 'It's how the cat got trapped down there that puzzles me. It was so thin, it must have been down there for days. Sharyn says the minute she opened the door it sprang up the stairs, out of the darkness, like a creature from a horror movie. It was trying to get past her, I s'pose, but she thought it was leaping for her face.'

'And she lost her balance fending it off, and fell?'

'Something like that.' He came to a halt, saying with surprise in his voice, 'You know, Tone. If that fall had been curtains for Sha, it would have slaughtered me. I didn't realize till this happened just how much Sha means to me.'

Tony came to a halt a couple of feet ahead of him and turned to face him, his astonishment transparent. 'I knew you were pretty concerned, but I thought you were more worried she'd lost the baby. I mean, I've never really reckoned you and Sharyn as being a permanent couple. I've always had the feeling there was still someone else in your life, someone you've not let on about.'

Johnny's eyes slid away from his. 'Yeah?' he said, as if genuinely taken aback that his twin should have thought such a situation possible. 'Well, what happened to Sha has shown me I'm not up for those sorts of capers. She's still in St Thomas', but you know that, don't you?'

As Tony nodded, Johnny began walking to the far side of the warehouse again. In some respects it was a good thing that Tony no longer seemed able to read his mind, as he had when they'd been kids. It meant his affair with Tilly was something he didn't have to defend or explain – and with Sha in hospital after nearly losing the baby, that was a relief. He missed the mental closeness, though. Most of all, he missed the fact that *he* couldn't read Tony's mind. Sometimes he wondered if he ever had been able to, or if the ability had only ever existed in his imagination.

He slowed down, saying fiercely: 'This pig's ear where Sha's mum is concerned – how do you really feel about it, Tone? And what the fuck are we going to *do* about it?'

'Maureen and the old man?' Tony quirked an eyebrow. Though not wearing a suit, as Johnny was, his style of dress nowadays was a far cry from the T-shirt and jeans he'd habitually worn when he'd first arrived back in England. Broad-belted white trousers sat snug and low on his hips; his vivid-patterned black-and-mustard silk shirt had a Sulka label, the black linen jacket that, hooked by his thumb, was slung over one shoulder, was Italian. 'What *can* we do?' he said dryly. 'The very fact that Maureen left for Spain with him this morning, while Sharyn's still in the hospital, shows the sort of commitment there is between the two of them. And as the old man's never given a toss what we think about anything, I can't see him starting now, can you?'

They'd reached the grimy windowed cubicle that jokingly served as an office.

'How long d'you reckon it's been going on?' Johnny asked, kicking the door open. 'It could have been going on for years, couldn't it? Fuck. It could have been going on even when Mummy was alive.'

Mummy? *Mummy?*

Coming from Johnny, the childish diminutive was so unexpected, so bizarre, that Tony rocked back on his heels, stupefied by shock.

Johnny, oblivious of what it was he had said, or the effect it had had, seated himself on a battered swivel chair and swung his feet on to the desk.

Tony wasn't oblivious, though. He was slipping and cascading backwards through time, eight years old and with Johnny in their childhood bedroom, acrid smoke billowing around them as they clawed at the window and Johnny screamed: *'Me, Mummy! Me! Me!'*

'Are you okay?' Johnny was looking at him in concern. 'You don't look quite the ticket. Are you sure you want to do the business as planned? You could always do it tomorrow night – though my having got Cheyenne's uncle a ticket to the Boxing Championships tonight is too good an alibi to waste . . .'

'I'm fine. Cheyenne's putting everything in place now, down on the ground floor. The place will go up like a torch, and there are enough bales of cloth to fool the fire investigators into thinking our fictional Mr Bee has lost his entire stock.'

'Then as long our fictional Mr Bee is up to the questioning he's going to receive, we have no worries.'

'D'you have doubts?' Tony's eyebrows pulled together in a sudden frown. 'I know Cheyenne's uncle has never pulled a stunt like this before, but he's not likely to grass if things go pear-shaped, is he?'

Johnny shrugged. 'He might do. It's always a risk when you're dealing with someone who's basically straight – but it's because he's got no criminal record that he's so ideal as a frontman. If the fire investigators rumble he's using a false identity and that the insurance claim is bogus, he'll get done for fraud, but there'll be no links back to us or to any of our other long-firm jobs.'

'Unless he grasses.'

'Unless he grasses,' Johnny agreed. 'But, with luck, the situation won't arise. Even if it does, if he knows what's good for him he'll keep shtum. So stop worrying.'

There came the sound of someone taking the stairs from the ground floor two at a time. A moment later, Cheyenne strode into the cavernous first-floor storage area.

'Little Donnie's just arrived,' he said as he came to a halt in the doorway beside Tony. 'Don't know why he's here. We don't need him for anything, do we?'

'Nope.' Johnny folded his hands behind his head. 'If you've got everything ready for tonight's fire, there's nothing else to do. The stock – all except for the worthless stuff we're leaving – has all been sold. Your uncle knows what's expected of him. Everything's sweet as a nut.'

'No, it isn't.' Little Donnie came across the warehouse floor at a trot, pushing past Cheyenne and barrelling straight into the office. 'Take a butcher's at this, Johnny. It could mean trouble.' Breathlessly he threw a copy of the *Evening Standard* down on the desk. 'Page two, far right-hand column.'

Johnny swung his feet from the desk and reached for the newspaper.

'What is it?' Cheyenne asked Donnie, as Tony moved up beside Johnny to read over his shoulder. 'Has someone been shooting their mouth off?'

'Nope,' Donnie snapped. 'But it looks as if Jimmy Jones is about to be exhumed.'

The news item in question, which was accompanied by a photograph, carried the headline: **NEW HIGH-RISE BLOCK TO BE DEMOLISHED.** Tony leaned further forward to read the small print.

A twelve-storey block of flats, built on an Old Kent Road bomb-site in 1966, is to be razed to the ground. The state-of-the-art building, made from an innovative system of pre-fabricated sections, has proved unstable. The stainless-steel bolts holding the sections together have begun to corrode and a local council official has confirmed that, after several structural inspections, the building has been condemned. Residents are being rehoused on the new Ferrier Estate at Kidbrooke, and demolition work is to start immediately.

'Jimmy?' he said incredulously, turning to Johnny. 'Is that where you put him? In the foundations of this block of flats?'

'Yeah.' Johnny was still regarding the newspaper musingly. 'Seemed like a good idea at the time. We buried him in the rubble below a lift-shaft the night before they poured the concrete in.' He grinned. 'You don't reckon it's Jimmy being buried there that's caused the corrosion, d'you?'

Little Donnie sniggered.

Cheyenne said tersely, 'It ain't funny, Johnny. I arranged workers for that building site, remember? If they find the body, they'll soon put two and two together and realize it's Jimmy. Then what? The police already have you fingered as being responsible for his disappearance. Once they have a body, they'll soon build up a case – especially if they go through the names of the contractors who were working that site when Jimmy went AWOL and realize that I was one of them.'

'It's true, Johnny.' There were white lines around Tony's mouth. 'It could get very tricky.'

'Well, I'll worry about it if and when it does, but not before.' He pushed his chair away from the desk and stood up. 'If everything's organized here, let's move. This place is too bleedin' depressing for comfort. I'm off to St Thomas' to visit Sharyn. You three can do what the hell you want.' He picked up the newspaper and tossed it into a wastepaper basket. 'And no talking about Jimmy. All that's likely to happen is that another block of flats will be built on the existing foundations and he'll carry on decaying, undisturbed.'

Little Donnie sniggered again.

Cheyenne, who had far more at stake than Donnie, didn't look convinced.

Tony said, 'I'm going to hang on here and give everything a final once-over. Tell Sharyn I hope she'll be home soon, and I'm glad the baby is okay.'

'Will do.' Johnny paused in the doorway and shot him a grin. 'Don't worry about Jimmy, Tone. He was a non-event when he was alive, and he's going to remain a non-event. Trust me.'

With his hands once again in his pockets, he strolled off in the direction of the stairs, Little Donnie and Cheyenne close behind him.

Tony reached down into the wastepaper basket and retrieved the newspaper. The block of flats depicted in the photograph was one he and Johnny drove past almost daily. How on earth could Johnny not have been tempted to tell him that he'd buried Jimmy in its foundations? And how could he be so uncaring when it was a near cert that the body would now be found?

As he heard the doors to the street open and then bang shut he looked down at his watch. It was ten past five. Six hours to go till his self-appointed time for torching everything. Listlessly he walked out of the office, wondering how he was going to kill the intervening time. There was Cheyenne's handiwork to inspect, of course, but Cheyenne was a craftsman. Everything would be in order. All that he would have to do was strike a match and toss it.

It would be easy.

It would be child's play.

He came to a halt at the far side of the warehouse floor where doors set in the outside wall, thirty foot above the street, enabled goods to be winched up and into the building from the backs of lorries parked immediately below.

Would he be able to do it? What would happen when he smelled smoke and saw flames once again?

He reached a hand out to the massive hook and chain that hung down from the winch high above him, his fingers curling at head height around the cold metal, his jaw clenched so tightly that the veins in his neck stood out in knots. He mustn't think about that other fire. If he did, he'd lose his grip on things entirely. What he had to do was concentrate on the next step in his grand scheme of things – and the next step was keeping Johnny happy by successfully torching the warehouse for him.

He breathed out slowly. There wasn't much light in this part of the warehouse and not much debris for the fire, either. He wondered whether he should chuck some oily rags on the floor or whether Cheyenne had intentionally not done so because of all the heavy, non-combustible metal in that part of the warehouse. The girder that supported the winch, running the breadth of the ceiling and extending several feet out over the street, was of steel, as was the chain. There were similar arrangements, in the same area, on every floor. For the first time it occurred to him to wonder if it was going to be a problem.

A small smile tugged at the corner of his mouth as he reminded himself that, if it was a problem, it was his only problem. His father and Maureen and Albie were all well on their way to the Costa del Sol by now. He had survived breathing the same air as Albie and would never have to breathe it again. Albie wasn't returning to London. When the holiday in Spain was over, he was flying directly back to Canada from Marbella.

The relief was so great he felt giddy with it. No more Albie. No more having to blank his knowing, sly glances. No more heart-stopping reminders of the terror he had felt as a child, curled up on the straw in the cold and dark of the cubbyhole in the barn roof, knowing that Albie was climbing the ladder towards him.

Sweat broke out on his forehead and with his free hand

he wiped it away. It was over. Finished with. Long gone. He'd made his plan of retribution and it was one that was moving towards a conclusion on oiled wheels. Albie had been a product of the nightmare done to him; not its initial instigator. He had to keep remembering that. And he had to keep remembering his favourite proverb: *Though the mills of God grind slowly, yet they grind extremely small.* His smile flickered a little deeper. Where he was concerned, it was true. It was very, very true.

From the floor below him, the sound of the door to the street being opened and then banging shut, snapped him out of his reverie. Who the fuck was it? Had Cheyenne forgotten something? Or had Johnny come back to have a private word?

Footsteps began mounting the stairs. Footsteps that weren't Donnie's and that certainly weren't Johnny's. Footsteps that were part of the nightmare memories he'd just dragged himself free of. His hand tightened on the chain leading up to the winch. The giant hook, hanging at shoulder height, began swinging very slightly.

It couldn't be Albie. *It couldn't be Albie.* Albie was aboard an aeroplane heading for the Costa del Sol. He was allowing the horrors of the past to physically merge with the present, and that way lay madness.

'I'm over at the winch,' he shouted, forcing careless nonchalance into his voice, certain that it must be Cheyenne.

There was no immediate reply, and then the person who had entered the building and climbed up the first flight of stairs began walking across the warehouse floor towards him.

'What's this, laddie?' Albie asked, running a hand over his close-cropped hair. 'You didna used tae tell where you were hiding, did you?'

The broad, carefully preserved Glaswegian accent, sent a charge like an electric shock down his spine.

'What the fuck are you doing here?' Tony whispered, his voice cracking. 'You're supposed to be on your way to Spain!'

Albie grinned, his lips thin and tight against his teeth. 'Your auld man wanted me to take care of a wee piece of business for him. When it's done I'll be on the first flight out tae Marbella.' He cocked his head to one side. 'It's no been verra' easy tae have a word with you wi' Marco around. Now he isna', I thought I'd take advantage.'

'Christ, but you're pushing your luck, Albie!' His voice was back under his command, but it still wasn't the voice he wanted. It wasn't a voice whose menace would stop Albie dead in his tracks. There was too much old remembered fear in it; too many memories of begging and pleading. 'I'd rather eat shit,' he said unsteadily, the blood surging through his veins in a dark, dizzying tide, 'than speak to you.'

'Would you, laddie?' Albie regarded him consideringly. 'But at least you havna blabbed to your auld man. Which is why I wanted these few wee words.' In the dim light his eyes were as small and mean as a snake's. 'Marco's going to be putting more work my way – and I dinna want anything spoiling things. And if anything was said tae him, I'd hate tae have tae tell him the way it really was. The way as a wee un you begged and pleaded tae be able to suck ma cock. The way you always loved it up your tight wee arse . . .'

Tony's hand hadn't moved from the chain hanging from the winch. Now, slowly, he slid it lower, grasping the neck of the hook.

It was a movement Albie never registered. He was

enjoying himself too much. Enjoying torturing with words, just as he'd once tortured with deeds.

'Your wife would no doubt like tae know your real preferences as well,' he was saying, the light catching on his cracked front tooth. 'It'll explain tae her why she's getting no satisfaction in bed – and she isna'. I can tell by looking at her that she hasna' had a good shagging since the day you took up with her . . .'

Tony lunged forward, the hook in his hand, the chain rattling down from the winch above him as he hurled the murderous weapon towards the centre of Albie's forehead.

There was an instant of realization in Albie's eyes; a split second of disbelief and terror as he registered the horror of the manner of his death, and then, as he vainly attempted to throw himself clear, the hook slammed between his eyes and blood and bone and brains flew.

The winch continued rolling on its metal track, jerking him, impaled, across the floor in a skidding bloody trail.

As it finally eased to a halt, Tony moved with speed. He had to be certain Albie was dead. And if he was dead, he had to free his body from the hook. This area of the warehouse wouldn't bear the brunt of the fire. He needed Albie on the ground floor, where the blaze was going to start.

Breathing hard, he crossed to Albie's side, slithering slightly on hot, sticky blood. Albie had no identity in England that mattered. No one would report him missing. Marco had left him behind to handle unfinished business, and it was bound to have been unfinished business of a violent nature. Marco would assume that he'd come to grief trying to carry it out. If there was any kind of retribution, Tony was confident it wouldn't be coming his way.

With hands that were perfectly steady, he began going through Albie's pockets. Albie's remains would be found, of course. His bones. His teeth. Marco would know then. Or he would if he knew that Tony and Johnny had been running a long firm from the premises and that the fire was their doing.

He slid a passport from Albie's inside jacket pocket. Did the old man know about this particular venture of theirs? Just as Marco didn't keep them informed about his business activities, so they didn't keep him informed about theirs. It was just possible he wouldn't know.

Tony eased a thick wad of notes from Albie's trouser pocket. If Marco didn't know, the only people who might cotton on that Albie was the charred corpse were Johnny, Little Donnie and Cheyenne.

He removed a signet ring and dropped it into his pocket. Little Donnie and Cheyenne didn't count and he'd be able to handle things with Johnny. It had always been intended that the fire investigators would assume the blaze had been started either by vagrants seeking shelter in the building, or kids who had broken in and been acting the fool.

Now it could easily be supposed that two vagrants had broken in and one had murdered the other before firing the building in an attempt to avoid identification of the body.

He removed the wristwatch and then began the hideous task of trying to remove the hook from Albie's skull, or, since this was impossible, removing Albie's skull from the hook.

No one was going to report Albie missing and after an absence of twenty years from England, it was unlikely that the police would be able to determine his identity by any other means.

Skin and blood and gristle and shattered bits of bone clung between his fingers and under his nails as he finally succeeded in extricating Albie from the hook.

There were always prison dental records, or course, and he didn't know if, before he'd left for Canada, Albie had done time. One thing was for sure, though, a vagrant wouldn't be wearing the halfway decent casual clothes that Albie was wearing. In case any remnants of clothing survived the fire, they'd have to be suitably shabby and untraceable. Nothing that had been bought in Canada. Nothing that had come from anywhere but a charity shop.

As he finally dragged Albie's body away from the chain and hook, he glanced down at his watch. There was plenty of time to organize suitable clothing, but little to effect the change-over. Albie's body was beginning to stiffen already. By the time he left the building and returned with other clothes, rigor mortis would have set in and the task would be impossible.

He heaved Albie's body over on to its side to check the label inside his fairly worn sports jacket. Harry Fenton. Very British and not too expensive. It could have come from a charity shop. That wouldn't be too much of a problem.

Beginning to breathe a little easier, he checked the labels on every other item of clothing Albie was wearing. Albie had been a slob. His underpants were from a chain store and grey enough to pass muster. His shoes were old, battered loafers.

He stood up, aware that the blood he'd been kneeling in was saturating the lower part of his trousers. It didn't matter. He'd be destroying everything that he was wearing. Or he would when the task in hand was over.

Dragging Albie's body to the ground floor wouldn't

be easy, but it wouldn't be impossible, not if he first heaved him on to a length of cloth from one of the rolls downstairs. Then, remembering that the hook would most certainly survive the fire, all that remained was to wipe it clean.

After he had finally finished using it.

Once again he reached out for the hook, dragging it the few necessary inches along the winch. The question of dental records was so unlikely to be an issue that he knew he had absolutely no need to do what he was about to do.

It didn't matter

He wanted to do it.

Pulling the hook down, he knelt on one knee beside Albie and then, having rolled him again on to his back, he took a firm hold of the neck of the hook and began smashing it time and time and time again into Albie's mouth.

Chapter Seventeen

It was February and freezing cold and the phone call came in the middle of the night. Both Maureen and Amber had been expecting it.

'That'll be Johnny!' Maureen called out as she hurried past Amber's bedroom on her way down to the hall to silence the insistent ringing. 'It'll be about Sharyn. She must have gone into labour.'

Amber swung her legs out of bed and looked at the clock. It was three in the morning. Sharyn was already two weeks overdue and, as far as Amber was concerned, it was bloody typical of her that, after keeping people in suspense for so long, she'd finally gone into labour in the middle of the night.

As she heard her mother saying tautly, 'Yes, Johnny. Right. We're on our way now,' she groaned and reached for jeans and a sweater.

Other women might have babies with very little fuss, but it had always been obvious Sharyn wasn't going to be one of them. When their mother had gone off to Spain with Marco, Sharyn's prime concern had been that she would be back in England for the baby's birth. And she'd insisted that Amber, too, promise to be at the hospital as well.

'Is it all systems go?' she asked unnecessarily as her mother came flying up the stairs, a luscious silk nightie skimming her ankles.

'Yes. Her waters broke an hour ago and he took her

straight to Greenwich Hospital. It'll be ages before the baby is born – first babies always take their time – but you know your sister. She wants us there.'

As her mother hurried back into her bedroom to throw on some clothes, Amber zipped up her jeans. Was she mad, or what? If the boot was on the other foot, she couldn't imagine Sharyn turning out in the middle of a winter's night to sit uselessly in a maternity waiting-room, for God only knew how many hours, for her.

'Come on.' Incredibly her mother was already dressed – after a fashion – and again at her bedroom door, her turbulent mahogany-red hair pulled hastily into a ponytail that made her look twenty-five, not forty-five.

Resignedly Amber pulled her sweater over her head and tugged on a pair of boots. The last five months hadn't been easy and now, when something was happening that was good rather than bad, Sharyn was making as much drama out of it as she could.

As if, she thought moodily, hurrying down the stairs in her mother's wake, there hadn't been enough drama. First there had been Albie's disappearance between London and Marbella. It had been a disappearance neither Johnny nor Tony had seemed much alarmed by.

'He was going out on a later flight to the old man's, so he could do a bit of business for him in London,' Johnny had said. 'I don't know what it was that Dad had trusted him with, but he obviously wasn't up to it. Either that or he's done a double cross and skipped off with cash he should have been handing on to someone. The truth will out, given time.'

Subsequent emerging truths had been so unpleasant that Albie's disappearance had been sidelined.

'Workmen have found a body buried beneath a block

of flats they were demolishing on the Old Kent Road,' her mother had said to her one morning as she flicked through the previous day's *Evening Standard*. 'Can't be very nice for the people who've been living above it for the last few years.'

As she slid into the passenger-seat and her mother put the Mini Cooper which Marco had given her into gear, Amber marvelled at how totally unconcerned she'd been. The block of flats in question had been uncomfortably near to where she lived, but there'd seemed to be nothing else noteworthy about the news article.

And then the rumours had begun to fly.

The Richardson brothers, big-time South London gangsters who had come a cropper some years ago and were now both serving long sentences for torture and murder, had always been rumoured to have disposed of the bodies of their victims in the concrete foundations of flyovers, bridges or buildings. The body found in the Old Kent Road was clearly one of their bits of handiwork.

And then it was reported that the building was only five years old. As the Richardsons had already been behind bars when it was being built, it put them in the clear.

Then came the other rumours.

As her mother veered out of narrow streets into a near empty and brightly lit Jamaica Road, Amber marvelled at just how long it had taken her to cotton on to the fact that the body was possibly that of Jimmy Jones.

In her heart of hearts, she'd known that Jimmy was dead, but she'd spent years trying to convince herself otherwise. If he was dead – and if Johnny had killed him – then she was partly responsible. She was the one who had come up with the hare-brained idea that Jimmy could have been responsible for Zoë Fairminder's death. And she had told Sharyn, who, following her own agenda, had told Johnny.

'What time is it?' her mother asked as they left Rotherhithe on the Lower Road towards Greenwich. 'D'you think we'll be able to get a cup of tea or coffee when we get there?'

Amber glanced at her watch. 'It's three twenty-five. And they're bound to have a hot-drinks machine in the waiting-room. It's practically a brand-new hospital.'

The rumours that the body was that of Jimmy Jones were soon so rife that it was a surprise to everyone when Johnny wasn't arrested and questioned.

If it was also a surprise to Johnny, he never let on. 'Jimmy did a runner,' he'd said to her comfortably when she'd tentatively broached the subject one evening in the Prince. 'There's no need for you to be worrying on my behalf, Sis.'

'Sis' was his new name for her. 'I've always wanted a little sister,' he'd said at his and Sharyn's wedding. 'Now I've got one – and she's a cracker.'

He had eventually been arrested and taken to Tower Bridge nick for questioning, but three days later he'd emerged unscathed without any charges having being brought.

'The bastards are still trying, though,' Tony had said to her when she asked him what was going on. 'Johnny isn't out of the woods, yet. Not by a long chalk.'

The tension for Sharyn had been enormous. 'Johnny can't be arrested for murder!' she'd wailed. 'Not now! Not when we're about to have a baby!'

Even Johnny had begun to look ever so slightly stressed.

Marco had flown back from Spain – though whether

his return was prompted by Albie's disappearance or Johnny's experience at Tower Bridge nick, Amber hadn't been sure.

Little Donnie had had no doubts. 'Marco will be giving giant sweeteners to the blokes in the Met who matter,' he'd said confidently. 'Johnny isn't in any danger. Not with Marco reaching deep into his pocket.'

The belief that the police could be bought provided the price was high enough was fairly universal, but it wasn't one she shared. She *knew* a copper. Really knew one. And the very idea of Rob Gowan being bought was laughable.

As always when her thoughts veered in his direction, Amber jerked herself savagely back into the present moment. Thinking about Rob Gowan was pointless. And wondering if he was one of the officers who had questioned Johnny was worse than pointless; it was horror-movie stuff.

'D'you want me to phone Dad when we get inside the hospital?' she asked, forcing her thoughts on to a different track as they entered the hospital car park. 'He'll want to know that the baby's on its way.'

'D'you reckon?' Maureen brought the Mini to a halt with such abruptness Amber banged her head on the windscreen. 'Or is this just another attempt to remind me I should be on a guilt trip where Tommy is concerned?'

'Why do you always refer to Dad as Tommy when you talk to me about him? You never do it when you're talking to Sharyn! And, yes, I do think you should be on a guilt trip. Everyone does. Dad only came out of nick three months ago, and what did he come home to? He came home to you not being there. He came home to the realization that you were having an affair with Marco!'

Maureen stepped out of the Mini and slammed the driver's door with such force the little car rocked. 'Christ, Amber! You're seventeen! Surely you're old enough by now to realize you don't know everything about my life with Tommy? Why won't you just take it from me that my affair with Marco wasn't an earth-shattering surprise for him? He'll come to terms with it . . . He *has* come to terms with it. He and his landlady are already out and about, arm in arm.'

She began walking at furious speed towards the hospital entrance.

'If you want to wake the two of them up with the news that Sharyn's gone into labour, then by all means do so,' she said, pushing open the plate-glass doors as Amber stormed after her. 'Only don't be surprised if you get a flea in your ear for your trouble. Maternity?' Without pausing for breath, she threw the word queryingly at the young woman on Reception. 'My daughter was admitted an hour or so ago. Which way is it?'

The high heels of the fashion boots they were wearing clicked noisily on the linoleum floors as they headed off in the direction indicated.

With great difficulty Amber kept silent. Here, in a hospital in the middle of the night, was not the time and place to start an unholy row with her mother.

As they walked into the Maternity Unit's waiting-room, Johnny strode to meet them. 'Maureen! Glad you're here,' he said, moving as if to kiss her on the cheek.

Amber saw her mother sidestep swiftly in order to avoid the physical contact. She didn't think Johnny would be much put out. Since Maureen had gone off to Spain with his dad, Johnny had hardly been able to bring himself to speak to her, let alone kiss her. That he'd nearly done so now showed just how distracted he was.

'They reckon the baby is going to be born quite soon,' he said. 'I'm going back into the delivery room to sit with her. They said I could stay with her for the birth.'

Even though he'd got out of bed in the middle of the night and dressed hurriedly, he was still wearing a suit, shirt and tie. The tie, though, was pulled loose at the neck and the top button of his shirt was undone.

'Tony's here,' he said, stepping aside so that they could see the seated figure he'd been obscuring. 'I'll tell Sha you're here.'

Quite obviously taking his father-to-be role very seriously, he hurried back to Sharyn's side. Maureen acknowledged Tony and then sat down near a coffee-table piled with magazines. Amber sat down next to Tony.

'I don't know why the three of us have been roped in to being here,' she said, still in a bad mood after her war of words with her mother. 'It isn't normal, surely? I'm surprised Sharyn didn't want Angie and your dad here, and Little Donnie and Cheyenne as well.'

Tony shot her his rare, but attractive, smile. 'It's Sharyn's big moment. She needs to know it's making an impact.'

She opened her mouth, about to say that, when she had a baby, she'd do it very differently, and then closed it again, smartish. That Angie couldn't have a baby wasn't something she'd ever heard Tony mention, but harping on about the baby she hoped she would one day have didn't seem exactly sensitive, under the circumstances.

Nor did she particularly want to ask him about Angie.

'Our marriage isn't working,' Angie had said to her bleakly a week or so ago. 'It isn't because of anything major. There isn't another woman. He doesn't beat me. He doesn't keep me short of money. Rather the reverse. It's just he doesn't seem . . . *interested*. We hardly ever have sex and, when we do, it's a non-event. Why he wanted to marry me in the first place, I can't imagine. He doesn't seem to *need* me at all. And I need to be needed, Amber.'

Amber wasn't sure that she needed to be needed. For some reason she didn't understand, Fast-Boy certainly seemed to need her. A year or so ago, when she'd been a tad younger and a lot more impressionable, she'd found Fast-Boy even giving her the time of day unbelievably exciting. Now, though, it was different. She still wanted to be his friend – she would always want to be his friend – but she wasn't sure she wanted to be his lover ever again.

The incident when he'd been so violent towards Angie had disturbed her deeply. Even though she was on terms with so many people who were violent, before Fast-Boy beat up Angie in the club, she'd never *seen* any violence first-hand before. And she hadn't liked it. She hadn't liked it at all.

It had made her think a lot more deeply about what it was that Fast-Boy did. True, he seemed to lead a charmed life where the police were concerned. Apart from one twelve-month stretch a couple of years earlier, he'd never been collared for anything. The incident he'd done time for had been one where he'd been completely unarmed – and it had been a rare event. Usually Fast-Boy went about tooled-up and she knew that, if he were caught, his sentence would be seven or eight years, maybe more.

Even worse – real nightmare country – was the prospect of his one day being in a position where he put his gun to use. 'You must be joking,' he'd often said to her. 'What kind of an eejit d'you think I am, Red? I go tooled-up to frighten the shit out of people so that I *don't* get trouble. I'm too cool a customer to lose my head, no matter what the scenario. Stop grieving about it. It isn't ever going to happen.'

'Johnny's taking this father-to-be lark very seriously, isn't he?' Tony said, breaking in on her thoughts. 'I've never known him be so hyper over anything. It looks like he and Sharyn are going to walk happily into the sunset, after all.'

'Yes.' She forced a smile, wondering what Tony would say if she were to tell him that Johnny was having a passionate affair with Tilly Conway. Perhaps, now that the reality of fatherhood had really hit home, Johnny would end the relationship. She certainly couldn't see him leaving Sharyn and going off to Spain with Tilly. Not when leaving Sharyn would also mean leaving his new-born son behind.

From the direction of the delivery room there came the unmistakable sound of a baby's cry. Her mother dropped the magazine she had been reading. Tony rose to his feet.

The doors leading to the delivery-room suite flew open and Johnny came bursting through, his face radiant. 'It's a girl!' he shouted euphorically. 'I've got a little girl! Can you believe that, Tony? Christ! I've got a daughter! *A daughter!*'

'Lola Buttercup,' Maureen said in agonized disbelief, half an hour later as they drove away from the hospital in the pale light of early dawn. '*Lola Buttercup*. Lola sounds like a stripper's name and Buttercup sounds like a heifer's! I didn't particularly want Sharyn to call the baby after me, but I did think she and Johnny would choose Sheelagh for her second name.'

She slammed the Mini into third gear, speeding through Rotherhithe at well above the legal speed limit. 'Marco's going to go ape-shit. Lola isn't even Italian. It's short for Dolores or Carlotta or some other Spanish name. Is that why they chose it? Now that Marco intends living permanently in Spain, is Johnny thinking of moving out there, too?'

'I shouldn't think so.' With a stab of alarm Amber remembered what Tilly had said about Johnny's plans for Spain. What if he intended leaving Sharyn behind but taking Lola with him? The prospect was so monstrous she choked on her breath.

'I'm not surprised you're choking,' her mother said, circumnavigating a roundabout and cutting towards Jamaica Road. 'Telling people your niece is to be given the moniker Lola Buttercup is enough to make anyone choke.'

As soon as it was nine-thirty she rang David Lampeter and cried off going into work. 'My sister's had her baby and I've been at the hospital with her all night,' she said, with slight exaggeration. 'Count today as one of the days holidays due me. I'll be in tomorrow.'

'What are you going to do?' her mother asked when she came off the phone. 'Are you going back to the hospital to spend some time with Sharyn?'

'No. Johnny will be there and I expect you'll be going back and Angie will most likely be visiting. I thought I'd go and find something really nice for a christening present. There's a super jeweller's in Blackheath Village. I'm going to catch a bus and spend the morning there and then maybe have a walk on the Heath.'

'In February?' Still suntanned from her long stay in Marbella with Marco, Maureen shuddered.

'Why not? We don't all have second homes on the Costa del Crime.' Without waiting for her mother's reaction to this last nasty dig about her affair with Marco, she swung out of the house wearing a scarlet beret that clashed hideously with her hair; an ex-army greatcoat that she'd bought in a charity shop and that buried her to mid-calf, and knee-high black leather boots.

Lola. Lola Buttercup. It was so unexpectedly imaginative that she found it hard to believe it was a name Sharyn had chosen. Unlike her mother, Amber approved. As she sat on the top deck of a bus, trundling towards Blackheath Village, she wondered what name she would choose when she had a little girl. Daisy? She liked the name Daisy, but perhaps cousins called Daisy and Buttercup would be a bit too much. It was a pity, though, if Sharyn had cornered the market where a flower name was concerned as there were so many pretty ones: Poppy, Pansy, Rose . . .

She continued daydreaming as the bus turned off before Greenwich and began crawling in heavy traffic up Blackheath Hill. Bo Kitten would be a nice name, and even more unusual than Lola Buttercup. Idly she wondered if it should be hyphenated or not, and then told herself she was being ridiculous. It had been hard enough trying to imagine Johnny as a caring father. Trying to imagine Fast-Boy as one was impossible.

She got off the bus and made her way to Black's Jeweller's. There were lots of high-quality secondhand things in the window, as well as new, but somehow she didn't fancy the idea of a secondhand christening present. She walked straight past the display window into the shop and very firmly asked to see brand-new silver

Christening bangles. Choosing one, and asking for it to be engraved with the name 'Lola Buttercup' was fun, and she was in a fizzingly good mood as she strode out of the shop and on to the pavement.

'Hi,' Rob said, puncturing her euphoria at a stroke.

He was leaning against the waist-high railing that protected the narrow pavement from the busy street, so obviously lying in wait for her that she wondered how long he'd been following her. Had it been just since she got off the bus, or had he followed her all the way from Bermondsey?

Tightening her lips, she prepared to march straight past him.

He caught hold of her arm. 'I need to have a word, Amber,' he said, swinging her towards him. There was nothing officious in his tone. Only genuine concern and misery.

Thinking that if she'd any sense she'd tug herself free and jump on the next passing bus, she snapped, 'There's nothing you can say that I want to hear. You're a copper. You could have told me you were a copper, right from the off. But you didn't, because you were hoping to get information from me about my friends and family – information I wouldn't have known I was giving.' Her voice shook with the force of the anger she still felt. 'If you think I'm even going to talk to you, much less resume a relationship with you, you're wrong.'

'OK. You've made your point.' His voice was even terser than hers. 'And yes, you're right in that I first asked you to come for a drink with me in the hope I might glean some information about Johnny Martini. *But that isn't why I continued seeing you.* I love you. I know you don't believe me, but it's true.'

At the word 'love' she flinched, and he pulled her

nearer, holding her by both shoulders. 'I know the kind of difficulties there are, but if we really want to, Amber, we can sort them.' His gold-flecked eyes were pleading. 'We can . . .'

'No!' Violently she pulled away from him. 'Johnny is family. He's my *brother-in-law*. And you're a detective-sergeant at Tower Bridge nick.' For some reason she couldn't quite fathom – unless it was emotional reaction to Lola's birth – tears burned the backs of her eyes. 'You've had him in there, questioning him about the body that was found in the foundation of the flats being demolished in the Old Kent Road. Were *you* one of the coppers questioning him?'

As she read the answer in his eyes, her throat closed so tight she could hardly get the next words past her lips. 'And you think our difficulties are something we can sort? Never, Rob. Not in a million years!'

She swung away from him, heading not towards the Heath, where, if he caught up with her, she would have no way of escaping him, but towards the nearest bus stop.

She needn't have bothered depriving herself of her walk.

He didn't follow her.

He simply remained where he was, watching the crimson red of her beret as she wove her way between the pedestrians enjoying Blackheath Village's many boutiques and bookshops. She'd been right, of course, in saying that their difficulties were insurmountable. He didn't want to leave the Force; couldn't even begin to imagine doing such a thing. And she'd been right in assuming he was one of the coppers who had been in on the questioning of Johnny Martini.

Her crimson beret disappeared from view and desultorily he eased himself away from the railings and began walking back to his parked car. Johnny had handled himself well under questioning. He'd been insultingly at ease, sitting with one leg crossed over the other, displaying a glimpse of louche purple silk sock. 'Yes,' he'd freely admitted, 'I was probably one of the last people to see Jimmy alive. I wanted a word with him and when he came out of Petty France after picking up his passport, I gave him a lift back to the gaff he'd moved into, north of the river.'

'Where, north of the river?' Ramsden had asked.

'Dalston.' Johnny had said with a shrug. 'In Verona Street, near to the Krays' gaff in Vallance Road.'

'What was he doing over there?' Rob had chipped in. 'Jones was a South London boy. Bermondsey was his patch. Not Dalston.'

Johnny's electric-blue eyes had met his, insultingly amused. 'He was running scared. We'd had a ruck and so he went looking for protection. He thought Ronnie and Reggie would give him it, but he over-estimated his own importance. They found him as much of a nuisance as I'd found him. So they said goodbye to him. Permanently.'

'You're saying Jones' death is down to the Krays?'

'I'm saying it wasn't down to me. Now, gentlemen, is there anything else I can help you with?'

Rob opened his car door and slid behind the wheel. The address Johnny had given for Jimmy Jones in Dalston had been checked out. 'Yes,' the old dear who lived there had said. 'Mr Jones was with me over the dates you're querying. He was a very nice young man. Very quiet.'

'I'll bet he was very quiet!' Colin Ramsden had snorted in fury. 'So quiet she not only didn't hear him, she didn't see him either! If Jimmy Jones even sniffed the air of Dalston, I'll eat my hat.'

Rob turned the key in the ignition and revved the engine. The outcome of Ramsden's interview with Johnny had been a setback, but not a major one. Though Forensics hadn't as yet come up with anything that would tie Jimmy's death to Johnny, there was still time. And if Forensics didn't come up trumps, there were other ways of garnering the kind of evidence that would stand up in Court.

He slid the Cortina into gear, wondering what Amber's reaction was going to be when Johnny was finally charged with Jimmy Jones' murder. Whatever it was, he would probably never know about it, for he doubted if she would speak to him ever again.

He eased the car into traffic, his pain nearly beyond all bearing.

That evening, in the Prince of Wales, champagne corks flew and brandy-chasers crammed every table. 'Ain't it wicked, seeing Johnny so happy?' Little Donnie said to Tony as he squeezed past where Tony and Amber were standing. 'I reckon we'll be celebrating it being a little boy next time, don't you?'

As Donnie was swallowed up in the throng, Tony raised his eyebrows slightly. 'Do you reckon Donnie's right?' he said to Amber. 'Is this baby going to be the first of many for Johnny and Sharyn?'

'Absolutely.' It wasn't a flippant reply. Amber knew her big sister. Sharyn's reasoning would be that the more children she and Johnny had, the less likelihood there would be of his ever leaving her. 'Sharyn's made Johnny happier than he's ever been in his life,' she said. 'Incredible though it may seem, I think Johnny has just realized that he's really a family man.'

Tony turned and looked across the crowded bar

towards his twin. Johnny *was* happy. Happier than he'd ever seen him.

'Poor Sharyn,' Cheyenne's girlfriend said as she squeezed past them, a brandy cocktail in each hand, 'It's a shame she can't be here to share in the celebrations. When does she get out of hospital, Amber?'

'Ten days from today. And don't worry about Sharyn not being able to wet little Lola's head. Her way of celebrating is to shop. She's already arranged that the first day she's home, she's going to leave the baby with our mum while I take her up town to shop to her heart's content.'

If Tony was listening to them, he gave no sign.

He was still watching Johnny, his blue eyes thoughtful, his mouth a tight, hard line.

'I don't know why we're doing this for Sharyn,' Angie said nine days later as, together, they blitzed Johnny and Sharyn's flat and filled it with vases of fresh flowers. 'She wouldn't bother to do this to welcome either of us home from hospital.'

'No, she wouldn't.' Amber shot her a grin as she cleaned a glass-topped table with a mixture of vinegar and water. 'Perhaps we're really doing it for Lola.'

Angie's mouth tugged into a smile, but the smile didn't mask the lines of strain around her eyes. She put down the vase of flowers she'd been arranging, saying with sudden abruptness, 'I've left Tony.'

Amber stopped her cleaning. 'Blimey,' she said, shocked. 'When? Where are you living? What does Tony think? Does he want you to go back?'

Angie ran a hand through her shoulder-length Afro. 'I did it two days ago,' she said, sitting down on the arm of Sharyn and Johnny's white leather sofa. 'At the moment I'm back with my mum – though I don't think Fast-Boy's realized yet there's three of us in the house again.'

The winter-wool maxi-length skirt she was wearing was the colour of burnt umber. She'd teamed it with a biscuit-coloured shirt and boots the colour of butterscotch. Now, fingering a long rope of topaz-coloured beads, she said: 'I'm not going to be staying at Mum's indefinitely. I've rented a house, out on the Isle of Grain. It's a bit dilapidated. I wondered if you'd come down there with me and help me to get it into shape? Paint and decorate it, that sort of thing.'

Kneeling on the floor, the cloth she'd been wiping the table with still in her hand, Amber rocked back so that her weight was on her heels. 'Of course I will. But are you saying that there's no chance of you and Tony working things out?'

'No . . . we're just not . . . compatible.' She stopped fingering her beads. 'What about you and Fast-Boy, Amber? What's happening there? Are the two of you eventually going to get married?'

'I don't know. I don't think so. Like you and Tony, we're not truly compatible. We're very good at being friends, but when it comes to the other thing . . .'

Her voice tailed off. Lovemaking had been magic with Rob, but she'd never told anyone about him and now, when he was one of the officers trying to nail a murder on Johnny, wasn't the time to start – not even with someone as trustworthy as Angie. Instead she said, 'Fast-Boy's just such an unknown quantity, Angie. He never tells me about the jobs he pulls, but I do know he goes in armed. I don't want to be married to someone who might one day kill someone – or someone the Flying Squad will be able to fire at, if they ever succeed in cornering him.'

Angie slid down on to the sofa proper and clasped her hands so tightly in her lap that her knuckles shone. 'He's my brother, Amber,' she said unnecessarily, 'how do you think I feel? The first time I knew he was hiding guns at home I nearly died with fright. I was only sixteen.' She gave a tight little smile. 'And I did the unforgivable. I told Sharyn. She obviously told Johnny because ages afterwards the police raided the house. By then it didn't matter because Fast-Boy had begun keeping everything at Jed's, but he knew damn well that I was the only person who could have talked – and who I would have talked to.'

'And he thought Sharyn had told Johnny and that Johnny had grassed on him and told the police?' Amber's face had gone bone-white.

'Yes. And he thought right. It's the only way it could have happened. I've never known him be so furious about anything. It's the only time he's ever threatened to kill me and believe you me, Amber, I wouldn't have put it past him. He's always been determined to even the score where Johnny's concerned. If he knew anything about this business with Jimmy Jones, he'd be doing some informing, I'm sure of it.'

For once, Amber wasn't remotely interested in Jimmy Jones. 'Angie,' she said nervously, 'there's something you have to know. It wasn't Sharyn who told Johnny that Fast-Boy had a gun hidden in the coal bunker. It was me.'

'You?' Angie stare at her. 'But how could it be? This happened *years* ago, Amber. You were only a kid. How could you have known anything about Fast-Boy's goings on, then?'

'I was in the bedroom, beneath the bedcovers, when you and Sharyn were talking. I heard you tell her and . . . and I thought it was something Johnny should know about. As you say, I was only a kid, and I think I had some crazy idea that Fast-Boy might use one of his guns to shoot Johnny down in a pub. It was about the time George Cornell was shot in the Blind Beggar and, well . . . I always had a crush on Johnny. I thought that by telling him I was doing him a good turn.'

'Jesus, Mary and Joseph,' Angie said reverently. 'And all these years I've thought it was just another case of Sharyn shooting her mouth off.' As their eyes held and they began realizing the wrong done to Sharyn, they began to giggle, knowing that it was all so long ago, it didn't matter.

'Let me show you a photo of the cottage at Grain,' Angie said, still giggling as she got up and began searching for her handbag. 'It's absolutely super. Only two bedrooms and a tiny, tiny kitchen. From my kitchen window all I can see are reed beds and the sea wall and, beyond it, acres and acres of water and sky.'

The next afternoon, leaving the deliciously beautiful Lola Buttercup in the doting care of her grandma, Amber played the supportive sister role to the hilt.

'I want to go to Biba,' Sharyn said as she fiddled with her hair and Johnny rammed a couple of wads of notes into her handbag, each one thick enough to choke a pig. 'It's where all the models and pop stars and film stars shop.'

Behind Sharyn's back, Johnny flashed Amber a happy grin. 'Then tell Wodgie to take you straight there,' he said to her, as if having had a baby had rendered Sharyn unfit to give directions to the driver. 'He knows London like the back of his hand. It won't be a problem.' He returned his attention to his wife. 'And make sure Amber has a little spending spree, too, Sha. Have you looked at all the flowers she's stuffed into this flat? It looks like the Chelsea Flower Show.'

How Sharyn could bear to tear herself away from Lola Buttercup, Amber couldn't even begin to imagine. As they sat in the back of the Mark 1 Zodiac, she said so.

Sharyn immediately took offence. 'I hope you're not trying to make out I'm not being a good mother? Because if you are, Amber, you're way out of order. *Way* out. I'm going to be a *wonderful* mother. I love my baby to bits. It's just that I've had months and months of wearing clothes fit for an elephant and I want to have something to show off my figure again.'

'It's a bit soon,' Amber retorted waspishly. 'Your figure won't be back to normal for a while, surely?'

Sharyn shot her a look fit to kill. 'Film stars get their figures back immediately after they've had babies and *I've* got *mine* back.'

'Perhaps if madam tried a bigger size?' the glamorous young shop assistant said hesitantly.

'I don't *need* a bigger size. This *is* my size.'

Sharyn was now beginning to sound more tearful than angry, and Amber sighed. Why she'd let herself be talked into coming shopping when, by rights, Sharyn should have been at home with Lola, still getting her strength back after the birth, she couldn't begin to imagine.

'Let's give it a rest, Sharyn,' she said gently. 'Why don't we go for a cup of tea, or maybe a glass of wine? We can always come back another day. Johnny will let us have a car and driver any time we want.'

'I want nice new clothes *today*.' Sharyn said with mulish stubbornness. 'Besides, we've only been here half an hour. Wodgie isn't coming back for another two hours.'

'Perhaps this dress . . . ?' the assistant said hopefully, swirling a Kaftan-type dress in front of Sharyn.

Sharyn winced. 'No,' she said with what was, for her, remarkable brevity. 'It looks like a maternity dress.'

'I think we should go home,' Amber said decisively. 'If Wodgie isn't waiting for us when we leave the building, we can get a taxi.'

'No.' Sharyn no longer looked as if she was about to burst into tears. 'We can get a taxi, but not to go home. We'll go to Selfridges. Selfridges' clothes *always* fit me.'

The shop assistant looked pained, obviously tempted to point out that Selfridges' clothes would only fit her if they were in sizes larger than the ones she was presently trying to squeeze herself into. Before she could say a word, and before Sharyn caused a monumental scene, Amber said, 'OK, Sharyn, we'll go to Selfridges. But if you don't find what you want there, it's straight home. Agreed?'

'Agreed.'

Out in Kensington High Street there was no sign of Wodgie and there wasn't a taxi to be had.

'Let's go by tube,' Sharyn said, as yet another black cab sped past them, occupied. 'High Street Ken station is only a couple of minutes away.'

'Are you sure you're up to it, Sharyn?' Amber regarded her sister doubtfully. 'You only had a baby eleven days ago. By rights, I don't think you should even be out shopping, much less getting on and off crowded tube trains. Why don't we go for a coffee while we wait for Wodgie to come back for us?'

'No!' Like a spoilt child, Sharyn stamped her foot. 'I do wish you'd stop fussing, Amber. I've had a baby, not just come out of hospital after being fitted with artificial legs!'

'OK.' Knowing the trouble there would be if she didn't, Amber gave in with all the grace she could muster.

Despite it being such a bitterly cold day, the High Street was crowded and the tube station was more crowded still.

By the time they'd got their tickets and gone down the escalators to platform level, Sharyn was beginning to look dangerously pale. Cursing herself for having been so weak-willed as to have agreed to their travelling by tube in the first place, Amber said, 'I'm just going to fight my way through the crush to the sweet kiosk, Sharyn. I think we both need a couple of bars of chocolate to keep our blood-sugar levels up.'

Sharyn nodded, looking distinctly unhappy at the situation she had put herself in. The platform was as crowded as if it was the rush-hour. Not only that, in order to get to Oxford Street and Selfridges, they'd have to change at Notting Hill Gate on to the Central Line.

With increasing anxiety, Amber left Sharyn to battle her way to the front of the platform while she fought a way through to the sweet kiosk at the platform's rear. A train was speeding into the station and, as she asked for two Kit-Kats, she hoped to God Sharyn wouldn't be daft enough to get on it without her.

It was then, as from behind the chest-high counter the woman reached out for her money, that all hell broke loose.

For the rest of her life she never knew which came first. The terrible screeching of the train as it came to an emergency stop, or the uproar of screaming and the shouts of: 'Someone's fallen!' 'A woman's thrown herself under the train!'

She knew, even as she whirled around, who the woman was.

'Sharyn!' Shouting Sharyn's name at the top of her voice she began pummelling her way through the crowd as they ghoulishly surged forward in an effort to see if the body was visible on the tracks. 'Sharyn! SHARYN!'

Dimly she was aware of a tall young woman pushing her way through in the opposite direction, the one person moving against the flow.

'Sharyn!' Amber was sobbing as she finally got to the front of the shouting crowd. 'Sharyn!'

Her handbag was still teetering on the lip of the platform where it had fallen. The train had halted a good dozen yards further on. Of the body beneath it, there was no sign. It was there, though. Everyone knew it was there.

The tube driver was on the platform, and the guard was running the length of the train to reach the place where Sharyn had fallen. Station staff were shouting out that no one was to leave the scene. People on the train – behind the automatically locked doors– were nearly as hysterical as the people on the platform.

In the midst of the mayhem, Amber was aware only of her own voice, as she screamed, and continued to scream, her sister's name.

Later – how much later she was never able to tell – some sort of order was imposed. People were herded away from the edge of the platform. 'It's my sister!' she sobbed as they tried to move her away. 'It's my sister! My sister!'

Someone sat her down. Policemen were everywhere. Names and addresses were being taken. Station staff were shouting instructions to each other. Firemen arrived. Ambulancemen arrived with a stretcher.

Amber wasn't screaming now. She was moaning and in torment, her hands covering her face, the tears spilling through her fingers as the long, grotesque task of retrieving Sharyn's body began.

Chapter Eighteen

Because of the necessity for an inquest, the funeral couldn't be held until four weeks later. Incredibly, no one blamed Amber for Sharyn's death. Not her mother. Not Johnny. Not the Coroner. No one.

'Why should they, Amber?' Angie asked compassionately after a verdict of accidental death had been given. 'It wasn't your fault. Everyone knows how obstinate and strong-willed Sharyn could be. She wanted to go shopping and, if you'd refused to go with her, she'd have gone alone.'

'If she'd gone alone she'd never have opted for travelling to Selfridges by tube,' she'd said, heartsick. 'She'd have waited for the driver and car Johnny had arranged for her. I *knew* it was all too much for her the instant we were inside High Street Ken station. She was pale and looked as if all the stuffing had been knocked out of her . . .' She began crying. 'And all I could think of doing was to . . . was to buy *chocolate,*' she'd said between heaving sobs. 'I should have taken her straight back up into the fresh air . . .'

'It wasn't your fault she pushed a way through to the very edge of the platform.' Angie was been sharply forceful. 'It was such a typically dozy thing for her to have done when she was feeling faint. I suppose, though, she just wanted to be one of the first on to the train, so that she could be certain of getting a seat.'

Taking into account that the tragedy had occurred on

the same day that Sharyn had been discharged from hospital after having had her first child and that none of the many witnesses questioned had seen anyone push her or act in a suspicious manner, it was a conclusion the Coroner had shared. Sharyn, in a state of post-parturitive exhaustion, had fainted and fallen beneath the wheels of the oncoming train. Now, on a fiercely windy March morning, they were laying her to rest.

'Ashes to ashes,' their family priest was saying. 'Dust to dust . . .'

Held in Maureen's arms, submerged in a shawl, Lola Buttercup began making small mewling sounds. It was more than could be borne. Angie gave a strangled sob. Tears streamed down Maureen's face. Wearing a black Crombie overcoat, black leather-gloved hands clasped tightly in front of him, Johnny groaned, looking like a man on the edge of an abyss.

Tony put his arm round his twin's shoulders and, at that moment, even to Amber, they looked so alike as to be indistinguishable.

'Our Father, which art in heaven . . .' As the young priest began leading them in the Lord's Prayer, she saw her father holding on to the arm of the woman he had begun living with.

The relationship suddenly didn't seem to matter, just as her mother's relationship with Marco no longer seemed of the slightest importance.

'Thy kingdom come, Thy will be done, in earth as it is in heaven . . .'

Amber couldn't say the words. Her lips wouldn't move.

When Sharyn had been alive, she'd spent hardly any time with her. Even when they'd been small children, they'd never been close. Now, though, if only she could turn her head and see her – hear her complaining how it had taken her ages to find anything to wear, and that the wind had ruined her hair – she would have given anything. *Anything.*

'It's over, Amber.' The speaker was Marco. 'Let me help you back to the car.'

'But we can't go!' Wildly, Amber looked towards the grave. She'd never realized before that graves were so deep. Or that they could be so wet. The clay sides were slicked with moisture and, at the bottom, beneath the coffin, water was beginning to ooze. 'I can't leave Sharyn here!' Her voice rose hysterically. 'Sharyn was scared of the dark! I can't leave my sister in that hole! I can't! *I can't!*'

Marco's arm, as it slid around her, taking her weight, was like an iron bar. 'Come along, *cara.*' His low growl of a voice was tender. 'You're strong. You can survive this.'

Despite her nearly demented protests, he half forced and half carried her to the nearest black stretch-limousine and then, as she collapsed on its rear seat, slid in beside her, his arm still round her shoulders.

'It was my fault,' she sobbed, clinging to him for comfort as if doing so was the most natural thing in the world. 'I shouldn't have left Sharyn on her own, not even for a minute. I should have known it was too soon after Lola's birth for her to be out shopping. I should have known she might faint . . .'

As the car began to move, he rocked her comfortingly in his arms. Amber wasn't even aware of how bizarre his open show of concern for her was. The burden of her grief and guilt was too great. It was so great she couldn't even begin to imagine how she was going to be able to live with it.

*   *   *

Maureen watched their limousine sweep away in the direction of the cemetery gates and then, looking like a ghost, her eyes darkly ringed, her face deathly pale, she stepped into the car nearest to her, Lola still in her arms.

Johnny and Tony joined her and, as they did, the tears rolled down her cheeks and on to Lola's shawl. Sharyn had died just when she'd been so happy at becoming a mother and now she would have to be a mother to Lola.

As the limousine sped out of the cemetery into the main road, Maureen looked across at Johnny. His grief was naked – and sincere. She didn't think it would last for long, though. And when it was over – when he embarked on a long string of live-in girlfriends – what would happen to Lola then? Would Johnny want each new girlfriend to play 'Mummy' to Lola? Would her little granddaughter be passed around like a parcel?

She hugged Lola tightly, fearful of the future; fearful of what Marco was now saying to their daughter – of just what details of his relationship to her he was accidentally, or purposely, revealing.

'You're too much like me not to be able to weather this grief,' he said to her, when her hysterical calling of her sister's name had finally ceased. 'You're my daughter. But you'd already guessed that, hadn't you?'

She pulled away from him, her eyes meeting his. 'Tommy Bailey's my father,' she said steadily. 'He brought me up. He loves me. Whatever is now happening between you and my mother, don't try to reclaim me from your shared history. I don't want to know.'

There was a beat of time. And then another.

'Fine,' he said at last as the limousine swung past the Prince of Wales and slowed to a halt. 'I admire your loyalty to Tommy, and I won't physically try to reclaim you as my daughter in any way whatever. But if you ever need me, I'm here for you. Understand?'

On legs like cotton wool she stepped from the car. 'I won't be needing you, Mr Martini.' Her heart felt as if it was being squeezed into extinction. 'You're not the kind of man I want my father to be.'

He flinched as though he'd been struck. She didn't care. He'd been right in thinking he'd told her nothing she hadn't guessed long ago, but the day she'd buried her sister was no day for openly acknowledging that she was Johnny and Tony's half-sister.

People were already beginning to gather at the house for the traditional wake. Ignoring them, not wanting to speak to anyone, she went upstairs to the room she had, for most of her life, shared with Sharyn.

The teddy bear that had been Sharyn's night-time comfort as a child still lay on her bed. Shoes she hadn't wanted to take with her when she'd moved into her smart new home with Johnny lay in an untidy pile in the corner of the room. Odds and ends of her make-up lay on the dressing-table next to a sympathy card that Rob had sent. From downstairs there came the sound of laughter as Irish relations began swapping yarns and pitching into the whisky.

It was all too much for Amber to take. Knowing she'd give way again completely if she stayed in the house, she turned her back on the sight of the teddy bear and left the room.

Five minutes later she was in a nearly deserted Prince of Wales and Happy Harry was asking her whether she wanted bitter lemon with her vodka, or tonic water.

'Bitter lemon,' she said, seating herself at a corner table in the aptly named snug, a corner of the pub that was usually appropriated by middle-aged ladies such as Little Donnie's mother and Mrs Flynn. Today, although a fire was burning in the grate, it was blessedly empty.

'Everyone is at your sister's funeral,' Happy Harry said lugubriously, setting a glass of vodka and a bottle of bitter lemon on the table in front of her.

Through the window a black stretch-limo could be seen moving slowly down the road towards her home.

'Your mother didn't want the wake to be held here,' Harry said, not hiding his regret at all the custom Maureen's decision was losing him. 'She didn't think a pub was appropriate. I reckon she's still thinking of your sister as being little more than a kid.'

'I suppose she was, to Mum.'

It was the first time she'd ever had anything even approaching a conversation with Harry and she was too numbed by grief to find his presence intrusive.

'Yeah, I s'pose.'

What Harry did next took her completely by surprise. He seated himself at the other side of her table in order to carry on the conversation.

'I'm sorry about what happened to Sharyn,' he said, his eyes avoiding hers, as she'd noticed most people's did when they offered their sympathies. 'I remember her from when she was a little kid. Johnny too, of course. Especially Johnny.'

Amber poured a splash of bitter lemon into her vodka. Johnny. What the hell would Sharyn have said if she'd known that her little sister was also her husband's half-sister?

'Johnny was always a bugger.' Now Happy Harry had launched into reminiscence mode, there was no holding him. 'I took this pub over directly I was demobbed. It

312

was the only pub standing this side of Jamaica Road. The Germans had bombed the whole area to smithereens – anything near the docks was blasted to pulp. The opposite side of the road to your place was one big bomb-site. Johnny and Tony, and the gang of kids that Johnny always had at his heels, used to spend hours playing war games on it.'

He lit a cigarette. 'I was one of the first British soldiers to enter Belsen – bet you didn't know that, did you?'

He was right. She hadn't. The information was so unexpected it even pierced her own mental agony. No wonder he always looked as if it would kill him to laugh. An experience like that would destroy the capacity for laughter in anyone.

'I brought a German helmet home,' Harry continued, now well into his stride. 'When Johnny was about seven, I gave it to him. He never had it off his head. Playing at being a German SS officer and starting the most God-Almighty fires on bomb-sites – it was all he ever did.'

'Was Tony the same?' she asked, forcing herself to take some interest.

'Nah. Tony just did whatever Johnny wanted him to do. And then there was Fast-Boy, of course. He was an odd kid. And Johnny doing for his dog made him even odder.'

Amber took a drink of her vodka. Fast-Boy. What on earth would Fast-Boy say if she were to tell him that Marco Martini was her father?

'What happened to Fast-Boy's dog?' she asked, wondering if she was now going to learn the reason for their abiding hatred.

'It wasn't really a dog, more a pup. A little mongrel.

And what happened to it was near-enough an accident – kid's stuff. Though I always felt responsible.'

Until now, she'd only been listening to him with half an ear. Now he had her whole attention. 'How could you have been responsible?'.

Happy Harry remained silent and for a moment she thought he wasn't going to tell her. Then he said, an odd note in his voice, 'I told him too much. About what I'd seen in the war. About Belsen. Kids are ghoulish little buggers. They always want to know the worst.'

He stared down at the tip of his cigarette. 'SS doctors did medical experiments on the Jews in the camps. I don't have to tell you what kind. I'm sure you know. One experiment was to see what degree of cold could be tolerated by the human body. They put Jews into tanks of freezing water and then recorded their body temperatures until they froze to death – and, of course, the length of time it took them to die. God knows what kind of mentalities those Nazis had. All I can say is, I'm glad I'm English. Anyway, Johnny thought it was something he could incorporate into his war games. There were cats going missing for weeks.'

'And then Fast-Boy's dog?' Amber put her drink down, her hand shaking violently.

'Puppy,' Harry corrected. 'Johnny's "experimentation tank" was a tin bath that had been ripped out of his house when his dad got a new bathroom put in. It was down at the bottom of the Martinis' garden and Johnny filled it with ice that the butcher let him have – he used to cart it home in a wheelbarrow – and water from a garden hose. It did the job all right. Fast-Boy was everywhere, asking if people had seen his puppy. Muffin, he called it, or some silly name like that. I dunno who told him they'd seen Johnny carrying it home. All I know is

314

that when Fast-Boy barged into the Martini's back garden, Muffin had icicles all over him and was breathing his last.

'Oh God!' Amber pressed her fists against her mouth, certain she was going to be sick. 'Oh Christ!'

'There was a fight between them so bad all the street knew about it. Course, Johnny said he hadn't meant for the puppy to die – though I know differently. Marco Martini told Mrs Flynn he'd get Fast-Boy another dog – this time a pedigree – but when he did, Fast-Boy wouldn't take it from him. Funnily enough, I don't think many people remember the incident. A week or so later, the Martini home went up in flames and then there were real tragedies to have to come to terms with. Sheelagh Martini was a nice woman. Everyone liked her. And, like your sister, she died too young.'

Amber never told Fast-Boy – or Johnny – what Happy Harry had told her. For the remainder of March and all through April she simply endured each day, grieving for Sharyn and, when not at work, helping her mother look after Lola.

That Maureen would take on the task of caring for Lola was something Johnny had taken for granted. 'My worry is what he'll decide to do when he's got over the shock of Sharyn's death,' her mother said unhappily. 'I don't want Lola being looked after by a succession of his girlfriends. He hasn't got a girlfriend in tow, yet, has he? Because that's when the difficulties are going to start.'

'No,' she said, hoping she was speaking the truth. Certainly, the minute she'd returned to work after the funeral, Tilly had been absolutely adamant that her affair with Johnny was over.

'Mr Martini wouldn't allow Johnny to take Lola out

of your care, would he?' she asked. Ever since he had told her that he was her father, she had steadfastly refused to refer to him as anything other than Mr Martini. It was distancing, and that was how she wanted things.

'No,' her mother said. 'But Marco's back in Spain. No matter what his wishes, things could still get iffy.'

Looking at her mother's face, Amber had known that Maureen, too, wanted to be in Spain. And, because of little Lola, she couldn't be.

'If you wanted to join him, I'd give up work and look after Lola,' she said. 'It wouldn't be any trouble. It's something I'd like to do.'

'You're only eighteen,' her mother said. 'You're too young to be tied down with your sister's child. And it's my responsibility.'

She had left the room abruptly at that point and, with so many other things weighing on her mind, it was a suggestion Amber hadn't raised with her again. Night and day, the fact that she was Johnny and Tony's half-sister – and that they clearly didn't know – dominated all her thoughts. What if she told them? Would it make things easier between them? Or would it make things impossible? Whenever she thought back to the days when she'd fancied Johnny like mad, living in the hope that he would one day make her his girlfriend instead of Sharyn, she came out in a cold sweat. Then she remembered that neither her mother nor Marco would have let it happen.

In May, Johnny was questioned again about Jimmy Jones' death. And released without being charged. 'Tossers,' was all he'd had to say about the police when he'd come strolling into the Prince of Wales, straight from Tower Bridge nick.

In June, there was news of Albie. 'He's in Scotland,' Tony said when Maureen, not for the first time, wondered aloud what on earth had happened to him. 'He's taken up with another woman – which is why he did a bunk. If Marco had known about it, he'd have torn him limb from limb. Family pride and all that.'

In July, Amber saw Johnny walking into a cinema in Leicester Square, his arm round Tilly Conway. She was with Tony at the time. Ever since she had learned the truth about her relationship to him, she'd begun spending more time in his company and, when they'd accidentally met in the street, he on his way to Charing Cross Station and home, she on her way from Charing Cross to a meeting with Fast-Boy, she'd decided she had enough time in hand for an early-evening drink with him.

'Have you seen Angie lately?' he asked as they strolled from Irving Street into Leicester Square, looking for a watering-hole that appealed.

'Not since last Monday. She's gone down to the Isle of Grain for a few days.'

Angie and Tony's separation was now official and, as far as anyone could tell, reasonably amicable. What he thought about Angie's rented cottage out on the Thames Estuary was something no one, not even Angie, knew.

'How d'you think Johnny's doing?' he suddenly asked her. 'Do you think he's finally beginning to get over Sharyn's death?'

It had come as a surprise to nearly everyone just how hard Johnny had taken Sharyn's death. He'd looked physically ill for weeks.

Amber, who knew she wouldn't get over Sharyn's death ever, had been about to say that she didn't know how Johnny was feeling, when he and Tilly walked clearly into view some twenty yards or so ahead of them.

There could be no possible misinterpretation of the kind of relationship between them. Her head was resting on his shoulder as they walked, and his arm was round her waist.

'Je-*sus!*' Tony said emphatically as they both came to a shocked halt. 'I guess I've got my answer. He's getting over it. Has *got* over it. Who is she? Do you know?'

'Oh yes.' Amber's voice was unsteady, her face bloodless. 'Her name is Tilly Conway. She's a friend of mine – an *ex* friend of mine. We work together.'

'*That's* Tilly Conway?' Tony was looking utterly gobsmacked. 'But I thought Johnny's affair with her was over ages ago, before Johnny and Sharyn married.'

'I didn't know you knew about his affair with her.' As Amber watched Tilly and Johnny enter the cinema together, she felt as if her heart had calcified to stone. She, like everyone else, had believed Johnny had been truly grieving for Sharyn. And he hadn't.

Tilly had been lying when she had said that her affair with Johnny was over. It had never been over.

Savagely, she wondered if they had even seen each other the week of Sharyn's death and the day of her funeral.

'If Johnny ever told you his affair with Tilly was over, he was lying.' Her voice was bitter. 'Their affair was still ongoing when he married Sharyn. I knew, because of working with her. When Sharyn died, Tilly told me she wouldn't see Johnny again. I believed her. Which just goes to show how gullible I can be.'

'And me.' The words were said with deep passion.

She looked across at him, suddenly very grateful that he was with her. Over the last few months, Tony had been the most supportive brother possible to Johnny.

Now, like her, he'd realized just how duplicitous Johnny could be.

'Let's have those drinks,' she said, glad that she could at least respect one of her half-brothers. Johnny was a prize bastard and their father's reputation for violence was so chilling it was best not to think about it. Tony, though, was not only near-legit, he was also wonderfully sane. It was a comfort, of a kind.

'. . . So you can go and join Marco in Spain,' she said crisply to her mother later that evening. 'I've made a decision and I'm sticking with it. I'm giving up my job – I hated it anyway, it was so boring you wouldn't believe – and I'm going to live on Social Security, plus whatever you and Marco and Johnny toss my way – and look after Lola. Not only do I *want* to look after her, I *need* to.'

It was true. And it was also true that nothing on earth would make her change her mind about chucking her job in. She wasn't even going to work her notice. She couldn't, because she never wanted to see Tilly again.

'But surely you're coming into the office to clear out your desk?' David Lampeter had said to her when she had telephoned him at his home to announce her decision. 'And what about the unfair workload you're leaving on Tilly's shoulders? I thought you were her friend?'

'I was her friend, but *was* is the operative word,' she'd said in a voice brooking no argument. 'I'm her friend no longer. And if you want to tell her so, please feel free.'

When David Lampeter broke the news to Tilly that Amber had let him down by giving up her job without

319

agreeing to work her notice, she immediately guessed the reason.

Her first reaction was relief that Amber *wasn't* coming into Lampeter's again, because she wouldn't have put it past her to have flown at her, tooth and nail.

Her second reaction was satisfaction. Now that Amber so obviously knew about her and Johnny, there was absolutely no reason for him to insist they keep their relationship a secret. It wasn't as if he was a married man any more. He wasn't. He was a widower. He could date whomsoever he pleased. And he could re-marry any day he wanted to.

She'd wanted to see him immediately, to tell him what had happened, but their arrangement was that she didn't phone him, he phoned her. And never at the office, in case Amber answered the phone. So when he phoned Lampeter's later that morning, she knew immediately that he must have heard from Amber.

'We need to talk, sweetheart,' he'd said, sounding as if he was in a hurry and speaking from a phone box. 'Some friends of mine are having a celebration tonight on board one of the party boats. It's fancy dress and it'll be fun. I'll see you've got something to wear. There's going to be a band and there'll be plenty of champagne. The boat is the *Mary-Jane*. She leaves Westminster Pier at nine o'clock, returning around midnight. I might be a little late, so wait for me on board. Corner the little open section of deck in the stern, just beyond the lower-deck saloon where everyone will be dancing, Having champagne there, beneath the stars, will be more romantic than being in with the crush.'

He'd rung off before she had the chance to ask him if what he needed to talk about, was Amber.

At lunchtime an invitation to the party and a box

with a milkmaid's dress in it had been delivered to Lampeter's. *Just so they'll let you on board if you arrive before me,* the handwritten message read.

For the rest of the day she'd wondered if, as they drank champagne alone in the stern, he would ask her to marry him.

A minor disappointment, when she arrived at Westminster Pier, was that he wasn't there, waiting for her. At the foot of the gangplank a member of the crew took her invitation from her and she boarded along with a crush of other people, all elaborately costumed.

To reach the lower deck saloon, where a three-piece rock group was already tuning up, she had to squeeze past a Scarlet O'Hara lookalike; a mermaid; a merman; two pink Easter rabbits; a nearly naked man with a trident, who she could only imagine was supposed to be Neptune; and a whole gaggle of St Trinian's schoolgirls.

Slipping the long, silver-linked chain strap of her evening bag over her head and under one arm, so that the tiny bag rested on the skirt of her Old English milkmaid costume, and carrying the shawl she'd brought with her as protection against any chill river breezes, she wriggled a way through the throng, finding with something like relief that most people were heading for the top deck, and that the lower saloon cabin was still relatively empty.

At the far end of the cabin, narrow doors led out to the stern and a section of open deck so small it could accommodate only two French café-style chairs. Putting her shawl on one of them, she seated herself on the other and glanced down at her watch. It was five to nine. The *Mary-Jane* would be sailing in five minutes – from somewhere deep in the bowels of the ship, engines were already beginning to throb – and there was still no sign of Johnny.

The dusk was beginning to deepen rapidly and lights were beginning to sparkle amongst the trees all along the Embankment. From where she was sitting she could see people still boarding: a couple dressed as Batman and Robin; a man – or she assumed it was a man – in a champanzee costume; a Nell Gwynne complete with a basket of oranges and stunning cleavage. There was still no sign of Johnny and it occurred to her that, even if she did see him, if he was in fancy dress, she probably wouldn't recognize him.

The noise of the engines changed, crew members began busying themselves with ropes, and then the gangplank was raised and Tilly felt a stab of panic. Where *was* Johnny? If he wasn't on board by now, he wouldn't be able get on at all – and she could no longer disembark.

Not relishing the thought of being alone for three hours with a party of people she didn't know, she rose to her feet, picking up her bag and shawl, wondering where she should start searching for him. The crowded top deck? The even more crowded bar? The lower saloon, which was filling up a little now as the band got into its stride?

She'd opened the doors, about to enter the cabin that was almost as long as the boat, when she saw him coming down the companionway. He was in fancy-dress, but she would have known him anywhere. Slim-hipped and sexy, he was wearing a Lone Ranger outfit, complete with black mask and a low-slung gun-belt and silver-handled gun.

She stepped back on to the minuscule deck area, leaving the door open so that he could easily join her. The rock group were playing a pale but deafeningly loud imitation of Dave Edmunds' 'I Hear You Knockin''.

'I thought you weren't going to make it,' she said, smiling up at him as he closed the doors behind him, blocking out some of the noise.

She slid her arms up around his neck in anticipation of his kiss.

He didn't lower his head. Instead he removed his mask.

When she saw his face – and the expression on it, she stepped back swiftly, saying bewilderedly, 'What's this about? What's the matter? Why do you want to talk to me? I don't understand . . .'

'I needed to talk to you away from the family because I need to talk to you *about* family, and this was the best I could come up with,' he said, taking a hip flask out of his back pocket and handing it to her. 'Here – have a swallow of this. It will help keep the river breezes at bay. We can slaughter the champagne later.'

Numbly she did as he suggested, grateful for the brandy's searing warmth. Lola – that was what he wanted to talk to her about. This was going to be all about the impossibility of marrying, without taking Johnny's ridiculously named daughter into the equation.

'This is about Lola, isn't it?' she said.

He nodded and she took another deep swallow of brandy.

'Can't Amber's mother go on looking after her? She is her granny, after all.'

From the saloon, 'I Hear You Knockin'' had given way to an ear-splitting rendition of Rod Stewart's 'Maggie May'.

The doors crashed open to reveal an inebriated Neptune, steadying himself before launching himself forward. A cowboy-booted heel backslammed the door in his face. Neptune, not fancying a ruck when he was half-naked, retreated.

'Maureen might be persuaded to continue caring for her – but what Lola needs is someone who's going to be a mother to her, not a granny.'

The *Mary-Jane* was out in the centre of the Thames now, her decks crammed with dancing partygoers. As she approached Lambeth Bridge, dusk deepened to darkness and the river breeze began making itself felt.

Not liking the way the conversation was going, Tilly wrapped her shawl round her shoulders and leaned against the waist-high deck rail.

'I'm eighteen,' she said tightly. 'I'm not ready to have kids of my own, let alone take on someone else's – especially not Sharyn Bailey's.'

It was the wrong thing to say.

She knew it immediately.

He closed the distance between them in a split second and, as the *Mary Jane* nosed beneath the cavernous overhang of the bridge, he whipped her legs out from under her. As she staggered against him, completely taken by surprise and unbalanced, he tipped her up and over the rail.

She screamed, but her screams were drowned by the sound of fifty partygoers belting out 'Maggie May'.

Then, she too, was drowning. Drowning in black, oil-polluted water that choked her throat and flooded her nose and burned her eyes. She needed air; needed the surface; needed to be able to swim. Instead, as she struggled to fight a way upwards, a current like a vice pulled her ever further downwards. Her chest was exploding. Her ears bursting.

As the *Mary Jane's* partygoers sang happily, champagne corks popping as, with Lambeth Bridge at their backs the launch ploughed on towards Vauxhall Bridge, the Tate Gallery to the right, the gaily lit Albert Embankment to the left.

Behind, in the boat's long, rippling wake, a strappy silver sandal bobbed to the surface and began floating downstream, unaccompanied.

Chapter Nineteen

It was David Lampeter who broke the news to Amber.
'It's incredible,' he said in a stunned voice, breaking all
precedent by telephoning her at home. 'Her parents
phoned me with the news this morning and the police
have just been to see me. They wanted to know if the
balance of her mind might have been disturbed: what
was her work situation, here at Lampeter's? Did I know
if she had any personal problems . . . ? I told them I was
her employer, not her friend, and that I didn't have a
clue. *You're* her friend, Amber. Or were. Do *you* know
of any reason Tilly would throw herself from the back
of a Thames party boat?'

'Tilly's dead?' Amber didn't answer his question. She
couldn't. For one thing it was ridiculous. Tilly would
never commit suicide. Why should she? She was young,
pretty – and she had the boyfriend she'd always wanted.
But Tilly *dead*? It didn't make sense. It wasn't possible.
The only person who would have wanted Tilly dead –
if she'd known about her affair with Johnny – was
Sharyn.

And Sharyn couldn't be responsible for Tilly's death,
because she was deep beneath the ground in Hither
Green Cemetery.

'They found her body close to Lambeth Pier. Her
evening bag had a shoulder strap and she was wearing
it across her chest, the way girls do when they want to
keep their bags safe and their hands free . . . ' David

Lampeter's voice was unsteady. 'It was still on her when she was found. There can't be any mistake. There was a club membership card in it and her provisional driving licence, both in plastic wallets.' His voice became even more unsteady. 'Her father said he hadn't known she was going out on a party boat. Her parents never knew where she went in the evenings. Talking to him was absolutely hideous, Amber. He was so distressed. So bewildered.'

'It must have been an accident,' she heard herself saying as her brain reeled. 'It can't have been suicide. It must have been an accident. She must have had too much to drink and fallen . . .'

'Fallen?' Angie stared at her as if she'd taken leave of her senses. '*Fallen?* You mean she fell like I did? Like Sharyn did? Like Zoë did?'

They were seated at the kitchen table in Angie's mother's house, Lola asleep in a carry-cot nearby.

Amber wrapped her hands tightly round a freshly made mug of tea. 'How could it be anything other than an accidental fall?' she said, feeling as bewildered as Tilly's father had. 'Zoë's fall and your fall only made sense if Sharyn had caused them out of jealousy.'

As Angie gasped, her eyebrows flying nearly into her hair, she said, 'God forgive me, Angie, but that's what I thought. Sharyn knew Johnny was going to start seriously dating Zoë and that night at the Prince, the night she died, Sharyn left the pub minutes before Zoë. Because Johnny had just given her her marching orders, she left in a lot of distress. Then, when you fell and there were so many similarities . . .'

'You never told me you thought Sharyn was responsible for my fall. How come you didn't tell me?' If the subject under discussion hadn't been so serious, Angie's incredulity would have been almost comic.

'Because she was my *sister* . . .' Amber's voice cracked and broke. 'I feel so bad, Angie, knowing I accused her of causing Zoë's death and so nearly causing yours, and not being able to tell her I now know that she didn't and that I'm sorry!'

Angie watched her fighting back tears of grief and remorse and then said, 'Let's make a list.'

'A list?' Amber stared at her blankly. 'What kind of a list?'

'A list of all the accidents. All the falls. All the things they have in common.'

She got up from the table and walked across the kitchen to where a shopping notepad, with pencil attached, lay on a shelf near the door.

'Let's begin with Zoë Fairminder,' she said, picking up the notepad and walking back to the table with it. 'Let's think of all the common denominators.'

She wrote down Zoë's name and underlined it. 'She was Johnny's girlfriend . . .'

'No, she wasn't. She was about to *become* Johnny's girlfriend. She was Fast-Boy's girlfriend.'

There was a moment's awkward pause. 'OK,' Angie said at last. 'She was my brother's girlfriend and your boyfriend's girlfriend. And her death was considered to be accidental. A barricade was removed, either by negligence or horse-play, from around a deep pit and, in the dark, Zoë fell into the pit and broke her neck.'

Against Zoë's name, Angie wrote: *A fall into a pit. DEAD. Circumstances suspicious. Open Verdict given.*

'It couldn't have been Johnny,' Amber protested. 'What would have been his motive? And besides, from the moment Zoë left the pub with Fast-Boy to the time

I left the pub and found her body, Johnny never moved away from the bar.'

'You're not saying it was Fast-Boy who did it, are you?' Angie's voice was sharp. 'Because it wasn't. He and Zoë went outside *together*. If he'd removed the barricade, she would have seen him do it. And as your dad pointed out at the time, she'd hardly have fallen into the pit then, no matter how nicely he'd asked her to.'

'I never did think it was Fast-Boy.' Amber's face was taut and strained. 'I'm just pointing out that it couldn't have been Johnny.'

Angie put a cross next to Zoë's name, as if acknowledging that her death might not fit the pattern she was trying to establish. She took a drink of her tea and then said resolutely, 'OK, Deirdre Crosby . . .' adding Deirdre's name beneath Zoë's.

'Deirdre died in a car crash,' said Amber. 'She'd only just passed her driving test and had been drinking. No one else was involved.'

'I know.' Angie stared down at the name, the pencil still in her hand. 'But she crashed because her brakes failed. And when brakes fail, it's always possible they've been tampered with. The Coroner gave an Open Verdict, remember?'

'I remember.'

'So? Do I leave Deirdre's name without a cross?'

Amber nodded.

'Abbra Hornby,' Angie said. 'D'you remember Abbra? She went out with Johnny all through the summer of 1968 and then she fell off the platform of a moving bus and almost got run over by a taxi. She and Johnny were never seen together afterwards. Johnny went back to dating Sharyn. What Abbra did, I don't know.'

Amber's silence was profound. Reluctantly, Angie

pencilled another cross, this time against Abbra Hornby's name.

'And then there was my fall,' she said heavily, adding her name to the list. 'You're not going to ask me to put a cross next to my name, too, are you?'

'No,' Amber said unhappily. 'But you've no proof there was foul play, have you? And Johnny wasn't the only person either at Take Six that night, or in the vicinity. Sharyn told me she was there, too. She'd been sure Johnny was secretly meeting you at the studios and was there to try and find out for certain. And she saw Tony there.'

'Tony?' Now it was Angie's turn to look blank. 'Tony wasn't there, Amber. Why should he have been?'

'Perhaps because, like Sharyn, he was jealous. According to Sharyn, Tony was just as aware as she was that you and Johnny were having an affair.'

Angie sat very still for a few moments. At last, she said, 'I don't want to speak ill of Sharyn, Amber. Not now she's dead. But she always did tell fibs. And Tony wasn't there that night. If he had been, he would have told me. As for the idea that he was there arranging for me to fall – no, it's not possible. It all happened before he had asked me to marry him. It was when he *must* have been in love with me. If anyone caused my accident that night, it was Johnny, not Tony. Just as he never went out with Abbra Hornby after her accident, he never again went out with me. Besides . . .' she looked down at her list, 'how or why would Tony have been responsible for any of the other accidents? He barely knew Deirdre Crosby or Abbra Hornby, and he didn't know Zoë at all. He only arrived home from Canada the night she died and, though he was in the pub that evening, at the same time she was, he never even spoke to her.'

Angie waited. When Amber made no attempt to break the silence, she said in a tight voice: 'And then there's Sharyn. She fell *twice*. Once down the wine-cellar steps – and don't ask me to believe that the cat got into the cellar by accident, because I don't believe it. Someone had half-starved it and put it in there, knowing full well it would fly up the steps like a bullet when the door was opened, and that the shock would be enough to make anyone lose their balance – especially a pregnant woman.'

'And Sharyn's fall at the tube station?' Amber asked, her face ashen. 'I was there, remember? And one thing I know for an absolute certainty. Johnny wasn't in the crush of people around Sharyn when she fell. If he'd been there, there's no way I could have missed seeing him.'

'He must have been there.'

'He wasn't. The only person who pushed out of the crush *away* from what had happened was a woman. Everyone else was either too riveted with horror to move or they were ghoulishly trying to get a glimpse of Sharyn's body.' Her voice was raw with remembered horror. 'Either way, Johnny wasn't there. He simply wasn't there, Angie. Truly.'

Slowly Angie drew a cross next to Sharyn's name and *Accident One. Accident Two* she left uncrossed.

'And Tilly,' she said finally. 'Tilly was Johnny's girl-friend. You told me that she was his girlfriend even before he married Sharyn. And Tilly didn't throw herself off the back of that boat. You've been on party boats yourself, Amber. The deck rails are waist-high. She would've had to climb halfway up to have been high enough, or unsteady enough, to topple over into the river.'

'There'll be an inquest,' Amber said through dry lips. 'We'll know more, then.'

'There was an inquest on Zoë Fairminder and Deirdre Crosby and Sharyn,' Angie said fiercely. 'Two Open Verdicts and one Accidental Death. And those verdicts were *wrong*, Amber. I can feel it in my blood and bones.'

Amber reached out for the notepad and swivelled it round so that she could read Angie's list.

X *Zoe Fairminder*. *About to become Johnny's girlfriend. A fall into a pit. DEAD. Circumstances suspicious. Open Verdict given*

Deirdre Crosby. *Johnny's girlfriend. Traffic accident due to brake failure. DEAD. Coroner's decision: Open Verdict.*

X *Abbra Hornby*. *Johnny's girlfriend. Fall from a moving bus. Could have been killed. Was Injured.*

Angie Martini, née Flynn. Johnny's girlfriend. Fall down flight of stone stairs. Circumstances suspicious. Badly Injured.

X *Sharyn Martini, née Bailey. Johnny's wife.*

    Accident One: Fall down wine-cellar steps. Near miscarriage.

    Accident Two: Fall at tube station under oncoming train.

    DEAD Coroner's verdict: Accidental Death

Tilly Armstrong. Johnny's girlfriend. Fall from a boat. DEAD

Despite the three crosses indicating doubt, it was still a list that made disturbing reading. Six girlfriends of Johnny's, all dead or injured. *And those were only the ones they knew about.*

She remembered what Happy Harry had told her about Johnny as a child – about the way he had killed Fast-Boy's dog. Despite all Johnny's surface likeability and charisma, he was violent. There'd been the incident when, according to Cheyenne, he'd held Jimmy Jones by his ankles out of a sixth-floor window. And there was the common gossip as to his being responsible for Jimmy Jones' death. Plus, he couldn't possibly run his personal protection and security businesses if he wasn't a man who thrived on intimidation and fear. But was being violent – in the way that Johnny undoubtedly was – the same as being psychotic?

And he would have to be psychotic to be responsible for even one of the deaths, or attempted deaths, listed on Angie's notepad.

And he was her half-brother – a secret even Angie wasn't privy to.

And he was Lola Buttercup's father.

One thought after another chased around her brain. If she picked up the telephone and spoke to the police – which was what her instincts were telling her she should do – she would be grassing on her own flesh and blood.

But it would only be grassing if the investigation proved that Johnny *was* responsible for even one of the 'accidents' on Angie's list.

Recalling the sight of Sharyn's body as it was finally retrieved from beneath the train, she pushed her chair away from the table.

'What are you going to do?' Angie asked as she watched her walk to the telephone.

Amber picked up the receiver and began dialling a number she knew well. 'I'm going to show your list to a policeman I know,' she said.

He suggested that they meet at the Trafalgar in Greenwich. With the manner of Tilly's death so raw in her mind, a pub overlooking the Thames would not have been Amber's first choice, but she gritted her teeth, knowing that the only important thing was that they met. Rob would know whether Angie's list and suspicions – and her suspicions, too, – were viable or pathetically laughable.

The Trafalgar, because of its position on the river, its nearness to the *Cutty Sark*, and the fact that it was of interest in itself, being such an old and historic pub, was always crowded, and Amber was grateful for the general hustle and bustle. The noise level would lend privacy to her conversation with Rob and, amongst a throng of other drinkers, they would be barely noticeable.

'Hi,' he said, rising to his feet as she walked across the old, uneven wooden floor to the table he had cornered. 'I take it this is business, not pleasure?'

The table was directly in front of a leaded window giving superb views of the river. 'Yes.' She averted her eyes from the sight of a boat ploughing upstream towards Westminster. She'd made the reason she wanted to see him clear when she had telephoned him. She hadn't wanted him to think she'd had second thoughts about breaking off with him and that she was hoping for some kind of a reconciliation.

The problem was, the instant she'd set eyes on him, love, longing and lust had surged through her with such intensity her knees had wobbled.

'I've got you a Bacardi and Coke,' he said, indicating the glass and bottle on the table. 'Didn't think you'd want to wait while I fought through the crush at the bar.'

'Fine. Thanks.' She sat down, her knees still wobbly, though now their unsteadiness was as much at the thought of what it was she was about to do as the feelings Rob Gowan was so ace at arousing in her.

'What is it?' he asked, sitting down beside her with his back to the window so that he had all the activity taking place in the bar in view. It was the sort of thing he did automatically as a policeman. And, as a policeman, he knew instinctively that Amber was about to impart information. He waited, his curiosity intense.

'It's this.' She was wearing a searing pink T-shirt and

lime-green cotton dungarees. From one of her many pockets, she took Angie's list and laid it on the table in front of him.

It was, she knew, fairly self-explanatory. Nevertheless, she hadn't expected him to understand the situation quite as quickly as he did.

'Christ,' he said softly beneath his breath, but not in surprise. It was more in satisfaction that long-held suspicions were being given credence.

'It's not my list,' she said, almost defensively. 'It's my friend, Angie's.'

'Angie Martini? Tony's wife?'

'Yes – but they're not living together any more. They've separated.'

'Tell me about her fall,' he said, his eyes on the sheet of notepaper.

'Don't you want any other explanation?' She'd been so psyched up to give one that she felt almost irritated by his not asking. 'And don't you want to know about the three names that come before hers on the list?'

'No.' His pleasantly good-looking face was grim. 'I've had a bee in my bonnet for yonks about the number of Johnny's girlfriends who've come to physical grief in one way or another. Zoë Fairminder, I know about. I've seen her autopsy report and I've read the inquest findings. Deirdre Crosby, I also know about and, as in Zoë's case, I've read all the official reports. I know about Abbra Hornby's accident because her parents were selling a house through Lampeter's at the time. They'd told David that their daughter was Johnny Martini's girlfriend in order to impress upon him the kind of person their daughter ran with – in case he tried to short-change them – and they told him about the near-escape she had, falling from a moving bus in Trafalgar Square. I know nothing about the other accidents and fatalities – apart from Sharyn's, of course.'

He came to a stop and then said awkwardly. 'About Sharyn . . .'

Tears burned her eyes. 'Let me tell you about Angie first,' she said, wondering how on God's earth she was going to be able to re-live and re-tell what had happened at High Street Kensington tube station.

As succinctly as she could, she told him about Angie's affair with Johnny, way back in the winter of 1966. She told him about their meeting-place – and the people who knew of it: herself, Sharyn, Tony. And possibly, though she wasn't sure, Marco. And then she told him about the fall from Angie's perspective. 'Seconds after the lights went out, as she was edging her way down the stairs, she said it was as if a snake suddenly whipped against her legs at ankle-height – and certainly she fell exceptionally hard. She fractured the neck of her pelvis. Her pubic bones were crushed. Her shoulder dislocated. Because of all the damage to her pelvis and the lesions, due to leaking blood, she can't have children.'

She paused and took a much-needed drink.

Wisely he remained silent.

'Afterwards,' she said, putting her glass back down on the table, 'when Angie could walk again, she went back to the building to look at where she had fallen in daylight. She found a disused pipe at one side of the step and an air vent at the other, both at the same height – ankle-height. The pipe showed signs of having had something looped round it, and she's convinced it was a wire that had been stretched across the step and tied to the air vent – and that was the "snake" she felt against her legs as she toppled over and plunged down the entire stone flight.'

'You mean she believes someone tried to kill her?'

'Yes.'

'Who found her?'

'Johnny.'

His decision to speak with Angie Martini officially was immediate.

'And Sharyn?' he prompted.

Amber drew in a deep, shuddering breath. 'Sharyn and Johnny's flat was . . . is . . . pretty sumptuous and it has its own wine cellar. When Sharyn was four months pregnant she fell down the steps and nearly lost the baby as a result. No one thought the fall sinister. She'd just had a row with Mum and she'd gone home upset and angry. When she opened the cellar door, a cat sprang up out of the darkness at her and she lost her balance and fell.'

'Her cat? Her and Johnny's cat?'

'No. It was a half-starved stray. We all thought it had got trapped in there after having slipped into the house, or that it had entered the wine cellar through the air vent. But Angie reckons the cat had been put in the wine cellar with the purpose of scaring someone – Sharyn – half to death when they opened the door. She thinks the cat was also purposely half-starved to make it even more desperate to escape. As for the second accident . . . the tube accident . . .'

She was unable to continue and he covered her clasped, clenched hands with his. 'Unless you have something to tell me that wasn't in the Coroner's Report, you don't need to go through it all again, darling.'

The endearment was, he knew, totally out of order when she'd made it so clear she didn't want their relationship to revert to what it had once been, but he could no more have prevented himself from using it than he could have prevented himself from breathing.

'You've read it?'

'Oh yes. I read it to see if Johnny could possibly have been behind it.'

'And he couldn't, could he?'

'Not unless he, or one of his minions, was there and you kept the information to yourself.'

'No. Never.' Her voice shook with emotion. 'I wouldn't protect anyone if I thought they'd had anything to do with Sharyn's death.'

'And Tilly?' he asked, aware how close she was to breaking down. 'Is this the Tilly who worked with you at Lampeter's? I didn't know she'd died.'

'It only happened two days ago. There hasn't been an inquest yet. I don't have any details. Only that she fell from a party boat on the Thames and drowned.'

'And she was Johnny's girlfriend?'

'Oh yes.' There was a world of bitterness in her voice. 'Tilly has . . . had . . . been Johnny's girlfriend for a long time. Even before Johnny's marriage to Sharyn. Johnny told Tony it was over when he and Sharyn married, but it wasn't. And Tilly vowed to me it was over when Sharyn died. But it wasn't.'

She took another sip of her Bacardi and Coke and then said, 'I bumped into Tony up town last week. He was on his way to Charing Cross Station and I was on my way to meet . . . well, it doesn't matter who I was going to meet. I had time in hand and so it seemed a good idea to have a drink together. I've always got on well with Tony and . . .'

For an insane moment, the temptation to tell him of her true relationship to Tony and Johnny nearly overcame her. 'Anyway, we were walking through Leicester Square when we saw Johnny with Tilly. He had his arm round her waist and her head was on his shoulder. I telephoned your brother-in-law the next morning and told him he wouldn't be seeing me in the office again. I couldn't bear the thought of continuing to work with Tilly. I didn't ever want to see her again. And now,' she added, pain raw in her voice, 'I shan't.'

He was silent for a moment or two and then he said, 'You were right to come to me with the list, Amber. It's true that Johnny isn't implicated in even one of the accidents or fatalities, but, like your friend Angie, I think it's sinister.' He slipped the list into his pocket.

'And you'll find out if it is, one way or the other?'

'I'll do my best.'

First, he'd have to convince Ramsden that such a catalogue of deaths and accidents warranted further investigation – and that wouldn't be easy. He did, though, now have a tool with which to have another go at cracking Little Donnie. It would need a good few half-truths. He'd have to convince Donnie that there was real evidence against Johnny where these 'accidents' were concerned and, most particularly, that Johnny had been responsible for Deirdre's death. If he could do that, then the chances of Donnie grassing up Johnny for Jimmy Jones' murder were high.

'Leave it to me, Amber,' he said as she rose to her feet. 'Trust me.'

It was something Johnny often said and she winced. 'Yes,' she said, knowing that, in Rob's case, he meant it. 'Thanks, Rob.'

She turned away from him, walking out of the pub at a speed he was quite sure indicated how reluctant she was to be in his presence – unless he could be of professional use to her.

Well, that at least he could do.

He'd speak to Ramsden about the names on the list,

but first he'd have a quiet drink with Little Donnie.

As he rose to his feet and began heading in the direction of the main entrance and the pub's public telephone, he wasn't thinking about the things he intended saying to Little Donnie.

He was jealously wondering who it was Amber had been on her way to meet the evening she and Tony saw Johnny with Tilly.

Amber made her way home not knowing which she felt worse about; handing over Angie's list or turning her back on Rob when she'd wanted, more than anything, to stay with him.

Knowing that Angie would be in no hurry to be relieved of the task of babysitting Lola, she decided to make a detour to the Prince of Wales. She'd only had one drink while she was with Rob and she was definitely in need of another.

The minute she stepped inside the pub and Johnny called out, 'Amber! Thank God. Have you heard the news?' she knew just what a monumentally bad decision she had made.

He was the very last person she wanted to see, but she couldn't immediately turn her back on him and leave.

'What news?' she asked, knowing full well and walking towards him with feet like lead.

He was standing at the bar with Tony and he looked terrible. Ever since Sharyn's death he had lost all his air of slick sophistication. Now, though still suited and booted, nothing about him looked crisp any more. He seemed haggard and careworn and years older than his twin.

'Tilly's dead,' he said, looking so dazed that Amber was filled with the sudden conviction that he couldn't possibly have had anything to do with her death. 'I know you didn't know that there was anything going on between me and Tilly, but there was. I was thinking that perhaps she'd make a great step-mum for Lola – and now she's dead. Christ.' As he picked up a generously full balloon-glass of brandy, his hand was shaking. 'Everyone I've ever loved has died. D'you know that?'

His speech was slurred and it was obvious that the brandy he was now drinking was only the latest of many. 'Zoë died, Sharyn's died. And now Tilly's died.'

Amber bit back the temptation to remind him about Deirdre Crosby. Perhaps he hadn't been in love with Deirdre. Perhaps Deirdre belonged in another category.

'Steady on, Johnny.' Tony's concern, as he put an arm round Johnny's shoulders, was touchingly obvious.

Watching him, Amber knew that some time in the very near future she would tell him that his father was also her father. If she knew Tony at all, he would be more pleased by the news than shocked.

'I already know about Tilly,' she said, not wanting to feel any more deceitful than she already did. 'Mr Lampeter rang me with the news this morning. Tilly's father had telephoned him and . . .' She'd been about to say that the police had also had a word with him, but decided that any mention of the police would only be an aggravation.

'I'm like Typhoid Mary,' Johnny said with sudden vehemence. 'Everyone she came into contact with died, but not her, even though she was the carrier of the disease. And every woman I love – or even come near to loving – dies. A woman would have to be mad to come within a yard of me. She'd have to have a death-wish!'

From behind the bar, Happy Harry said, 'Vodka and bitter lemon, Amber?'

She shook her head. 'No. I hadn't realized how late it is. Mum left for Marbella this morning and Angie's babysitting Lola for me. I need to get back. I said I'd only be gone for an hour, and that was three hours ago.'

She began beating a hasty retreat to the door, not wanting anyone to ask her where it was she had been.

'Lola,' Johnny said, his voice cracking on something that sounded like a sob. 'Thank God I've still got Lola, Tony. Thank Christ, I've still got my little daughter!'

The emotional temperature was so charged that the second Amber stumbled out into the street she gasped for air. Johnny was either an actor deserving of an Oscar, or a man almost destroyed. Whichever he was, he was also a father whose thoughts were turning to the one thing still left in his life: Lola Buttercup.

And Lola Buttercup was the only thing that she now felt she had in her life.

What if he took Lola away from her?

What if – horror of horrors – he decided he wanted to look after Lola himself?

Chapter Twenty

Rob found Little Donnie in the same pub they'd met in previously. It wasn't a meeting Donnie had agreed to without strong persuasion. Only when Rob told him that the alternative to a voluntary chat was a much more unpleasant kind of chat in Tower Bridge nick, had Donnie been convinced of its necessity.

'So what the fuck is this about?' he said as Rob bought two pints of lager in. 'You need to watch the way you're behaving, Rob. You're getting illusions of grandeur. You ain't an inspector yet, you know.'

The temptation to say that he soon would be, was nearly too much for Rob. Instead he took a typed list out of his pocket and laid it on the bar in front of Donnie.

In essence, it was the list Amber had given him. What he'd done, though, was to flesh out the details of what had happened to each girl and to add remarks which left little doubt as to Johnny's responsibility for each accident.

'What the fuck is this?' Donnie eyed it with derision. Then he saw his sister's name. 'Hey!' he said, his manner changing instantly. 'What are you doing, carrying my sister's name around on you? And on Met headed paper? That's a fucking liberty! That's way out of fucking order!'

'Read the list, Donnie. Work it out for yourself.'

Donnie read it.

It took a little time.

'What the fuck is this?' he said again, though this time with bewilderment, not derision. 'Are you pigs trying to make out Johnny's even sicker than he is? Why would he be killing all his girlfriends off? It don't make sense.'

'Where Johnny's concerned, does it have to make sense? You said yourself he was a sicko.'

'Yeah. Well. Not *that* fucking sick.' Donnie looked at the list again. 'This Fairminder bird, for instance. Why would Johnny have done for –' He stopped abruptly.

'Why would Johnny have done for Jimmy Jones if he himself had arranged for Zoë Fairminder to fall to her death?' Rob said, making an inspired guess. 'You tell me, Donnie. And you tell me why Abbra Hornby is willing to testify that Johnny pushed her off the platform of a fast-moving bus . . .'

This was such a blatant lie that he had his fingers crossed as he said it.

Donnie frowned, beginning to look unsure.

'And what about your sister's death?' Rob persisted, presenting another of his strongly held suspicions as if it were an incontrovertible fact. 'Her brakes failed. There was no evidence they'd been tampered with. The Coroner gave an open verdict. But we've got an unofficial statement from an apprentice mechanic who was working for the guy who did the tampering for Johnny. Once Johnny is safely behind bars for Jimmy Jones' murder, he's going to make an official statement and is prepared to go in the witness box. Johnny Martini is responsible for your sister's death, Donnie. And for Zoë Fairminder's death. And Sharyn Bailey's. And Tilly Conway's. Now, are you going to give me the gen on Jimmy Jones' murder, or not?'

'Are you tellin' me this is for real?'

344

'Absolutely.'

Still Donnie hesitated.

Rob took a drink of his pint and then said conversationally, 'How old would your sister have been if she hadn't tangled with Johnny? Twenty-three? Twenty-four?'

'Twenty-three.' Little Donnie's eyes were suspiciously bright. 'I'm going to kill the fuck. So help me God, but I'm going to swing for him! I'm going to fucking kill him!'

'People don't swing for murder these days, more's the pity. And you couldn't kill Johnny. You'd be no match for him and you know it. Instead of getting mad, why not get even?'

He paused to let his words sink in, and then said again, 'So . . . what's the gen on Jimmy Jones' murder, Donnie? Did Johnny do it? Did you see him do it?'

''Course I fucking did. Johnny always liked to have an audience. I wasn't nearby, though. I didn't have a fucking thing to do with it. And I didn't have anything to do with getting rid of the body, either. That was down to Cheyenne.'

'Drink up.' Rob's voice was taut as a bow as he tried not to show his elation. 'We're going to Tower Bridge so I can take a proper statement from you.'

'Yeah, well, just one thing before we do . . .'

He was looking his usual shifty self again and Rob hoped fervently that he hadn't counted his chickens before they'd hatched.

'What?' he asked.

'I'm not so worried about Marco now he's retired to Spain, but I don't fancy the thought of grassing Johnny up and going in the witness box to testify against him if his twin is still running around loose.'

'Tony?' Rob's eyebrows lifted. If Tony Martini was someone to run scared of, he didn't know about it. 'I thought Tony was legal.'

'Nah, don't you believe it. Tony runs the long-firm scams for Johnny. Has done for four years. Mebbe five. And the last one he ran for him, he torched the building and they made a double killing by claiming on the insurance. Cheyenne's uncle was the front man for them.'

Following a pattern that Rob had noticed with a lot of grasses, once Donnie had finally started, there was no stopping him. 'And that wasn't really so much of a double killing as a treble.'

He sniggered.

Rob waited.

'There was a body found in the remains of the building,' Donnie said, sounding almost gleeful at the prospect of putting away not just one of the twins but both of them. 'A tramp's. Know which fire I'm talking about now? Only the bloke who died wasn't a tramp. And he was dead before the warehouse went up. Me and Cheyenne and Johnny didn't know a thing about it till afterwards, when an uncle that Tony couldn't stand went missing. Then we all put two and two together, but we didn't say nothing. Why should we? Johnny never even told his dad.'

'OK.' Rob let his breath out very slowly. When Donnie gave his statement in Tower Bridge nick, Colin Ramsden was going to be over the moon. His own promotion to Inspector would proceed like wildfire and, more importantly still, once Johnny was on remand, witnesses who could pin one – maybe even two or three – of the accidents on Angie's list on to Johnny, would finally feel safe enough to start coming out of the woodwork.

He'd done a good day's work. Ahead lay the real

work. Gathering proof that Johnny had been responsible for Sharyn Bailey's death.

The next morning found Angie pushing Lola's pram away from the main road and up the only slope Bermondsey possessed. In the row of shops that lay at the top of the slope, a small supermarket had just opened and she wanted to check it out.

'You're surely not volunteering to spend hours looking after Lola *again*,' Amber had said, knowing very well that she was. 'I might as well get another job and let you look after her all the time.'

'Except that you don't want to,' Angie had responded with a grin. 'We could both look after her, I suppose. Even though me and Tony are now officially separated, I've no intention of going back to office work – or any other boring nine-to-five job – and neither have I any intention of taking money from Tony. Not when it's Johnny who's his pay-master. I've decided to rent a stall in Bermondsey market and make hats and sell them. You could help me if you wanted. With your odd-ball fashion sense and skill with zany colour combinations, I reckon you'd be pretty good at making hats.'

She positioned the pram at an angle outside the entrance door of the supermarket and put its brake on. It was a hot day and Lola was lying fast asleep on a cool cotton sheet, shielded from the sun by a parasol sunshade.

As she went into the supermarket she reflected that everything she'd said to Amber had been absolutely true. Amber *would* be ace at making hats. They could have a little workshop down at the cottage and then drive back to Bermondsey on market days to sell their stock. For the first time in ages she became aware that she felt almost happy. Was it because she was beginning to see a future for herself away from any involvement with Tony? Or was it because the doubts and suspicions of years had finally been put on to someone else's shoulders? And not just anyone's – a Detective-Sergeant's.

She picked up a wire basket, perusing the well-stocked shelves as she pondered the amazing fact of Amber having had a romantic entanglement she had known nothing about. Even more amazing was that the entanglement had been with a policeman. It explained, of course, why Amber had kept their relationship secret. It was hardly a connection the Martinis would have been happy about.

She put a bottle of HP sauce and a bag of sugar into her basket. There were six aisles and the cash till and exit were about fifteen yards from the entrance. If not exactly Sainsbury's, it was certainly a step-up in convenience from their rather scruffy local grocer's.

She was just beginning to make her way back down the third aisle when an elderly lady next to her gave a gasp of alarm. 'Oh dear!' she said, a box of soap-powder in her hand as she looked towards the window and the street. 'Oh *dear!*'

Angie followed her gaze to see what it was that had alarmed her. An exceptionally tall woman, wearing a black-and-white chequered headscarf and a black coat, was walking across the road away from the supermarket with such little regard for the heavy flow of traffic it was a miracle she was still on her feet.

And then Angie saw that it wasn't the woman's safety the elderly lady was concerned about.

It was Lola's.

The pram was no longer parked at a safe angle on

the pavement, facing in towards the building. Instead it was facing directly down the slope.

And it was moving.

She dropped the basket she was carrying and began to run, making the split-second decision that she stood more chance of halting the pram in its tracks if she could get ahead of it than she would by trying to catch up with it.

The exit, then. She needed to make for the supermarket's exit, not its entrance. *And she had to get there before the pram rolled past it.*

She was shouting as she hurtled down the aisle towards the cash till, vainly hoping that someone nearer to the exit than she was would be able to run ahead of her into the street and catch hold of the pram's handle.

No one did, because there was no one in a position to do so.

The elderly lady was way behind her, still clutching her box of soap powder. The girl on the cash till had seen what was happening and was giving squeaks of horror, but that was all. Trapped in the little closed off area in which she sat, she was making no move to vault out of it.

Angie skidded round the end of the aisle, sending a pile of ornately stacked baked-bean cans flying. Why was there no one around? It was a busy weekday morning, so why was there no one in the street? The pram was still trundling past the long window frontage, gathering speed. She smashed a way through the narrow aisle at the cash till and careened towards the plate-glass exit door.

She had to be in time. *She had to be.* Once the pram sped past the exit door it would be only yards from the busy main road that formed a junction with the sloping street.

349

Her hands were slippery as she yanked the door open. The pram had passed her. She was aware of someone on the far side of the street shouting. Of car horns tooting. Of herself screaming. With her heart feeling as if it was about to burst, she launched herself in a flying rugby tackle, her hands closing on the pram's handle.

The pram didn't come to an instant halt. Rocking from side to side, it dragged her with it and then, as her weight finally ground it to a near halt, it toppled over, skidding on its side, spilling Lola Buttercup on to the hard pavement.

There were people now. Lots of people. Someone wearing a shop-assistant's overall was scooping a crying Lola Buttercup up into her arms. A gentleman was righting the pram.

'Are you all right, dear?' someone else was asking her in concern.

'I think she's broken her arm,' another voice was saying. 'I think we should call for an ambulance.'

Angie had enough experience of broken limbs to know very well that she'd broken her arm. Her arm, though, and the pain screaming through it, was not her immediate concern. 'Lola?' she said, desperately craning her head in Lola's direction. 'Is Lola hurt? Is she all right? *Is she all right?*'

'She's not very happy, dear,' the woman holding her said. 'But she doesn't seem to be hurt. Still, it'd be best to have her checked over by a doctor, wouldn't it?'

'There's an ambulance on its way,' said the well-dressed gentleman who had righted the pram and was now picking up the parasol. 'They'll check the child over.'

Utterly ashamed for doing so, Angie began to cry. The depth of her fear had put her into such a state of shock that she couldn't help herself. What if she hadn't caught hold of the pram in time? What if it had careered into the busy main road?

What if Lola Buttercup had died?

In the hospital, when Amber arrived, she burst into tears again. 'It was . . . awful,' she said at last. 'One minute I was wondering if I should get cocoa or if Ovaltine would make a nice change, the next all I could see was the pram beginning to roll down the slope towards the road. I love Lola just as much as you do, Amber. If anything had happened to her, I would never have forgiven myself. And there was just *no one* there to catch hold of the pram. The tall woman in the chequered headscarf didn't even seem to realize what was going on behind her. The girl at the cash till was just *stupid* and . . . and . . .'

Tears ran down her face and dripped on to her hospital nightie. 'And I can't believe I didn't put the brake on properly. I never checked it. I was thinking about how nice it would be if the two of us moved in together and began a business together, making hats – and I was so busy thinking about that, that I never checked whether the brake was really and truly fast down.'

'Stop torturing yourself over it, Angie,' Amber said firmly. 'Apart from your broken arm, no real damage has been done. Lola doesn't even have a graze. She's in a cot down on the children's ward, but only until I've finished visiting you. Then I'm taking her home.'

Angie wiped her tears away with her fingers. 'I only think of the cottage as home, now. It's so quiet and peaceful on the Isle of Grain. What I'd like is for you and Lola to live down there with me. As soon as they let me out of hospital – and it won't be long, once I've been down to the plaster room and they've set my arm – I want to go straight down to Grain. I need to be there. It calms me down.'

'I could do with a bit of calm myself,' Amber said wryly, remembering how hateful it had been, running into Johnny in the Prince of Wales. 'What d'you say about me going down there today, with Lola?'

'And me joining you the minute I leave here?' Angie's face brightened immeasurably. 'I'll have to come down by mini-cab. I won't be able to drive, not with my arm in plaster. You'll have to take a cab there, as well. It'll cost a fair bit. It must be thirty miles, but it'll be worth it.' She hesitated a minute and then said, 'Would you mind if I asked Fast-Boy if he'd like to join us?'

'Why should I mind?' Amber suppressed a flush of guilt, aware that, with Rob so powerfully in her thoughts, it wasn't a prospect that was sending her into raptures. 'He is my boyfriend.'

'You know there's no phone down there, don't you?' Angie's eyebrows pulled together in a slight frown. 'Perhaps it might be an idea for you to ring your policeman friend before you leave. Just in case he has any news.'

Given that it was only twenty-four hours since her meeting with him, Amber knew that Rob having news was highly unlikely. Nevertheless, letting him know where she was, seemed a sensible idea.

After she left the ward and, before going to collect Lola, she went down to the reception area, where there was a large bank of public telephones.

'I'm sorry,' said the WPC who answered Rob's extension. 'DC Gowan is in a meeting. Can I help you?'

The answer was emphatically no, but Amber didn't say that. Instead, she found herself saying, 'This is a personal call and I'd really appreciate it if you would give him a message from me. Please tell him Amber phoned – and that Angie and Lola have been involved in an accident. Angie is in Ward Six at Lewisham Hospital and I'm taking Lola, who is unhurt, down to Angie's cottage on the Isle of Grain. I'm going to be there for a few days and will be out of contact as there's no telephone.'

'OK.' The WPC's voice indicated that she wished Rob wouldn't make so free with his extension number. 'Will do.'

Forty-five minutes later, with Lola fed and changed and gurgling contentedly in a carry-cot beside her, Amber was seated in the rear of a mini-cab heading out of London and into north-east Kent.

It was the first time since receiving the telephone call from the hospital saying that Angie had been admitted, that she'd had any real time to think.

And she wanted to think, for there was something nagging at the corner of her mind; something she couldn't quite catch hold of; something she knew was both important and unpleasant.

It was mid-afternoon now and as the cab skirted Blackheath and then settled down to a steady speed on the A2, Amber rested a hand on the rim of the carry-cot and closed her eyes.

What had happened to the pram outside the supermarket had been an accident. It had to have been. However sick in the head Johnny might be, he would never harm his daughter. Why, though, would he have harmed so many girls he had apparently been in love with?

If, she thought.

If he had harmed them.

Though she had no difficulty at all in believing him capable of killing Jimmy Jones, she still balked at the idea of his killing Deirdre and Tilly – and Sharyn.

As she thought of her sister, her eyes flew open. The images she was seeing in her mind's eye too horrific. *Had* Johnny been in the tube station? Had he perhaps been 'guised up to prevent her recognizing him?

There had been very few men in the crush on the platform and none who were wearing heavy beards or hats or sunglasses, or any of the other usual methods of disguise. Women shoppers had been very heavily in the majority and the only woman who stood out in memory was the tall woman pushing against the tide of people craning forward to see over the lip of the platform to where Sharyn had fallen.

Her heart jolted with such violence that she thought it had stopped.

A tall woman wearing a chequered headscarf.

An headscarf identical, according to Angie, to the one worn by the woman who had walked away from the supermarket and across the road as Lola's pram had begun to roll. And it was a hot summer's day. Why would the woman Angie had seen have been wearing a headscarf and coat?

The answer was that she wouldn't have been, not unless the headscarf and coat were intended to disguise her identity.

Or his identity.

She gave an agonized cry and the mini-cab driver swung his head around, saying anxiously, 'Do you want me to stop? You're not going to be sick, are you? If you suffer from car-sickness, you should have told me.'

'No. No I'm not sick.'

It wasn't true. She felt more vilely sick than she'd ever felt before in her life. The only person she knew who was adept at disguising himself as a woman was Fast-Boy. And the person at the tube station and the super-market couldn't have been Fast-Boy. It couldn't.

They were well clear of Greater London now, speeding down on the A207 towards Dartford.

She remembered Angie telling her how the only time in his life that Fast-Boy had ever threatened to kill her had been the night she went to meet Johnny at Take Six; the night she'd fallen and been lamed for life. And she thought of how Fast-Boy must have felt when Zoë had told him she was jilting him to become Johnny's girl-friend. And of the way he had hit Angie in the night-club, the night before her wedding. Not only hit her, but kicked her as she lay in a crumpled heap on the ground.

And then she remembered that, as she'd left her, Angie had been about to ring Fast-Boy and ask him if he'd like to spend a few days down at the cottage with them. If he were to drive there on his bike, he could quite well be there by the time she arrived.

And if he was . . . ? Then what? What was she going to say to him? *Excuse me for asking, darling, but were you responsible for my sister's death? And have you just tried to arrange a similar accidental death for my baby niece?*

Her heart began beating so erratically it hurt.

She was being ridiculous. She was behaving like some-one mentally deranged. The very idea that he was respon-sible for Sharyn's death and the incident with the pram was ludicrous. Laughable. But now that the idea had lodged in her brain, she couldn't shake herself free of it. She was going to have to talk to him about it, either at the cottage or somewhere else.

She lifted Lola Buttercup out of the carry-cot and held her chubby body close to her for comfort, suddenly feeling that instead of heading towards sanctuary; she was heading towards disaster.

Chapter Twenty-one

He wasn't there. Her relief, when the mini-cab driver dropped her off at the cottage and she saw that there was no Harley-Davidson parked anywhere in sight, was immense.

Hoisting the carry-cot from the rear seat, she put it down on the grass that edged the rough track they'd just bumped down. Then, having fumbled in her shoulder bag for her purse, she paid the driver.

'You sure this is where you want to be?' he said doubtfully, eyeing the lonely vista of reed-beds and estuary. 'What are you, a bird-watcher or something?'

'I'm just a person who likes peace and quiet,' she said, wryly amused and hoping fervently that, for the next few days, peace and quiet was what she was going to get.

'Each to his own,' he said, stuffing the money she had given him into his shirt pocket. 'Can't say I'd like it out here. Don't think anyone would, unless they liked fishing.'

He slewed his car round on the dried mud of the track and headed back towards civilization, bumping and swaying over the ruts which marked the course of the last heavy rainfall, a cloud of dust hanging thickly in his wake.

Feeling slightly cheered by her brief brush with normality, she picked up the handles of the carry-cot in one hand and a bagful of groceries with the other and turned towards the low, white weather-boarded cottage.

It had been built as a smallholding. The lean-to attached to it, once home to a couple of goats, was now used only for storing paraffin and coal. A couple of rickety sheds, standing in what the estate agent had imaginatively called a back garden and covered in cloudy-blue ceanothus, housed remnants of rusting farm implements. From the rear it looked out towards the Thames Estuary, bearing the brunt of brutal north-east winds, a Virginia creeper clinging tenaciously to its walls. A couple of hundred yards or so away, the sea wall could be seen and, earlier in the year, she and Angie had walked along it, enjoying the salt-spray laden air and the sight of large flocks of geese and ducks.

A smile tugged at the corner of her mouth as she slipped Angie's key into the lock and turned it. Perhaps she was more of a bird-watcher than she'd given herself credit for. If she weren't careful, she'd soon be knowing sandpipers from lapwings.

'Now then, Lola my darling,' she said, putting the carry-cot down on the sofa in the oak-beamed sitting-room. 'We're home and Auntie Amber is going to make you up a nice bottle of baby milk.'

Lola gurgled and blew her a raspberry.

Amber blew her one back.

The sitting-room was cosy – Angie had seen to that. She'd painted the walls the colour of burnt umber, filling the chimney alcoves with bookshelves for acres of orange-spined Penguin paperbacks. The sofa and armchair were piled with deep yellow cushions and in the window embrasure was a window-seat with more cushions. There was a rocking-chair that had come from Bermondsey Market and that Angie had painted a bright green; an open fireplace with a shining brass fender around its hearth and a gold-framed Impressionist print of a woman with a child in her arms above it. The floor was wood, covered with a scattering of muted-coloured rugs that the two of them had picked up in various London markets.

Grateful that it wasn't winter and she didn't have to faff about filling paraffin heaters to back up a coal fire, she took the bag of groceries into the kitchen. A bottle of milk for Lola; a cup of tea for herself. Then she'd think about food.

She plugged the electric kettle in, noting with satisfaction how much more cheery the kitchen looked than when she had first seen it. Instead of being covered in flaking green distemper, the walls were now painted sunshine yellow and there were gingham curtains at the windows and pots of herbs on the window ledge.

Attractive as the cottage was, now it had Angie's distinctive personality stamped on it, she wasn't sure how she felt about living there. It was just too isolated. Too lacking in mod cons.

Deep in thought, she spooned milk powder into Lola's feeding bottle, aware that there was an alternative. With her mother now in Spain again – this time on an apparently permanent basis – Angie could easily move in with her. Then they could spend long weekends down here, but not be down here entirely.

There came a loud rap on the front door and she dropped Lola's feeding-bottle with a clatter.

Out on the estuary there could be no casual callers.

Fast-Boy had arrived.

She walked back through the house to open the door to him, taking deep, steadying breaths. She didn't *have* to confront him with all the dreadful possibilities that had raced around her mind on the drive down. She could wait until Angie was with her. In fact, it was only right that she spoke with Angie first.

Forcing a smile she was far from feeling, she opened the door.

The person on the doorstep wasn't Fast-Boy.

It was Tony.

She was taken totally by surprise. That Tony might be in the habit of paying visits to the cottage was something that had never occurred to her.

'Angie isn't here, Tony,' she said, feeling as if she should make some sort of an apology. 'She's broken her arm and is in Lewisham Hospital.'

'I know. It's the reason I've come.'

Wearing a black T-shirt and a grey Italian suit, he strolled past her into the cottage's low-ceilinged sitting-room and suddenly – seeing him out of context, away from his usual haunts and without his being in Johnny's shadow – he looked almost like a stranger.

'I'm sorry,' she said as she followed him into the room, bewildered. 'I don't understand.'

He looked towards the carry-cot where Lola was kicking fat little feet.

'I've come for Lola,' he said. 'I'm taking her to Spain. Tonight.'

It was such a bolt from the blue she could hardly comprehend it. 'But you can't!' she protested, knowing very well that, if he wanted to, he could. 'Lola's *my* responsibility.'

'I have to.' His square-jawed face was uncompromising. 'Lola isn't safe here, Amber. She isn't safe anywhere the old man isn't on hand to keep an eye on her. You must realize that yourself, after what happened this morning – and especially after what happened to Tilly Conway.'

The room swam.

'Oh God,' she whispered devoutly, pressing a hand to her mouth, not having to ask him what it was he meant; knowing only too well.

She swayed and then, knowing her legs were about to give way, sat down abruptly on the sofa, next to the carry-cot.

'It helps that you so obviously know what I'm talking about,' he said grimly. 'Christ, but it's a nightmare, Amber. I've known ever since we were kids that Johnny's a psycho; ever since he started the fire in which our mother died. One of the reasons I came back from Canada was so that I could keep an eye on him; hold him in check.'

He ran a hand over his hair. He still wore it in a hippy-looking ponytail and it was smooth and flat to his head. 'I never thought it would come to this, though.' A pulse began pounding at the corner of his jaw. 'I never thought he'd try to harm his own daughter.'

'But . . . do you know for sure that he has?' She was clutching at straws and knew it –besides, far better that it was Johnny who was a raving psychopath than Fast-Boy.

'I know it was Johnny who tipped Tilly Conway over the side of the *Mary-Jane*,' he said, the pulse still pounding. 'He told me so himself. And I've always had doubts about the way Sharyn died. That being the case, I don't have any doubt at all that, if an accident took place this morning, to Lola, then it was Johnny who was responsible for it.'

Lola, now hungry, began to cry.

Amber rose abruptly to her feet, latching on to the need to feed her as if the task were a life-line, her thoughts and her stomach churning. *Why* would Johnny have thrown Tilly into the Thames? It didn't make sense. And as for Sharyn . . . She clamped down on her thoughts with iron will. She mustn't think about Sharyn. Not just now. Not just yet.

He followed her into the kitchen. 'I'm sorry I'm having to confirm whatever doubts you already had,' he said, his handsome face haggard with stress. 'But the minute Angie rang me and told me what had happened to her and Lola, I knew Johnny had passed a point of no return.'

As he was talking, she was moving like an automaton, shaking Lola's bottle, mixing together the milk powder and cooled boiled water

'And I know that I have to take Lola to Spain,' he said, as she squeezed milk from the bottle's teat on to the back of her hand to check its temperature. 'With your mother there, it's the obvious answer. She can care for Lola, just as she used to care for her here, and the old man will be on hand to make sure Johnny keeps his distance.'

She went back into the sitting-room, lifting a distressed Lola from the carry-cot.

There were so many things she wanted to ask; things so horrific she didn't know how to put them into words. As she began feeding Lola, she was thinking about the fire. If Johnny was responsible for the fire, then Marco must know. How on earth had Marco come to terms with the knowledge that Johnny's action had resulted in his wife's death? And how had Tony ever come to terms with it?

'I'm booked on a flight from Gatwick this evening,' he was saying, sitting on the arm of the sofa, so tense there was no mistaking his intention of leaving at the soonest possible moment.

Hysteria rose up into her throat. His taking Lola to Spain was the most obvious and the safest thing to do – but she wanted to be the one to take her there. She didn't want to let Lola out of her sight. Not for so much as a minute.

'I'll make Lola another bottle, for you to take with you,' she said, stalling for time, seeking refuge in practicality in order not to go mad at the thought of all the questions that needed answering.

What, for instance, was Tony going to do about Johnny's confession of responsibility for Tilly's death? Was he going to go to the police? Even as she asked herself the question, she knew the answer. Tony would never grass on Johnny, not in a million years; no matter what it was he had done. And what about all the other accidents on Angie's list? Did Tony know about them? And did he know for sure if Johnny had been responsible for them? Had Johnny made other confessions over the years? If so, it was no wonder Tony was always so buttoned-up and unforthcoming. A lifetime of keeping those kinds of secrets would take its toll.

Lola had finished her bottle – or as much of it as she seemed to want – and she lifted her against her shoulder. She would have to tell Rob what Tony had told her. Someone as mentally ill as Johnny couldn't possibly be allowed to remain on the streets. He needed psychiatric help in a secure, psychiatric hospital.

'I'm going upstairs to put a dry nappy on her,' she said, the words 'mentally ill' pounding in her brain like a tom-tom. He was her half-brother. They shared the same heredity. Lola Buttercup was his daughter. Did that mean that they might one day suffer from some kind of mental illness, too? And what about Tony? Tony was his twin. His *identical* twin. Surely it was biologically impossible for one of them to be mentally ill and for the other not to be?'

She carried Lola upstairs, into the bathroom, and then heard a sound that a little while ago she had been dreading and that was now like music to her ears. It was the distinctive engine-note of Fast-Boy's Harley being ridden at speed down the rutted track.

A few minutes later, as she dropped Lola's wet nappy into a bucket, the front door opened and she heard Fast-Boy's startled greeting: 'Hi, Tony. What are you doing here?'

She walked downstairs, Lola in her arms. As she entered the sitting-room, they looked towards her. 'Tell him,' she said to Tony. 'Tell him. Because if you don't, I will!'

'Tell me what, Red?' Fast-Boy slung his black leather bomber jacket over the rocking-chair. 'About Angie's accident? I already know.'

'About the fact that Johnny was responsible for it,' she said tightly, aware that Tony had gone as white as a sheet and that it had never occurred to him she would tell anyone what it was he had told her. 'About the fact that on Saturday night he threw the girl I used to work with into the Thames and left her to drown.' She kept her eyes firmly on Fast-Boy, knowing very well what it was she was doing.

That Johnny had told Tony he was responsible for Tilly's death couldn't just be her word and no one else's because, when push came to shove, she knew it was something Tony would deny ever having said. She had to make him tell Fast-Boy as well. And the only set of circumstances in which he was ever likely to be pressured into doing so, were the circumstances here and now.

'Your friend, Tilly? The blonde-haired girl?' Fast-Boy's fine-boned face never gave much away and it didn't do so now. He looked towards Tony, an eyebrow quirked. 'This is interesting, Tony. Tell me more.'

Tony gave a heavy, almost theatrical sigh. 'I don't need to tell you about Johnny, Ewan. You, of all people, already know.'

'Oh yes. I know.' There was a wealth of dark meaning in Fast-Boy's voice as he crossed the room and flopped down into the armchair. 'But I don't know about Red's friend's death. And I don't know about Johnny rigging this morning's little accident.'

His eyes flicked to Lola, and Amber trembled as she saw how intense the expression of concern in them was. Fast-Boy might be acting indifferent, but in reality he was anything but. In getting Tony to tell him all that he had told her, she had probably been taking a step too far, too fast.

'Tilly was Johnny's girlfriend,' Tony said bluntly. 'She and Johnny were aboard a Thames party-boat. According to him, they had a barney and he lost his temper with her and tipped her over the side.'

'Mr Lampeter phoned me with the news after her body was found,' Amber added. 'The police don't know who she boarded the *Mary-Jane* with. They don't know that she was Johnny's girlfriend.'

Fast-Boy was looking at Tony with a very strange expression in his eyes. 'And Johnny told you that he was aboard the *Mary-Jane* with Tilly and that he helped her into the Thames?' he asked. 'And this was Saturday night? Saturday night just gone?'

Tony nodded. 'And as I suspect he's also responsible for tampering with the brakes of Lola's pram this morning,' he said, taking a step towards Amber and lifting

Lola from her arms, 'I'm going to take Lola to Spain, where she'll be safe.'

'Safe from Johnny?'

Tony settled Lola into the crook of his arm and nodded.

'And you're taking her – when?'

Tony began walking towards the door. 'I'm booked on a flight this evening from Gatwick. I'm taking her now.'

'No, you're not.' Fast-Boy rose to his feet.

Tony stopped walking.

Amber's eyes widened.

'Saturday night, Johnny couldn't have been anywhere near the *Mary-Jane*,' Fast-Boy said with cool certainty. 'At eight-o'clock he was in the same pub I was drinking in, in Soho. And at ten o'clock, after the two of us had had a little skirmish in Dean Street, he was in the cell next to mine in Bow Street nick. And he was there all night, as half a dozen cozzers will be happy to testify.'

Tony didn't move, but something changed in his eyes and in his face. Suddenly he didn't look like the Tony Amber had known for six years. Suddenly he really did look like a stranger.

'And this morning at eleven o'clock when, according to Angie, Lola's pram was hurtling towards one of the busiest main roads in Bermondsey, Johnny was again in nick.' Fast-Boy's voice was implacable. 'He was arrested at ten o'clock this morning and taken to Tower Bridge police station where he was charged with the murder of Jimmy Jones. Word is, the Filth are looking for you, too. Something to do with a warehouse fire and a body. I'm not sure of the details, but I expect you are. So . . . all in all, I think you'd better leave Lola here, don't you?'

'No, God damn you!' he snarled. 'I don't!'

Coming from Tony – always so icily in control of himself – the explosion was obscene. 'I'm not going to let Johnny have Lola!' His teeth were gritted, his lips white. 'He loves her. She means too much to him. I'm not going to let Johnny have *anyone* he loves!'

Like a snake sloughing off a long unwanted skin, the personality they'd always believed was his visibly slipped and slid and slithered into disintegration.

There was an instant of time in which Amber thought, *This isn't happening. He didn't say that. He couldn't have said that. He didn't mean it the way it sounded.*

And then she saw his eyes and knew that he had meant every single word.

As realization began finally to dawn, she said half-believingly in a voice scarcely recognizable as her own: 'Just as you didn't allow him to have Zoë, Tony? Or Deirdre . . . ?' She paused, her lips dry. 'Or Sharyn?'

He whipped around to face her. 'Yes,' he said, all pretence abandoned. '*Exactly* as I didn't allow him to have them. And do you know why?' His eyes, so like Johnny's eyes, blazed with a passion out of control. 'Because Johnny robbed me of everything. He robbed me of my mother. My home. My happiness. My *innocence*. That's why I came back. To level the score. To get my own back. To make Johnny *pay.*'

Fast-Boy didn't ask what monstrous act Johnny had committed to warrant such retribution. Instead he said softly: 'Zoë? You caused Zoë's death?'

Ice slithered down Amber's spine.

She knew Fast-Boy.

She knew exactly what he was capable of.

His bomber jacket was only yards away, slung over the back of the chair. There would be a gun in its pocket. Fast-Boy never went anywhere without a gun. She even knew which gun it would be. It would be the .38 snub-nose revolver – a gun he always referred to as a 'tidy little fucker'. Small enough to conceal easily, but carrying a fairly big round.

And Lola Buttercup was still in Tony's arms.

Her heart lurched and seemed to stand still. Somehow she had to get Lola out of the room; out of the house. And she had to do it *now*.

'Lola needs changing again,' she said in a voice so raw she didn't know how she was getting the words past her throat. 'If you give her to me . . .'

Fast-Boy's voice cut across hers like a knife through butter. 'You moved the barricade from the workmen's pit? It was you, the night you got home from Canada?'

Tony nodded. 'Yes,' he said, as if it was no big deal. 'I knew no one would suspect that I'd done it. Why should they? I didn't know Zoë. I'd never even spoken to her. What I knew, though, was that Johnny was crazy about her. As he drove me home from the airport, Zoë was all he talked about. So I started as I meant to go on.' As if it was the sanest thing in the world, he said: 'I robbed him of Zoë just as he had robbed me of my mother.'

Fast-Boy hadn't been given his nickname for nothing. He moved fast, but not fast enough. Tony was yards nearer the rocking-chair and, even having hold of Lola, he'd yanked the gun free of the jacket seconds before Fast-Boy could have even hoped to have laid hands on it.

To Amber, it seemed as if there was no pause – not even an instant's – between Tony diving for the gun and his pulling the trigger.

The noise was deafening in the small confines of the room.

Fast-Boy ricocheted backwards, hitting the ground, clapping a hand hard against his upper thigh as he did so.

Lola, terrified out of her life by the crack of the gun, began screaming at the top of her lungs.

Amber hurtled to Fast-Boy's side, knowing that if he didn't die from this gunshot wound, he would surely die from the next. Tony's cards were on the table and there could be no going back. They were all going to die. Her. Fast-Boy. Lola.

She seized a cushion from the sofa, pressing it against the gaping hole in Fast-Boy's biking leathers, trying to staunch the sticky flow of hideously dark blood.

'It's OK, Red,' she heard Fast-Boy say on a gasp of pain. 'It's OK.'

It wasn't OK and both of them knew it.

She sprang to her feet, intent on rushing upstairs to search for any first-aid box that Angie might have.

'Forget it,' Tony said, reading her thoughts, a red-faced, screaming and hiccuping Lola Buttercup still held tightly in one arm. 'You don't think I'm letting you out of this room, do you? I know you, Amber Bailey. You'd be on the Harley like greased lightning.'

It was a thought that hadn't occurred to her, but he was right.

'And if you did that,' he continued, Fast-Boy's gun still in his hand. 'Then I'd kill both of them. Ewan *and* Lola.'

She met his eyes and knew he was speaking the truth. It wasn't Johnny who was sick. It was his twin.

Why hadn't she realized it before? Why hadn't she listened to Sharyn, when Sharyn had told her that Tony had been at Take Six the night of Angie's fall? Why hadn't she realized that his excessive self-control was a necessity; his way of keeping smouldering depths of hatred tightly reined? Why hadn't she realized that his buttoned-up repression wasn't merely odd, but downright creepy?

With a deep, tearing groan Fast-Boy was heaving himself into a sitting position against the wall of the room, the cushion – dark, ugly stains seeping through it – pressed hard against his thigh, his face grey.

He wasn't going to be able to help her. The only person who could possibly get the three of them out of the nightmare they'd been plunged into was herself.

'Give me Lola,' she said, steel entering her soul; knowing if she had to kill him in order to save Fast-Boy and Lola, she would do so without hesitation; without even the slightest remorse.

'And have you make a dash for it with her?' He gave a mirthless laugh and, moving the gun from his right hand to his left, he hoisted Lola on to his other arm.

Lola's terrified screams had quieted into hiccuping sobs and Amber knew that in a few more minutes, despite being held so uncomfortably, Lola would be fast asleep.

She went and sat down on the floor next to Fast-Boy, knowing that the important thing was to keep Tony talking; that if she could keep him talking long enough she might even be able to save their lives.

'Why?' she asked stonily. 'Why did you do it?'

Still covering them with the gun, he took a step backwards, sitting on the seat in the deep embrasure of the window.

'Because Johnny robbed me of everything,' he said again, as if stating the obvious. 'He knew Mum loved me best – she used to take me everywhere with her. That's why he started the fire. Johnny was *always* starting fires. He wanted to prove it. He wanted to prove that she would save me and not him.'

Beside her Fast-Boy made a sound. It was almost one of amusement.

'Only she didn't.' The skin was tight across Tony's cheekbones, his lips bloodless. 'Johnny was screaming "Me, Mummy! Me!" and she fought her way through the blazing house and it was Johnny she grabbed hold of, Johnny she died saving. If it hadn't been for Johnny . . .' his voice shook. 'If it hadn't been for Johnny, we'd both have been saved by the firemen. If it hadn't been for Johnny, she wouldn't have died. And if it hadn't been for Johnny, I would never have been sent to Canada, away from his influence. To Canada and Albie.'

There was a moment, as his eyes became oddly unfocused, when she wondered if she would be able to rush him. As she tensed herself, giving Fast-Boy a quick look to signal what she was about to do, Tony was again reliving the claustrophobic dark of the cubbyhole in the barn roof. He could hear Albie's voice; smell his stale body odour; feel his hands. Hands that had reached beneath the old horse-blanket for him; hands slippery with sweat that had tugged his trousers down and had probed and pushed, explored and violated.

Then he saw Amber's movement and he jerked the gun so that it was pointing at her head. 'Don't even think about it,' he said softly.

Fast-Boy's breathing was becoming increasingly rasping. 'Sorry, Red,' he said with difficulty as her eyes flew to his in an agony of concern.

She nodded, understanding what it was he was really saying. That he couldn't help her. Couldn't get to his feet no matter what.

She moved so that she could hold the cushion in place

for him, his blood seeping beneath her fingernails. 'Tell me,' she said to Tony, fighting down the sobs rising in her throat. 'Tell me how you did it. How did you push Abbra Hornby from the platform of the bus. You're Johnny's double. How come she didn't see you, didn't recognize you?'

'Abbra Hornby?' For one minute he looked totally blank, unable to recall who Abbra Hornby was. Then he said with a glimmer of amusement. 'I took a leaf from Fast-Boy's book. I dressed as a woman.'

She let out a long, low breath.

'I wore sunglasses as well. And I was always behind her. Recognition was never an issue.'

'And Deirdre Crosby? Her brakes failed. And they failed because of you, didn't they?'

'Yes,' he said. 'They did.'

It was almost as if they were having a perfectly normal conversation. Lola had now fallen into an exhausted sleep and he was holding her on his knee with one hand, the gun in the other. From behind him, the early evening sunlight shone on the smooth glossiness of his hair and winked on the gold of his thickly braceleted wristwatch.

'And then,' Amber said, knowing that, not only was she capable of killing him, but that she would kill him, 'there was Sharyn. You were the woman in the chequered headscarf, weren't you? You pushed her in front of the train and then forged a way through the crush towards the exit. How did you manage to do it without anyone seeing you? Not one witness mentioned you . . .' Her voice was vibrating with so much emotion she broke off in mid-sentence, not wanting him to mistake her grief for weakness.

'Why should they have mentioned me?' He looked extraordinarily relaxed. All the vicious anger of earlier had ebbed and Amber felt a seed of hope. If she could bring him back to normality – or what passed with him for normality – then maybe she could persuade him to give her Lola and let her get help for Fast-Boy; maybe she could even convince him that neither she nor Fast-Boy would talk.

'I never put a hand on Sharyn,' he said, his voice so indifferent the hair on the nape of her neck stood on end. 'I was at least two people deep behind her when she went toppling over the platform edge.'

'Then how . . . ?'

As Fast-Boy groaned again and appeared to slip into unconsciousness, Tony adjusted Lola into a more comfortable position on his knees and said, 'I had an umbrella with me. And I simply slid it between the people in front of me, into the middle of Sharyn's back . . . and pushed. You see, I didn't know then about Johnny's affair with Tilly. I really and truly thought that with Lola's birth he'd suddenly become a devoted family man. Stupid of me. He's my twin. I should have known better.'

'And Tilly? How did you persuade Tilly to meet you on board the *Mary-Jane*? Or did she think she was meeting Johnny?'

'Well, of course she thought she was meeting Johnny. She also thought she was going to the private party of one of Johnny's friends. In reality, it was simply a standard fancy-dress jaunt on the Thames. Anyone could go, as long as they bought a ticket. I liked the idea of being disguised by a mask and not attracting attention.'

'But when you met her on board, she must have know you *weren't* Johnny?' Amber persisted.

'Actually, I don't think she did, not instantly. I didn't try to fool her, though. There was no point. And when she realized I wasn't Johnny, she didn't attempt to leave.

Not when I told her I had family business to discuss with her.'

'And you threw her overboard and left her to drown in the dark? All because you wanted to make Johnny suffer?'

Her voice was fogged with the horror of it.

'I killed three people . . . and I'll probably kill more . . . to show Johnny what's it's like to lose everything he loves.' The savagery was back in his voice with a vengeance. 'Johnny lost nothing! Our mother wasn't the centre of *his* life. And he didn't lose his home. Have you any idea what Northern Canada is like? How ferocious the winters are, with snow so thick it's above your shoulders, and with the temperatures way below freezing? And Johnny didn't lose his childhood! He didn't have to live life alone, with no friends, no companionship, no *love*. He didn't have to live with a pervert whose only entertainment was to have me as a plaything he could hurt and humiliate and get sexual satisfaction from! He didn't have to live with *Albie!*'

Beside her, Fast-Boy moved and then, incredibly, he began to laugh.

'And you blame Johnny for all this, do you? You think it's all Johnny's fault, because Johnny started the fire?'

Tony flinched, a tremor running through him, and Amber's throat tightened. Fast-Boy provoking him further wasn't going to help them get out of the cottage alive. Not unless Fast-Boy was doing it on purpose; doing it as part of a plan he had in mind.

'Shut up!' Tony hissed. '*Shut up!*' In his arms Lola woke with a start and then, seeing Amber, began cooing happily.

'I don't know how to break this to you, Tony,' Fast-Boy said, the saturated cushion still pressed against his thigh, 'but Johnny never started that fire.' He leaned his head back against the wall, savouring the moment, spinning it out for as long as possible, before saying with deep satisfaction: 'I did.'

Both Amber and Tony stared at him.

Tony spoke first. 'I don't believe you. I don't believe you, you cunt! *I don't believe you!*'

'It's why I felt so bad about your mum dying. It never occurred to me she'd come back and do what she did. And I didn't know you were in the house, either. I thought Johnny was in it, alone.'

He grinned, and what the effort must have cost him, Amber couldn't even begin to imagine.

'I'd overheard my mother saying your mum was going down to the shops. She always took you with her and it never entered my head that she mightn't have done.'

'But why?' Amber asked bewildered. 'Why would you do such a thing?'

'Muffin,' said Fast-Boy, beads of perspiration breaking out on his forehead as his loss of blood began kicking in with a vengeance. 'I did it because of what Johnny did to little Muffin.'

If either of them had even faintly disbelieved him before, they did so no longer.

'It was easy enough to do.' He winced, trying to pull himself a little further into a sitting position against the wall and failing. 'My old man sold black-market petrol all through the war and when the war was over it was a habit he continued. There were enough jerry-cans of petrol in the shed in our garden to have set London alight, let alone one house.'

To say that he now had Tony's complete attention was an understatement. With rising hope Amber wondered if this was Fast-Boy's intention; if he was trying to get

Tony so engrossed that he would put down the gun and move away from it.

'The old man said Johnny had done it,' Tony said stubbornly, the pulse at the corner of his jaw in evidence again. 'I heard him. I heard him tell my aunt that it was because Johnny had wanted to see who Mum loved best. Me or him.'

'Yeah, well, funny enough, a bit of that is true.'

Fast-Boy hauled himself another few feet along the wall so that he was in reach of the chair. Tony didn't attempt to stop him. As Fast-Boy dragged another cushion from it, to replace the cushion sodden with his blood, Tony simply waited for him to continue talking.

'It's something Johnny had loud-mouthed about doing. He was jealous to death of you. Everyone knew that. That's what gave me the idea of how to protect myself after the fire got so out of hand; after your mother died. I knew there'd be a police investigation, but I was more scared of your dad finding out that I'd done it than I was of the police. So I went to see him.'

He was speaking with such difficulty now that, even though he was being so stunningly successful in engaging Tony's complete attention, Amber wanted him to stop. She didn't know how much blood he had lost, but it was a lot. His skin had taken on an almost translucent sheen and was hideously cold.

'You spoke to the old man?' Tony's voice was incredulous. 'You told my dad that you'd started the fire?' He shifted Lola into a different position on his knee. She had begun clapping her hands and blowing bubbles and it was obvious to Amber that he was finding it increasingly difficult to hold on to her.

'No,' Fast-Boy said, closing his eyes briefly and then opening them again. 'I told him about what Johnny had been threatening to do. And I told him that I'd seen him do it. I told him that I'd seen him with the jerry-can of petrol.'

'Christ,' Tony whispered, looking as if he'd been pole-axed. 'Fucking *Christ!*'

Dazedly he walked towards the sofa, dropping Lola unceremoniously into her carry-cot.

It was then that Fast-Boy moved.

While Tony had his back towards him, he levered himself upwards and hurled himself on him.

Amber leapt with him in perfect synchronization, her target Tony's gun arm. Only the gun was no longer in the hand it had been in. As he'd dropped Lola into the carry-cot, he'd transferred it back into his right hand and this time, as he twisted round and fired, there could be no doubt at all as to the outcome.

Fast-Boy was blasted backwards, blood pumping from his chest.

Even before she reached his side, she knew he was dying – and dying fast. As she sobbed hysterically, cradling his head on her lap, his eyes met hers for one last time. 'Sorry . . . Red . . .' he said, 'love . . . you . . .' And then blood bubbled from his mouth and his head fell to one side.

She couldn't stop screaming. She knew she had to regain control, because she knew she had to kill Tony, but for an endless age she couldn't do so.

'Murderer! Monster! *Psychopath!*' she screamed from the floor beside Fast-Boy's body, his blood on her hands, on her dress, on her face. 'You're not just killing everyone Johnny loves! You're killing everyone I love as well! And do you know what the worst part about it all is? You're my *brother!* My half-brother! How could I have a brother so evil and sick? A brother fit only for Broadmoor?'

She pushed herself to her feet, stumbling against the green rocking-chair, no longer screaming but sobbing in great, jarring, juddering sobs.

'The old man's your father?' It was an idea that had obviously never previously occurred to him.

Whether it had or hadn't, Amber didn't care. She'd got herself under control now and her brain was racing. She wasn't going to die in this room and she wasn't going to let Lola die, either.

'It doesn't make any difference,' Tony was saying after a long pause. 'Half-sister or not, you'd never keep quiet about all this, would you? And I need to keep to my agenda where Johnny is concerned.'

He was talking about Lola.

Fear seized her heart with such crippling intensity that she didn't how she could still be continuing to breathe.

'What are you doing to do to her?'

'I think I'm going to have you drown her,' he said. 'The assumption is going to be that Fast-Boy came here to see you and that you had a God-Almighty lovers' row. You shot him. I'll wipe the gun free of my fingerprints and make sure that yours are on it. And then I'm going to make it look as if you left the cottage, walked to the estuary, and drowned Lola before swimming out until you could swim no further.'

'And your car tracks?' she asked, dry-mouthed. 'How will you explain those away?'

'I could have come down here earlier,' he said. 'The cottage is my wife's, after all. And why would I have any reason for murdering you, Amber? Or Fast-Boy? It's common knowledge that I always got on well with Fast-Boy. It was he and Johnny who were enemies.'

It was very neat. Very straightforward. And she realized that it depended on one thing entirely.

There could be no bullet wounds on her body. She couldn't be fished out of the estuary with a bullet in her back. Not if, in order to satisfactorily explain Fast-Boy's death, her death was to be perceived as suicide.

Lola was crying again, kicking chubby legs in distressed agitation. Knowing what it was she had to do; knowing that she was going to have to run faster than she'd ever run in her life; knowing that everything depended on her being able to start the Harley into life before Tony caught up with her and that she would have to do so with Lola in one arm, she said: 'I can't bear Lola crying. Let me pick her up.'

'OK,' he said – and smiled.

She walked to the carry-cot and, as she bent over it, he lifted the gun high and with great economy of movement brought it smashing down on to her head.

Chapter Twenty-two

The pain, as she returned to consciousness, was like no pain she'd ever before experienced. She knew where she was. On the floor in the sitting-room at the cottage. She knew that Lola was with her, for she could hear her making mewling sounds in the carry-cot on the sofa, just above her head.

She didn't know where Tony was, though. She didn't know if he was standing nearby, waiting for her to show signs of life so that he could smash her into unconsciousness again.

Blood from her head was trickling into her mouth and down her neck. Tony was going to kill her and Lola. He was going to fire the cottage and take her unconscious body – and Lola's – down to the estuary and drown them.

She moved her head. Pain rocketed through her, but no blow came. Gingerly she moved some more, opening her eyes and pulling herself into a sitting position against the sofa.

Fast-Boy's body lay only yards away, his eyes still open.

There came the sound of someone moving something large and metallic around. The noise wasn't coming from the kitchen, though. As she fought wave after wave of dizziness, understanding dawned. He was in the lean-to. The sound she could hear was Tony moving paraffin cans around in the lean-to.

How long would it take him to remove enough cans for his task of starting the fire? Not long. Paraffin cans weren't heavy. If she was going to run for her life – and Lola's life – then she had to do it now.

She pushed herself to her feet and bent over the carry-cot. Lola took one look at her blood-smeared face and began to cry.

Amber didn't blame her.

'Hush, my darling,' she said, picking her up and holding her close against her blood-sodden dress. 'Hush. Please hush.'

She turned with her towards the door, stumbling against the rocking-chair as she did so. Then she hesitated. She couldn't leave Fast-Boy with his eyes open. Still holding Lola, she bent down on one knee beside him. 'Love you,' he'd said as he died. She closed his eyes knowing that, in her own way, she had loved him in return.

One paraffin can clattered against another. What if he was already bringing them back into the house? No way would she be able to struggle with him. A puff of wind would blow her over.

She forced herself upright once more and, as Lola continued to cry, walked unsteadily out of the room, across the hall and towards the already open front door.

Once on the doorstep, looking out over windswept grass towards the track, she rocked back on her heels.

The Harley wasn't there.

Tony had moved it – and the likeliest place for him to have moved it was the lean-to.

In all that vast, bleak, flat landscape there was nowhere to run; nowhere to hide.

Which meant he would simply have to shoot her in the back; for at least that way she would have some satisfaction. That way she would at least know that she had ruined his plans.

With Lola still crying, she began to run. It wasn't a very straight run, for she found it impossible not to weave from side to side, as if she was drunk. And it wasn't a very fast run. She couldn't see clearly for the black dots swimming against her eyes, but she knew she was heading in the right direction; along the track that led – eventually – to a seldom-used road. That led – eventually – to a busier road. To shops and houses and help.

How many miles until salvation? Two? Three?

And how many yards had she covered? Twenty? Thirty?

She was never sure, afterwards, which came first. The faint sound of car engines or his furious cry as he came out of the lean-to and saw her.

She heard him drop the cans he was carrying. Heard him begin to give chase.

The breath rasped in her throat and pounded in her ears. He would have to shoot her. He would have to spoil his precious, tidily made plans. She was staggering now, barely running at all, the ground a swirling mirage of dry earth and coarse grass and grey stones. Why had he still not shot her? Why couldn't she hear his feet pounding after her?

There was nothing ahead, only the track leading across the uncompromising flatness into seeming infinity. No help. No sanctuary. And then she realized that the sound of car engines wasn't being carried on the wind from a road so distant it wasn't even in sight.

The cars were on the track she was on and they were speeding towards her. And not just two cars, but three. A car she didn't recognize in front and cars she did recognize behind. Police cars; the most beautiful, most blessed sight in all the world.

The lead car slewed to a halt only yards in front of her, her reflection in its windscreen. Her hair was matted with blood from her head wound. Her face was streaked and smeared with it. Fast-Boy's blood was saturating her dress and, in her arms, Lola Buttercup was crying fit to bust a gut.

'Dear Christ!' Rob shouted as he leapt from the car and sprinted towards her.

'Tony's behind me!' she gasped as she fell against him. 'He's got a gun, Rob. He's killed Fast-Boy.'

With his arm around her, Rob shouted orders to the driver of the second police car, that had overtaken his car and pulled up alongside them, engine running. 'He's armed! Draw up nearer the house and radio in for back-up and an ambulance. *And don't try and confront him.* Wait for me.'

To Amber he said, 'I'm going to get you to hospital just as fast as I can, but first I have to deal with this. I want you to get into the back of this car *and stay there* till either an ambulance arrives or I get back to you. Do you understand?'

Her relief was so sweeping, so total, that she was tempted to ask him where, in her condition, he thought she might go? Instead she thought of Fast-Boy and began to weep.

Rob was running to the third car, yanking a door open without waiting for it to come to a complete standstill. Seconds later, as she collapsed on the back seat of what had been the lead car, she saw both his car and car number two sweep to a halt only yards from the cottage.

It was only then that she realized there was no sign of Tony. Hadn't he been behind her, after all? Or had he seen the police cars approaching long before she had, and turned back?

'Come on out, Martini! We know you're in there!' she heard Rob, now out of the car, shouting through a megaphone.

And then Tony was at the cottage door, one hand in the trouser pocket of his hand-tailored Italian suit, the other still holding Fast-Boy's gun.

He looked slim-hipped and relaxed and very, very handsome.

'Come on, Tony!' she heard Rob shout. 'Be sensible. Give yourself up!'

Two uniformed policemen had emerged from the second car and another two had scrambled out of the third. Rob had come prepared for trouble, but she could tell from the tense way the men were standing that they hadn't come armed.

It wasn't a situation Tony could shoot himself out of, though. There were too many of them. Just as she'd had nowhere to run, now it was his turn.

She wondered why, when he'd seen the cars and known that he was trapped, he had even bothered returning to the cottage. And then she noticed that the paraffin cans she had heard him drop to the ground when he had begun to chase after her were nowhere in sight.

She knew, then, what it was he had returned to do.

She knew what it was he was so nonchalantly waiting for.

There was no indication of fire; no wisp of smoke, no shooting tentative flame. One minute the weather-boarded, oak-beamed cottage was serene under the daffodil sky of early evening. The next there was a loud crack as the sitting-room windows splintered and flames gushed out, licking greedily upwards.

Tony paused for a second and then turned, walking back into the house.

Rob began running for the cottage and then, just as he reached the doorway, just as he was about to hurl himself through the belching smoke after Tony and as she was scrabbling like a wild thing to open the car door, her hands slipping and sliding, sticky with blood, the gunshot came.

She no longer tried to get out of the car. With a fist pressed to her mouth she fell back against the seat, knowing what he had done. Knowing that it was all over. Knowing that Lola was safe.

For a long moment Rob didn't move. He simply stood, one arm raised to shield his face from the heat of the blaze. Then he turned and began walking slowly back to the car.

As he opened the door, and as Lola finally stopped crying, she said, 'Would you take me home, please, Rob?' Her face was so bleak it tore at his heart.

'I will, by way of the hospital,' he said, having no intention of waiting for an ambulance that could still be fifteen minutes or so away, and knowing she was thinking of Ewan Flynn and knowing better than to put his arm around her.

Leaving the men he'd brought with him to wait for the fire service to arrive, he slid behind the wheel, turning the car around, beginning to drive as gently as possible, back down the track.

As he did so, he looked in his driving-mirror at the scene they were leaving behind. There wouldn't be much for the firemen to find when they arrived. Against a sky fading to dusk, flames were leaping roof-high.

Acutely aware of Amber's grief, knowing the fire wasn't only Tony Martini's funeral pyre but Fast-Boy

Flynn's as well, he turned his attention to the road ahead, already mentally composing the first lines of the report he would have to make.

Chapter Twenty-three

It was December. For weeks after the deaths of Tony
Martini and Fast-Boy Flynn, Rob had only seen Amber
intermittently. There had been her statement to take. A
long, long statement as she catalogued all that Tony had
told her and Fast-Boy with regard to Sharyn's death, and
the murders of Zoë Fairminder and Deirdre Crosby and
Tilly Conway.

He had been able to tell her just why he had arrived
on the Isle of Grain accompanied by two cars of
uniformed officers. 'It was when I got your message,
Amber,' he'd said. 'I went to the hospital and spoke with
Angie and it was just a gut feeling.'

Then there had been the inquests.

He'd barely known how to talk to her at Fast-Boy's
inquest. Her hair had been shaved where she'd had
medical attention for a fractured skull. She'd been so
pale and so quiet it had almost been like being with
another person.

Her mother had been with her – and Marco Martini.

Considering that it had been Marco's son who had
tried to kill her – and who had killed Maureen Bailey's
eldest daughter and Fast-Boy – it had been an odd situation.

It was made even odder when she had told him that
Marco was her father.

If it had been something he should have guessed, he
hadn't.

Johnny had come to trial not long afterwards and been sentenced to life for the murder of Jimmy Jones. If Rob still had a care for his career – and he had – then it should have been enough to ensure he had no further thoughts of trying to resume his relationship with her.

It wasn't.

If Amber would marry him, then the Force would have to accept his marriage, or he would leave it and find another career.

The question of whether Amber would or would not marry him never came up, though.

She hadn't said as much, but he knew she was too emotionally shattered to want a relationship of any kind. She needed space and, for three months, he had given her it.

He looked down at the beautifully wrapped Christmas present he was carrying. When he gave it to her, he was going to tell her that he loved her and wanted to marry her.

'She's over at Greenwich Park,' Maureen Bailey said when she opened the door to him, a ten-month-old Lola Buttercup held on one hip. And then, as he walked back down the short path, she called after him: 'She's there on her own.'

Coming from a woman who had no time for coppers, it was quite startling encouragement.

Once at the park, he found her easily enough. In December, not too many people were sitting around on park benches.

She looked up at his approach, saw the box in his hands and gave a glimmer of a grin.

'Is this a visit by Santa Claus?'

'Could just be,' he said, sitting down beside her.

She was wearing a military-style coat that reached to

her booted ankles and a Russian-style, imitation fox-fur hat. From beneath it, her hair flamed in spicy red curls towards her face.

'Congratulations about the promotion,' she said.

It was his turn to give a glimmer of a grin.

'Thanks.'

The seat she'd chosen to sit on faced the boating pond and the breeze was ruffling the surface into small, steel-grey waves.

'It's so near New Year, I wondered what your plans for the future are,' he said, wanting to know what she had in mind, before he told her what was on his mind.

'Mum's going to go back to Spain with Marco. Angie is going to move in with me and help me care for Lola. We're going to make hats and sell them at Bermondsey Market.

He was silent, aware he fitted into her plans nowhere at all.

'Won't Lola be a little lonely,' he ventured, 'being brought up by two single women? Don't you think it might be a good idea for her to have a cousin or two to play with?'

She turned her head, her eyes, as they met his, full of the kind of cheeky impudence he hadn't seen in them since Sharyn had died. 'Are you offering to supply them, Detective Inspector Gowan?'

He toyed with the gaily wrapped present he still hadn't given her. This wasn't the way he'd meant to do it, but it was as good a way as any.

'Yes,' he said. 'I am.'

She giggled and took the present from him. 'Then when I'm in the mood to have a baby, I'll give you a ring.'

'I'm first in line, then?'

'Oh yes,' she said, feeling happiness stealing once more through her veins. 'You're most definitely first in line, Rob.'

He didn't move to kiss her; didn't try to put in more explicit words the offer he had just made and that she had accepted. He didn't need to, for there would be time enough. All he needed to do now was to watch her open the present he had given her. And as he did so, his heart was singing like a skylark's.

Looking for Mr Big
Maggie Hudson

Deena King is a barrister. A tough, moral, professional woman who has made a highly successful career putting criminals behind bars. Al Virtue is a South London villain, the brains behind some of the most daring heists the capital has seen. Only once has he been called to pay for his crimes, and Deena King was the prosecuting QC.

But now they must form an unlikely alliance, for Deena's son and Al's daughter have vanished from college. As the trail leads from the London underworld to the headquarters of a Colombian drug cartel, it soon becomes apparent that the forces of law and order are following an agenda in which the safe return of the young students is not a priority – and Al and Deena are unwitting pawns in a deadly game.

'Stunning – read this or we send the boys round'

MARTINA COLE

'Hudson has a voice of her own . . . a highly enjoyable read'   *The Times*

ISBN 0 00 651455 3